Anna Bell lives in the South of France with her young family and energetic Labrador. When not chained to her laptop, Anna can be found basking in the summer sun, heading to the ski slopes in the winter (to drink hot chocolate and watch – she can't ski) or having a sneaky treat from the patisserie – all year round!

You can find out more about Anna on her website – www.annabellwrites.com or follow her on Twitter @annabell_writes.

D1328801

Note to Self

Anna Bell

ONE PLACE. MANY STORIES

HQ
An imprint of HarperCollins*Publishers* Ltd
1 London Bridge Street
London SE1 9GF

www.harpercollins.co.uk

HarperCollins*Publishers*
1st Floor, Watermarque Building, Ringsend Road
Dublin 4, Ireland

This edition 2022

1
First published in Great Britain by
HQ, an imprint of HarperCollins*Publishers* Ltd 2022

ISBN: 978-0-00-846763-0

MIX
Paper from
responsible sources
FSC™ C007454

This book is produced from independently certified FSC™ paper
to ensure responsible forest management.

For more information visit: www.harpercollins.co.uk/green

This book is set in 11.1/15.5 pt. Bembo by Type-it AS, Norway

Printed and Bound in the UK using 100% Renewable Electricity at
CPI Group (UK) Ltd, Croydon, CR0 4YY

To my UKC girls – Sarah, Sonia, Christie and Ali – the mind boggles what our eighteen-year-old selves would have written to us. Thanks for all the memories we made then and for the new ones we continue to make.

Dear Future Me,

You only went and bloody did it, didn't you? Did what we said you'd never do: grow up. Don't you remember, we were supposed to always be young, always know what's in the charts, always be down with the cool kids? But let's face it, I've never been down with the cool kids, so there's really no hope of that happening. Unless I've seriously under-estimated myself.

My mind is boggling at what your life might be like. Are there flying cars? Do people live on Mars? Did you finally reduce your unread emails to zero? I can't begin to imagine.

So, what do I hope of me in seventeen years' time? Mainly I hope you're happy. And not the kind of on-paper happy that's all about shiny cars and executive flats. I mean proper cheeks-ache-from-too-much-smiling-and-laughing-type happy. I hope your life is busy and full of love and friendship and that

you're finally comfortable in your own skin.
I hope that you are being true to yourself
and that you've become the woman you should
have been and the one that you wanted to be.

   But most of all I hope that you haven't
fucked it up and that you didn't lose him,
again.

   X x

Chapter 1

I sometimes think that I am the only person in the world who doesn't enjoy their birthday. There's that assumption that the day has to be special and better than any other day of the year: the most fun had, the best meal ever eaten, the most love felt. There's always so much pressure that it inevitably feels like you're setting yourself up for a fall when it doesn't live up to expectations. And this year, on my thirty-fifth birthday, for some inexplicable reason I'm feeling it even more.

I've never been that bothered about getting older. I didn't have a midlife crisis when I hit thirty and I don't dread the thought of turning forty or fifty, so I can't put my finger on why all week I've been freaking out about turning thirty-five. It's not even a special birthday.

I might not have the husband or children I once expected to have at my age, but I have so many other things to be grateful for. A flat all of my own. A boyfriend who's sweet and funny, who isn't in a hurry to fast-track our relationship. I'm co-director of a successful business. Yet, despite all this, I can't shake the feeling that turning thirty-five is significant somehow.

I quicken my step towards the café where I'm meeting Dad and Layla, hoping they'll distract me from my thoughts. A breeze

3

whips around me and I pull my cardigan across my chest. It might be June and almost a midsummer's day, but there's nothing midsummer about today's weather at all.

I immediately locate my dad in the corner of the café when I walk in.

'There's the birthday girl,' he shouts, loud enough for the rest of the customers to hear. He folds his newspaper and places it on the table, before standing up to give me a big hug. 'Happy birthday, love. Thirty-five, eh?'

'Thanks for reminding me.' I peer around the table, trying to spot any discreetly placed birthday decorations. Dad knows I hate any kind of fuss on my birthday. 'I'm glad to see you *finally* listened to my no-decorations rule.'

I catch the slight twinkle in his eye as he tries to suppress a smile.

'What have you done? The whole reason I agreed to meet you here, and not the office, is to keep this low-key.'

My dad and I are co-directors of an office supply company and in years gone by he's decorated my desk with balloons, banners and streamers, and there's always a speech. I hate speeches.

The bell above the door of the café jangles, and in breezes Layla, one of our work colleagues, who over the years has become my best friend too. A waitress walks out from behind the counter with a tray of hot drinks and Layla nearly takes her out with the two pink foil helium number balloons that pop out from behind her.

'I'm so sorry,' she says, trying to wrestle the three and five under control. 'Happy birthday, Edie.'

'Did *you* forget to send Layla the no-fuss memo?' Dad laughs, oblivious to my eye roll.

I grit my teeth, standing up to give her a hug, and she tucks the offending balloons around my chair.

'No one is letting me forget how old I am today, are they?'

'By the time you get to my age you need all the reminders you can get,' says Dad, standing up. I can't help but crack a smile, as, deep down, I know they're only making a fuss because they care. 'I'll go order us some coffees; two flat whites?'

'Perfect,' Layla says, and I nod.

As Dad goes to queue for the drinks, Layla pulls out an expensive-looking box of chocolates and slides them over to me.

'Thank you, you know you didn't need to.' She'd already given me her present when she took me on a fancy spa day at the weekend.

'Couldn't resist. Besides, I couldn't show up empty-handed – I had to give you something on your actual birthday. Speaking of gifts, I'm dying to know what Miles got you!'

'Oh, I don't know yet, I'm not seeing him until tonight.'

'Didn't he sleep at yours last night?'

'No, because I'm seeing him *tonight*.'

'You two' – she shakes her head – 'there's nothing to stop you seeing each other two nights in a row, you know.'

'I know, but just because we're having fun dating, doesn't mean to say that we have to live in each other's pockets. We both like having our own space, and seeing each other a couple of times a week suits us fine. Besides, a birthday is just another day.'

'I feel like you should come round and do a TED talk about that in our house. Try convincing the twins that their eighth birthday is like any other day.'

'Isn't their birthday in October? That's months away.'

'I know, but that hasn't stopped them from lobbying for every bit of the not-even-released-yet Liverpool football kit, an Xbox, a zillion games for the aforementioned Xbox, an iPad.' She takes a deep breath. 'Anyway, this is not about them, this is about you. Where's Miles taking you to dinner? Somewhere fancy, I hope?'

'The Chambers.'

'Ooh, that is proper swanky.' She lowers her voice and leans across the table. 'You know that's a proposal restaurant, don't you? I think I read in the local paper that they get on average two proposals a week.'

My whole body stiffens.

'We're definitely not at that stage.'

She gives me a knowing smile. 'Maybe tonight will prove otherwise.'

My stomach's started to churn even though I know she must be wrong. We've only been together five months.

The coffee machine starts to whirr away in the background and Dad comes back over and takes his seat.

'What have I missed?' he asks.

'Edie is going to The Chambers tonight for dinner with Miles.'

'Oh, you'll have to let us know what you think. I was thinking that perhaps we could book it for our Christmas do this year.'

'Blimey, business must be good,' says Layla. 'That's a step up from last year's trip to the pub across the road.'

'I think winning a place on the council tender should be reason to celebrate,' says Dad.

'Just because we're a preferred supplier doesn't guarantee that anyone will order from us,' I say. 'It might be best to play it safe this year and go all out next year when we know if it's made a difference.'

'Come on, Edie, I've got that dress from Whistles that's just itching to be worn again. It would be the perfect occasion,' says Layla, pleading with her eyes.

'You and that Whistles dress.'

'Well, if someone would get married already I'd have somewhere else to wear it.' She gives me a pointed look.

The waitress comes over with a tray and I'm relieved of the interruption until I notice with horror that she's got an almond croissant with a lit candle in it. She breaks out into a loud rendition of 'Happy Birthday' and Dad and Layla don't miss a beat joining in. The rest of the patrons of the café sing along and my cheeks burn. I try and sink down in my chair, but between Dad singing at the top of his lungs and the pink helium balloons advertising my age, there's no escaping it.

The waitress places it down in front of me and I mutter a thanks before I blow out the candle. Dad pats me on the back and Layla claps her hands.

'Thank you for that complete embarrassment.'

'Come on, it's your birthday; we just wanted to make it special. You know it's only a fraction of what your mum would have done,' says Dad. 'Jan always loved birthdays.'

My heart burns at the mention of Mum. He's right though; she would have done something completely over the top. She would have filled the whole café with balloons and there would have been a cake the size of a table, and it certainly wouldn't have had one solitary candle on top.

I can't help but feel sad. My birthdays have never been the same since she died seventeen years ago. Each one serves as a painful reminder that she's no longer here. I've almost reached the point now where I've celebrated more without her than I did with her.

Dad senses the shift in mood, and he puts his hand over mine. He doesn't say anything, but he doesn't need to; his being here knowing how I'm feeling is good enough.

'So how long have you got before you need to go?' I say, trying not to slip down a melancholy rabbit hole.

Layla's a governor at the school that her twin boys attend, and she's roped Dad into doing a careers talk there this morning.

'In about twenty minutes. You should come,' says Layla.

'Um, that's OK. I thought I might just potter round and go to the shops.'

In truth, I hadn't really thought about what I was going to do after I left them. It was a last-minute decision to take the day off, mainly motivated by the weird feeling I've had surrounding this birthday.

'Why don't you come with us?' says Dad. 'I feel like I haven't seen you properly for ages. It would be nice to spend the morning together at least.'

'Dad, we work together every day. We see plenty of each other.'

'Yeah, but it's different when we're in the office. I just feel like we haven't caught up a lot lately.'

I don't want to point out that it's his fault, so instead I take a bite of my croissant. He's always busy with Julie, the woman he's started dating.

'You know I don't really like those kinds of events, I'm never very good at answering questions on the spot.'

8

'It's not like you'll have to say anything, just come and watch my talk.'

'The boys would love to see you to wish you happy birthday,' says Layla.

The two of them are ganging up on me, but it's not like I have anything better to do and perhaps it'll distract me from thinking about my birthday.

'OK, why not.'

'Good,' says Dad, a triumphant look on his face. 'Now, that almond croissant looks really good. I might just get one for myself.'

'Dad! You know you're supposed to be cutting down.'

'Don't worry, I didn't have any breakfast at home.'

That's not really the point and he knows it.

'Plus, it's not every day your baby turns thirty-five.'

'Tell me about it,' I say, wishing that everyone would stop reminding me.

Chapter 2

We arrive at the school in plenty of time for Dad's presentation and are greeted by Claudia, the twins' teacher. She wastes no time getting straight to the logistics of how the talk's going to work.

'First, we'll introduce you to the kids,' says Claudia, 'then we've got the perfect story lined up for you to read, if that's OK? It's about a boy deciding what he wants to be when he grows up, and then we'll finish off with a Q&A. It'll be nice and informal, so hopefully the kids will all get to join in.'

My dad is grinning like a Cheshire cat. He's the complete opposite of me in that he loves public speaking. Dad's the face and the spokesperson of our company and I'm the behind-the-scenes–making-sure-everything-happens person; it's why we make such a good team.

'Right, so we'll get you a—' Claudia's interrupted by Dad's phone ringing. He excuses himself from the conversation and retreats over to the other side of the room. 'As I was saying, I'll just go and grab your visitor passes before I take you to the class,' says Claudia. She heads into the glass-walled office in the corner.

'You'll have to report back, Edie, and let me know if the twins behaved themselves in class,' says Layla.

'You're not going to watch?'

'No, I've got a meeting with the head teacher – governor stuff.'

'Oh, well, I'm sure the twins will behave as they normally do.'

'That's why I'm worried.'

I laugh but stop when Dad walks back over with a frown on his face.

'Everything OK?' asks Layla.

'No, actually, Julie let herself out of my house and she's locked her car keys inside.'

'Oh, gosh,' says Layla, as Claudia returns, passes in hand.

'I'm going to have to leave and give Julie my spare key; otherwise she won't make it to work on time.'

'You can't go,' I say to Dad. 'What about the kids?'

Dad looks at Claudia in a panic then glances over at me. 'Why don't you do it, Edie?'

'Er, yeah, sure, I can take the keys to Julie.' It might be a little awkward since I've never met her before.

'You haven't got your car and you're not insured on mine. No, I mean, you do the talk instead of me.'

'Oh, that's a great idea!' Claudia chips in, her face lighting up. 'In fact, not to be rude, Gary, but we're always looking at ways for the kids to become more aware of gender equality. And who better to speak to the kids than a young, female CEO like Edie. I'm sure it would be incredibly inspiring.'

'But I haven't got a speech prepared,' I stutter.

'You don't need one, it's all going to be very relaxed.'

'It's not only about being unprepared . . .' I try and think of a reason that sounds less pathetic than admitting that I'm scared of talking to a class of children. I wipe my clammy hands on my jeans.

'Couldn't Julie get a taxi to work, or Layla could do the talk instead?'

'Please,' says Layla. 'Your job title is way more impressive than mine; besides, I've got that meeting.'

My heart starts to race.

'It's just a story and a Q&A, and I'll guide you through it.' Claudia's using a gentle voice like I imagine she uses when she's trying to reassure the children.

'You've got this, Edie,' says Dad, squeezing my shoulder before he hurries off to rescue Julie. The irony isn't lost on me that I came to spend more time with him, and I've ended up covering for him whilst he goes off to her, again.

As I enter the room, the sight of thirty plus excited seven-year-olds sitting cross-legged on a square of carpet is even more terrifying than I could have imagined. Beads of sweat start to form on my forehead and my mouth goes dry.

I follow Claudia with shaky legs, wishing I had her air of confidence as she strides across the classroom. She's every bit the cool teacher I would have loved to have had as a kid, with her tight corkscrew curls that frame her face, and dressed in a mustard-coloured turtleneck with a black dungaree dress and stripy tights.

She claps her hands together and the noise level starts to fall until there's silence.

'Right then, raise your hand if you like pens.' Nearly every hand shoots up. 'OK, what about notebooks? And pencils? And chocolate biscuits? Well, that's what Edie's company sells to different offices. Now you're going to hear all about it.'

★

Despite my nerves I manage to make it through the introduction to my job and the story without incident, with the children still more or less concentrating.

'OK, class,' says Claudia, 'I've got a very important question and I want you to think long and hard about it. What do you want to be when you grow up?'

They suddenly snap to attention pondering one of life's deep questions for a seven-year-old. Adults ask children it all the time. It's a bit of a cruel trick in a way, making them dream big, convincing them they can be anything they want, but how many people actually get their exact dream job? Don't most people have to adjust their life goals based on the hand they're dealt? The resources they have, the grades they get, the opportunities that are available to them. Or, in my case, the life they inherit when everything falls apart.

'Let's see, does anyone want to be a firefighter?' asks Claudia, pausing to see a show of hands. 'OK, a few. How about an astronaut? . . . A doctor? . . . Chef? . . . Actor? . . . Business owner? How about you, Scarlett?'

'I want to be the prime minister or a zookeeper.'

'Excellent choices. Lucas?'

'A sorcerer.'

'Like a magician?'

'Like a wizard,' he says, his eyes widening.

'Magic, I like it.' Claudia nods. 'Now what do you think Marcus in the book wanted to be?'

Hands shoot up and she points to a boy at the back.

'Um, everything? But he looked happiest in the pictures when he was an astronaut.'

'He did look pretty happy in that picture and maybe that was what he wanted to do the most. But isn't that the best bit? That there are so many options and possibilities of what he could do?'

'Yes, he's lucky. He'll grow up to be *a man*,' says Scarlett, twiddling hair around her finger.

I bite my lip and try not to laugh as she seems to have morphed from a seven-year-old into a fully grown woman.

'You'll be able to do all those things too. Edie is living proof that you can achieve great things if you work hard for it,' says Claudia, swooping in quickly.

Scarlett doesn't look convinced, and I try hard not to smile. She's so feisty that I have no doubt in my mind that she'll be smashing glass ceilings whatever she decides to do.

'And what did you want to be, Edie, when you were our age?' asks Rohan, one of Layla's twins.

'Oh, um, I . . .' I'm caught off guard by the question and my mind's gone blank. 'I'm not sure, maybe at your age . . . I probably wanted to be a ballerina or a bobsleigh driver.'

The kids pull confused faces and Claudia, who must be close in age to me, laughs.

'There was a film . . . bit of a long story,' I try to explain. 'But then when I got older, I dreamed of changing the world, becoming a lawyer or even a teacher.'

'I overheard my mum saying once that no one actually wants to be a teacher. She couldn't think of anything worse,' says Kiran, Layla's other son. Layla's earlier fears suddenly make sense.

Claudia puts her hands on her hips. 'I'll have you know that I always wanted to be a teacher. I used to line up my soft toys and take the register and read them books when I was a little girl. Besides, who else is going to put up with you all?' she says with a cheeky smile to the children.

'I think your job sounds way cooler,' says another one of the boys, pointing at me. 'Do you get to boss people about?'

'Well, I am the boss, but part of being a good manager is that you don't boss people about, but you enable staff to—'

'What's the point of being a boss if you can't be bossy?' says a girl. 'Do you ever make people cry?'

'No, never. Or at least not intentionally; there *was* one time, but it was a big misunderstanding . . . Does anyone want to know about stationery?'

A hand flies up and Claudia calls on the boy.

'Do you have one of those pencil sharpeners that you put the pencil in and it makes that grrrrrr sound and it comes out all sharp?'

'I do, we also sell them.'

'Wow.' The whole class looks impressed. 'Do you have it in your bag?'

'Sadly not.'

'Anyone got any more questions?' asks Claudia over the sighs of disappointment.

'Are you married?'

'Um . . . no.'

'Do you have a Ferrari?'

'Do you have a horse? My dad won't let me get a horse, but I bet you have lots of money, so you have one.'

The children have perked up and they're no longer waiting to ask their questions and they're shouting out whatever pops into their head all at the same time and I'm turning this way and that trying to answer them all.

'How many kids have you got?'

'Um, none . . . yet,' I say, feeling flustered.

'You better hurry up,' says a girl at the front. 'My mum's always moaning that she's too old for all this and that she should have had me earlier.'

First Layla and the talk of proposals and now the kids telling me I should have kids . . . I tug at my blouse; it suddenly feels very warm in here.

'How old are you, exactly?' says a boy, squinting and trying to appraise me as if to answer his own question.

'I'm thirty-five, today, actually.'

There are gasps before they break into a spirited version of 'Happy Birthday' that even startles Claudia.

'What did you get for your birthday, Miss? I got Minecraft Lego.'

'We're getting a little off topic here, so I think that it might be time to wrap this up. Good job, Edie. Shall we give her a round of applause?'

I'm treated to some deafening applause before the bell rings.

'OK, line up, Mrs French will take you out to the playground.'

They leap up and start pushing and shoving their way into a line and the teaching assistant leads them out.

'And then there was peace,' says Claudia as the last child leaves.

'I don't know how you do it.'

'You get used to it.' She puts the chairs we were sat on back by a nearby desk. 'You were so good with the kids. Do you spend a lot of time around them?'

'Me?' I slip my handbag onto my shoulder. 'Not really.'

'You were a natural. You know, I'm a trustee for a literacy charity and we're always looking out for people to help and I think you'd be perfect for it.'

'A charity, right, I'm sure the company could sponsor you.'

'Thanks, that's kind, but what we're desperate for are volunteers: people who will listen to the children while they read.

'The charity's called Big Little Readers. You might have seen it in the local news when it was launched last year?' I shake my head. 'Essentially, it's run out of the library and volunteers go in pairs to people's houses to read to kids who don't get the same support as others do. Maybe the child's parents are busy juggling multiple jobs, or having to care for the child's medically ill siblings, or they just need additional help that the parents themselves can't give. Every household has a different reason for needing the charity, but the volunteers are there with the same purpose: to be attentive and to help inspire the child to read.'

'What a great idea,' I say.

'It is and it's had amazing results.'

'And you want me to volunteer? I think today was a bit of a fluke, to be honest. I don't really know how to talk to kids.'

'You could have fooled me earlier.'

She walks over to her desk and roots around in her drawer.

'Here's a leaflet with more information. Why don't you have a read, and then if you're interested' – she scribbles on the back – 'that's my email address.'

She hands me the paper and I take it.

'Um, thanks. I'll think about it,' I say to be polite, but knowing that today was a one-off.

She guides me back into the reception, where I find Layla leaving the head teacher's office. We say our goodbyes to Claudia and head outside.

'Well, how did it go?' asks Layla. 'Did the twins behave themselves?'

'Yeah, it went well, and the twins were good.'

I decide not to tell her about the teacher comments Kiran made. What she doesn't know won't hurt her.

I pull my phone out of my bag to turn it off silent. I see that I've got a message.

Miles
Happy Birthday Edie! Looking forward to the next stage in our Love Story tonight ☺ xoxo

I groan.

'What is it?' asks Layla.

'I've just received the corniest text ever.'

I turn my phone round for her to see and she laughs.

'Who knew Miles was a hopeless romantic at heart? You have to admit, though, that all signs point to a proposal tonight. The restaurant. And that text message. Someone may be Mrs Cole by the end of the night,' she says, nudging me.

I get a sinking feeling in my stomach, praying beyond hope that she's got it all wrong.

Chapter 3

I open the door to Miles, or at least I presume it's him. He's laden like a pack horse with bags draped over his arms and his face is obscured by an enormous bunch of flowers.

'Hello, birthday girl,' he says.

He tries to lean down, and we do our best to kiss but the lilies get in the way. We pull apart and he attempts to hand me the flowers.

'Hello yourself. What is all this stuff?'

I take a bottle of wine that Miles is about to drop, and he manages to catch a garment bag that was slipping off his arm.

'All in good time,' he says.

I notice his overnight bag on his back that's bulging at the seams, a contrast to its usual state as Miles usually travels with only the essentials.

I walk over to the cupboard under the sink and pull out a vase. I fill it with water and place it on the kitchen island. I'm about to arrange the flowers when Miles places a small turquoise bag next to me. It's Tiffany blue. I stare at it, Layla's words about the proposal fresh in my mind.

'So, big night tonight.'

My heart starts to beat a little bit quicker.

'Yep, although it's just another year older. It's no big deal.'

Miles leans on the kitchen island and raises an eyebrow.

'But tonight is a double celebration.'

I look down at the unspoken Tiffany bag.

'Double celebration?' I squeak. We have not been dating long enough for it to be anything small and sparkly. But that bag.

'The council tender,' he says. 'I saw it on your company Facebook page.'

'Oh, right, *that*.' I breathe a silent sigh of relief.

Miles and I have been dating for about five months and it's that perfect limbo stage of a relationship before we decide if things get serious, and, if my past form is anything to go by, where things fall apart. It's an unspoken rule between us that we'll see each other a few nights a week, usually alternating between whose flat we stay in, but it's not expected. There are no assumptions that we'll be each other's plus ones to events if we don't want to go. Yet, whilst we've got those boundaries in place, we're also comfortable enough around each other that I don't mind if he sees me first thing in the morning make-up free with massive bedhead, and he's unfortunately perfectly comfortable parading around in his flat in the pair of bright-orange fisherman trousers that he bought when travelling in Thailand. Ones that are quite frankly so hideous that they should have been confiscated at customs.

'I thought you would have been excited. Hopefully it's going to bring in a lot of business.'

'Fingers crossed,' I say, trying to find some enthusiasm. Winning the tender means we're on the preferred suppliers list for the county council, which means all the council-run organisations – anything from the museums to country parks to the main offices themselves – now have the possibility of ordering from us. Doors that, up until now, were previously closed to us.

'You never know, it might lead to an offer from a bigger company wanting to buy you out.'

'You know I could never sell the business.' I walk over to the coat hook and slip a light jacket over my dress.

Miles is a corporate lawyer and he's used to the cut-throat world of global mergers and acquisitions. No matter how much I try and explain the family business and loyalty we have to our staff, he doesn't get it. I could never sell it and risk what would happen to them.

'Maybe if the offer was high enough it might be too good to refuse.'

'I think you get Porter's confused with one of the multi-million-pound companies you deal with.' I decide to change the subject as we're never going to agree. 'So, what time is the reservation for?'

'Ah, about that,' he says. 'I cancelled it.'

I sigh with relief. It must mean there's no engagement on the horizon if we're no longer going to *the* proposal restaurant.

'I hope you don't mind,' he continues, 'but I thought it would be more romantic if we did something just the two of us here. I've got everything we need.'

'Oh, OK,' I say, surprised. 'That sounds lovely.'

He smiles and slides the Tiffany bag towards me. 'Here's your present, by the way. Happy birthday.'

I flick the hair out of the back of my jacket and pick the bag up, my hands trembling. I try and read his face but he's not giving anything away. I pull out the box, which is thankfully too big for a ring, and I begin to relax. I flip open the lid expecting jewellery, only to be confused by the solid lump of silver in front of me.

'It's a wine bottle stopper. The one you've got looks to be on its last legs.'

I glance over at the stopper that's poking out of an open bottle of red. It's got a ceramic Portuguese cockerel on top, and it's at least seventeen years old. It was a present from a holiday Mum and Dad went on the summer she died. It was probably a last-minute purchase at the airport, one that she thought I'd take to university that September and lose. But it was the last thing she ever gave me and because of that it's become one of my most treasured items.

'Oh, um, thanks.' I turn the super-sleek, beautifully designed silver stopper over in my hands. I don't tell him what the cockerel stopper means to me. Miles isn't one of those people who wants to know everything about me and the life I've lived before him; he baulks at hearing anything even remotely emotional, and sometimes – like now, when grief is tightening its grip around my heart – that suits me just fine.

'So, what have you got planned for us tonight?' I ask, putting the wine stopper back in its box.

'It's a surprise. I just need to set a few things up.' He looks down at his bulging rucksack. 'I know it's your flat and every-thing, but I need you to disappear for a little while. Ten minutes or so.'

'OK. I'll go in the bedroom.'

'Nope, I need that too. How about you wait downstairs in the foyer.'

I think for a minute that he's joking, but he starts to usher me out.

'Ten minutes?'

'Fifteen minutes, max,' he says, closing the door behind me.

I head downstairs and settle myself in the faux leather chair next to the main entrance. I can't help laughing at what a strange day it's been. From having my life picked apart by a class of seven-year-olds to being chucked out of my own flat whilst Miles does goodness knows what to it.

It might not have been the day I imagined I'd have, and certainly not one that would meet most people's expectations of a birthday, but it's been good enough for me. And one that didn't warrant the uneasy feeling I've had all week.

I pull my phone out of my jacket pocket and text Layla the news that we're no longer going to The Chambers. Then I check my emails. I'm scrolling through the usual marketing ones when I spot what looks like a very sophisticated phishing scam. It's an email with my name as the sender. I'm about to delete it but then I spot the subject line and it sends shivers up my spine: Note to My Future Self.

It can't be.

I click open and hold my breath.

Dear Future Edie,
    Hello, from the past!!!!!!!!!!!!!!!!
    Now don't freak out - it is me! Or should
I say you 17 years ago if I've got my
maths right. In case you can't remember,
I'm writing this from the reception desk
at Hartland's Holiday Park. It's so quiet
in here today as there are free cocktails
by the pool and, unsurprisingly, no one is

popping in with their usual questions or complaints.

But I'm not writing to you just because I'm bored; I'm doing it because today is a momentous occasion. It's my 18th, whoop! Which of course means it's your birthday too – Happy Birthday – God, you're so old now ;). Mum's already had a giant cupcake-shaped cake delivered. Will I ever be old enough for her not to go over the top with the birthday celebrations?

Tonight, I'm heading out with the gang to a pub in Westerly for my first legal drink! I can't wait to shove my ID right in the bouncer's face now that I'll no longer be trembling in fear that they're going to let everyone else in but me.

All morning, Soph, Douglas, and Joel have been discussing how I should properly mark turning 18. Douglas thought I should get a tattoo, but Soph mentioned something about writing a letter about goals and it reminded me of a website Mr Cross had told us about in an English lesson once, where you could email yourself in the future. So here I am! And if you're reading this then it's worked!

I probably should have picked a landmark age to send this to, like 30 or 40, but I'm excited that, as of today, I'll be ticking that 18-34 box on forms, which means you'll be eligible for the 35 and over box, and we all know that's who the real grown-ups are!

What's it like to be a proper adult and to finally have this whole life thing sussed? I hope that you're living life to the fullest. Don't worry, I won't hold it against you if you haven't been bungee jumping or skydiving – yawn. I hope instead that you've embraced every second of life, and you've done lots that has both scared you and made you smile :)

Let's hope you've figured out your life plan and that Mum and Dad haven't sucked you into 'the firm' (said in my best mobster-impression voice). I bet you're changing the world, aren't you? That you became a barrister or something, fighting for injustice. I hope you're generally kicking arse (ass?) and that Mum and Dad have finally forgiven you for not taking Business Studies at university!

Obviously, you'll have found the secret to having a super ethical job that sticks a middle finger up to the man yet still pays mega bucks, and then you'll be able to afford more than the value noodles that I've been living off since arriving at Hartland's, and maybe your drink of choice will be more sophisticated than a Blue WKD.

Now, obviously you'll be married to Scott; I know that he is most definitely the one.

But, in case you're not, I can hardly bring myself to type that, is your husband really fit? Did you have a big wedding? I'm guessing you've got kids? One? Two? Three? FOUR? Mum was teasing the other day saying she wanted lots of grandkids.

It must be so weird to have lived through all this and have grown up the other side. I envy you so much. You'll have your shit all sorted. I'm sure you'll probably look back on this time with fond memories. The summer you escaped from the parents. Plus, in a few months you'll be (grades willing) at the University of Leicester. Don't people say that university years are the best of your life? How depressing will that be to graduate and think that my best years are behind me.

Although, I seriously think that this job might be the best time of my life. I've made such good friends and it just never stops. There's always something going on – and the work isn't that bad.

Now, Mr Cross said that we should include a note to self – an inspirational message from the past to give you a kick up the old bottom. So here goes. Do something you wouldn't usually do. From what I know of adults, they always live within their com-fort zones, like they've forgotten that real

living happens when you step outside of it.
Remember, your comfort zone does not have
a brick wall built around it.
 Much love,
 A lot younger you x x

It takes me a second or two to process what I've just read and then I go back to the start and I read it another three times to make sure I'm not hallucinating. Goosebumps creep up my arms.

It breaks my heart to think of eighteen-year-old me. She was so care- and worry-free, living her life in a way that I'd forgotten I had once done. She sounded so young, and she had no idea what was coming her way and how it would change her life forever.

I don't often think about the long summer at Hartland's. It's so hard to remember all the fun I had over those few months without thinking about how it ended abruptly when my mum died. Without the guilt around her death creeping in and weighing me down. Without me thinking about falling in love with Joel and how he broke my heart.

I'm about to read it a fourth time when a message from Miles pops up on the screen telling me it's time to come back to the flat.

Miles. I remember where I am and prise myself out of the chair, my legs unsteady as I walk back on autopilot.

It's dark when I get there, and I flick the lights on.

'Hey, turn them off,' says Miles, appearing at the end of the hallway. 'Woah. You look like you've seen a ghost.'

'I almost have,' I whisper.

Miles takes my hand and leads me into the lounge. It's dark in there too and he guides me to the sofa. He perches on the edge, sitting stiff and upright and it takes me a second to work out why. He's wearing a tux, only it's a little snug and it looks like it's restricting his movements.

I scan round the room, there's a blanket on the floor and there are scores of glasses housing lit tealights. Rose petals are scattered over the floor, and there's the most delicious smell coming from the oven.

'Did you do all this? It looks amazing.'

'Yes.' He straightens his bow tie. 'I googled "romantic evenings in" and followed their recommendations.'

I can't help but suppress a smile. Googling romance is such a typical thing for Miles to do. Still, he's gone to a lot of effort to execute it beautifully.

'I like your tux.'

'It's a little tighter than it used to be,' he says, trying to tug it down. 'We're going to have a picnic inside and watch a movie. I've got some Camembert in the oven. I thought if I was going to do cheesy, we needed cheese.'

I splutter a laugh and I blink back a rogue tear.

'Edie, what's happened? Even in this light you look pale.'

'I'm fine,' I say, my voice wobbling. 'I just received an unexpected email from someone.'

'Who was it from?'

I open my mouth to tell him, but I worry if I do that he'll laugh and think I'm weird that I wrote to myself, or, worse, that he'd want to read it.

'It was from an old friend that I'd met the summer after my A levels. We worked at a holiday park in Dorset together.'

He doesn't put two and two together to realise that's the year that my mum died.

'Oh, right,' he says. 'Do you need to write back or take a moment?'

I wipe under my eyes and I attempt to smile. I can't think about it now. Miles has gone out of his way to do all this for me.

'No, it's fine. So, what film have you picked?'

'*Love Story*. The website said pick a love story, so I assumed it would be perfect.'

I scrunch my eyes shut. That's depressing on a good day, let alone after reading the email that I've just received.

'What? Don't you like it?'

'It's just . . . it's a bit sad.' That being a massive understatement.

'Oh, really? It's not romantic?' His face falls.

'Well, it is,' I say, trying to give him credit, 'but it's also a story of heartbreak too.'

'Oh, I should have done better research.' He looks so disappointed. There he is in his tux, which he might rip through at any moment. He's gone to so much trouble.

'It's fine, we can stick *Bridget Jones* on instead.'

I need something that's funny and warm and something that can distract me from the maelstrom in my mind.

'Perfect. Pop it on and I'll get the cheese out and we can start our cheesy night.'

He gets up like a mechanical robot.

'Edie, do you mind if I change first? I should have perhaps tried the tux on beforehand.'

'Change away. Thanks for making the effort.'

He bends down and kisses me and we hear an unmistakable sound of ripping and we both wince.

Miles shuffles out and both of us can't help laughing at how silly he looks. It momentarily lifts my mood, but, when he disappears, thoughts of the email flood back.

'Bloody hell,' I mutter, closing my eyes.

I wonder if somewhere in the back of my mind I was expecting this email and that's why I've felt anxious about turning thirty-five.

My head's spinning and all I can think of is the next instalment, because I might not remember what I wrote but I do remember that once I started sending emails to the future, I couldn't stop.

Chapter 4

The summer before I started university, I'd had my heart set on going interrailing. I'd been dating my boyfriend Scott for almost two years, and back then that felt like a lifetime. I'd been heartbroken at the thought that he and his best mate were going away for a whole month around Europe. On one of the many occasions when I'd been moaning about our impending separation, he'd invited me to tag along, and I'd jumped at the chance. The only slight complication was that I'd have to convince my parents, who'd ultimately be funding the trip, to let me go.

Despite the comprehensive presentation about the cultural experiences I'd have and how I'd pay them back working at university, my parents weren't thrilled about the idea. At first, I thought they were saying no because they wanted to exploit a cheap labour source by having me work at Porter's over the summer, or that they wanted to keep me close for our last summer together before I moved away. But then they tried to make me see it through Scott's friend's eyes and how I'd be turning him into a third wheel on his own trip. They suggested that I concentrate on earning money for university and that Scott and I could go the year after. And when they put it like that, a trip just the two of us did sound more appealing, especially when we could visit places like Paris and Venice, the cities of love.

'So, I take it you think I should work for you at Porter's then?' I said with a groan.

My dad went to speak, but my mum put her hand on his arm and interrupted him.

'Actually, I think you should go to Hartland's. The summer I spent working there changed my life.' She looked over at Dad and they shared one of their sickeningly in love glances. 'Lionel's still there, running the show. I could give him a shout.'

It was a story I'd heard many times before: Mum met Dad when she was working at the reception at Hartland's Holiday Park when she was sixteen and he was holidaying with his friends. Mum got roped in to judge a knobbly knees competition in which Dad was taking part. He might have got last place in the competition, but he ended up with her phone number, so he always said he was the true winner.

We used to go there on holiday a lot when I was little. It was a special place for our family. But as the business started to do better, they had the money to holiday abroad and instead we visited Westerly for daytrips.

'You never know, you might meet the man you're going to marry there just as I did.'

I groaned. 'I've already met him, and he's going interrailing.'

Mum and Dad exchanged looks; they didn't need to say what they were thinking.

'I met Scott when I was sixteen, same age as you, Mum.'

Dad bit his lip trying not to laugh.

'And I bet if Dad was going interrailing you'd have gone with him.'

'I couldn't have afforded it. And neither can you. Work the summer, and then go travelling with Scott next year. I promise you'll have just as many adventures working at Hartland's.'

I'd scoffed, thinking that she was quite delusional, but I thought if I didn't agree to go they'd only make me work at Porter's and I didn't want to spend a second summer there.

It wasn't until I was standing with my backpack staring at the entrance sign to the holiday park that I wondered how my parents could think it was in any way comparable to a European travel adventure.

The T was hanging precariously from the entrance sign and I wondered if that was indicative of the rest of Hartland's, like it had seen better years.

'Are you sure you're going to be OK?' Dad asked. 'We can park the car up and come in if you like?'

They were both standing on their respective sides of the car, equally reluctant to get in. I wanted to jump back in the car and tell them there'd been a mistake. I might have been bored out of my brain at Porter's last year, but its familiarity was suddenly appealing. I hadn't expected to feel so scared to leave my parents.

'I'll be fine, you go,' I said, trying to be brave. I knew that university was only a few months away. I was going to have to stand on my own two feet then. My parents wouldn't always be there in the car whenever things got too scary.

'OK, well, if there's any problems we'll be at the hotel until tomorrow night. And any problems after that we're only forty minutes up the road,' said Mum.

'What, if you drive like Michael Schumacher?'

Dad laughed. 'Remember, we pay the bill for your mobile, so make sure that some of the calls are to us.'

I was ready to fly the nest, desperate for my own space, yet at the same time I didn't want to leave my parents. Even though I'd never admit it out loud with all my teenage embarrassment, I was worried how I'd cope without them.

I'm not saying we had one of those magical relationships where my parents were my best friends and we never had a cross word. They drove me crazy a lot of the time and they interfered in everything. But they were still my parents and they were always there when I needed them.

'If you're sure you're going to be OK?' said Mum again.

'I'm sure.'

I waved as they got back in the car and I turned towards the entrance. I needed to get a grip; it wasn't like I was never going to see them ever again.

When I was little, I remembered Hartland's being a magical place, not only because it's where my parents fell in love, but also where fun could be found around every corner. I made my way through the open gates and headed to the portacabin reception. I was surprised at how small and unglamourous the site looked – nothing like it did in my memories or on the website.

The receptionist behind the desk was a young woman about the same age as me. She had straight blonde hair that was layered heavily to make it look almost spiky at the edges, and she wore a bright-red T-shirt with a name badge that read Elizabeth.

'Can I help?' she asked, looking me up and down.

'Um, yes, I'm a new member of staff, Edie Porter.'

She looked me up and down again, seeming no more impressed than she had the first time.

'I've got a list somewhere. Ah, here we are, Edith?'

'Yes, but everyone calls me Edie.'

'Right, well, Edith, here's your key.'

She pulled out a photocopied map and drew a big circle.

'Looks like you're sharing with me and Sophie. Hope you're tidier than she is.'

She handed me the key and turned straight back to her computer.

I wasn't expecting any kind of welcoming committee, but I'd hoped for a smile at least.

'Is there any other information I need to know? Am I going to be meeting Lionel today or . . .?'

Elizabeth looked up like it pained her to do so.

'You'll meet him at four p.m. at the team meeting. It'll take place in the staffroom at the bottom of the staff accommodation.'

'Thanks . . . Elizabeth, is it?'

'It is to you!'

I snatched the keys and turned away, not bothering to ask any more. I scanned the road, hoping my parents' car would still be there, but they'd gone.

'You look like you're about to do a runner,' said a man with a Scottish accent. He was wearing a bright-red T-shirt that matched Elizabeth's and a shell necklace around his neck. His longish light-brown hair was bleached at the tips and I wondered if it was from the sun or if he'd dyed it. I guessed he was a little older than me, but not by much.

'Is it that obvious?'

I was on the verge of tears and I was doing everything I could to hold them in.

'Ah, don't tell me you've just had a run-in with Ms Randall-Perry. Otherwise known as Elizabeth and only Elizabeth. Don't worry, we don't all bite like her. What did you do, call her Liz, Lizzie, or Beth? She doesn't approve of name shortening.'

'None of the above; she found out that I was sharing a room with her.'

He winced and pulled a face.

'No wonder you were tempted to run,' he said with a laugh. 'Come on, I'll show you where your room is. I'm Douglas.'

'Not Doug or Dougie, just Douglas?'

'Oh, please, do not make me sound like I'm like Elizabeth. But yes, just Douglas. People have tried to call me Doug in the past, but I just don't suit it.'

'Nice to meet you. I'm Edie.'

He shook my hand and insisted on carrying my bag for me. He gave me a running commentary of the different areas of the campsite as we walked through. He pointed out the caravans where they put young people who made all the noise, the leisure complex in between, the fancy lodges that were closest to the beach. He told me the best shift rotation was night security and the bin runs were the worst. He was a wealth of information, only the more he told me about life on the campsite, the more daunting the job sounded. Where was the fun Mum had promised?

'Here we are,' he said as we reached what looked like an old 1950s motel. There were three identical-looking floors, all with external walkways sheltering the doors. 'There's a staffroom there at the end of the other block. This is my bedroom, by the way; you might want to remember that one,' he suggested with a cheeky wink.

'Douglas, you're not hitting on a yet another member of staff, are you?' said a woman leaning over the railing.

'Of course not. Would I possibly do that when it's against

the code of ethics in the staff handbook?' he shouted up before turning to me. 'But when did rules ever stop anyone?'

'Douglas,' shouted the woman again.

'That's your roommate, Soph.' He sighed and did a mock bow. 'I'll leave you in her capable hands.'

He walked away and I made my way up the stairs.

'Don't mind Douglas, not all the boys that work here are as incorrigible as him. You'll get used to him and his ways. I've known him for years; he's my cousin Joel's friend from boarding school. You got a boyfriend?' Unlike Elizabeth she had a wide, welcoming smile.

'Yeah, his name's Scott.'

'Nice. I've got one called Billy. Well, he's not my boyfriend, we're not exclusive or anything, but you know. He's in a band. They play here on a Friday night, so you'll get to see him then. I'm Soph, by the way.'

'Edie.'

'Lovely to meet you.' She looped her arm through mine and pulled me into one of the open doors. 'Come and see our flat.'

I wasn't expecting the Ritz, but I found myself in a corridor where the walls looked like they were made from cardboard. There were two doors either side of the corridor, and a small fridge with a microwave balanced precariously on top at the end. Calling it a flat seemed overly generous.

'That's Elizabeth's room. Don't ever make the mistake of going in there and touching anything; if a thing is out a millimetre, she'll know about it. This is my room.' I glanced through the open door to a room with a bright-purple bed-spread and a collage of photos Blu-tacked across one wall. 'That's the bathroom. And this is you.'

She flung open the door to a bare-looking room that had a small double bed with a green plastic mattress on top, a long, tall cupboard and a chest of drawers.

'It's a bit basic, but we don't spend a lot of time in here. To be honest, most of the time you'll be working and if we're not we're at a party or at the beach. I'm a local, so stick with me as I know where all the best places are.'

I slumped the backpack off my back and stared at the prison-like walls. Soph was rattling off pubs and bars in the town and I was only vaguely listening.

Everything was so overwhelming, and it hit me all at once; I was really doing it.

'I've got some Archers in my room, fancy one with lemonade? You know, a toast for the summer?'

'Yes,' I said, nodding to Soph. 'I'd love one.'

'We're going to be great friends, Edie. I can tell.'

Her whole face lit up and suddenly the place didn't seem so bad after all.

Chapter 5

I haven't been able to stop thinking about the summer at Hartland's since I got the email from the past a week ago. It's been manic in the office since we got on the council tender, sending out quotes, meeting new clients. Usually, I throw myself into work more than usual when I want to escape real life, but even that's not working.

The email has got too deep under my skin and opened the floodgates to memories that are popping back in my mind thick and fast. It was such a bittersweet period of my life that it's too painful to think about. My brief taste of freedom whipped away in a flash.

'Are you ready to go?' asks Layla. She's got her jacket on and her handbag's slung over her shoulder.

'It can't be that time already, is it?'

I look down at my monitor and see that it's 12.30 p.m. and time for the lunch I agreed to.

'Don't tell me, you're not going to be able to make it?' Her hands automatically go up to her hips.

'She's going,' says Claire, the office manager, overlooking her glasses. 'She's been miles away today; I reckon she could have gone to Australia and back.'

'I haven't got anywhere near what I wanted to do done.'

'Don't worry,' says Claire, 'it'll still be here when you get back. Knowing you, you'll work late anyway.'

Claire's worked at the company since I was a little girl, and occasionally, like now, I catch her looking at me not as her boss, but as that same little girl who needed telling what to do.

'Come on.' Layla flashes a triumphant grin. I know I'd be fighting a losing battle if I tried to protest.

We walk on autopilot to our favourite café tucked along one of the back alleys in town. We always say we should go somewhere different, but we never do.

'How's everything with you? Apart from the boys and their birthday lobbying?'

'Oh, you know. I'm trying to plan the military operation that is also known as the school holidays. The kids do need a break, but six weeks?'

'What's in the plan so far?'

'Let's see. Both boys want to do a football camp, which will almost require us to take out a second mortgage, but I feel like any opportunity to get them off a screen is worth taking. Then I'm trying to schedule in the grandparents to take them for a couple of days a week, but that's proving tricky. I tell you, my mum has a more active social life than I do with her lawn bowls and her baking club.'

'You know, if there's anything we can do to help, then do say. You could bring the boys into work or if you need to work from home, we could fit around your schedule.'

I think of the summers I spent hiding under one of my parents' desks, drawing on the old printing paper with the perforated edges with as many highlighters as I could get my hands on.

'Homeworking is always very welcome, but coming into the office is my break, my sanctuary. Plus, the boys would just be hooked into their devices at home, so the more I can get them out of the house the better. We'll cope somehow. Sorry for the rant.'

'Rant away. That's what I'm here for.'

'I think I'm done now,' she says, taking a deep, cleansing breath. 'So how about you? How come you're so distracted today?'

We reach the café and I hold the door open for Layla to walk through. We wave at Sue the owner and plant ourselves on a table in the corner.

'It's a little weird.'

'Like, what kind of weird? Like sexually weird? Is Miles into something?' Her eyes light up.

'Um, no.' I try and stop disturbing images of him in rubber popping into my mind.

'If it isn't Miles then, what is it?'

I'm hesitant to tell anyone but at the same time if I don't tell someone I'm going to lose my mind.

'I got an email from myself that I wrote seventeen years ago,' I say in a hurry like I'm ripping off a plaster.

Layla looks at me, confused.

'Who wrote it?'

'I did, seventeen years ago. I used this website where you input the date in the future that you want it sent, along with the email address of the recipient, and I guess it stores the info on a server and sends it at the requested date.'

'That sounds like something out of a film.' She doesn't look any less confused. 'Well, come on then. What did the email say?' She's raising her eyebrow so much it's almost lodged in her hairline.

'It was pretty cringey. It was supposed to be this whole inspiration-to-your-older-self thing. I was only eighteen. It was when I was working at a holiday camp.'

'You worked at a holiday camp? I didn't think you'd ever worked anywhere other than Porter's.'

It's the first time in a long time that Layla looks genuinely surprised at something I've said.

'It was the only other job I've had. I worked there for a summer.'

'How did I not know this? Where was it?'

'Westerly in Dorset.'

'Oh, I've heard that part of the world is supposed to be lovely. Tim's always saying we should go on holiday there with the boys.'

'You should. It's a gorgeous area. Westerly itself is on the river and has all these different colour houses that line it. Then there are the quaint villages that have chocolate-box cottages covered in thatch and pubs with those crooked wooden beams. Not to mention the nature reserves full of heather and the beaches.'

If I close my eyes, I can smell the heather and hear the waves crashing against the rocks.

'Sounds wonderful.'

'It is.' I almost choke on my words. I haven't been to Westerly since that summer and my heart almost aches thinking about it.

It's probably changed so much over the last seventeen years. I've often thought about going back, but I've always chickened out at the last minute.

Sue comes over and takes our order and, when she leaves, Layla holds her hand out expectantly and I wonder what she's doing.

'Are you going to let me read it?'

I hesitate, before I find my phone in my bag. It's not like there was anything particularly embarrassing in there and the truth is I need her to understand what's in it so I can talk about it. I hand it over.

I watch her face as she reads it. Her expression's switching from a look of concentration to one of amusement.

'Who was Scott?'

'Oh, he was my boyfriend from home; he ended up cheating on me and we broke up that summer.'

Layla nods and carries on reading.

It's agonising waiting for her to finish; I'm anxious to hear her thoughts.

'You sound so different,' she says, looking up, wrinkling her face in confusion. 'I never would have guessed you wrote this. You sound so . . .'

'Fun?'

'I was going to say energised.'

'Ha, that's a polite way of saying that I'm boring now.'

'No, it's a polite way of saying that you're no longer eighteen. None of us would sound how we did when we were that age – thank goodness. In all honesty, I don't think I'd be friends with that Edie now; she'd exhaust me. Give me Edie who likes the occasional spa day and box set bingeing any day.'

I laugh. 'Thank you, I needed to hear that.'

I take my phone back and slip it in my bag.

'You know . . .' She starts to move the salt and pepper shaker around on the table, avoiding eye contact. 'It might not hurt to take her advice a little and step out of your comfort zone once in a while.'

'You're siding with past me?'

'Not siding. It's just, it might not hurt to shake it up a little. Not timetable your life so much that your office manager can predict your every move. Perhaps not going to the same café every week.'

'I'm not that predictable.'

'Here you go, the usual, just the way you like it,' says Sue, putting down our coffees in front of us.

Layla bites her tongue, trying not to laugh.

'I like routine,' I say, pulling my Americano towards me.

'We all do; in fact, living with the twins I crave it. Maybe I'm just secretly jealous of yours.'

'I don't have a life to be jealous of.'

'Oh, no, perfect-sized flat in a gorgeous building overlooking town, company director at thirty-five. Good-looking boyfriend. No, nothing to be jealous of at all,' she says, snapping a breadstick.

'Come on, you have a great life.'

'I know, and I'm so lucky, but sometimes I fantasise about a life where it's just me in a silent flat and no one to clean up after but myself.' I lose her momentarily to the fantasy. 'I'm just saying, it's nice to take a look at your life every so often, isn't it? Shake it up, try something new. Like next week, we'll try a different café for lunch.'

'Shhh, don't let Sue hear you.'

Layla laughs.

'I love that you wrote to yourself. What a great idea. Did you do it again?'

'I did, quite a few times that summer, if I remember rightly. It's all a bit hazy because time passed so differently then. I was only there for about twelve weeks, but it felt like I fitted a year's worth of living in each one.'

'Wow, so this is the first of many?'

'Uh-huh, I'm just waiting for the next one to arrive.'

Layla sips at her drink, leaving a layer of foam on her lips. I gesture to it and she brushes it away.

'Do you keep in touch with any of those friends?'

'Not really. Soph and Douglas tried to at first, after I left when Mum—' The word gets stuck in my throat because I so rarely tell the story.

'It was that year that she died?' She tilts her head, and her face softens.

'Yeah, it was a few days before I was due to leave. Soph did come to visit me a couple of times after that and she'd send me Christmas cards, but our lives were just so different, what with me working and she at university. It sounds petty, but it hurt to keep in touch with her and Douglas because they were living the life I wanted to and couldn't have.'

Layla reaches out and squeezes my hand.

'It was such a difficult time for you. You've got to remember that you were so young. Imagine that girl who wrote that email suddenly having to run a company and look after your dad with all the stuff that happened to him. From the sounds of it, you got thrown in at the deep end.'

Layla joined the company a few years after me and she didn't witness first-hand the aftermath of when my mum died and when Dad's drinking went out of control. Those were the worst years of my life. By the time she started work, Dad had sorted himself out, and I'd accepted that Porter's was where I was meant to be. Dad helped me with a deposit to buy my own shoebox-sized flat and I'd started my Open University business studies course. I'd said it was because I wanted to get a degree, but it was mainly to keep busy to ensure I didn't have time to think about things that hurt.

'I bet if this was a movie the emails would be magical and you'd be able to write back to yourself,' says Layla, snapping me out of my thoughts.

'What and offer past me advice?'

'Uh-huh, although it could be dangerous. How does it go in the movies? With every little tweak to the timeline comes life-altering repercussions. You mention something you think is innocent to your past self and, next thing you know, one minute we're sat here, the next we've disappeared. Can you imagine if you told yourself not to start at the company? You never would have met me as, without you on the interview panel, I probably wouldn't have got the job.'

'Don't say that; the office wouldn't be the same without you and we all know it. But imagine if I could change the past . . .'

I could tell past Edie not to let Mum drive the night she died. Or I could tell her not to pick up the phone when Mum rang. Or not to have got so drunk in the first place. Or not to have confronted Joel. There were so many things I could have done differently that night that would have stopped my parents from getting in that car accident.

I hadn't realised that a tear had fallen down my cheek until Layla hands me a serviette.

'Oh Edie, I wasn't thinking. Of course, there'd be so much you'd want to change.'

I wipe my face, trying to stop the guilt taking hold.

'It's fine. It's just all been a bit of a shock.'

Sue comes over and puts our plates in front of us and I'm grateful for the interruption.

'You promise you'll tell me when you get others?'

My mind boggles when I think of what else I'm going to get. There's no doubt Joel will play a starring role in most of them. I'm not sure I want to be reminded of that crush in vivid detail.

'Promise,' I say, wondering if I mean it. I don't know if I want to tell her about Joel because, after all these years, it still feels every bit as painful.

The chat with Layla at lunch allowed me to finally concentrate on my work for the rest of the afternoon. It's only now that the office has started to thin out at the end of the day that my mind's started to wander there again.

'I'm off; don't stay too late,' says Dad, putting on his suit jacket and turning off his computer monitor.

'I won't.' I rub at my eyes. 'I was thinking of going soon. Did you want to grab dinner?'

He pauses and I notice that he's a little flustered.

'Actually, I'm um . . . meeting Julie tonight; she's cooking me dinner so I um . . .'

'Oh, right. That sounds nice.' I'm forcing enthusiasm into my voice and I know it probably sounds false, but I can't help it. It's not like I'm not pleased that my dad seems to have finally met someone that he likes – it's taken him long enough – but I've been so used to him always being there in the past. Now, when I ask him to do things, he's often busy or he's out when I nip in to put healthy food in his fridge.

'Yeah,' he says, 'um, but we're looking forward to having lunch with you at the weekend. It'll be nice for you to finally meet her.'

I notice the use of the word 'we' and it stabs at my heart as 'we' used to mean him and Mum.

'I'm looking forward to it too,' I say, trying to make myself mean it. He's never been serious with any of the other women he's dated, and I have no idea how it'll make me feel to see him with an actual girlfriend.

'You know Miles is more than welcome if he wants to come.'

Miles has met my dad a couple of times, but only at after-work drinks. I'm about to bat his invitation away, but maybe it would help having an extra person there when I meet Julie. Miles would be able to plug any awkward silences with the random fun facts he likes to come out with at times.

'I'll check if he's free.' Dad looks pleased. 'I think it's supposed to rain tonight; you might want to take your brolly for the walk home.'

He nods and retreats over to the coatstand and takes out his golf umbrella. 'What would I do without you looking out for me?' he says, holding it up as he passes.

I wonder if I should call it a day too, but I don't fancy going home to an empty flat and Miles is playing five-a-side football tonight. I shut down my work anyway and pull up the email from my past self, reading it for the billionth time. Only this time when I get to the end, instead of clicking out of it, I hit reply.

Ever since Layla talked about emailing back, I've been wondering what I would say to my old self if I got the chance.

Dear Past Edie,
    Surprise! It's a very old you, one that I don't imagine you'd recognise at all. In some ways you'd be pleased to know that

I am successful, in that I own my own home, I have a nice boyfriend (not Scott, who was a cheater - DUMP HIM!!!). His name is Miles, he's clever and knowledgeable about random things, he's tall and kind and he's always trying to encourage me to be the best I can be. He's also got a well-paid job, so I guess he ticks all your boxes. I have a best friend called Layla, who I also work with, which means that I always get to see her.

I also have a very good job and I'm lucky because I'm actually a company director. You'll be less impressed to hear that the company is Porter's but at some point you'll realise that it was never really a choice; it was something that I had to do for Dad. And whilst I never did make it to an actual university (there's a bumpy ride coming, but you'll get through it), I managed to get my degree in business studies.

My life might not look anything like your life did back then and you might be disappointed with how I turned out but everyone has to grow up. And comfort zones are called comfort zones for a reason and sometimes it's nice and comforting to stay in them! Especially if you've been through what I have.

Tell Mum that you love her more, don't

answer the phone to her when you're drunk,
and give her extra hugs.
  With love, Edie x x

'Idiot,' I mutter out loud to myself after I've written it. From the corner of my eye, I catch Aaron looking over at me. I was so lost in my own little world that I'd completely forgotten I wasn't alone. I cough to cover up my outburst and turn back to my PC. Embarrassed, I go to delete the email but accidentally hit send and it disappears before I can stop it.

Layla is right though; on paper my life sounds great, but I can't shake the feeling that eighteen-year-old me would be disappointed with how my life has turned out.

'Working late?' says Aaron, walking past. He comes to a stop at the corner of my desk.

'I'm just finishing up. How about you?'

'I'm just printing some bits then heading off. We're doing a warm-up session for the Impensonators tonight.'

'Oh, what's that?'

'Our improv team. Instead of impersonators, we're the Im-*pen*-sonators because of, you know, working here.'

'Right, of course.'

'It's the annual improv battle competition coming up. Hey, we're always looking for more team members. You're welcome to come along tonight, see if it's your cup of tea.'

'Oh, um, thanks for the offer, but I'm busy tonight.'

Improv is the stuff of nightmares. Not only do you have to perform in front of people, but you also have to be good at making entertaining things up on the spot.

'Well, even if you don't fancy taking part you should come along and watch one of the battles.'

'Yeah, that sounds good.'

I really should go and see the team in action at some point. They formed after a staff night out to a comedy club. Aaron and Yas bonded over a love of comedy and signed up to an improv workshop. When they emailed the rest of the office to see if anyone wanted to join, Hayley and Dave signed up along with them. Last year they competed in a competition play-off throughout the summer, and I guess they're doing it again this year.

He retrieves his printouts from the communal printer and I try and ignore the niggle about comfort zones. Improv would be the perfect way to get out of mine. A shiver runs down my spine; that's a step too far. It's not like I need to listen to the advice of my teenage self, is it?

I glance back at my inbox, sighing with relief when I get the failure-to-send message; at least no one in a tech office somewhere gets to read my reply.

I click on the original note-to-future-self email and I move it to an archive folder. If there's one thing that I've learnt over the years, it's that looking back on the past and what might have been will only ever lead to heartbreak.

Chapter 6

Miles arrived early to pick me up to take me to Dad's house for Sunday lunch and he wasn't hanging around on the drive over either. When we pull up on the drive he practically runs towards the front door.

'Slow down,' I say, struggling to keep up with him. 'You're acting like the flipping Road Runner from *Looney Tunes*; I can't keep up. We haven't got Coyote running after us, have we?' I look behind me, pretending to check.

I'm expecting him to crack a smile or to give me some fun fact about *Looney Tunes* cartoons, but he does neither.

'What's with you?' I ask.

'I'm just nervous; it's the first time your dad's invited me to his house.'

'It's no big deal, it's just lunch.'

I feel a tiny bit guilty now that I'd only invited him to take the pressure off meeting Julie alone.

'Hello, I thought I heard voices. Come in, come in.' Dad races back to the kitchen almost as fast as Miles has been running about; it must be catching.

There's a hive of activity in the kitchen, with saucepans bubbling over and chopping boards and vegetable peelings covering most of the work surface. He opens the oven to baste what looks like a turkey.

'Isn't it just the four of us?'

'I know, I know. But I wanted everything to be just right.' Dad's hair is sticking up in all different directions from the steam and he looks well and truly flustered. He quickly shuts the oven door. 'Right, sorry about that. Now I can say a proper hello. How are you keeping, Miles?'

'Good, thank you. Here.' He digs into the bag that he's carrying and presents Dad with a box of chocolates and a bottle of wine.

The smile slides off my face as he passes Dad the bottle.

'I'll take that, shall I?' I say, intercepting it. I know that I'm being ridiculous; it's not like my dad is suddenly going to start drinking again just because his hand makes contact with a bottle, but I can't help myself.

Dad narrows his eyes at me before he turns back to Miles.

'Thank you for the chocolates, and for the wine too.'

'We'll take the bottle home with us,' I say, hugging it to my chest. 'Dad doesn't drink.'

'Oh, sorry, I didn't know.' Miles throws me a look of panic. 'I should have picked up on it. I just assumed when you didn't drink at the pub it was because you were driving. It's totally my fault.'

'No, it's mine. I should have mentioned it,' I say.

'It's no secret that I'm an alcoholic. It was a hard time for all of us. I can't say I blame Edie for wanting to forget about that period of our lives.' He slips the tea towel he was using as an oven glove over his shoulder.

'It's OK, there's really no need for you to explain,' says Miles, gesturing with his hand.

'Oh, I don't mind. After Edie's mum died, I went out of control,' Dad carries on regardless. 'I count myself lucky that thanks to my incredible daughter I managed to get sober.'

'I had no idea.'

'Then maybe that's a good thing and I've not scarred Edie for life with it.' Dad attempts to laugh and I half smile but the truth is I was scarred, which does make it even more weird why I haven't brought it up with Miles over the last five months. 'I've been sober for fourteen years now, and I'm fine with people around me drinking, but I just don't like to keep it in the house.'

'I'll go and put it in the car,' Miles offers.

'I'll go, it's my fault.' I squeeze him on the arm, feeling even more guilty. I guess that if I'm going to bring him into situations like this I should open up to him more.

As I walk down the hallway, I can't help but overhear the conversation happening in the kitchen and I stop to listen.

'So Edie mentioned roadrunners earlier and it made me think of an interesting fact; did you want to hear it?' asks Miles.

I knew he'd have a fact about it.

'About the TV show?' Even from afar, I can detect the confusion in Dad's tone.

'No, the birds in the wild.'

'Oh right, go on then.'

'Roadrunners are actually members of the cuckoo family.'

'Really?'

Dad doesn't sound impressed. It's a shame because I always thought Dad would be one of the few people who would get Miles's random facts; after all, he and Miles are quite similar in a way – Dad's always telling me about odd things he's read in the paper or seen in a documentary. I almost turn back towards the kitchen, wondering if they need a bit longer to get to know each other before they're left alone.

'Well, did you know that they're quick enough to eat a rattle-snake?' adds Dad.

'What? Now, that is impressive,' says Miles.

I hear the genuine tone of enthusiasm in both of their voices, as Miles starts telling him about rattlesnakes.

I head outside, content in the knowledge that the two of them have found some common ground.

I open the car and I sit down, sliding the offending wine bottle into the footwell. I know I should have told Miles about Dad before now, but, much like my mum's death, it's a period of my life that I'd rather forget.

It all happened so gradually that I didn't realise for a while that he had a drinking problem. I guess in my naivety I had misconceptions of what an alcoholic looked like. At first we all cut him a bit of slack over turning up for work late. I put it down to his being almost the opposite of me: whereas I threw myself into work and wanted to be in a place that reminded me of Mum, Dad almost couldn't bear it.

He'd always liked a beer after work, even when Mum was alive, but after the accident he turned to wine, a large glass of red, which soon turned into a bottle, and then two bottles. Back then I was still living at home and at first he hid it so well. He always bought the same brand and hid the empties so that I didn't realise he was drinking so much. But then he started to get lazier about going to the bottle bank and empties started to accumulate at a rapid rate. The bottles began to be opened as soon as he got home and I no longer waited for him in the mornings because he never got up in time.

The final straw came when he was late for work one morning and I went into his office to find a file and I discovered a bottle of whisky hidden at the back of a filing cabinet. At first I tried to tell myself that it was a holdover from another era, when drinking at work was just part of the thing you did, only when I examined the label I discovered it had been bottled less than six months ago. It was one thing to be drinking after work, but not during.

I'd poured it down the sink and phoned him but when he didn't pick up I'd gone home. I'd raced up the stairs to find him lying on his front and my heart had stopped, fearing the worst. I'd rushed forward, only then noticing the smell. I'd looked down at my feet and seen the big, wet stain on the carpet and I'd known instantly that it was urine.

A shadow falls over the car, which startles me out of my thoughts, and I look up to see a woman standing there.

'Um, hello, are you by chance Edie?' she asks.

I hadn't really given a lot of thought to what Julie would look or be like. She appears to be around Dad's age, with shoulder-length dark hair that's been loosely curled, and she's wearing a floral maxi dress that shows off her curves.

'Yes, um, hello, you must be Julie.' I climb out of the car and we stand there, staring at each other.

'How do you do.' I hold my hand out, wondering when I've ever been so formal.

'I'm good, thank you,' she says, shaking my hand as if she's afraid of breaking it. 'I've been looking forward to meeting you; your dad talks about you all the time. He's ever so proud of you.'

'Ah, um, thank you. He talks of you too.'

She beams back and dimples appear on her cheeks. She looks over my shoulder at the door.

'Should we go in? I bet Gary's in a right muddle with the cooking.'

'He absolutely is.'

I shut the car door and am about to lead the way when she walks straight into the house.

'Ah, love, you're here,' says Dad, walking over and kissing Julie on the cheek and taking her by the hand. My legs feel unsteady by the sight and I cling on to the breakfast bar. 'I've been waiting to introduce the two special women in my life to each other and it looks like you've done it yourselves.'

'Oh yes, I've wasted no time,' says Julie.

Dad beams at her before looking back at me, and I try hard to match his enthusiastic smile. He gives me a little head bob as if I've given him approval and then he turns to introduce her to Miles and the three of them start chatting. I can't let go of the breakfast bar. Dad's dated other women since Mum died and I've met a couple of them, but this is different. This reminds me of how he used to look at Mum.

'Edie?' says Dad, and I look up at him. 'Did you want to sort out the drinks?'

Before I get a chance to react, Julie heads over to the fridge.

'I'll get them,' she says, and she pulls out a selection of juices, before she navigates to the right cupboard and gets out the glasses. There's a familiarity to her movements; she looks right at home as she prepares them all.

'So, what's cooking today then?' she asks, handing us glasses of grape juice.

'Well, if it ever cooks, it's roast turkey. I was going for a kind of family Christmas meal vibe.'

'In July,' she says, laughing.

'Exactly. But it's running a little behind schedule.' Dad lifts the lids of his saucepans one by one, grimacing at the contents.

Dad is always behind schedule with his cooking and usually I have to swoop in and take over if we're ever to eat at a reasonable time. I'm just about to offer when Julie shakes her head and goes and grabs the much-neglected apron off the back of the door and slips it over her dress before she shoos Dad away.

'What are we up against?' She lifts up the same saucepan lid that Dad had, and she laughs with him as they peer down at it.

'Take a proper seat, Miles, Edie,' says Dad, ushering us over to the dining table in the corner of the kitchen.

I do as I'm told, but I still can't get used to taking a back seat at Dad's house.

The meal was every bit worth the wait. Julie did a great job of rescuing it and ensuring that everything was cooked on time and it tasted delicious. She spent most of the meal asking us questions and, as I put down my knife and fork, I realise that I still know very little about her.

'So, Julie, Dad says that you're a physio.'

'That's right, I specialise in neurological conditions, so people with illnesses such as MS and Parkinson's or who have had strokes or brain injuries.'

She's finished her meal too and she picks up the cloth napkin from her lap and folds it on the table as she talks.

'It must be really rewarding,' says Miles.

'It can be. It can be frustrating too, what with the limitations of their injuries or illnesses, but I guess the days when you make that difference and make someone's life a bit easier and a bit better in quality, those are the days that I take as a win.'

I see the pride in Dad's eyes and if I was under any kind of illusion that Julie was just another woman that Dad was dating, that look has well and truly shattered it. Miles was right; today was a big deal, but not because he was invited to lunch, but because Julie was. I've always hoped that Dad would one day find happiness with someone again, but I never expected for it to hurt so much.

'I'll get dessert, shall I?' says Julie.

She starts to take the plates and when I go to stand up, she tells me to sit back down.

I watch as she and Dad work almost in sync with each other as they get the dessert out of the fridge and the side plates from the cupboard.

'This looks amazing,' says Miles as a large banoffee pie gets placed on the table.

'Julie made it; she's a wonderful dessert maker.'

'It's ever so easy.' She begins to cut the slices and hands them out.

Dad goes to squirt extra cream on it.

'I don't think you need any more than that, there's already hundreds of calories in it,' I say.

'Edie, you fuss too much.' He squirts a little from the can.

'I probably should have made something less calorific,' says Julie, as she takes his plate and scrapes the cream off into the empty side of the pie dish and reduces his slice to a smaller one. 'There you go.'

She hands him back his plate, and I wait for him to pick up the squirty cream in defiance, but he doesn't.

'Oh, you're probably right,' he says, taking a bite. 'It's delicious. Worth every calorie.'

I stab a little too forcefully at the biscuit base and a bit flies across the table. For so long I've been the one to keep Dad on the straight and narrow, trying to reduce his fat intake in the hope of lowering his cholesterol, and now Julie's only been on the scene five minutes and I already feel like he no longer needs me.

'Your dad mentioned you did the talk at school for him when I'd locked myself out. I felt terrible.'

'Don't worry. It was fine.'

'I was telling Julie how brave you were considering you hate all forms of public speaking.'

He gives her a knowing look. It makes me feel vulnerable knowing that he and Julie not only talk about me but that he's also telling her my fears.

'Actually I kind of enjoyed it. And the teacher even asked if I'd like to volunteer for a children's charity that reads to kids to try to encourage a love of reading.'

'She did?' says Dad, surprised.

'Yes, she did. She thought I'd be good at it.'

I go on to explain what Claudia told me of the charity.

'That sounds so worthwhile,' Julie says, nodding encouragingly.

'Aren't you worried about what you'd be walking in to?' says Miles. 'All those problems that the kids might have.'

Typical Miles; I'm sure 'always think the worst' was drummed into him during his law degree.

'Yes,' says Dad. 'Plus, I'm sure she'd understand that you with the kids was a one-off, that it wasn't your kind of thing.'

I hadn't really given it much thought before but hearing Dad automatically assume I won't do it almost makes me want to give it a go. I know past Edie would have approved. This would well and truly be something out of my comfort zone.

'Actually, I think I'm going to give it a go.'

'Good for you, Edie, it'll be rewarding,' says Julie.

'I think so.'

She points at the banoffee pie. 'Anyone for seconds?'

Miles nods through his last mouthful and she scoops him up another slice.

'It was delicious,' he says.

'If you think those are good you should try her scones. They're so good her village has asked her to bake them for the tea tent at their fête.'

'Stop it, you'll make me blush,' she says, her cheeks flushing. 'But speaking of the fête, it's next weekend if you fancy coming along.'

'I love a cream tea, so I'd normally jump at the chance to say yes,' says Miles, 'but I'm going to Florence on a stag do.'

'A stag do in Florence?' Dad laughs. 'I know since I got sober and older I haven't been on that many stag dos lately, but Florence? That's a first.'

'Why not? Men have evolved since the days of heading to the pub and drinking for hours straight. Have you booked tickets for the Uffizi?' asks Julie. I'm about to laugh out loud at the thought of Miles going to an art gallery on a stag do, but to my surprise Miles starts to nod.

'Yes, we booked them a few weeks ago. I mean, obviously we have other stag do activities lined up, but you can't go to Florence and not go there.'

'Too true,' says Julie.

'Fun fact about the Uffizi: did you know that the *Mona Lisa* once hung there? An Italian Louvre worker stole it before the First World War because he wanted it hung in Florence. When they recovered the painting the curator asked if it could go on temporary display there, so it did.'

'Fascinating,' says Julie, her eyes lighting up. 'Just talking about all that art is making me want to go back and visit. Have you been, Gary?'

'No, I haven't.'

'We'll have to go. You'd just love Florence and Sienna's nearby and their art collections are amazing too.'

I'm about to tell her good luck getting my dad to go on holiday. He's not really seen the point of them since Mum died, but before I get the chance he nods.

'I'd love to. All that Italian food and wine.'

I'm flabbergasted.

'Excellent,' says Julie. Dad raises his eyebrows and she beams back. I get the impression that if they didn't have company they would have kissed. 'But next week, how about coming with us to the fête, Edie, if Miles is away?'

'Um maybe, I'll have to see,' I say, not knowing how comfortable I'd be spending the day with just the two of them.

'Of course, you must be very busy. I'll clear up these plates, shall I?' says Julie and I get the impression that she's disappointed.

We all start clearing away the plates and I can't help but feel that I've spoiled the end of the dinner. For years I've wanted my dad to find someone and be happy, but I don't think I was properly prepared for how it would make me feel.

Chapter 7

Over the last ten days I've been checking my emails more than usual, eagerly anticipating the next note to self as I can't remember how soon after the first one that I wrote the second one. I'm about to log off my office computer, when I check my personal email one last time. I get butterflies in my stomach when I see that it's finally arrived.

I look around to make sure no one is paying me any attention, and of course the few people left in the office aren't.

Dear My Lovely Future Self,

How are you doing this fine day? Now, I know you weren't expecting to hear from me again, especially so soon! But I really enjoyed writing to you the other day. It felt a bit cathartic to talk about what's going on. I'm having the best time and I really want to tell everyone about it, but it's hard to explain it to anyone who's not here.

I only give Mum and Dad edited highlights because they worry over every mention of me going out drinking and hanging around with boys. I think things were different in Mum's day and she took her actual work a lot more seriously. LOL.

And then there's Scott who should get it; he's exploring the world too after all. On the very rare phone calls that we manage to co-ordinate he sounds bored when I tell him about our pub golf or the lilo races we have in the pool. He tells me of the different art galleries and landmarks that he's visited, making it out that he's having philosophical debates with all these cool travelling buddies. He's constantly making his adventures sound better than mine, when really it just sounds to me like he's getting stoned in every city he visits and talking bollocks.

I think that was a long-winded way of saying that it feels right emailing you, because you'll totally get this! Because you know the gang and you know that whilst it sounds like we're messing about and just drinking our way through the summer you'll know that there's more to our friendship than that. You know, the conversations we have in the wee hours round the campfire. And we talk about the future and how our lives are going to change come September when we all head off to uni; well, Douglas is going on a second gap year, but the year after he'll be going to uni.

I even love the work too. My favourite is when I'm on the kids' club rotation as then you really get to act like a big child. We do arts and crafts and play games. There's something so invigorating about the summer holidays because the children are excited all the time and it's sort of infectious. It's making me glad that I picked English Lit, so that my options are open in case I want to go into something like teaching. I dunno. I guess running a kids' club on a campsite is widely different to running a classroom and having to mark homework and to plan lessons. I know it's not all playing with parachute silks and face painting, but it has made me think.

Anyway – I love it here so much and I know I've only been here three weeks, but I don't want it to end. Can you believe that I almost didn't come? The night before I came here, I was petrified, and I drafted an email to Lionel telling him I couldn't do it. I'm so glad that I didn't listen to that little voice in my head. If there's one thing I've learnt so far from being here – and my one bit of advice that I still hope you're following – it's that you shouldn't talk yourself out of doing something just because it seems scary. Who'd have thought before this I'd be happy getting on a stage

and leading people in the 'Cha-Cha Slide'
;)?

Remember, you are capable of more than you ever expect. My note to self this time is to be brave and be bold. Make those leaps.

Laters dude.

X x x

I'm a little bit in love with old me; she's feisty and uncompromising, and, for a minute, I feel like I've just had one of those conversations with one of my girlfriends. The ones that are like pep talks that gee me up and make me think I can take over the world. Like when I used to talk to Soph or Joel back in the day.

My eyes linger on the note to self to be bold and be brave. Back when you're eighteen, everything seems possible, but when you grow up, you realise that it's not so easy.

I might have filed the first email into my archive, but I haven't been able to archive my thoughts as easily and I've started to think about the woman I used to be, the one who listened to what I wanted, and the one who really believed that there weren't walls around comfort zones. It's made me realise that I've hidden behind a routine and work for the last seventeen years, trying to keep out all of these memories, all of this thought and hurt. Just reading that new email reminds me how alive I used to be and it makes me wonder if maybe, just maybe, a little bit of that old me is still inside.

Before I can stop myself, I dig out the leaflet Claudia gave me about the charity and I type out a quick email letting her know that I'm interested in finding out more. I hit send before I can change my mind.

I stand up, full of nervous energy about what I've just done, and head to the kitchen. Layla's there washing some of the cups up and Yas is drying them and they're laughing.

'Oh, hi, Edie,' says Yas, looking up as I walk in. She's trying to compose herself and Layla's giggling away. 'Sorry, I was just filling Layla in on us getting through the first round of the play-offs; Aaron and Dave were pretending to be a pantomime horse.'

She finishes the drying up and puts the cups away.

'I heard you made it to the next round. I'm thrilled for you.'

'Yes, let's hope we can beat last year's place when we got knocked out in the third round. You'll have to both come and see us.'

'Yes, we'll have to try and organise something,' I say.

'Do,' she says before she heads out.

'You're working late tonight, no school pick-up?' I say to Layla as I fill the kettle with water.

'No, Tim's mum is staying for a few days.'

'Ah, that's why you're here over your hours.'

She pulls a face. 'It's not that I don't like her, it's just that I like to give her quality time with her precious grandchildren.'

'Uh-huh.' I don't believe a word of it.

'So, distract me from what's going on at home. Have you had any more emails?'

'I just got one.'

'And? What did it say?'

'Much the same as the first one. More about how much fun I was having with my friends and how I loved it there.'

Layla pulls the plug from the sink and the water starts to gurgle as it goes down the plughole.

'Have you ever thought about getting back in contact with them?'

I shake my head.

She gives me a look that lets me know she doesn't believe me.

'From time to time, I've wondered what has happened to them, but I've never done anything about it.'

'Well, the emails are a sign that you should! These days you can look anyone up on Facebook or Instagram.'

'Not if you don't have an account.'

'I forget you don't do social media.' She puts her cup back in the cupboard. 'What about LinkedIn? You have one of those profiles, right?'

'I do, I've never thought of that.'

'It's worth considering.'

She looks at her watch and then does a theatrical sigh.

'I really should get going, can't put home time off forever . . . unless there's some big work emergency?' She looks hopefully at me.

'I've got nothing, unless you're much better than me at coming up with some last-minute excuse.'

'Where's Yas and the rest of the improv crew when you need them,' she says with a laugh. 'See you tomorrow?'

'You will indeed. Have a good evening with Tim's mum.'

She skulks off with a resigned sigh and I make my cup of tea before hurrying back to my desk to bring up LinkedIn. I'd never thought of using it for anything other than a work tool. Claire made us make profiles a few years ago and apart from looking up the odd client I haven't used it much.

I pull up the search bar and type in 'Sophie Marsden' and hit return before I lose my nerve. There are several listed and it takes me a few scrolls to find the right one. But then I see one who looks familiar and works for a PR firm. The last Christmas card I had from Soph was just after she'd graduated, and she was working in PR in London. I click on the headshot and it's unmistakably her.

It's so strange to see adult Soph's résumé. The list of agencies she's worked for is impressive, and I notice her latest company is based in Poole, not far from Westerly. My hand hovers over the connect button and I'm tempted to send her a message, but what would I say?

I click back into the search bar, about to type in Joel's name, just to see if he's there, but I shut the site down quickly. Even after all this time, it still hurts to think of him. There's something comforting and equally terrifying knowing that they're all there, only a click away.

I turn my attention back to the spreadsheet I'm working on and I try with all my might to focus on the figures, but I can only think of the words from the email and I end up caving and re-reading it again. I'm wondering if I should call it a day when the main office line rings. The office has thinned out, so I pick it up, relieved by the distraction.

'Porter's Office Supplies, Edie speaking.'

'Ah, hello there,' says a very posh-sounding voice. 'I see that you offer supplies for people working from home.'

'Yes, we do.' I look over the top of my PC to see what members of the sales team are still in so that I can transfer it, but there's only Lucinda left and she's on another call. 'All of our sales team are on other calls at the moment, but I can get some details and get them to be in touch.'

'If that's not too much trouble.'

There's something in her voice and the way that she's elongating her words that makes her seem familiar, but I can't place it.

'No trouble. What sort of business do you run?'

'Um, well, it's a sort of a discreet one. It's just for . . . well, just for my fans, if you get my drift.'

'OK . . .' Why didn't I let the phone ring out? 'And what sort of supplies did you want?'

'I saw that you did bespoke orders and that you sell novelty products and toys and I just wondered what you meant by toys?'

'Um, usually it's along the lines of yo-yos or stress balls, that type of thing.'

'Stress balls you say,' she says with inflection. 'Hmm, that could work. I also had this idea with some other types of toys.'

'Why don't I get your name and number and I'll get my colleague to call you back?' I say, wanting to end this weird phone call.

'OK, perfect. The name's Elizabeth, Elizabeth Randall-Perry.'

My jaw hardens and my arm goes rigid.

'Elizabeth,' I practically whisper, the word catching in my throat.

'That's right, Elizabeth. Not Liz, not Lizzie, not Beth, E-liz-a-beth,' she pronounces, syllable by syllable.

There's only one person who took the piss out of how Elizabeth stressed her name.

'Soph?'

'Ha, surprise! Did I have you going there for a moment?' she says with a cackle. 'I'm so sorry, I couldn't resist. When I got the notification from LinkedIn that you'd looked up my profile, I was so ridiculously pleased. And then when I saw you were still at your dad's company, I thought I'd phone.'

'And almost give me a heart attack?' I say, relieved that it's her. My heart's still racing and I take a few deep breaths to try and calm it down. For a split second I'd thought it was Elizabeth on the phone.

'I'm so sorry, it was just when I was looking up your company's phone number online I was thinking of our summer at Hartland's and I thought I'd have a little fun. I wonder what she's up to? I'm sure wherever she is she'll be there sucking the fun out of it. I bet she's one of those Facebook trolls that joins all sorts of weird and wonderful groups and then pounces on everyone with all her negativity.'

'Or maybe she got nicer as she grew up?'

Soph cackles again down the phone. 'Nah. Some people are bad eggs for life.'

'Well, whatever she's up to, I can't imagine she'd have a kinky subscription site.'

'No, I'm guessing she wouldn't. But I reckon there'd be a market for that kind of thing – you know, bossy, slightly scary. I bet she'd make a killing. Someone would find her sexy.'

I think of Joel and instantly my heart constricts.

'So speaking of what people are up to, how are you? What's new?' She's talking as if we haven't spoken for a few weeks, rather than fifteen years. 'Your dad must love that you're still at the company. How is he?'

'He's better than he was. After Mum, well, he got in a really bad place,' I say choosing my words carefully. 'He's much better now but I still like to keep an eye on him.'

'Ah, I bet. And what about you? Are you married? Dating? Single? Other?'

'Dating. I'm seeing a guy called Miles; he's nice. Nothing serious at the moment.'

'Oh, are you still at that exciting stage where you go on dates and shave your legs?'

I laugh. Soph always had that way to put you at ease and it's like all the years are falling away.

'I guess we are, although it's been five months now, so we're just starting to move out of that stage.'

'Oh, you're in the transition from honeymoon to real life.'

'I guess.' I try not to think about my reaction to the Tiffany bag. 'How about you? I see that you're working in Poole.'

'For my sins. I work for a boutique agency. That's PR spin for tiny little back office. But the people are lovely. Only I'm not there at the moment, I'm on maternity leave. I'm a mum, can you believe that?'

I cannot imagine Soph as a mum because in my head she's still the eighteen-year-old from the email.

'That's amazing, congratulations. Boy or girl?'

'Boy. Alfie, he's five months old. I'm not sure who's more surprised, me or him, that I've kept him alive, but here we are.'

'That's brilliant, Soph. I'm really happy for you. Are you married or . . .?'

'No, but consciously not. Brett and I have been together for coming up seven years. He's a musician.'

Of course he is. She always had a type when we were at Hartland's. They were always different but had the same things in common. Leather jacket. Longish hair. Played a guitar. Soph had terrible taste in men over that summer, but I guess we both did.

'Why am I not surprised? So how's maternity leave?'

'I'm going to cover Alfie's ears, he's having a snooze on me,

72

but I actually miss work. How wrong is that? You spend your life dreaming of a time that you don't have to go to work but then the minute you're not there you miss it. Or maybe it's just that I miss having adult conversations and having someone else to make me a cup of tea – or getting to drink a cup of tea whilst it's hot. Sorry, Edie, I'm rambling. Alfie was up four times last night and I really don't see real people anymore; I think I've forgotten how to talk.'

'Do you not go to baby classes to see other mums?'

'Oh, I do. I have some lovely ladies that I met at the NCT classes and they're great, but we only ever talk about babies and how much we want to kill our partners, and we have these weird conversations that take an hour to have but in reality it feels like we only said about three lines to each other as in the meantime we're dealing with the babies and fussing over them and then forgetting where we were in the conversation.'

'That sounds . . .'

'Dull. I know.'

'It doesn't, just different. I can't believe you're a mum. So are you living in Poole?'

'No, I live in Westerly. Can you believe that I came back here? I was so bloody defiant that I was going to leave and then about three years ago, when Brett and I finally admitted defeat that we'd never be able to afford to buy anywhere with a vague London postcode, we bit the bullet and moved back. It's a bit of a cheesy thing to say but it did feel like coming home though, plus it's super handy to have my mum on the doorstep for a bit of babysitting. Not that we ever really go out as we're always so bloody knackered. I never get any sleep.'

'Sleep's overrated. What was it Douglas always used to say? Sleep when you're dead.'

'Yes, because we were idiots then. Idiots that did not appreciate how amazing actual sleep in a comfy bed all by yourself actually was. So typically Douglas though. You know he hasn't really changed.'

'Do you still see him?' *love*

'Yeah, him and Joel are still pretty close. He lives up in London and works in the City. He's married and got a kid.'

'Douglas or Joel?'

My heart starts to hammer in my chest. Of course, it would only be natural for Soph to mention Joel; she's his cousin.

'Douglas, obviously. Could you imagine Joel working in the City? No, he went and did his engineering course and he works on yachts.'

'That's what he wanted to do.'

'I know, good for him, right? He's worked all over the world. A few years in Sydney, a stint in the Caribbean. South of France. We've had some great holidays visiting him. He worked on this one superyacht for this American family who used to get him to charter the yacht from Connecticut to the Riviera just in case they fancied a day on the water during their holiday and often they'd go on it for a day. A day. Can you imagine?'

Joel always did know what he wanted to do and it's reassuring to think that he's living somewhere many miles away from here.

'Ah, Edie, it's so lovely chatting to you on the phone. I'm so glad you looked me up, but what would be even better is if we could do it in person. Why don't you come down and meet Alfie and Brett? We could do it one weekend.'

'Me come down to Westerly?' My palms are getting clammy just at the thought. I haven't been there since I left Hartland's and I can't imagine going back.

'Yeah, I mean I could come and see you, but I don't often have the car at weekends as Brett takes it, but I could catch the train. I think I only have to change at Bournemouth. Alfie does like the train, although I've never done it on my own with a pram, but I'm sure it's doable. I'm sure someone would help me off with it.'

'It sounds like it'll be easier for me to come to you but—'

'If you wouldn't mind.' She practically jumps at the suggestion. 'Are you free this weekend?'

I think of the invitation to Julie's village fête. Dad's still hounding me to go with them, but maybe if I explain Soph had got back in touch and invited me down he might let me off.

'Actually, my boyfriend's on a stag do so I'm at a loose end.'

'So you'll come?'

'Yes.'

'You will?' She's just as surprised as I am that I've said yes.

'I will.'

'Amazing. I'm going to give you my number and you can text me as I don't have a pen and Alfie's asleep on me. Then I'll text you directions and we can make a plan. Perhaps we can do a barbecue on Saturday afternoon.'

'That sounds nice.'

She does a little squeak down the line. She rattles off her number and I jot it down, promising to text.

'Thanks for making my week, Edie; I can't wait to see you.'

We say our goodbyes and I put down the phone and stare at it. A shiver runs over my body.

I think of my new note to self. Going to Westerly to see Soph is exactly the type of thing past me would want me to do; I just hope that I'm brave and bold enough to actually go through with it.

Chapter 8

The traffic starts to lighten as I turn off the main road towards Westerly. Everyone else is heading off to the thatched cottage villages or the golden beaches further towards the coast. The town of Westerly boasts a nice little street of waterfront houses, but they're on the banks of the river rather than the sea, and it doesn't get the same number of day trippers as other more picturesque towns in the county. But it's a big, bustling market town nonetheless.

I come to a roundabout on the edge of the town and Hartland's Holiday Park is signposted. I grip the steering wheel tighter, almost tempted to drive right round the roundabout and head back home, but I make my way to Soph's.

I find her house, a thin well-kept semi-detached with a small garden and driveway in the front. I'm almost glad that she lives on a modern housing estate that could be in any town and that I don't have to go to the town centre that's full of memories.

She opens the door before I even get to it. She looks completely different and not only because she's got a baby balanced on her hip. Her hair that was once blonde and ironed straight is in loose waves that are almost brown. She's wearing leggings with a long T-shirt over the top. It's the most clothes

I've ever seen her wear; she lived that summer in tiny shorts or skirts.

'You're here! I was just watching by the window as I didn't want you to ring the doorbell. For once it's this man that's up,' she says, grabbing hold of Alfie's little hand as he giggles, 'but Brett is fast asleep and I didn't want to wake him or he'll be a right grump. But I'm so pleased you're here.'

She pulls me into a hug and I try not to squish Alfie.

'Hello, and hello you.' I'm not brilliant with babies and Alfie hides his face against Soph. 'You look like you haven't changed at all.'

'You're just being nice.' She runs a hand over her face. 'I have wrinkles, and this hair is not my natural colour, and these bags under my eyes, I hope I didn't have those when we knew each other. I feel like I haven't slept in years.'

'That's how I felt when we were working at Hartland's.'

'You're right, maybe I did have such big bags then too. You know, these sleepless nights are so different to those sleepless nights.'

I love the fact that she still talks a million miles an hour, just like she did when she was a teenager, like one long stream of consciousness.

'Sleep when you're dead,' we both say, laughing.

'Oh, I've missed you. Come on in.'

She ushers me into the kitchen.

'This little monster hasn't been up from his nap long. It'll be a nightmare getting him to bed.'

She tickles him and looks at him with so much love. It's weird seeing someone that you once saw dance on a bar in their underwear and downing funnels of beer now responsible for a baby.

I hand her the bottle of champagne that I've brought with me and she thanks me and puts it in the fridge.

'A bit more upmarket than the Archers and Pernod we used to drink.'

'Oh, don't.' My stomach lurches at the thought.

'You know, since we spoke, I keep thinking back to that summer at Hartland's. I haven't even begrudged the night feeds. Last night I even woke up Alfie as I was laughing so hard. Do you remember when the entertainment staff all got food poisoning and we had to go up and lead the Saturday night show?'

I close my eyes tight. 'I think I'd blocked that out of my memory for good.'

Soph starts to really laugh and I join in. We'd dressed up as The Pussycat Dolls, or at least a family-friendly version with less provocative dancing and more clothes, and performed a spirited version of 'Don't Cha'. I can still picture Douglas in the little dress of Soph's that he'd borrowed for the occasion.

'All I can say is thank goodness that was before everyone videoed things on their phones.'

There's a light tapping noise coming from the front door.

'Oh, I'll get that.' She walks off towards it and I look out of the window at the garden beyond, thinking how homely her house is.

'Look who decided to pop by,' says Soph, coming back in doing jazz hands as Douglas appears behind her. He stops still in the doorway when he spots me and pushes his sunglasses on top of his head.

'What the—' come his dulcet Scottish tones.

He looks almost exactly like he used to only with more lines and wrinkles; signs of a life lived. He's still got a full head of hair yet just as untamed as it used to be. He used to be one of those naturally good-looking guys who had a long fangled styling process to make his hair appear as if he'd just rolled out of bed, yet the messy hair he's sporting today doesn't seem quite as deliberate. 'Edie?'

I nod to confirm it, still too stunned to say anything.

'Bloody hell.' He drops the overnight bag he's carrying to the floor and leans over towards me. I expect him to give one of those grown-up air kisses but instead he wraps me up in a big warm hug.

It's only as he pulls away that I notice that his skin looks ashen and his eyes a little bloodshot.

'I can't believe you didn't tell me Edie was coming.'

'I wanted it to be a surprise.' Soph goes on to explain how she couldn't resist inviting him down. 'Hang on, is Suzie not with you? And Isla?' She looks towards the front door.

'No, they couldn't make it, what with the short notice. Playdates and activities, you know what it's like when your seven-year-old has a better social life than you.'

'I've got all that to look forward to, haven't I?' Soph says to Alfie.

'Is there a beer going?'

Soph glides over to the fridge and pulls one out and hands it to him. He does a swap and gives her the magnum, which she pops in the freezer.

'We were just reminiscing about our Pussycat Dolls performance.'

'Oh, then I'm going to need something stronger than this beer. In fact, why don't we open the champagne? This is an occasion for us all to celebrate. The gang all being back together.'

'Hadn't we better wait for Joel to get here?' says Soph.

My heart feels like it stops.

'Joel's coming, here?' I stutter.

'I hope so,' says Douglas. 'I'm staying with him tonight.'

'I thought you said that he was working abroad?' It was one thing edging out of my comfort zone to what felt like an adjacent country, but this feels like I'm about to cross a continent.

'He was, until he broke his ankle, then he wasn't allowed to work with plaster on so he stayed with Mum whilst he recuperated. Then typical Joel, always landing on his feet, he got offered a job at the local boatyard and he decided to stay for the summer.'

'Right,' I say, quietly breaking out into a cold sweat.

'So, what are we saying, yes to the champagne?' Douglas raises his eyebrows.

'It'll be warm,' says Soph, pulling a bottle of Prosecco out of the fridge. 'We can drink this until it chills.'

I look at the bottle and remember my car parked outside. I'm torn between wanting to drive away and wanting to drink the whole bottle.

'I shouldn't, I'm driving.'

'You can stay over if you want to have a drink. I can't promise it will be the best sleep you've had as Alfie will probably scream the house down.'

'Are you sure that would be OK?'

'Absolutely. I would have asked before, but I didn't want to put too much pressure on you.'

Douglas doesn't hang around popping the cork and Soph scrambles to grab some glasses.

They're distracted with the Prosecco and I sit down at the kitchen table before my legs give way. I can't imagine what it's going to be like to see Joel again after all these years. I thought I was in love with him, but reading the emails from the past has made me realise how young we were and I wonder if it was just lust. A mixture of hormones and being away from home for the first time.

Douglas hands me a glass and I down it almost in one.

'Yes, Edie, just like the old days.'

He downs his too and then fills us both up with another glass.

'Shall we go outside?' asks Soph.

'Great idea.'

I follow the others out and we sit on deck chairs and Soph pops Alfie onto a blanket in the middle.

'So, Edie, I don't see a ring on your finger. Not married?'

I laugh at him. Trust him to have noticed that.

'No, I've got a boyfriend, Miles; nothing serious.'

'Best way to be.'

'Says the married man.' Soph raises an eyebrow before she gets down on the blanket with Alfie.

'Hush now. So tell me, what else have you been up to since we last saw you?'

I fill in a few of the blanks, not that there are many, and then I turn the questions on him.

'Soph was saying you live up in London? Dulwich, wasn't it? Must be nice.'

'Hmm. Yeah it's OK.'

'Nice place to raise kids. How old's your daughter again?'

'Seven.' A small smile of pride creeps over his face.

'I'm guessing it's a good age?'

'Kind of, although she doesn't need me like she used to.'

'I'm sure that's not true.'

He shrugs.

'I bet you're great with her though, lots of fun.'

'That's me, fun Douglas,' he says, holding his glass out in a toast and downing the rest of his drink. He tops his up and then tops up mine. I didn't even realise it was empty. He goes to top up Soph's but she pulls hers away.

'Do you remember that time we got drunk on a bottle of champagne after those guests left?' I say.

'Oh, I do remember.' Soph cringes. 'We stole it before house-keeping could get to it and then drank it on the beach. I think that was the first time I'd ever drunk it.'

We start to swap hazy memories from our time in the holiday park and the drinks keep going down nicely, which is just about helping to block out the thought of Joel arriving.

'I'm going to make a cup of tea,' says Soph, getting to her feet. 'I can't carry on drinking at that rate when looking after Alfie. Anyone want anything?'

'Maybe some music,' says Douglas.

'Oh yes, I'll make a playlist when the kettle's boiling.'

Alfie starts to whimper when Soph goes and Douglas sits on the blanket and picks up a toy to give him.

He starts to fill me in on his hangover and what he was up to last night, and a few minutes later, Soph appears to the sound of 'Don't Cha'.

'Oh, don't. I still get PTSD from this song.' Douglas puts his hands over his ears.

'Come on, I bet you still remember the moves.'

Soph points a finger at him, but he's having none of it. He uses Alfie like a human shield.

'Someone has to do it with me. Edie, you remember it, right?'

I haven't heard the song in years but my body still instinctively knows the routine. The three glasses of Prosecco I've drunk probably explain why I let her pull me up. I soon find myself strutting down towards the garden fence. We turn and attempt a slut drop, but we don't make it as far down as we used to. Then, as the music builds at the end of the chorus, we shimmy round to the final 'Don't cha', pointing our fingers out towards Douglas and Alfie. But my body freezes as I stare in the direction of where my finger is pointing. Joel.

He looks directly at me and I almost forget about the others in the garden. He still looks good. His hair's shorter than it used to be but it's still long enough to be tousled. He's wearing a black T-shirt, black jeans and his arms are tanned.

'Edie,' he says. There's no warmth in his eyes like the others had, and his lips are curling.

Douglas gets up and slaps him on the back.

'I see someone else didn't know about the mystery guest. You want a glass of Prosecco?'

Joel nods.

I slowly regain the power over my hand that was frozen in a point and it drops to my side.

'Your face is a picture.' Soph picks Alfie off the blanket and takes him over. Joel tickles Alfie's stomach before he gratefully takes the glass Douglas hands him, drinking it quicker than I did.

'Easy, Joel, it's a long afternoon ahead,' says Soph.

'Sorry, I was thirsty after the ride over here.'

'You know, water works well when you're thirsty. I'll get you a glass when I'm on my way back; I think this little man has done something in his nappy and I'll go and change it.' Soph holds Alfie like he's a suspicious package.

My legs are unsteady walking back over to my chair and it takes both of my hands to keep my glass steady as I finish the rest of it.

Joel sits down on the chair furthest away from me.

'And I thought I was surprised.' Douglas goes to top up his glass only to find the bottle empty. 'I guess the magnum will be chilled enough by now. Don't have too much fun without me.'

He looks between us, clearly picking up on the tension.

'What are you doing here?' asks Joel, staring at the rug on the floor. It bothers me I didn't even get a 'hello, how are you?', just a straight-up blunt question. Why's he mad at me after all he did?

'Soph invited me. She phoned me at work after I'd looked her up on LinkedIn one day. If I'd known you were coming, I wouldn't have—'

Douglas comes out before I can finish that sentence. He pops open the bottle and both Joel and I automatically hold our glasses out.

'Isn't this fun? The old gang back together,' says Douglas. 'How many years has it been? Twelve? Thirteen?'

'Seventeen,' I say without having to think of it.

'Man, we're old. Well, you're lucky, Edie, this is the longest time since then that Joel's been in the country.'

'So lucky,' I mutter under my breath and I feel his eyes burn into me.

'If there hadn't been that storm, and mister clumsy over here breaking his ankle, Joel wouldn't be here. Although it's pretty much healed now, I bet he and his itchy feet will be off again in no time.'

'You never did want to settle down.'

'Speaking the hard, honest truths, Edie. I like it.' Douglas laughs and high-fives me. I didn't mean it to sound so bitchy, or maybe I did. I need to stop drinking.

'What are we talking about?' Soph walks back over the lawn with a freshly changed Alfie.

'We're just wondering when Joel's going to be off again.'

'You can't go anywhere. Alfie would miss his uncle Joel too much.'

'At least someone would miss me.'

'I'd obviously miss you too,' says Douglas. 'I'm surprised you haven't been tempted back to Cannes.'

'That's where Joel's girlfriend works,' Soph adds.

I try and nod, ignoring how it feels like I've been punched in the gut. I've got a boyfriend and, even if I didn't, Joel's the last person I'd ever want.

'For the moment at least,' he says, taking a swig of his drink.

'She works on superyachts too, and the two of them are always off on one adventure or another,' says Soph.

'You know, I'm not against her whisking you away somewhere more exotic.' Douglas winks at Joel.

'Do I look like a travel agent?' he says, shaking his head. 'Always trying to get a free holiday.'

Douglas shrugs. 'Can't blame a guy for trying.'

The Arctic Monkeys song that was playing stops and it's replaced by 'Filthy/Gorgeous' by Scissor Sisters.

Soph bursts out laughing and points at Douglas.

'Oh no, not this song,' he says with a groan. 'This reminds me of the time that guest locked me in her caravan for days.'

'Why do you think I added it to the list?'

'I'll have you know that was a very traumatic experience. She locked me in from the outside, and the window only opened about ten centimetres.'

'Come on, weren't you only stuck inside for a few hours?' says Joel.

'Was that all it was?' I start to laugh.

'It felt like days.'

'Didn't she have claws or something?' says Soph, scrunching her hand like a claw, causing Douglas to shudder.

'That's right, you had those scratches down your back.' I can see it so clearly in my mind.

'They were just long nails,' says Joel, shaking his head. 'You've blown this way out of proportion.'

'I looked like I'd been mauled by a tiger. I couldn't take my shirt off outside for a week; my tan totally faded.'

'Didn't you still sleep with her a few times after that?' Joel rolls his eyes and tops up his drink.

Soph starts to cry-laugh.

'Did I? I think I had Stockholm syndrome. But hey, why am I the only one that's getting dragged through all this? That summer we were all guilty of some shockingly bad lapses in judgement.'

I find myself looking at Joel and he stares hard back at me, causing me to shiver.

'Soph, what about the time you—' starts Douglas.

'No, don't tell that story,' she says, holding her hands up.

'You don't know what I was going to say.'

'But I bet it was nothing that I'd want Brett to overhear.'

'Are my ears burning?'

I turn towards the house and my mouth drops open. All this time I've been curious to meet the man who tamed Sophie.

I imagined he'd have shaggy hair, an old band T-shirt and sleeves of tattoos, exactly the type she used to go for, but I couldn't be more wrong. He's wearing long blue shorts and a fitted floral shirt. He's cleanly shaven with neatly styled blond hair and not a tattoo in sight.

'Sorry, everyone. Late night last night. I was playing a proms in the park.'

I'm stunned; I'd assumed when Soph said that he was a musician that he was in a band, not a classical musician.

'I did tell him that he didn't need to get up early with Alfie this morning.'

'You needed your sleep,' he says, giving her a quick kiss, before making the rounds. He shakes the boys' hands and then turns to me.

'Ah, you must be Edie, so nice to have you here.' He gives me air kisses on both cheeks. 'Now, what didn't Soph want me to hear?'

The evening passes in a blur of stories and half-baked memories interchanged with anecdotes from the others' meet-ups over the years. I try to ignore the little pangs of jealousy at how well they all still know each other, thinking about how, if things had been different, I might have been there too.

Alfie's gone to bed, and we're still sitting outside. Brett's got the firepit going and we're all wrapped up in Soph's blankets as, despite the sunshine this afternoon, it's still chilly in the evening.

Joel and I haven't spoken to each other since our interaction earlier. We've tried to ignore one another as much as we can, which is fine by me.

'Do you ever wonder why Lionel didn't fire us?' says Joel,

after Soph finished a story about when we'd got stuck in the bottle store. 'We were all terrible at our jobs and we did things that I'm sure would have been grounds for dismissal.'

'Back in the day, I think he was just desperate for any of his employees to stay the whole summer.'

'What's it like now?' I ask.

'It's gone all upmarket.' Soph pulls her blanket further round her. 'It's all wooden lodges. I could take you out and show you tomorrow, if you like?'

I pause for a moment. It might be one step too many down memory lane.

'I need to head back early.'

'Perhaps next time you're down, because you have to come back; my mum could babysit Alfie and we could organise a night out like old times. Boy, do we need one. Don't we, Brett?'

'We certainly do.'

'I mean, we have date nights but all we talk about is Alfie and how tired we are, which is lovely, honestly,' she says, turning to Brett and stroking his cheek, 'but sometimes I just want to wear my old outfits and go out, out.'

'No complaints from me. I've been trying to get you into one of those little skirts for ages,' says Brett, raising a suggestive eyebrow.

'I'm always up for going out, out,' says Douglas. 'Just tell me when and where.'

'I'm sure Mum wouldn't mind babysitting Isla too.' Soph looks at him brightly.

'Oh, um, yeah, I could see if they want to come, but they're going to be spending a lot of the summer with Suz's mum in Suffolk.'

'That's a shame. Edie, you'll have to bring Miles.'

'Hmm, yeah, maybe.' If today is anything to go by, I don't think I could put myself through another evening with Joel. I'm definitely going to keep in touch with Soph and Douglas, but it's clear to me we're no longer a gang of four.

'So that's settled then, we're going to do a night out in town.' Soph claps her hands together.

'It'll be busy in the summer,' says Joel. 'You wouldn't be able to get a seat in the pubs with all the tourists.'

It sounds like I'm not the only one who doesn't want a repeat of tonight.

'Ooh, grandpa,' says Soph. 'Then we'll do it before August and all the hordes descend down here. Strike whilst the iron's hot and all that. We're busy next weekend, but how about the weekend after?'

'I'm in,' says Douglas, without hesitation.

'I can't.' Joel finishes his drink. 'I'm going to Cannes.'

'Edie?'

With Joel away, I don't hesitate. 'Count me in.'

'Yay. I'm looking forward to it already,' says Soph, reaching over and giving my hand a squeeze.

I'm looking forward to catching up with Soph and Douglas again without Joel and his cold eyes boring into me. I don't understand why he's mad at me; he's the one who broke my heart and set in motion the chain of events that led to the worst night of my life.

Chapter 9

THEN

I first met Joel when I found him lying naked in my bed a few days after I'd arrived at Hartland's.

The first few days had been a shock to the system and I'd quickly learnt how full-on it all was. The camp mantra amongst the staff was definitely work hard play hard. The long shifts and rotations around different parts of the camp seemed relentless, and after we finished it was time to go out. There was always a party somewhere: in town, on the beach, a silent disco in the club after it finished. After a few nights I was exhausted; I had no idea how I was going to survive the entire thirteen weeks.

By the night I met Joel I was running on fumes. I'd just finished the late shift in reception. I'd hidden from Soph and Douglas, who had been talking about getting a taxi to another campsite to go clubbing with a few of their friends and there was no way that I had the energy for that. Instead, I'd gone back to our accommodation and headed straight for the shower and got dressed in my flannel pyjamas, the ones my mum had bought me and that Soph had dubbed my passion killers. I was so knackered I didn't care. They were warm and cosy and I was set to flop straight into bed.

I flicked on the light to my bedroom and got the shock of my life. There on my bed was a naked man curled up in the foetal position on top of my duvet cover.

He opened his eyes, looking round, confused.

I was completely paralysed, my body rigid with fear, too stunned for the flight-or-fight mechanism to kick in.

'What are you doing in my room?' he said, putting up one arm to shield his eyes from the light and the other to grab a pillow to cover himself up.

'Your room?' I screamed, my voice coming back. I looked over my shoulder; three steps and I could be out of the main door and on the walkway. 'This is my room.'

He laughed and rubbed at his hair. He had the type of long hair that made you want to run your hands through it.

'Very funny. Did Douglas send you? I wouldn't normally be complaining about a beautiful woman walking into my room but it's been a long day.'

My cheeks flushed that he'd called me beautiful. There was a smile on his face that was a little bit cheeky and those eyes . . . They were so dark I felt like I could get lost in them. I tried to keep focused. He was still a naked stranger in my bed.

I grabbed a hairbrush off the chest of drawers next to me and held it threateningly.

'This is my room,' I repeated, although with less conviction. My fear was ebbing away, and it was swiftly being replaced with butterflies in my stomach.

He rubbed his eyes before he squinted and looked down at the pillow.

My cheeks were starting to flush again as my brain repeatedly tried to remind me that there was a naked man on my bed. I tried to give off an air that I wasn't fazed by the situation and that this was totally normal, although in reality Scott was the only guy I'd seen naked. Scott. My cheeks flushed harder that I'd forgotten I had a boyfriend.

'Where's all my stuff? What have you done with it?'

'I haven't touched it. This is my room,' I said again, putting the hairbrush down as with every passing second he was seeming like less of a threat. 'These are the staff quarters. What part of the camp are you supposed to be in?'

'Very funny. I'm staff too. This is my room.'

Every time I looked at him I noticed a different feature of his body. His abs. His muscular legs. His hands, which he kept running through that hair.

'You are trespassing.' I tried to keep my voice level and even but I was flustered and I think he knew it.

'Trespassing? Oh, I get it. This is James or Douglas, isn't it? I've heard about these kinds of tricks where they move all your stuff round when you're out or asleep, just to freak people out. Where did you put it all? Don't tell me they've put it in the pool?'

He moved a little on the bed and the cushion started to slip. My eyes widened as he grabbed it back just in time.

'No one's put your stuff anywhere. This is where I've been living since I came here three days ago.'

'Will you two just try and keep it down?' said Elizabeth, storming out of her room. She was dressed in a nightie and had her hair in a myriad of plaits. 'Some of us are trying to sleep.'

The naked man looked at Elizabeth and then back to me.

'Fuck, this really isn't my bed, is it? There's no way Elizabeth would be in on a joke.'

'Very funny, Joel, and highly observant. Although not so observant that you didn't realise that you were on the wrong floor. You needed to go up another flight of stairs. This is flat four on the *second* floor.'

'Bollocks,' he said, turning to me, the full horror of the situation registering. He looked so peaky he was almost translucent. 'I'm sorry, I must be in the room above you. I was helping out with the limbo competition and I may have had a little too much punch.'

'The alcohol is only supposed to be for the guests,' said Elizabeth, exasperated. 'Now keep it down. I'm on sunrise reception duty and if I don't get eight hours of sleep, I'm a right bitch.'

I caught Joel's eye and he pulled the same smirk as I did.

She stormed back to her room and, in case we hadn't realised she was cross, she slammed the door so hard that the flat rattled.

'I'm sorry,' said Joel, in a lower, more apologetic tone.

'That's OK; I'm sure it's an easy mistake to make. These flats all look the same.'

'Yeah. Same room just wrong floor.'

I nodded before it dawned on me what that meant.

'You're from the room above me? Eww, you're the weird-noise-sex guy.'

'I'm what?'

'Figures that you'd turn up in my room naked.'

I picked up my hairbrush again, still unsure what I'd actually do with it. To think I'd been flattered when he'd called me beautiful, when he was probably at it with everyone.

'What? No? What are you talking about? I haven't even had sex.'

I couldn't help raising an eyebrow.

'*Here*. I haven't had sex *here*. I've only been here a week. Give me a chance,' he said, crossing his legs.

'Then what are all the noises and the grunting that I hear? Sometimes you're at it for hours. The bed keeps squeaking and then it's followed by grunting.' I wrinkled my face up even more. 'On second thought, don't answer that. I don't want to know what you were doing alone.'

Joel's eyes were blinking rapidly.

'I don't know what you're talking about. It must be coming from another room.'

'But everything's laid out the same, right? Your bedroom is in the same exact position just up there? There's squeaking and grunting.'

'Oh,' he said, sighing with relief. He laughed again and there was that smile. 'It's not what you think.'

'I don't want to know,' I said, turning my back, not so much that I didn't want to hear what he had to say but because that smile was dangerous.

'It must be when I'm doing my workouts. I've got a squeaky ab cradle and the grunting is when I'm doing weights. I've been trying to get a six-pack.'

I turned back to him and my eyes flitted down to his waist before my cheeks started to burn.

'Obviously I haven't been doing it for long,' he said, this time with a brazen wink.

Neither of us said anything and it took all my self-control not to cross the room and kiss him. I'd never felt that way about a stranger before and the way he was looking at me, it was like he felt it too.

The main door of the flat opened and Soph walked in and whatever spell we were under was broken.

'There you are. What are you wearing? You are not going to bed.'

I groaned. I'd been hoping I'd be tucked up asleep before she came back to change.

'Well, I would be if there wasn't some naked guy in it.'

'Hot,' said Soph, walking in before she put her hands over her eyes and yelped. 'Joel, gross. Put some clothes on. Oh, Edie, please don't tell me that you're hooking up with him?'

'No,' I said, following her out to the corridor whilst Joel scrambled to find his clothes. I wondered what exactly was wrong with him. He might not have a six-pack, but he was still cute. Not that I was looking. I had a boyfriend.

'That's my cousin, Joel.'

'Your cousin?'

'Yes, and I just saw his . . . Why don't you have a bigger pillow?'

'Sorry, I hadn't been expecting—'

'Right, unless you want me acting like a total bitch tomorrow, keep the noise down,' said Elizabeth, poking her head out of the door.

'You mean she hasn't been acting like a bitch this whole time?' whispered Soph.

Joel appeared fully dressed and we followed him out onto the wooden walkway.

'Sorry, about that . . . I still don't know your name.'

'Edie.'

'Sorry about that, Edie. I'll leave you to it, ladies in red.'

'Why did he call us ladies in red?' I asked, watching him walk away.

'Because of our work shirts. The entertainment team often put the song on at the disco – you know, 'Lady in Red' – and then the guys try and dance with us. It's so cheesy.'

We watched Joel hesitate when he got to the stairs.

'Do you think you can find it OK or do you need us to walk you?' Soph shouted.

'Goodnight,' he called, waving as he went up.

'He is so embarrassing.' Soph took my hand and dragged me into her room.

'I thought he seemed cute.'

'Oh, no. Don't do that. Joel is great, he really is. He makes an awesome friend, but don't fancy him.'

'I've got a boyfriend.'

'Uh-huh. When does that seem to stop people around here?'

'Scott and I are different.'

'Right, well, that's good. Because my mum always says Joel is like his dad. He's definitely a love-you-and-leave-you type of guy. Always dates, never settles.'

'Good job Scott's not like that.'

'The famous Scott, I can't wait to meet him next month. Now seriously, we're leaving for the club in twenty minutes.'

'I'm going to bed.'

'To do what?'

'Sleep. I must have sleep.'

'You can sleep when you're dead.'

She selected a dress from her wardrobe and thrust it at me.

Half an hour later we were in the taxi away to the next campsite, but all I could think about was my bed, or more specifically the man who'd just been lying on it.

Chapter 10

I don't think I really realised how small my comfort zone was until I started to try and break out of it. I've been happy with its smallness, it's suited me well over the years, it's kept me guarded and safe, but I'd forgotten the little rush of endorphins that you get when you step outside it.

The weekend in Westerly was exactly everything I didn't know I needed, even despite Joel being there. I can't remember the last time I reminisced like that. I've spent so many years avoiding that time in my life because of how it ended with Mum, but it was actually nice to think about the happy times before everything changed. It made me wonder if the old Edie might be on to something with her notes to self after all.

We're all a little guilty of getting old and getting stuck in a rut, aren't we? It's not to say there's anything wrong with my life per se. It's not like I'm blissfully unhappy but maybe it wouldn't hurt to push those boundaries a little and to maybe go along with what this next email says.

Which is why I've got the familiar heart flutter as there's one waiting in my inbox.

Yo, yo, Edie!

How are you??? It's getting busier here every week, with more and more parents sneaking their kids out of school ready to start the holidays. There's more of a family feel to the place now and less drunken students who have escaped their exams.

Scott's extended his interrailing and he's now on some Greek island. The phone reception is patchy at best, so I haven't spoken to him in about a week. Soph, meanwhile, is on her third bloke of the summer. He's a bass guitarist for a rock band who were playing in the local pub. I wish she'd just hook up with someone on site as we keep getting dragged around the county to watch random bands play.

On Monday, Joel and Soph took us to meet their grandma Hetty. She cooked us a full roast dinner, which ordinarily should have been a struggle to eat in the sunshine but it was absolutely amazing. I think it's the first time that I have eaten proper vegetables other than salad in my burger for the last month. Hetty's worried we're going to catch scurvy so she's told us to come again. She was great fun and I could see so much of both Joel and Soph in her.

Then, last night, we had a fancy dress night in the disco, and all of us staff made an effort. The theme was children's TV programmes, and, for some reason, Soph, Douglas, Joel and I were supposed to be going as the children from the *Chronicles of Narnia*. Only when I got into my outfit of long skirt, cardigan and shirt – all bought from a charity shop – Soph walks in dressed as She-Ra, in the smallest outfit known to man with golden headdress and everything. Then I found Douglas in red shorts and carrying a red float, à la David Hasselhoff in *Baywatch*. It was too late for me to change, so poor me and Joel were left in our Narnia outfits. Not our finest hour. We spent the whole night having to explain who we were and having to put up with the weird looks that followed. In the end we just gave up and hung out by ourselves in our super unsexy costumes.

Oh – I almost forgot your note-to-self challenge; don't worry I'm not going to send you out in fancy dress. When do you ever see adults in fancy dress out in town?!! It's to try something new in honour of the fact that Soph is dragging me along to a Salsa dancing lesson. I think she fancies the guy that's teaching it. It can be anything as long as you've never done it before – ooh er missus, your husband might be in for a treat ;)

Love ya,

Edie x

I start to laugh, only to realise that people walking past me in the street are giving me a wide berth and I try and compose myself.

'Hey, have you been waiting long?' asks Miles, walking up and kissing me on the cheek.

'Only a few minutes.'

I put my phone back in my bag, my cheeks hot from the last line in the email. Miles isn't exactly one for trying new stuff in the bedroom.

'Where do you fancy going for a drink?' he asks.

'Actually,' I say, thinking of trying something different, 'my work colleagues are taking part in an improv comedy competition. It's in a function room of a pub so we can still have a drink.'

'Sounds good to me.'

We start to ask after each other's days as we weave through the town. We've got another half an hour before the improv starts so we prop ourselves at the bar and order our drinks, and our conversation soon turns to the stag do Miles has just returned from.

'I'm still exhausted,' he says with a groan.

'All those art galleries tire you out?'

'There was a lot of walking. Plus, the night out got quite wild. We dressed Wes up in a skin suit that was like Michelangelo's David statue.'

'Please tell me there are photos.'

He pulls out his phone from his back pocket and starts to scroll, my mind already boggling.

'Ah, here we go.'

He goes to hand it to me, when it starts to ring. He makes an apologetic face and answers it. I can tell immediately from his tone that it's work.

I stand at the bar, trying not to feel too self-conscious when Aaron hurries through the pub.

'Aaron,' I call out.

He does a double take.

'Edie, you came? The guys will be so pleased that you made it.' He keeps looking anxiously over my shoulder.

'Is everything OK?'

'Yeah, it's fine. Or at least it will be when Hayley turns up; she's late and we're all a little jittery because the team that we're battling was the one that knocked us out last year.'

'I'm sure you'll be fine.'

'Maybe the extra support in the audience will help.'

'Hopefully it will.'

He's always so confident at work but he looks really nervous. Miles walks back up to us; he's distracted, texting on his phone, his brow furrowed and he only notices Aaron at the last moment.

'Hello,' he says.

'Miles, this is my work colleague, Aaron. Aaron, this is Miles.'

'Nice to meet you. I've got to warm up but I hope we can catch up properly after the battle. So pleased you're both here.'

'Good luck and I hope Hayley turns up soon!'

He holds up crossed fingers and heads back towards the function room.

Miles reaches over to pick up his pint, taking a large sip.

'Everything OK?' I ask.

'Yes and no,' he says, his phone pinging. 'There's a problem with a merger that we thought would sail through without any issues. The company selling has added an addendum which the buyers are refusing.'

'Do you need to go back into work?'

He pinches at the bridge of his nose.

'I don't think so, but I might have to make another call. But hopefully that'll be it.' He winces, looking apologetic.

'That's not a problem.'

'Right, well, I'll get this phone call out the way before it starts.'

He gives me a kiss on the cheek and heads back out.

I reach for my glass of wine and glance back over to the function room. Now Yas and Dave have joined Aaron and they're huddled round a phone looking crestfallen.

I pick up our drinks and head on over.

'Hello,' I say, trying my best to smile, but the closer I get the more I pick up that something is very wrong.

Yas looks close to tears and she tries to nod a hello.

'Hayley can't make it; she's fallen over and she thinks she might have broken her leg.'

'Oh no, poor Hayley.'

'I know, luckily Brian's there to take care of her. But it means that we haven't got enough for a team. It's a minimum of four.'

Now I understand the disappointment.

'Can't you get someone else?'

'Not at this short notice,' says Aaron. 'It's due to start in fifteen minutes. I don't know anyone that could get here in time . . . Unless.'

He looks up at me with an intent expression on his face. I can almost see the cogs turning.

'Oh no.' I shake my head and put my hands up in front of me. 'I can't do it.'

'I think it's the only way we could still do this.'

Yas and Dave look up, pleading with their eyes.

'But I couldn't get up there in front of all those people and I couldn't make things up on the spot.' I break out in a cold sweat.

'There won't be that many people watching,' says Dave, 'and we'll make sure we do all the donkey work. You don't even need to say anything, just kind of react a bit to what we say.'

Even the thought of that terrifies me.

'Please, Edie,' says Yas.

I hear the desperation in her voice. If only Miles wasn't having to deal with work or he could have stepped up. He would be much better at it than me.

I think of the emails and the memories I have of that summer at Hartland's. It's eerily familiar to the time when we were roped into covering for the entertainment staff as The Pussycat Dolls. At least this time I wouldn't be in danger of pulling any muscles with the dance moves.

I can't leave them in the lurch if I'm their only option. Besides, it would certainly count as trying something new.

'Are you sure that I wouldn't really have to say anything?'

Yas squeals and throws her arms around me, despite me not actually confirming anything.

'Not a thing,' says Dave, 'just follow us round on stage.'

'But if you want to say something,' says Aaron, 'you just remember the *yes and* rule.'

'What does that even mean?'

'It means that you go with whatever someone else has said, but then just build on it.'

My head starts to spin, not really understanding.

'Just follow our lead. You're going to love it,' says Yas, squeezing my arm tighter. 'You'll get such a buzz.'

Any hope of being rescued by Miles are dashed when I spot him out the window pacing back and forth, his hand on his head.

'Right, let's get you up to speed,' says Aaron.

I nod, not quite believing what I've got myself into.

'Give it up for the Impensonators!'

The small crowd in the function room claps, and behind a makeshift backstage, which is only really a red curtain, Aaron puts his hand out and Yas and Dave put theirs on top, and with a quick nudge of the elbow from Yas, I put mine in.

'On three, wing it,' says Aaron, and we all count and they whisper it before Dave holds the curtain up and we find ourselves right slap bang in the middle of the audience. The small audience is in a horseshoe around us, which makes me feel hemmed in; it's almost claustrophobic.

'OK,' says the host, 'let's crack on with our second group.'

The other team have already done their first session. The two teams rotate five times, with each improv session lasting five minutes. It doesn't sound so bad when you put it that way. Five minutes per sketch, twenty-five minutes in total on stage, but the clock at the edge of the room is ticking loudly and I know I'm going to feel every single second dragging along. Especially after hearing the other team from backstage. The speed at which they went with the suggestions and made something up on the spot was incredible and I can't imagine how we're going to do the same.

'So, your scenario is,' he says, plunging his hands into the three bowls on the edge of the stage, 'holidaymakers, in . . . an industrial refrigerator, and the key word is . . . goals.'

Right away Aaron is nodding and Yas looks excited. I can

only imagine I look petrified as Dave gives me a quick pat on the arm followed by a thumbs up.

'Well, this is not what the brochure said,' says Aaron, striding into the middle of the stage area. He's looking around, with his hands on his hips. 'These are not holiday goals.'

'They said it was going to be cold, but I didn't think it was going to be this cold. I didn't even pack a coat.' Yas rubs at her arms and starts to shiver.

'I'd assumed skiing or mountains, not a budget version of an ice hotel,' chips in Dave.

'That's the last time I book something I see from an Instagram influencer. Hashtag cool holiday.'

There's a ripple of laughter around the room.

'Hashtag chilled holiday,' I say, before I realise that the words have come out. There's another ripple of laughter, but that's nothing compared to the look of surprise and joy on my colleagues' faces.

'Hashtag cool selfie,' says Yas, holding her hand out, pretending she's got a phone, and she gestures with her arm for us to gather around. She snaps a photo on her imaginary phone. 'And again.' She moves her arm and the others change position. I'm too slow to move so I pull a face. 'Hashtag squad goals.

'Uh-oh,' she says, her face falling.

Aaron puts his hands back on his hips. 'What's wrong?'

She starts to pretend to hyperventilate, and it's as if she's acting out how I'm feeling internally. It's such a strange feeling, trying to think of something in keeping with the scene yet at the same time listening to what the others are saying and reacting to it. We've only been going a minute or so but I'm already exhausted trying to keep up.

'There's. No. Wi-Fi,' she says, and the others dramatically gasp. I stand back trying my best to look shocked.

'No Wi-Fi? But the brochure promised Wi-Fi,' says Dave.

'Brochure,' says Aaron from a laugh. 'When did you book the holiday? In 1995?'

Dave smiles and the audience titters.

'I'll have you know the little travel agency in town has brochures still and it clearly said Wi-Fi in black and white.'

'What will I do if I can't update my Insta followers?' says Yas. 'How will I validate my holiday? How will anyone know where I've been? I mean, is this even real if we can't post it on Facebook?'

We all look amongst each other and I wonder how the others don't laugh. They're so in character and so good.

'Maybe we're being filmed,' I say, looking up at the ceiling. 'Maybe this is some kind of reality TV programme.'

'Like, how would they cope in the worst hotel cut off from the world?' says Aaron, pushing forward and immediately staring up at the ceiling with me.

'What if we go *Lord of the Flies*?' says Dave; he's spinning round looking for the camera.

'If I was going to be on TV I'd have worn better clothes. How's anyone supposed to see my hot body under this arctic parka?' Yas starts to smooth her hair down and pouts her lips.

'At least you have a coat with you,' says Aaron. 'These Bermuda shorts are not doing anything for the cold.'

'They're not doing much for your legs either.' Dave winks.

'I thought you liked my legs?'

'You can tell you've been working out,' says Yas, jumping in as Dave's lips are starting to curl at the sides like he's going to laugh.

'I have, it's been a goal of mine to get calf muscles.'

We all look at his legs.

'But you know the cold shrinks them.'

'Uh-huh, along with everything else, am I right?' says Aaron.

'I bet there's no gym in this place,' I say at the pause.

'Gym? There's not even enough beds,' says Dave.

'There's only one,' shouts Aaron.

'What?' screams Yas. 'But if I don't get my beauty sleep then my face goes all puffy.'

'At least without Wi-Fi no one will be able to see you on your Instagram,' I say, getting braver. The audience are laughing along. I'm doing this. I'm actually doing this.

'That's true,' says Yas, nodding. 'How are we all going to fit in it?'

'Is it even big enough for one?' asks Dave.

Aaron lies down on the floor, contorting into different shapes until he's in the foetal position. 'Maybe if we all slept like this.'

They all get down on the floor and curl up and I know I have to follow them.

'You know, when I said I wanted to be in bed with two women,' says Aaron, 'this was not what I had in mind.'

'Where do we complain to the manager about this?' says Dave, standing back up.

'Maybe that's why they don't have Wi-Fi so you can't put a review on?' says Yas. 'Does this door even open?'

She tries to tug at an imaginary door. Aaron goes over to Yas and helps her to pull the door. Soon she's followed by Dave, and not wanting to stand on my own, I start to tug at it too.

'It's no good. It's stuck,' says Yas.

'Usually I dream about getting stuck on holiday, but not like this,' I say.

'This is definitely not holiday goals,' says Aaron, just as the buzzer goes.

The audience breaks out into a round of applause and my whole body goes hot like it's starting to burn. I can't believe I just did that.

Aaron reaches out and pats us all on the back and everyone mutters, 'Good job', before they give a quick wave and we head behind the curtain again.

The others squeeze me into a hug. 'You did so well.'

All of them congratulate me as we hear the host pull out more suggestions for the other team.

The rest of the sessions pass by in such a blur that I can barely keep up. In between performing and watching the other team, I don't have time to worry or get nervous about anything. I start to throw myself into the moment, ignoring the audience and just concentrating on the other members of my team. It's only now that it's all over that it's truly hit me what's happened tonight. I'm starting to feel light-headed and a little bit sick and the only thing keeping me upright are my fellow team members, who all have their arms around me as we celebrate the fact that they're through to the next round.

'You're our lucky charm,' Aaron tells me.

'Oh, I didn't really do anything,' I say.

'You did,' says Yas. 'When you were playing the rugby player at the dress fitting, it was genius.'

'I honestly don't where it came from,' I say, still not quite believing I'd actually gone through with it.

'You know you'll have to do the next round too,' says Dave. 'We're not letting a talent like yours go that easily.'

'Won't Hayley be back though?'

'Yes, but we can have five members, and it actually works better with more of us participating as it takes the pressure off a bit.'

'I'll have to see; I don't know if my heart can take it.'

'You'll get used to it, and that buzz, do you feel it?'

'I do,' I say.

The adrenaline rush is making me feel like I could do anything.

I'm dying to know what Miles thought of the performance, and I spot him by the entrance, searching the crowd for me; I give him a wave to let him know where I am.

'Edie, I'm so sorry you had to sit through that alone,' he says, taking hold of my hand.

'Wait, you didn't watch?' I say, deflated. 'Not any of it?'

'No, sorry, the call went on for longer than I thought. Was it good?'

'Uh-huh. Hayley was ill, so I took her place.'

'You took her place?' His eyebrows shoot up in surprise.

'I know, and it went OK. I mean, I was nowhere near as good as the others, but I spoke a few times.'

I smile and my nose automatically wrinkles. I can't remember the last time I experienced this kind of feeling.

'I'm gutted I missed it. But you did it. That's brilliant.'

'I know,' I say, looking over at the stage. My stomach is a flutter with butterflies. I actually did it.

Never in my wildest dreams this morning did I think I'd be performing improv in front of an audience of strangers late at night, or that it could have been as much fun. I'm almost looking forward to another email to see what it's going to challenge me to do next.

Chapter 11

Some days at work pass by in a blink of an eye, but today is not one of them. I can't seem to focus on any of the items on my to-do list.

I look over at Dad's desk, which is empty. I scan the internal calendar to see if he's got any external meetings or any explanation why he wouldn't be here at nearly ten o'clock. I notice that my Big Little Readers session is marked up as I'm leaving early, but there's nothing about Dad.

I pick up my phone to call him. Still after all these years whenever he's late I fear that he's been drinking again. I put the phone back down. There's probably a more logical explanation; he and Julie are getting close and maybe the traffic's worse coming from her house. I'll give him another half an hour.

I ping Layla a message on our internal messaging app in the hope of keeping me distracted and we meet in the kitchen.

'How was sports day yesterday?' I ask, flicking the kettle on before I notice the bloody scab on her arm.

'It was brutal. I tell you, we spend the day watching our kids, who aren't allowed to be seen as winners and losers, and then when they let the parents race, all those rules go out of the window and it's a fight to the finish line.'

'Sounds vicious.'

'It was. Luckily that's over for another year. Much like the school term, can you believe the kids break up today?'

'That's come round quickly. Have you got everything sorted?'

'I hope so. But enough about me, rumour has it that you were the star of the show with the improv team. How did that happen? Please tell me it was because of your emails.'

Trust the work rumour mill to have kicked in. The kettle boils and Layla takes over the tea-making duties.

'They might have played some part in getting me up on the stage, especially since I received a new email just before, telling me to try something new. But to tell you the truth, it was more down to the looks of disappointment on everyone's faces when Hayley couldn't make it; I didn't want to let them down.'

'I'm still in shock. Especially as I hear you're doing it again.'

'I didn't technically agree . . . '

'I don't think you have a choice. It's all Aaron and Yas are talking about. Besides, from the look on your face, it seems like you enjoyed it.'

I rub at my cheeks, which are starting to ache from all the smiling.

'You know, I thought I'd hate it and freeze up when it started, but I surprised myself by having a good time on stage. And people even laughed at some of the things I said.'

'I'm definitely coming to watch the next one. And whilst we're talking about things your emails have made you do, when's your next trip to see your friend Sophie?'

'Next weekend.'

Layla stirs in the milk.

'I'm so glad you're doing this, you know.' She takes the tea bag out and slides the mug towards me.

'Doing what?'

'Listening to your old self. Putting yourself out there. You'll keep me updated, won't you?'

'You'll be the first person I tell when I get another one.' Layla's been such a good friend to me over the years, I'm so lucky to have her in my life.

'Good, I'm looking forward to hearing the next instalment. And about your next night out with your old friends too. Right, I better get back to my desk. The big boss is a right slave driver.'

'Pesky bosses, they ruin everything.'

She laughs. 'I hope it goes well with the reading later on.'

'Thanks,' I call.

By the time I've made it back to my desk, I find my dad is sitting at his, his bright-orange tie acting like a beacon.

'Sorry I'm late,' he says when he spots me. 'I had to take the car to the garage and they were out of courtesy cars, so I ended up taking the bus.'

'A bus?'

'Yeah, although I could have walked and got here quicker, with the roundabout route it took.'

'Exercise might have done you good. Didn't your doctor say you needed to lose some weight?'

He laughs and tells me he's fine and not to worry so much, and I start to relax. One day I'll learn not to torture myself over Dad and that he can look after himself.

★

It's my first official volunteering session for the Big Little Readers. I had a meeting last week to make sure the paperwork for my background check was all OK and to complete a quick training session. But the majority of the training is done on the job. I've been teamed up with Arnold, a seasoned volunteer who's going to show me the ropes.

My shoulders start to tense as the manager Adrian introduces me to him. It's suddenly all becoming real.

'Relax,' says Arnold, 'the children don't bite. Or not that often anyway.'

He laughs, but it does nothing to ease my nerves.

'I haven't really done anything like this before.'

'You'll be fine. It's just reading a book, plus making a few silly voices here and there if you can.'

'I'll try my best.'

'You two are going to get on like a house on fire,' says Adrian, who's sitting across the desk from us. He glances down at the folder in front of him. 'Now, you're going to meet Lola, who is new to the programme. She's eight years old and currently lives with her aunt. Her mother died of cancer a few months ago and she's not in touch with her dad.'

It feels like the breath's being squeezed out of me as I imagine what it would have been like to lose my mum at such a young age.

I wonder if I should mention that I've lost my own mum, but I'm not sure I'm able to tell them without tears falling. Despite it having happened nearly seventeen years ago, certain things will trigger a memory of her dying and it'll knock me for six. Talking about my mum or thinking of memories can make me either happy or sad, depending on my mood, but occasionally I get propelled back to the moment when I found out that she'd died and I get that suffocating feeling that I'm never going to see her again.

'Edie, are you OK?' asks Adrian, looking up from the file.

I blink back a tear. I knew it would be emotional; I just hadn't expected I'd empathise so much. I want to ask him to assign me another child, but I know that's not how it works. All the kids are going to have a back story.

'Yes, sorry, I just can't imagine what she's gone through over the last few months,' I finally manage.

'I know, it's awful. Poor Lola. But we've found in a few similar cases that these visits can really help. An escape from everything that's going on in their lives.'

I nod again.

Arriving at Lola's house, I take a few deep breaths. I help Arnold to unpack the fold-up stools and the box of books from the car.

'I'll take the lead, to let you familiarise yourself with everything, but please do as much talking as you feel comfortable with today,' he says.

He's about to knock on the door when he stops and turns to me.

'Don't expect too much from the first session. Sometimes kids take a while to warm up to us.'

Before I can ask any questions, a woman opens the front door.

'Hello, come on in. I'm Kate, Lola's aunt.'

'I'm Arnold, this is Edie.'

We follow her into the lounge, where a little girl's sat watching the television. She doesn't look at us when we enter, staring straight ahead at the screen. Kate walks over and turns it off.

'Lola, these people are here to read some books with you. They've brought them from the library.'

The girl looks up at us and then back at the telly despite it being off.

'Lola,' says Kate again.

'It's all right,' says Arnold, putting down his little stool. 'Lola can join in later if she wants to. I'm just going to put the books down here and see if there's one I can read to Edie. She's new and hasn't heard all of the stories yet.'

'I haven't,' I say, my heart breaking for Lola and her hollow-looking expression. I recognise it from how I used to see myself in the mirror. It's a disjointed look, like you're there in body only and your mind's somewhere else entirely.

When I'd been considering volunteering, I'd been weighing up mainly whether I'd be brave enough to read to the kids, not whether I'd be emotionally up to the job. Miles had tried to warn me that it might be tough, but I hadn't listened.

'I'm thinking that perhaps I'd like to hear a story about an animal. A unicorn . . .' My voice is a bit shaky. I search Lola's face but there's nothing. 'Or perhaps something more exotic?'

'How about this one, it's about a whale?' says Arnold, taking it out of the box and beginning to read.

I'm not sure what I'd expected from these sessions but not the stillness and silence that is coming from Lola.

After Arnold's book comes to an end, I try a book about a princess. I even put on the kind of voices that would have made the improv crew proud, but there's still nothing.

We read another book, and then another. After each one Kate smiles.

'That was good, wasn't it?' she says, but Lola remains passive.

'You know, Lola, we can leave some of the books with you,' says Arnold at the end of the session.

There's a slight twitch from Lola. She doesn't move her head, just her eyes towards the box.

'That's kind of them, isn't it?' says Kate, and Lola props herself up a little straighter, her head now turned towards the box.

'What about one about llamas?' asks Arnold.

No reaction.

'Let's see,' I say, digging in. 'We've got one about racing cars, fairies, a Peppa Pig one, one about witches.'

She leans a little closer and I pull the book out and I place it on the sofa next to her.

She looks over it and she traces her finger over the raised edges of the witch's skirt.

Arnold raises an eyebrow at me and my heart pangs.

'Right, thank you, Lola, for listening to our stories,' he says. 'We really enjoyed coming to meet you and we'll be back to see you next week with some more books. Perhaps you could tell us if that witch one is any good.'

'It would be handy to know if you'd recommend it to other boys and girls,' I say.

Lola doesn't say anything else to us. Her fingers just stay on the book next to her. We take it as our cue to leave and Kate gives us an apologetic shrug as she walks us out into the hall.

'I'm sorry. She's not great with anyone at the moment, to be honest.'

'It's OK,' says Arnold. 'For most children it takes them a little while to warm up to our visits, but we know this is not always the case. Let's keep our fingers crossed.'

We say our goodbyes, and we load the books into the back of the car before we set off.

'You did really well in there,' says Arnold, pulling out of the drive. 'Especially as I could tell it upset you.'

'Was it that obvious?'

'Maybe to an old timer.'

'I'm usually fine,' I say, willing the tears not to fall.

'Grief's a funny thing, Edie; hit's you when you least expect it. My wife died ten years ago and yet sometimes it feels like it happened yesterday.'

'I'm so sorry.'

'And I'm sorry, for your . . . mum?'

I nod.

'You know, Adrian's a really top bloke. I'm sure if you spoke to him he'd switch you to another child.'

I might have considered it before we came but having seen Lola and the pain she's going through, I can't stop now.

'No, it's fine. I'm guessing that whichever child I'd be assigned to would have their own challenges. At least with her I can empathise with what she's going through.'

'And that might be a way for you two to connect. It might help her knowing that you understand how's she feeling.'

I bite my lip to ground myself with the pain. I don't like to talk about it, but maybe I should if it would help Lola.

'My mum, she died when I was eighteen. I just can't imagine how hard it would have been to lose her at Lola's age.'

Arnold purses his lips together.

'I know, it's unimaginable. When I think about my grand-children at that age.'

We drive along without speaking until we pull up at traffic lights.

'Is it always this exhausting? I feel like I've worked a whole week in just an hour.'

'Ha, I know, it takes me the next day to recover. Good job I'm retired,' he chuckles.

The light turns green and we're off again. I can't help but notice that, despite feeling exhausted, for the first time in a long time I feel like I'm doing something that's making a difference.

Chapter 12

I take hold of Miles's hand as we walk through Westerly. On one of our date nights, I mentioned the night out Soph had arranged and he seemed genuinely excited to be invited. We checked in to our B&B this afternoon and now we're heading to the pub to meet the gang. Westerly's changed a lot in the past seventeen years. The town centre's had a face lift; it's a little glossier and prettier, the Victorian buildings all freshly painted and decorated with hanging baskets, and bunting hanging between the old-fashioned streetlights. Yet, despite the gentrification, there's still enough of the old Westerly to make it seem familiar.

I walk past the pub where I had my first legal drink when I turned eighteen. Past what used to be a greasy spoon where we'd eat away our hangovers and that's now an upmarket seafood restaurant. I spot the old newsagent where Dad used to insist we bought our ice creams from when I was little as they were the cheapest in town.

Soph's chosen The Quays, which was one of our old haunts, and, like the town, when I step inside I notice it's had a bit of a makeover. There's a new slate floor underfoot and the bar is polished and shiny.

I spot Soph and Brett talking to a woman at a table in the corner and make a beeline for them.

'Hey, you came.' Soph stands up and wraps me up in a huge hug. 'And you must be Miles, I'm so thrilled you could come.'

He seems taken aback as she gives him a big hug too.

I lean over and Brett kisses me on both cheeks and then shakes Miles's hand. A woman with long, glossy brown hair is sitting at the table with them and she flashes a smile of perfect white teeth.

'Edie, this is Verity, Verity, this is Edie and Miles,' says Soph.

'Lovely to meet you,' she says with an American accent.

'Ah, is that an East Coast accent I detect?' says Miles.

'It is, I'm from Massachusetts.'

'Nice. I've got an aunt in New Hampshire.'

'Well, we won't hold that against her.' She flicks her hair over her shoulder. 'Sit, sit.'

I squeeze into an empty seat next to Soph and Miles rests his hand on the back of it.

'I'll get us drinks first,' he says, backing away. 'Edie?'

'I'll have a beer, thanks.'

'Anyone else?'

'We're all set.' Verity flashes her perfect smile again, then turns to me. 'Soph says that you all used to work together back in the day.'

'Yes, for a summer. Do you live in Westerly too?' I'm wondering if Soph's invited any more of her friends along. I guess I'd hoped that it would just be us.

'Actually, I'm only passing through on my way to the US.'

Douglas comes over and puts the drinks on the table.

He spots me and gives me a big hug.

'Is Suzie here?' I ask. 'I'd love to meet her.'

'No, Isla's got swimming lessons tomorrow morning, and it's complicated with logistics.'

'Haven't they finished for the holidays?' asks Soph.

'Must be the last one,' he trails off. 'So where's the famous Miles?'

I turn towards the bar and point to him, only my hand drops when I notice Joel walking towards us carrying two drinks.

'Tall guy?' asks Douglas. He has to ask me twice because at first I don't know what he's talking about; I'd forgotten we were talking about Miles.

'Yeah, that's him.'

Joel puts the drinks down on the table.

'Hello,' he says to me, his tone just as cold as it was at Soph's.

I watch him pass a drink to Verity and she puts a hand through one of the belt loops of his jeans. It's like I'm eighteen all over again and I feel the blood rushing from my head. It suddenly all fits into place now; this is Joel's girlfriend who was working abroad. She's all tanned and beautiful and I feel even more foolish that I thought I ever had a chance with him all those years ago if these are the kind of girlfriends he has.

'I thought you weren't coming,' I say, sitting back down, glad of the chair to support me. 'Weren't you supposed to be in the South of France?'

I wouldn't have come if I'd known he was going to be here.

'I was, but then Verity needed to fly back to the US, and she had the choice of stopping over in Paris or London.'

'So we thought it would make sense for me to come to Joel instead. And when I heard that Douglas was in town and that Soph was organising a night out, I knew I'd made the right decision.' She raises her drink in Soph's direction and they clink glasses. 'Although I did lobby for us to go to Bournemouth. This place is so quiet.'

'It's busy enough now that the tourists have started to arrive; Although it'll be so much worse next month,' says Brett.

Douglas pulls up a chair and leans across the table.

'So, Edie. Has anyone told you yet about my idea?'

'And what's that?'

Joel sighs. 'It's a terrible idea.'

'Douglas thinks we should play pub golf,' says Soph.

I wrinkle my nose; I haven't played that game in years.

Miles walks over and places a drink in front of me, and I introduce him to the boys before he sits down on my other side, his arm resting on my back.

'Miles, you look like the kind of guy who's played pub golf in his day,' says Douglas.

'I may have partaken in the odd round.'

'"Par" taken.' Douglas high-fives him. 'I like what you did there.'

It takes Miles a second to get his unintentional pun and he looks rather pleased with himself.

'You see, Miles is all for it, so I really think we're onto a winner.'

'I think it sounds like fun,' says Verity, clapping her hands together enthusiastically. 'But don't we need scorecards?'

'I borrowed a pen and paper from the barmaid.' Douglas holds them up.

'Of course you have,' Joel mutters under his breath.

'I can't even remember how we do this.' Soph peers at the grid Douglas is drawing on the paper. 'If a pub is par ten, we have to drink ten drinks – is that right?'

'Bloody hell, Soph, I think we'd be on the floor,' says Joel. 'No, it means that we've got to drink our drink in ten sips.'

'Oh, that seems a little tame.' She sounds disappointed.

'Well, if we were playing for eighteen holes, we'd be drinking a hell of a lot of pints,' I say.

'Oh, yeah, I guess,' she says. 'Wait a second, we're not doing eighteen holes tonight, are we?'

'No.' Joel fixes a stern look at Douglas. 'We'll do the nine holes. We used to go round the pubs twice, but now let's just do them once.'

'We used to have forfeits, didn't we?' says Soph. 'Although I guess assigning the night security shift is no longer applicable.'

I can't help but look up at Joel at this and he makes eye contact. That was always one of my favourite shift rotations largely because I got to spend time alone with him.

'Do you think we actually need to do the pub crawl bit of it?' asks Soph. 'Just that it's Saturday night and we'll struggle to get another table. We could stay here instead.'

'That sounds nothing like pub golf; it pretty much ruins the whole purpose, which was to rediscover our youth somewhat,' says Douglas. 'We will drink the whole nine holes as well as move pubs.'

'OK, Braveheart,' I say and Soph giggles.

Douglas raises an eyebrow and gives us both a scolding look, followed by one of his trademark charming smiles.

'Bloody hell,' he says, 'we've been talking about the rules for so long I've drunk my sodding drink. Anyone else need a fresh one?'

We all shake our heads. There's an awkward silence when he goes and I attempt to fill it.

'So, working in Cannes must be glamourous, Verity.'

'It's hard to see the glamour when you're working all the time, but it is a beautiful part of the world.'

'Which is why you should consider staying,' says Soph with a sigh. 'Do you know she wants to move to Florida and she's talking about taking Joel with her? That's way too far for us to visit as often, and expensive with flights.'

'Miami's a great city.' Miles picks up his drink. 'Are you able to get a visa to work out there easily, Joel?'

'It's complicated.' Verity turns to Joel and raises an eyebrow. 'But not impossible; there are definitely ways. It's just a great opportunity and guaranteed work with the yearlong good weather. Plus, better pay.'

'Not everything's about money,' says Joel.

'Those two have been on and off for years,' says Soph, lowering her voice and leaning towards me while the rest of them talk about the Floridan sunshine. 'They're as bad as each other, terrified of any labels that sound like commitment. But between you and me, I think this is them finally taking the next step. I mean, what's a bigger commitment than moving thousands of miles away together?'

I nod, wondering if that's true. It sounds like I had a lucky escape all those years ago as Joel was never going to be the type of man who settles down in one place and commits. I watch Verity slip her arm around Joel. She holds her phone out to snap a selfie and the two of them kiss. Maybe Verity's the one to finally make him change his ways.

Douglas sits back down, a fresh pint in his hand. 'Right then, let's tee off.'

He starts to down his beer.

'Woah, there.' I reach my hand up to his arm. 'We don't need any holes-in-one just yet. We've got a long night ahead of us.'

I notice that his eyes are ringed and heavy-looking again. I'm not sure if it's possible but he looks like he's aged since I last saw him a couple of weeks ago. I'm not the only one staring at him; Joel is too.

'Take it easy. We've got six sips to drink it in.'

Miles puts his glass down with half of it drunk; I think he'd had the same plan as Douglas.

'We get to chat though, right?' says Soph. 'I can't remember what we used to do on pub crawls.'

'It was pretty much just drinking,' says Joel.

'And dancing on bars. No, wait, that was you two,' Douglas says, pointing at me and Soph.

'Trust you to remember that, and it was only once or twice,' I say. '*Coyote Ugly* had a lot to answer for.'

'Oh my god, I loved that film. I so wanted to be a Coyote when I was younger.' Verity flicks her hair over her shoulder with attitude like she was acting the part.

'I'd love to have seen you dance on a bar,' says Brett, turning to Soph. 'Any chance you want to give it a go again tonight?'

'Yeah right. At eighteen I was as skinny as a rake, wearing something skimpy. There's no way they'd let me go climbing on a bar in my state and in this frumpy shirt.'

'You've just had a baby. And even then you're still the hottest women in the room – no offence, Verity and Edie.'

'None taken.' I'm really warming to Brett.

'Plus, who cares what top you're wearing. I would watch you dance regardless. Frumpy top, or you know my personal favourite is always no top . . .'

'Shhh, you're making me blush and embarrassing me in front of all of my friends. As my boyfriend you're slightly biased but thank you.'

He throws his arm around her, giving her a kiss, and she giggles as she pulls away.

Watching Brett and Soph together, I can see that he's nothing like the guys she used to go for, the ones who played it so cool with her that they were practically ice cold.

Douglas puts his empty glass down on the table.

'Yes! I did it in four,' he says.

'Take it easy, mate.' Joel's still staring at him. I'm almost relieved that I'm not the only one on the receiving end of his cold looks. 'We might be taking a walk down memory lane, but we're not eighteen anymore.'

'Tell me about it,' I say, looking at my barely touched drink.

Miles slams his drink down. 'In three,' he says proudly.

'Yes!' Douglas high-fives him and updates his scorecard.

Brett winces before picking up his drink. 'If you can't beat them, join them.'

By the time we've made it to the third pub — and on the fifth round, as we've compromised with two rounds in each — Douglas and Miles are in the lead, with the rest of us trailing behind.

'Come on, guys,' says Douglas. 'You're all flagging.'

I got the impression from Soph's barbecue that Douglas was a big drinker, but there's something about the way he is tonight that reminds me of Dad when he was out of control. His whole manner is off and it seems like he's trying to put on an act rather than be himself. Occasionally I catch glimpses of sadness and I wonder if that's the real him.

'I'm so tired,' says Soph, snuggling into Brett.

'What happened to this being our big night out? Our one big chance to go crazy,' he says, with a slur.

She sighs heavily. 'We got old, and I've got to go and pump and dump.'

Douglas raises an eyebrow, and his ears prick up like an animal's.

'That sounds interesting,' he says.

'Eww, get your mind out of the gutter,' says Soph, standing up. 'I've got to use my breast pump to pump the milk before my boobs start leaking. Alfie would usually be having another feed around now.'

'Ow, that's not quite what I had in mind.'

'We can all guess what you had in mind, Douglas,' says Verity as Soph heads off to the toilets.

'Right, what par are we on now?' asks Miles, standing up. 'I'll get the next round in.'

'Are we still even playing?' I tug at his sleeve to pull him back down.

'Of course,' says Douglas.

'I'm not sure I even drank the last round,' says Verity, turning to Joel.

He shrugs. 'Don't look at me, everything's been hazy since that whisky chaser. Is it time to go home yet?' He leans his head against the wall for support.

'You're such a cute drunk.' She pulls her phone out and cosies up to him, snapping another selfie.

Miles heads off to the bar. Brett leans over to talk to Joel and Verity, and I turn my attention to Douglas. I've been wanting to talk to him all night.

'You don't seem quite yourself.' I drop my voice to be discreet. 'Are you all right?'

'Myself?' says Douglas, in a loud thespian tone. 'I'll have you know that I've never felt more like myself.'

'You've been drinking quite a lot and I—'

'I'm fine. It's a pub crawl and it's not my fault I'm not a light-weight like the rest of you.' He tries to laugh it off, but it only highlights the lines and the redness on his face. It does nothing to reassure me.

Miles puts a tray of drinks down on the table.

'I'm pretty sure that I'm going to regret this tomorrow when I'm too hungover to properly see the sights of Westerly,' he says, sitting down. I go to take one of the drinks at the same time as Joel and our hands touch.

'You go.' He looks at me in the eye for the first time tonight without glaring.

'No, you have it.'

'There's one for both of you,' says Miles, dishing them out to us.

I rub my hand that touched Joel's with my fingers; it's still warm to the touch and it reminds me of how any time we used to find ourselves holding hands I'd get the same reaction.

'If you're in town tomorrow, you should join me and Joel, we're going paddle boarding,' says Verity.

'I'm sure they'd be too busy sightseeing to come.' Joel shakes his head, dismissing the idea.

'Not at all,' says Miles, his eyes lighting up. 'I've always wanted to try it. Can we hire boards locally?'

'Joel says there's a little shack in town where you can as I don't have a board. They hire wetsuits too.'

'Good job we bought our swimming gear after all,' says Miles, turning to me.

'Hmm.' The last thing I want to do is go out on the water with Joel. 'But didn't you book us into that spa on the way home?'

'I was going to, but the website kept crashing. I meant to phone them. Lucky I didn't, huh?' He pats me on the leg and I smile back, defeated. Looks like we're going paddle boarding.

'What have I missed? Is it time to go home yet?' asks Soph, sitting back down.

'What happened to sleep when you're dead?' says Douglas.

'I learnt that sleep is the elixir of life.'

'You can't bail out now.' Douglas looks round at us for someone to agree with him, but we all know the night's coming to an end. 'Fine. But if you're all going to be lightweights tonight then we should do this again, and make a whole weekend of it, so that none of us have any excuse.'

'I'd definitely be up for that,' says Soph before she claps her hands. 'We could go to Hartland's for old times' sake.'

Douglas bangs the table, startling Brett whose eyes had started to close. 'Genius idea. Let's do it over the summer.'

'Edie?' asks Soph.

'I'm not sure.'

I'm trying not to catch Joel's eye. Because I know it'll be difficult to spend a whole weekend with him, there of all places too.

'Come on, it'd be great,' says Soph, giving me one of those looks that I know all too well from when we were eighteen. It was one that had me dancing on bars alongside her. 'Promise me you'll think about it.'

'OK.'

'Is that an OK to you coming?' She reaches her hand across the table and squeezes mine.

'It's an "I'll think about it".'

She squeezes my hand again in excitement, as if I've already said yes. It's not that I haven't had fun tonight, being reunited with them all. But a whole weekend? And one at Hartland's, which is so full of memories. I'm not sure that any number of past emails could coax me into thinking that's a good idea.

Chapter 13

Paddle boarding sounded like a terrible idea last night, and that was before I woke up hungover and exhausted. Just the thought of it is sending shivers down my spine. I manage to shower and make it down for breakfast, but not even a full English has done anything to stop my head from pounding. Although my hangover is nothing compared to the one Miles has. He hasn't managed to make it out of bed yet. I'm fully prepared to text Soph and the gang to tell them we're going to have to give it a miss.

Alone at the breakfast table, I scroll through the news on my phone and then I check my emails and see that I missed a note to future self whilst we were in the pub. I click on it, pleased to be alone so that I can truly savour it. It feels even more poignant only being a few miles away from where I originally sat and wrote it.

```
Dear Edie,
    How's it all going in da future??? I know,
I read it and cringed too. I know I am not
50 Cent and not cool enough to pull that off.
But how are you? And how are the notes to
self going? I hope that you have gone out
of your way to do new things and well and
```

truly stretched yourself - metaphorically, obvs - we don't want any pulled muscles at your age.

Are you all set for summer? It's heating up here. The shorts are almost permanently on now and my legs, for the first time in years, have gone super brown. And they're toned too. Who knew the secret to amazing legs was walking miles and miles round the holiday camp every day and never sitting still for more than five minutes?

But despite it being really busy, I'm totally learning how to play the system a bit better and have started to do a sneaky bit of reading whilst on reception. I've been reading this book, called *Yes Man* that Joel lent me, and it's all about a guy who, unsurprisingly from the title, says Yes to everything he's asked. Soph and I decided to give it a go, of course with the proviso of being able to say no to men -obviously! So this email's note to self is to spend a day saying yes to more things.

Big love and sunshine kisses, Edie x x

'Did you want some more bacon?' asks the host of the guesthouse, bringing over a small casserole dish with a lid.

I'm about to instinctively refuse, as having to look out for Dad has made me watch what I eat too, even though I'm craving it, and then I stop: *say yes more.*

'Yes, please,' I say.

The woman seems pleased and scoops on another couple of rashers of steaming bacon onto my plate.

By the time I make it up to the room, taking with me the homemade cookies that I also said yes to, Miles is in exactly the same position as he was before.

'Hey, are you OK? Do you want me to cancel the paddle boarding?'

He opens one eye and shuts it tightly before he lets out a groan.

'I appear to have gone to some kind of floral hell. Why would the landlady decorate the bedrooms like this?'

'I'm guessing that her usual clientele don't play pub golf.'

'Hmm, but at least we were victorious.' He tries to scrunch his fist but even that's too much effort.

I don't point out that he only really won because everyone else had stopped playing. Soph had curled up asleep, her head resting on Brett's lap. Douglas had started drinking with another group at the other end of the pub and I don't want to think about why Verity and Joel made a swift, sudden exit.

'So, paddle boarding? I can text and cancel.'

He rubs at his temples.

'No, don't. I'll be quick in the shower.'

'Are you sure because—'

'I'll be fine. Give me five minutes.'

We make it down to the quay where we find Joel sitting on a wall, holding an extra-large reusable coffee cup. He's dressed in shorts and a T-shirt with flip-flops on his feet and sunglasses on top of his head. My stomach gives an involuntary flip. How is he even better looking than he was when we were younger?

'Woah, Miles, are you OK?' he says.

'I thought the fresh air might do me some good, but I'm not so sure.' He grips hold of the wall to balance himself.

'Verity's not too well either.' He points at her power walking down the river path with a bottle of water in her hand. 'She's trying to sweat it out.'

It's then that I spot Douglas on the grass in front of us, lying on his back, with a jumper covering his eyes.

'So many casualties. How are you feeling?' I ask.

'I'm all right. You?'

'I'm worried that I'm going to feel worse later.'

It's a beautiful spot we've picked to meet at alongside the river. There's not a cloud in the sky and the light's reflecting off the water, causing it to sparkle.

'Morning,' calls Soph, walking up to us with Alfie in the pram. She sounds much more chipper than the rest of us. She surveys the carnage around us. 'It's like the apocalypse.'

'Where's Brett?' asks Joel.

'He's gone to play a christening, can you imagine?' She pulls a face. 'He was looking rather green this morning. So it means I can't paddle board as I'm on Alfie duty.'

'I'll look after him,' says Verity, marching on the spot next to us. 'We can take it in turns.'

'Actually, I probably shouldn't do it. I had a Caesarean and I don't want to rip any stitches.'

'Pretty sure, they'd be healed by now, Soph. Alfie's almost six months old,' shouts Douglas.

'He lives,' she calls back to him, before muttering under her breath, 'for now.'

'Douglas, are you going to make it?' asks Joel.

'I might just go for a swim.'

'It'll be freezing.' Soph shivers and pulls a face.

'That's exactly what I need,' he says.

'If it's that cold, I'm not sure I want to do this, you know, in case we fall in, I say.'

'That's what makes it exciting,' says Verity. 'Plus it's good motivation to find your balance.'

'If she doesn't want to join in, that's her choice.' Joel gets down off the wall.

'Come on, Edie, you can't back out now. Trust me, you're going to love it.' Verity looks straight at me, raising an eyebrow.

I'm about to tell her I'd rather give it a miss, but then I remember that today is a day of saying yes.

'Yes, I'll do it.'

She pats me on the back and I don't miss the flash of annoyance on Joel's face as we get ready to go.

I arrive at the beach a hot, sweaty mess after the drive that seemed to take hours, despite it only being five minutes. I made the stupid mistake of changing into my wetsuit on the quay, so that I could use the changing cubicle, forgetting how hot neoprene could be, not to mention how uncomfortable it is to wear sitting down. Whilst Joel and Verity start to organise the boards on the beach, I try and pull the wetsuit out of all the places it got wedged into on the way over. Poor Miles is bent over double. He spent most of the drive like a dog hanging his head out of the window.

Verity walks over in bikini bottoms and a rash vest and holds out her phone to me.

'Hey, Edie, would you mind taking a photo of me and Joel?

Gotta have photographic evidence of all the love, right?' she says, slipping an arm round Joel's shoulders and pouting.

I try and ignore the ripple of irrational jealousy that flashes over me. Especially that he doesn't seem to be uncomfortable with her using the L word. I take a couple of snaps and then hand back the phone.

Soph settles herself on a towel and she tries to stop Alfie eating sand by encouraging him instead to place it on a sleeping Douglas.

'I fully expect him to be buried under it when we come back,' calls Joel, turning his attention back to the boards.

'That's the plan.' She winks back.

Joel runs through a quick briefing, which makes paddle boarding sound very straightforward.

'OK, so we're going to take this slow. To start off, we're just going to go on our knees.' Joel's slipped into full instructor mode. 'Ready?'

'On my knees,' I repeat, cursing past Edie and how she's got me into this mess.

I look at the water that appears so calm and still. Maybe it won't be so bad after all.

Verity's already drifting away from the shore. She's up on her board in no time, making it look effortless.

'It's all about balance, right?' says Miles, pushing off on his knees. He's drifting out towards Verity and she starts to give him tips on how to stand up. Joel looks out at them like he's itching to join them, and he climbs on his knees, about to push away, when he turns back to me. I still haven't even put my board in the water.

'Don't forget to fix your strap around your ankle in case you fall in,' he says, pointing down at it.

'Thanks for the vote of confidence.'

'Just best to be prepared. You've got nothing to fear falling in anyway, with your wetsuit on. At least you managed to get it on the right way round today.' He laughs a little before he catches himself and stops.

I instantly know what he's referring to: the very first time I put on a wetsuit when he took me for a windsurfing lesson.

'How was I supposed to know the zip went at the back? I'm sure it's a mistake that anyone could have made.'

'Uh-huh, do you know how many people I taught that summer and how many people put their wetsuit on backwards?'

'Maybe I was starting a trend.'

'One that didn't catch on.'

'You know, you tease me about that, but I still remember when you ate a pomegranate and started picking out the individual seeds.'

'Touché,' he says, finally laughing, and for the first time he looks at me with warmth.

It's the longest conversation we've had this weekend and it makes my heart ache for what we once had.

'Right, it's all about finding your balance,' he says, pushing his hair off his face before demonstrating. He stands up from his knees, and, holding his paddle in his hand, he pushes away from the edge. 'See, nothing to it.'

Miles is already standing on the board and, despite his raging hangover, he's making it look effortless as he paddles away with Verity. I'm worried Joel's going to paddle away with the others, and whilst I don't particularly want to be stuck with him, I don't want to be alone either. He gets a little way out but he turns back to shore. Climbing off his board, he holds mine steady.

I get on all fours on the board, and, once I'm on, Joel gently places his hands on my back to correct my posture and I try not to jolt at his touch.

'Just put your hands a little further apart on the paddle.' He lets go of my back and climbs on his own board and demonstrates how to hold the paddle and then how to use it.

I start to mimic him the best I can. I stay on my knees for a while until Joel suddenly stands up on his board. He looks forward and slowly spins his board round so that he's facing me.

'OK, we're going to get you up.'

'No, no, no, we're not, I'm happy on my knees. It's peaceful and it's great and—' I go to open my mouth again and to tell him another no when I stop myself. The last few weeks since I got my past emails have pushed me to the edge of my comfort zone and nothing particularly hideous has happened. Today is all about saying yes. 'What do I need to do?'

Joel smiles, and talks me through how I'm going to do it. Slowly I push one of my shaky legs up.

'You've got this, Edie, come on. Next leg. Keep looking up, don't look down.'

I get up on both feet and I am standing. I'm actually standing on my board.

'I'm up, I'm up,' I squeal and I look down to get my bearings and I start to wobble.

'Look at me, just at me,' says Joel, 'right here.'

'Are you trying to go all *Dirty Dancing*?'

'Not intentionally. Look into my eyes.'

'Now you've gone all Paul McKenna.'

He starts to laugh and so do I, which does not help my balance, and I start to wobble again.

'I'm going to fall, I don't want to fall.'

'Keep looking up.'

It doesn't help. My arms start to windmill and I instinctively drop my paddle and fall sideways off the board.

I hear Joel shout but not what he says as I hit the water, which, despite the wetsuit, is a cold shock. I'm only under for a second before my head comes back up and I gulp for air.

Joel crouches down on his board and reaches down to help me up.

'I won't let you sink.'

I remember the first time he said that to me. He'd been holding me so gently in the water, teaching me how to starfish on my back, my body tingling at his touch.

'Luckily neither will the foot strap,' I say, trying to push that memory out of my head.

'That's why you should always wear it. OK, to get back on, just push yourself up from the middle, don't kick out.'

I push myself like a beached whale onto the board and lie down prone.

'I'm going to stay here like this.'

'You can paddle with your hands.'

'Now this, this is much better.'

'Bit slow though and doesn't work your core.'

'My core's happy to be neglected. I don't need toned abs.'

My mind wanders to the summer at Hartland's to Joel and his squeaky ab cradle. I can't help wondering if he ever got that six-pack. Stop it, Edie.

'You were doing really well before, it would be a shame not to try again.'

'You're just being polite.'

'No, I'm not. Just keep looking up and your balance will get there. Are you ready to give it another go?'

'Yes,' I say, trying to mean it. I never realised how much my default reaction to any question is no. When did I get so negative?

It takes me a couple of goes to stand up, but when I do, I stay perfectly still.

'Now paddle,' says Joel in a gentle voice, trying not to spook me. 'Other way round.'

I turn the paddle and inch it slowly into the water and start to move it.

'I'm doing it,' I whisper, not wanting to jinx anything.

'You really are. Let's see how far you get.'

We're still going slow but with every passing second that I remain on the board I become more confident. I don't talk to Joel, I'm too busy concentrating on what I'm doing. Verity and Miles are far in front of us and they keep getting smaller and smaller.

'Did you want to go and catch up with them?' I ask.

'No, it's fine, I'm happy staying here.'

'Even if it's with me?'

The frost that's hung in the air between the two of us seems to have thawed, but it's left a lot unspoken.

'Edie,' he says, and I think he's going to say something more. He's looking into my eyes but it's not about getting me to balance; if anything it's having the opposite effect as my knees are going to buckle.

'I might need to have a little break,' I say, not sure how much longer I can keep upright without falling.

'There's a little beach over there, we can turn and head towards it.'

140

'You can just leave me there and pick me up on the way back.'

'It's fine, really. Put your paddle in like this and you'll turn.'

He demonstrates and I do my best to follow him. I end up back in the water but it's shallow and I walk the rest of the way. It doesn't feel as cold this time.

Joel makes it to the beach first and he helps me pull my board onto the sand and I sit down on it. I try and catch my breath and retie my hair into what's bound to be a really messy bun.

'That was amazing,' I say, looking back out at the water. 'I can't believe how peaceful it was.'

'I know.'

'I would have thought it was a bit tame for you. I thought you were all about adrenaline sports.'

He shrugs.

'Perhaps that's what happens when you get old. I still do kitesurf a lot, but Verity got me into paddle boarding last summer and it's nice just chilling on the water.'

Verity and Miles are well and truly out of sight now and I wonder how far they've gone.

'She seems really nice.'

'Yeah, she is.'

'Have you been together long?'

I dig my feet in the sand, enjoying the momentary feeling of having it between my toes.

'On and off for a while,' he says, sounding vague. 'Although I've known her years. Some of the yachting circles are quite small. We both worked a season in the Turks and Caicos and then she ended up in Cannes at the same time as me last year.'

'And now she's heading back to the US?'

'Yeah, she's thinking about it. She's got an interview for a job at a big resort in Florida. She thinks she might be able to get a job for me too, if I want it.'

'And do you?' My voice wobbles a bit saying it. I don't know why it would bother me if he did go.

'I don't know. It's hard to get a visa and if I did go, we'd have to live together and I'm not sure . . . but the job would be amazing.' He shrugs.

He's making it sound like his relationship with Verity is casual, but they're always cosying up taking loved-up photos together and he's considering moving to the US with her. Maybe Soph's right; this is them stepping up and taking their relationship to the next level, without admitting it to themselves yet.

'I bet it'll be nice for you to get back on the yachts. You must have missed it being here.'

He picks up a bit of driftwood and starts to peel the strands back.

'I miss bits of it. Being out on the water and the travel. But it was hard to have a life when you're not in charge of your own schedule.'

'I bet you saw some amazing places.'

'I did. But there are beautiful places here too. I've always loved this beach.'

I look up around me for the first time since we arrive and it's familiar.

'Is this the beach we used to come, to watch the sunrise?'

'Yeah, Kestrel beach. We used to walk through the nature reserve.'

I look over the treeline, trying not to let my head get too caught up in the memories of the times Joel and I spent here that summer.

'Look, Edie, I've been meaning to talk to you about things. To apologise for how I messed up our friendship with how I acted after . . .' He pauses and I don't think he can bring himself to say that we almost kissed. 'I was young and I didn't know any better and then when your mum died—'

'It's fine,' I say, shutting down the conversation because I don't want to think about how mad I was at Joel the night that she died. For a long time, I blamed myself for my parents' car accident. Joel too. If I hadn't confronted him, I would never have been in the state that drove Mum to get in that car. 'We don't need to talk about that. You're right, we were young and it was a long time ago. You know that Soph's got it in her head that we should all go for a weekend at Hartland's?'

'I know, it's like she wants us all to be friends again, as if no time has passed.'

'And if we're going to be friends, all of us,' I say, looking him in the eye so that he knows I mean he's who I'm really talking about, 'I think it's better that some things just stay in the past. I'm sure if we could go back, we would have done things differently.'

'I certainly would have.' He's staring back into my eyes and it takes my breath away. 'No need for things to get awkward.'

'None at all. We just forget it all happened. We pick up where we left off when we were just friends.'

'Just friends,' he says. 'Yeah, that's all, we ever were, right?'

He raises his eyebrow and attempts a smile and it breaks my heart a little bit. No matter whether it was real or not, or just in my teenage mind, he was the first man I ever really fell in love with, and he never even realised it.

'Right,' I say, nodding. It shouldn't really bother me after all this time that it didn't mean anything to him, but it does. 'So, that's all sorted then?'

'Yeah. I'm glad, because it's felt like we've been tiptoeing round each other.'

'I felt that too, but, as you say, no need.' I stand up and stretch my legs, my calves are tightening from the paddling.

'I'm getting really stiff. Should my calves hurt this much?'

He stands up and grabs his board.

'Probably, if you're not used to it. We should get going before you seize up. You ready?'

'I'm guessing no's the wrong answer.'

'No's usually the wrong answer,' he says with a laugh.

I'm tempted to bring up the *Yes Man* book he'd lent me when we were eighteen, the one I'd forgotten all about until I read the email this morning. But I don't because then I'd have to explain the note-to-self email to him and I'd feel embarrassed.

'Hey, there you are,' says Miles, paddling back in our direction. 'We were wondering where you'd got to.'

'How are you making that look so easy?'

'It's all about the bend in the knees,' shouts Miles. 'Come on.'

I follow Joel over to the shore, the freezing water lapping at my feet, and I'm pleased to be leaving the beach and all the bittersweet memories it brings back. We're putting the past behind us, and I've got to treat life like paddle boarding, looking forward and not looking back.

Chapter 14

THEN

When I arrived at Hartland's, I naively thought I'd spend my days sat behind a reception desk, as well as showing people to their holiday lodges. I hadn't envisaged how varied the role would be or how the rotation I'd enjoy the most was night security. I'm not entirely sure how much I could have done if something had kicked off in the middle of the night; Lionel hadn't given us any extra training, but apparently the big fences kept most people out and we were there to act as merely a deterrent.

Despite that fear, there were a lot of perks to the job. The first being that you had the morning off the next day and I could catch up on sleep without the threat of being dragged out on some kind of social adventure. Then there was a stillness at night in the camp that didn't exist in the day. Apart from a few rogue lodges whose lights were on late, the rest of the park was pitch black. The constant noise of conversations and children playing faded until there was almost silence, and, if the wind blew the right way, you could hear the water crashing against the rocks at the beach.

The best bit, however, was that you worked a buddy system and I was usually paired with Joel.

'Red Leader to Red One, do you copy, over,' came a mock American accent over the walkie-talkie.

'You realise I can see you from where I'm sitting,' I said into the static. I was sat at the sun terrace, watching him at the pool below.

'You didn't say over, over.'

'I can see you from where I'm sitting. OVER.'

'Come on, we need to have a comms check, every so often, just in case something actually happens, over.'

'I'll tell you something that is actually happening. When I went in and checked the reception, I found Elizabeth's secret supply of biscuits, over.'

'I'm there.'

Joel climbed up the stairs to the sun terrace to join me. We liked to sit there as we could see the rest of the holiday park and it was a perfect vantage point to watch out for trouble.

We sat in silence and ate the biscuits and drank lukewarm tea from a flask. It was the kind of companionable silence that felt natural; we didn't have to talk for the sake of it.

Joel's watch beeped and he looked down.

'It's quarter to five,' he said with a yawn.

'It's gone quick tonight.' We'd almost made it. This was the last hour of full darkness before the sun started to rise.

'It has.' He nodded and took another biscuit. 'How about we play a game?'

'A game?'

'Yep, would you rather. Like, would you rather eat sweets or chocolate? Or would you rather snog Bradley or Paul from S Club 7?'

'Easy, chocolate, hands down every time. And really S Club 7? Is that the best you can come up with?'

'OK, I'll try harder but you have to answer immediately, go with your gut. Books or film?'

'Books.'

'Spiderman or Superman?'

'Spiderman.'

Joel gave me a look.

'What? He swings on a web,' I said, turning my wrists over and pretending to ping webs. 'And all you need to defeat Superman is kryptonite.'

'And that's so easy to come by?'

'Hey, I didn't realise we had to justify the answers.'

'Yes, you're right. OK, horror movies or action thrillers?'

'Neither,' I said.

'You have to pick one, that's the rule.'

'But I don't watch either. Thrillers are always so far-fetched and horror movies scare the hell out of me.'

'What? You don't watch horror at all?'

'Nope, never have.'

'You've never seen any of the classics, *The Exorcist, Psycho, Halloween*?'

I shook my head.

'Not even *Scream*, or *Saw*?'

His voice was going high-pitched and I was convinced his eyes were going to pop out of his head.

'Nope, nothing that would terrify me.'

'Wow. Edie. You're missing out.'

'I don't think so.'

'So, what do you watch?'

'Romcoms.'

Joel pulled a face. 'Seriously? You said you don't watch thrillers because they're far-fetched, but romantic comedies aren't? Come on, they're built on a foundation of lies and the myth that happily ever after exists.'

'It does exist.'

'Really? In what universe?' he muttered under his breath.

'My parents are living happily ever after. They are truly in love.'

'How do you know?'

'Because you can just tell these things.'

'OK, maybe there are some exceptions to the rule. But you've got to admit that the way they get together in movies is always ridiculous, as well as the fact that it takes them so long to realise they're in love.'

'Do you think that it's always instant?'

'I think you know at first when you meet someone. You either fancy them or you don't. They always say that when you know, you know. And that's what it's like.'

'You say it like you're in love with someone,' I said, catching his gaze. 'Is there someone that you're not telling me about?'

He turned his head away and started to fidget.

'There is, you like someone. Who is it?' Joel had done his fair share of flirting with girls early on in the summer but lately I hadn't noticed him with anyone.

'It's no one.'

I didn't believe him, but even in the dim lighting I could tell he'd gone red. I guessed it was someone on the campsite. Janie who was in the housekeeping staff maybe, I often saw them talking. Or perhaps Mags from the entertainment staff. She was taking windsurfing lessons with him.

'What about you?' said Joel. 'Was it instant with you and Scott? Are you in love with him?'

I turned the cup in my hand. It was a question I'd asked myself many a time, especially with his visit to the holiday park looming.

'I think we're proof that it can take a long time.'

Joel did a thing with his eyebrows where one went up and one went down and he opened his mouth to say something, but he closed it again, like he'd thought better of it.

'What?'

'Nothing.'

'You were going to say something.'

'No, I wasn't. Hey, do you fancy going for a walk? We haven't made a round for a while.'

'You're trying to change the subject.'

'Maybe,' he said, standing up and holding his hand out.

I took it and he pulled me up, only he did it with just a little too much force and we almost crashed into each other.

'Sorry, you're lighter than you look,' he said, with a small laugh.

'Oi, watch it.' I hit him lightly on the arm. We hadn't moved any further apart and I noticed my breathing had become shallower.

'Let's go,' he said. He still had hold of my hand, and I didn't do anything about it.

I'd never really understood holding hands. Sometimes Scott had slipped his arm around me, and I sort of liked the feeling of protection that it gave me, but we rarely held hands. He had such long spindly fingers that it always felt awkward when I interlaced mine with his. But in that moment I got it. Mine and Joel's hands just fit together and it was like putting on a comfortable pair of shoes or slipping on an old jacket.

'You know, it's almost a full moon. We should go down to the beach and go for a moonlight swim.'

We were heading in that direction, not far away from the water sports hut.

'We can't do that. That's technically off site.'

Joel made a mock-shocked face.

'Come on, you can't play by the rules all the time. Do you think that no one bunks off night security? What about Douglas and Jill in the laundry? Or when Soph slept all night in the hammock by the pool? I think we've been extremely observant for the rest of the evening.'

'Well, the shift is almost over.'

'There you go,' he said, swinging our hands enthusiastically. 'What better way to mark the occasion than with a skinny dip?'

'There's no way you'll catch me doing that. Thankfully I've come prepared with my bikini underneath.'

I'd soon learnt to wear bikinis like underwear. I'd only brought a couple with me, but I'd spent my first few weeks' wages on Topshop's entire range of them.

'Spoilsport. I'll just grab some board shorts from the hut.'

'You keep them down there?'

'I have a full selection. Board shorts, diving shorts, Speedos.'

'Speedos?' I attempted to raise my eyebrow.

'They're more comfortable under a wetsuit.'

My mind was already picturing him in the Speedos and I tried to think of Scott instead.

After Joel quickly changed in the hut, and came out in a pair of board shorts, we walked down to the beach. I stopped looking over my shoulder when my feet touched the sand and

I saw the dappled reflection of the moonlight on the water. It looked so beautiful that it almost took my breath away.

I undressed quickly and Joel threw off his T-shirt and we headed into the water. I knew to ignore the initial shock as I inched in.

Joel on the other hand dived straight under and came up a foot away from me, splashing me in the process.

'You're such a wuss,' he said.

'Not all of us were born part fish. Have you always been so at home in the water?'

He raked his hair back and water droplets dripped off the tips.

'Pretty much. I used to go and visit my dad wherever he was working in the school holidays and he always spent that time out on the water. He was a pretty shit dad with most things, and during term time I rarely heard from him, but those one or two weeks a year when I'd stay with him always seemed to make up for it.'

'Is he happy that you're going to follow in his footsteps?'

He pushed himself back a little, treading water, moving backwards as I waded in deeper.

'I don't know. It's always hard to tell with him. He told me that if I needed any contacts getting a job after I qualified, then he'd help. But whether he was pleased?' He blew out his lips.

I couldn't imagine what it must be like to not have a parent who was rooting for you.

'I'm sorry, that must be really hard.'

He shrugged like he had the weight of the world upon his shoulders.

'It's like we've got the opposite problem. Your parents want you to join in the family biz.'

'I know, they'd have kittens if I ever did.'

'Do you think you will?'

'I hope not. I'd picked English lit to do at uni because I thought it left my options open for possibilities. And now I'm sort of glad as spending time with the kids in the kids' club is making me wonder about teaching.'

'I think you'd be great at it.'

'I just don't know how my parents would take it.' The water started to hit my chest. It was so cold.

'They started the company because that was their dream. I know I've only met them a couple of times, but I get the impression they'd want you to follow your own dream.'

'Isn't it scary though, all this? Making decisions that are going to affect the rest of our lives?'

'If there's one thing that my dad's taught me, it's that nothing has to be for the rest of your life. If you try something and it doesn't work, you can always find a plan B or go somewhere else, try something new.'

'Is it really that simple?'

'I think sometimes people overcomplicate it. But why would you spend time doing something if it makes you feel miserable? I don't think I'd take it to the extremes that he has, but I don't think that things are as set in stone as you think they are.'

I was submerged up to my shoulders, which was as good as it was going to get. I wasn't planning on going any deeper than that. Joel swam a little further out and pushed himself backwards, spreading his arms and legs into a starfish float. I watched him floating on the water; he looked so peaceful.

He stayed that way for a couple of minutes before he pushed himself back up.

'What? Why are you looking at me like that?'

I realised my head was tilted and my mouth was open.

'I don't know how you can let yourself go like that in the sea. I don't think I could put my head back in the water.'

'Why? Scared of getting your hair wet?'

'No, I'm scared of sinking, especially when you can't see what's below you.'

Joel swam a little closer.

'The only thing you should ever be scared of in life is not trying. Come on.'

He stood to the side of me. 'I've got you. Just push your belly up; imagine it's being pulled by an invisible puppet string.'

He placed his arm behind my back.

'Tip yourself backwards. I'll hold you up.'

'I can't do it,' I whispered.

'Yes, you can. You can do anything. I've got you.'

I turned and looked at him right in the eye before he rested his hand gently on the nape of my neck. I pushed my legs up and I tipped my head back. I could feel him cradling me, his fingers light on my neck, guiding it into place and causing my body to tingle.

I don't know how long I was floating for before I registered that he was no longer supporting me and I stood back up.

'I did it, I actually did it.'

'Told you,' he said with a smug look on his face.

I took a few deep breaths, taking it all in. 'I wish this summer would last forever.'

'Me too.'

Joel turned to look at me and my heart started to beat that little bit quicker.

'Come on,' he said, and I thought for a moment he wanted us to get out of the water, but he then pushed himself into a starfish and I followed suit. The two of us stared up at the moon. He reached for my hand and we entwined our fingers and it felt like we were the only two people in the world.

Chapter 15

The weekend at the beach seems like a distant memory after a few days back at work. It's always busy this time of the year; we're spread thinly with a lot of the staff taking leave over the school holidays. I'm just on my way out of the office when I bump into Dad coming back in from a meeting. He's eating the last bit of what looks like a bacon roll but he quickly tries to hide it, shoving the rest in his mouth.

'Good meeting?' I ask.

'Uh-huh, yes,' he mumbles through his mouthful.

'I'm just heading off for the Big Little Readers.'

'Good, good. Listen, I'm glad I caught you, you've been hard to pin down. You haven't popped round lately.'

'I know, I'm sorry. It's been so busy, what with volunteering and the improv group. Aaron and Yas have been trying to coach me some nights after work, and between that and watching the other battles . . .'

I feel a bit guilty because it's not just that I've been busy. Dad's been spending a lot of time with Julie and whilst I did think she was really nice, I'm having a harder time adjusting to it than I expected to.

'I heard they'd roped you into the improv. Julie and I will have to come and watch you sometime.'

'That would be great.'

'Speaking of Julie, her niece is getting married in September. It's our first official function as a couple.'

'Nice,' I say, tucking my hair behind my ear and trying to force a smile on my face.

'Yeah, we're both excited. I wondered if you could help with the outfit shopping?'

'Oh, right.' I take in his fluorescent pink tie with mini palm trees dotted over it and I think that it might not be a bad idea. 'We can't have you wearing one of those kinds of ties, now can we?'

'Oh, actually, I meant for you to go shopping with Julie. She was saying to me recently how she's jealous that a lot of her friends have grown-up daughters to go shopping with and I just thought it might be nice if she could borrow you.' He raises his shoulders. 'And it might be a nice way for you two to get to know each other.'

'Oh, um, OK, if we can find a time. Miles and I have got plans this weekend, and then the next weekend we're off to stay at Hartland's with Soph and everyone.'

'Well, it's not until the end of September, so hopefully you can fit it in.' I can tell he's disappointed but I'm worried if I tell him what's going on in my head he wouldn't understand. 'I'll give her your number and you can sort it out.'

'OK, but I better run. I don't want to be late for the volunteering.'

'Fine. Oh, and you know, you and Miles are welcome to pop over at some point during the weekend. Julie's going to help me put in some flowerbeds. Maybe we could do a BBQ?'

'Maybe. See you later.'

I close my eyes for a couple of seconds as I walk away, wishing that I wasn't pushing him away so much. I want to tell him why I'm acting weirdly towards him, but I don't want him to think that I don't like Julie, because that's not it at all. I should try to make more effort to find a way of moving past it and make the time for us to both sit down and talk through what I'm feeling.

'Are you not going away anywhere over the holidays?' I ask Arnold on the drive to Lola's house.

'Yes, I'm due to go to my daughter's house in Cornwall. Spend some time with the grandkids.'

'Nice. How many have you got?'

'Three. They're older now, teenagers, so they're not always crazy about spending time with their old granddad, but they humour me for a bit.'

'I bet they enjoy it really.'

'I hope so. They're good kids. When they're not out on their surfboards giving me a heart attack. My daughter wanted me to move down to be near them in Cornwall, but all that surfing, my nerves wouldn't be able to take it. You don't surf, do you?'

'No, I've never done it. I did paddle boarding last week, but that's a bit more gentle.'

Arnold pulls up at a red traffic light and cranks up the handbrake.

'I think I've seen it. It's the sport where people stand up on the board?'

'Yes, although I spent a lot of time on my knees and falling in the water.'

'I've never been one for the sea.'

I think back to how I used to say that too. How Joel changed my opinion of it. The traffic light changes, and Arnold turns on to the road where Lola lives.

'I wonder if she'll speak today,' I say, as we pull up outside of her house.

'Hopefully, but the main thing is she's engaging with us. She might not be saying it out loud, but she's listening; you can see it in the way she looks at the pictures in the books after that she's remembering the stories.'

'I hope so.'

Kate opens the door and she looks worn out. Her hair's scraped back into a messy bun and her eyes are ringed red.

'Hello, you two,' she says, trying to push a smile onto her face.

'Hello, Kate. How are things?' asks Arnold in his gentle voice.

She looks like she's on the verge of tears.

'Some days are better than others.'

'And that's what you've got to remember when you're having a day like today. That they're not all like this. Now, go and get a cup of tea and a biscuit and have a bit of a break whilst we read to Lola.'

Kate's eyes are glossy and I want to reach out and give her a big hug. I settle for the kind of smile that I've had from so many people over the years, one full of pity, and I'm well aware how inadequate it is.

When I walk into the lounge, Arnold is busy unloading the books and Lola is sitting on the sofa, her arms folded. On the surface it might look like she isn't interested in us being here, but the TV is off today and she's watching Arnold like a hawk as he places the books on the floor in front of her, telling her the titles as he goes.

'How did you get on with the book you had last week, Lola?' I ask, sitting down on a stool beside Arnold.

She doesn't reply but she picks it up from the side of her.

'Would you recommend it to any other boys and girls?'

She nods once.

'That's good. We'll put that on our thumbs-up pile then. Any ideas what you'd like to read today?'

She looks at the selection that Arnold has put in front of her, but she doesn't move towards any of them.

'How about this? It's about two witch sisters; one's supposed to be good and one's bad,' says Arnold.

She doesn't shake her head, so he starts to read, using his best funny voices.

For the next story, she points with her foot to another book on the floor and I pick it up and start to read it.

We manage to read her four books. I can tell she's listening and I have to remind myself that that's good enough.

We say our goodbyes to her and to Kate, and I climb in the car feeling deflated.

'Do you think we're doing more harm than good? I mean, maybe it's too soon to be going to see her,' I say.

'I think if she didn't want us to be there she wouldn't stay in the room and she wouldn't take the books,' says Arnold. 'Just like with adults in life, sometimes the people who need you there the most are the ones who don't say that they do.'

I close my eyes, letting his wise words wash over me.

'I just wish there was more I could do to help.'

'I know. But all we can do is keep on reading and hoping

that next week will get a little bit better. You could always talk to her about your mum?'

'Maybe,' I say, still not knowing if it's the right time or whether it'll hurt me too much to do it.

Arnold starts the car and I turn back and spot Lola looking out at the window. I wave but she doesn't wave back. I hope he's right, that next week we might finally see some improvement.

Chapter 16

I'm worn out by the time Friday comes along, emotionally after last night's session with Lola and physically after last weekend down in Westerly, but I'd agreed to meet Miles at the pub. His work colleagues all go out for Friday night drinks like it's enshrined in their work contract. It's a big deal to them if someone doesn't stop by for at least one drink. I used to go nearly every week, but lately with the trips to Westerly and catching up on work I haven't been, and with us heading to Hartland's for our trip with the guys next week, I feel like I should make the effort.

'Edie,' shouts Henry, one of Miles's colleagues, as I walk past the bar. 'We thought Miles was lying when he said that you two were still together; we haven't seen you in weeks. The rest are in the garden. What are you having?'

'Um, a lime and soda. Thanks, Henry.'

He looks a little taken aback.

'Driving somewhere, tonight?'

'Nope, it's hot and I'm thirsty.'

'Then a G&T?'

'Just a lime and soda, thanks Henry.'

He tilts his head and looks at me before turning back to the barman and ordering. I hover by him, ready to help carry the drinks.

There's an electric charge in the air as I walk through the pub, all the office workers ecstatic that the weekend has started.

Henry passes me three glasses, and I put them together in a triangle and make my way out to the pub garden where I find Miles in the midst of a group. He gives me a quick kiss and I hand him his drink.

'We were just talking about which altcoins are worth an investment punt.'

'Oh right,' I say, nodding, not really having any idea what they're talking about.

'Is this the Aperol spritz?' asks Renata, leaning towards me.

'Yes,' I say, handing it over.

'They're not still talking about cryptocurrency?' she says.

'I think they are.'

Renata does an exaggerated yawn in their direction.

'So how have you been? We've missed you. Or I at least have missed you, being stuck with these guys. Have you been on holiday?'

'No, I've been down to the coast for a couple of weekends and then work's been busy.'

'I know how that goes. Well, you look good for it. You've had some sun on your cheeks.'

'That was from not using enough sunscreen when I went paddle boarding.'

'Paddle boarding. Don't you mean paddle boring?' Renata laughs.

I think back to my time on the water with Joel and there was nothing boring about it.

'I found it relaxing. Have you ever tried it?'

'No, I'm more of an adrenaline junkie; I like to keep my heart rate up. I'm going wing foiling in a couple of weeks.'

'What's that?'

'Imagine a smaller paddle board that has a hydrofoil that hangs down underneath and it elevates the board out of the water so it feels like it's hovering. Then you have an inflatable that you hang onto that catches the wind and propels you along.'

'That sounds terrifying.'

'It's really not. Much easier than kitesurfing and looks pretty cool. You should give it a go.'

'Maybe I will.'

I'll have to mention it to Joel when I next see him; it sounds like it would be right up his street.

'So, what have you been up to?' I ask.

'What haven't I been up to?' she says with a cackle, launching into a precis of what she's been doing over the last month. She's one of those women who always reminded me of Soph, burning the candle at both ends and being completely unashamed of who she is and what she's doing. Only as Renata tells a story of her at a party with minor TV stars, it makes me realise how wrong I was about how Soph would grow up. Whilst she's still got that spark and energy, she's definitely calmed down with age. But from Renata's stories she's gone the opposite way and I can't help but blush when she reaches the punchline about her and a well-known children's TV presenter.

'Speaking of nights out getting out of hand,' she says, composing herself after the story, 'you nearly broke Miles at the weekend. He was a mess at work until at least Wednesday.'

'It was the pub golf that did it.'

'Pub golf,' she says with a snort. 'Is that what happened? I couldn't get anything out of him. He just said that something he drank had disagreed with him.'

'More like the amount he drank disagreed with him.'

Renata laughs and sinks back her drink.

'These go down far too easily. Do you want another?'

She gestures at the glass in my hand.

'No, I'm fine with this.'

'What is that, anyway? Looks interesting.'

'Lime and soda.'

'It's non-alcoholic?' Her eyebrows tell me exactly what she thinks about that.

'Yeah, I'm taking a breather from drinking for a bit.' I still can't face it after the pub golf.

'You're not pregnant are you?' Her eyes flit down to my stomach.

'No, I'm definitely not.'

'You're definitely not what?' asks Miles as he joins us, the guy he was talking to about crypto having disappeared.

'Pregnant,' says Renata. 'When Edie said she was off the booze I did that awful thing of assuming she was pregnant. Sorry, I didn't mean to offend.'

'It's OK, really. I think we've all done it,' I say, feeling guilty of wondering it over the years, even if I would never have been so overt as Renata to come right out and say it.

'I guess you won't have to put up with that for much longer,' Miles says, turning to me with a wink. 'You'll be past child-bearing age soon.'

'Thank you very much, I turned thirty-five not fifty-five.'

'You know, women keep having babies older and older these days, so you've got plenty of time,' says Renata.

'Not that that'll make a difference.' Miles takes a swig of his drink. 'Edie doesn't want kids.'

It takes me by surprise because I've never said that.

'Um, that's not quite true. I've always said that I didn't think I'd have kids.'

'Isn't that the same thing?'

'Not really.'

Renata's pretending to suck her drink through the paper straw, trying not to make eye contact with either of us.

'Were you still heading to the bar?' I ask her.

'Oh, yes, totally.' She sighs with relief. 'I'm guessing that you don't need a drink, alcoholic or otherwise. I'll just leave you to it.'

She hurries off and I turn back to Miles.

'I think this is something we need to talk about, don't you?'

'I don't know if we do. I genuinely thought you didn't want kids.'

'And that didn't bother you?'

He looks at me and then sighs, before leading me over to the edge of the pub garden. There's a low stone wall around the edge and he sits down on it.

'One of the things I've always liked about our relationship is that it's uncomplicated and you're not like other women who obsess about where things are going, or imposing timelines.'

'Right.'

My heart sinks because that's what I've always loved about it too. I've always liked that he doesn't root too deep into my past or want to know everything, but perhaps in keeping my past from him I haven't considered what that means for the future.

'I'm just saying that we shouldn't overthink these things. We're both enjoying it, we don't need to complicate it.'

'But you don't want children?'

He shifts on the wall like he's trying to get comfortable.

'Not really. I guess when you said to me that you never envisaged yourself having children I thought we were on the same page. I don't picture myself having them either. It's not to say in the future that I won't feel differently, but as of right now I don't want them.'

'Right,' I say, nodding. 'I guess I just assumed you would after hearing how fondly you talk about your nieces and nephews; how much you enjoy spending time with them.'

'Yeah, because I like them. I'm not a monster. But I can give those kids back, can't I? It's not the same as having your own.'

My head is spinning. Whenever I've thought of whether I'd want children it's always my mum that I think of. The pain of losing her plays heavy on my heart and I'm terrified at the thought that I could lose someone I love again, or that they might lose me. And that's before I take into consideration that Mum wouldn't be there to help me. My other friends with kids rely so heavily on theirs for advice and support, and I wonder if I'd always think there was something missing. They're the kind of thoughts that have scared me but I've never thought they'd stop me from having kids when the time was right.

'Look, this doesn't need to change anything between us, does it? I mean, it's still early days for us. We're having fun. And, as Renata said, you've still got a long time before any biological clock starts ticking.'

I don't point out to him that now I'm over thirty-five, I'd be considered a geriatric mum.

'I love the fact that we're uncomplicated and we're just seeing where things go. I'd hate for this to ruin anything.'

He puts his hand on my thigh and gives it a squeeze.

'I'm sorry if I upset you. Now, do you want me to get you another drink? Something alcoholic this time?' he says, like he's making a funny joke but it's a little too soon.

'I've still got this one,' I say, holding it up.

He leans over and gives me a quick kiss, one that's slow and slightly lingering.

'We're OK, right?'

'Uh-huh,' I say as he goes.

I'm left sitting on the wall, wondering what this means for us. It's really highlighted how little we really know each other, and it makes me wonder how many conversations I've avoided having with him that perhaps I should have had. All these emails from the past have made me think more of my relationship with Scott and I can't help but think I'm making the same mistake with Miles. If there was one thing that I learnt from that relationship, it's that maybe I should learn to trust my gut and start speaking up when something doesn't feel right.

Chapter 17

The summer at Hartland's was passing far quicker than I wanted it to. The school holidays meant that it was constantly busy, and I missed the quietness that came with having fewer guests and responsibilities and that had meant more opportunities to hang out.

It had become almost impossible for all four of us to get any time off together, and with Soph and I doing similar jobs, I was more likely to find myself having time off without her. Luckily for me Joel was often off when I was and we found ourselves spending more and more time just the two of us.

'I kid you not,' said Joel. He was sitting on the edge of the reception desk, his body shaking he was laughing so hard.

'I can't believe it!'

'I swear it's the truth.'

I wiped the tears of laughter from my cheeks, before I batted his arm to get him to stop telling me anymore. My ribs were aching from laughing too hard at his recollection of Douglas being chased around the campsite by a jealous husband.

There was a cough and I immediately remembered I was

manning reception. I turned towards the guest, using my best professional smile, only to see Scott standing there.

I stopped laughing, thinking that I was imagining him.

I hadn't seen him for two whole months, which, before I went to Westerly, sounded like such a long time, yet it had gone past in the blink of an eye. I was always so busy I barely had time to think about myself, let alone anyone else. I'd known he was coming but it was still a shock to see him in the flesh again.

He looked different. More tanned from his interrailing around Europe. The tips of his spiky short hair blonder than before and he was skinnier and taller than I remembered; he barely filled the T-shirt he was wearing.

'Hello, stranger.' He held his arms out and winked at me. When he'd winked at me like that in class I used to melt but now it seemed cheesy. 'Aren't you going to give me a kiss?'

I turned to look at Joel. He slid off the reception desk.

'This must be the famous Scott.' He held his hand out and Scott shook it.

'That's right, Edie's boyfriend.'

I walked round to the front of the desk.

'This is Joel. He's one of the water sports instructors.'

'Ah, cool,' said Scott. He took hold of my hand and pulled me towards him.

'I'll, um, leave you guys to it,' coughed Joel.

'Thanks, mate.' Scott pulled me in closer towards him.

'We'll see you later on.' I watched him walk away. 'We're going for a drink with him and the others later on. I'm so excited for you to meet everyone.'

'Me too, although I'm more interested in seeing you. I've

missed you.' He leant down and kissed me. It felt strange kissing him after so long.

'I can't kiss you here,' I said, pulling away. 'I'm at work.'

'It's been a long two months, Eeds.'

'It has.'

I felt disloyal, because I'd been having too much fun to miss him.

'You look different,' he said, taking a step back from me and looking me up and down.

'Do I?' I went to tuck my hair behind my ear but it fell straight back out.

'Yeah, I can't put my finger on it.' He reached down and tucked my hair in properly and stroked the side of my face. 'Are you going to show me where I can pitch my tent? I'm looking forward to giving you the grand tour.'

'Isn't it a two-man tent?'

'Uh-huh, but once we get inside there's lots for you to see.' He took my hand and pulled me in for another kiss and I tried to fool myself that the only reason I didn't want to kiss him back was that I was at work and didn't want to be caught.

One of the things I'd been looking forward to about Scott coming to Westerly was introducing him to the gang. It was so hard to do them justice on the phone and in emails. Yet, walking towards the water sports hut, where we'd arranged to have a quick drink whilst Soph and Douglas were on their breaks, I suddenly wondered why I made such a big deal out of it.

Scott reached for my hand and it took us a few attempts to clasp each other's fingers without it feeling awkward.

'What do you think of the place so far?'

'Yeah, it's all right, isn't it? For what it is.'

His words stung. All he'd done since he'd arrived was talk of his European adventure. Each time I'd tried to tell him about Hartland's he'd listened politely but I could tell from the look on his face that he felt his summer experiences were far superior to mine.

I spotted Joel hanging damp wetsuits on the rail outside the hut and I let go of Scott's hand and waved at him. Joel waved back, running a hand through his hair.

'Did you guys want a drink? We've got cold beers in a cooler,' he said as we got closer.

'That would be great, thanks, Joel.'

He headed off to get the beers and I sat down at the picnic bench. 'Are you going to sit down?'

Scott was busy watching Joel walk away.

'Yeah, sure.'

He sat down next to me and slipped his arms around my shoulder, pulling me in close to him. He kissed me on the lips, but when Joel arrived I pulled away, shuffling over a little, not wanting to make Joel feel uncomfortable whilst it was just the three of us.

'Hello, hello,' called Soph, walking up behind us with Douglas.

'Soph, Douglas, this is Scott.'

'I have heard so much about you,' said Soph, sitting down next to him.

'Haven't we just,' said Douglas, giving him a wave before he headed over to the cooler to get them drinks.

'All good, I hope.'

'Of course.'

My shoulders were tense; I hadn't expected to be nervous with them meeting, but it was like two worlds that existed separately were suddenly colliding.

'So, I'm sure you've been dying to hear all about what Edie's been up to since she's been here. Did she tell you about when we had to fill in for the ents team and we all got on stage and performed? Or when she was the assistant for that magic act?' said Soph.

'I still want to know how they did that sawing-in-half trick,' said Douglas.

'A magician's assistant never reveals her secrets.'

'You went up on stage and did all that?' Scott took a large swig of beer.

'Yeah, but only because I had to.'

'She was great at it,' said Soph. 'I mean, her as that Pussycat Doll with the mohawk wig. I can't wait until I get my photos developed.'

'I can't believe you still use a film camera.' Joel shook his head.

'Yeah, well, call me old-fashioned, but I like that surprise when you get them back.'

'I'll take my digital camera any day.' Joel reached into his pocket and pulled his out. 'Speaking of which. Look what I got a photo of.'

He flicked his camera on and searched through until he stopped at a photo of Douglas and a guy squaring up to him.

I started to laugh. The horror on Douglas's face was exactly how Joel had described it. I tried to explain the scenario to Scott, but he barely cracked a smile.

Douglas reached over to grab it but Joel pushed him away and it went back into his pocket.

'You're never getting your hands on it. Plus, I've emailed it to the lads from school anyway.'

'Like that, is it?' said Douglas, unamused. 'I'll just need to get a photo with you and Elizabeth.'

My head jerked to Joel.

'Elizabeth?' I said, confused.

'Shut up, Douglas.'

Joel stood up. 'Anyone for any more beers?' We all nodded and he quickly walked off to get them.

'What's that about Elizabeth?' asked Soph. She leant forward, eager for gossip.

'Elizabeth's got the horn for Joel,' said Douglas, raising his eyebrows.

'What?' she cackled. 'I couldn't imagine her having the horn for anyone. But Joel?'

He sat down at the table, barely meeting my eyes as he passed me the beer. I noticed his cheeks had reddened. What if he liked her too? What if Elizabeth was the girl he'd been talking about?

'Who's Elizabeth?' asked Scott, flicking the ring pull of his new can.

'She's the cow that we live with.'

'Edie, I've never heard you talk like that before,' said Soph.

'Well, it's the truth.'

'I know, I'm just surprised to hear you say it.'

I noticed that Joel was turning his beer can slowly on the table and wouldn't meet my eyes.

'She's the one that you said always shouts if you wake her up?' asked Scott.

'That's the one.' Soph launched into a story about Elizabeth and how we'd woken her the other night when she had a luminous

173

face pack on, but I couldn't pay attention I was too busy thinking what an awful couple Joel and Elizabeth would make. Even if Elizabeth wasn't a total bitch, they'd have nothing in common. She wouldn't even set foot on the beach because she hated sand.

Scott started to stroke my shoulder and I tried to ground myself in the moment. Why was I getting so worked up about Joel? I was with Scott and I was happy that he had finally come to visit me.

'It was scarier than the night we watched *The Exorcist*, wasn't it, Edie?' said Soph, laughing at the end of the story.

'You watched *The Exorcist*?' Scott turned to me, looking confused.

'Joel made me.'

'Because it's a classic. You can't go through life having not seen it.'

'I got my revenge by making him watch *How to Lose a Guy in Ten Days*.'

'Which was far more scary,' said Joel, brushing his hair out of his eyes.

'Well, it would be for Mr Scared of Commitment,' I said.

'Um-hmm,' said Soph and we high-fived each other.

Joel shook his head.

'We should be heading back,' said Soph, finishing her beer. 'Have a good night tonight. Where are you off to?'

'We're heading into town to get dinner. I guess we should get ready.'

'It was nice to meet you all,' said Scott, standing up. It sounded forced and I wasn't convinced he meant it.

We said our goodbyes and we started to walk away.

'I've worked it out,' he said after a while. I'd picked the scenic route to walk back, wanting to show off as much of the site to him as possible. We were almost at the beach where Joel and I had snuck off to do starfishes in the water.

'Worked what out?'

'What's different about you.'

A family passed us, weighed down with inflatables, towels and beach bags, trying to wrangle their sandy children along.

'What? My legs have got more toned?'

'No, it's not that.'

We were at the edge of the path and I stopped walking. 'Did you want to sit on the beach?'

He peered over the wooden railing at the beach and the sea beyond.

'Shall we just go back to the tent? It looks like it's going to rain anyway.'

I glanced up at the sky, which was laden with dark clouds.

'Fine.'

We took the path away from the sea and found ourselves following the family back through the shortcut of mobile homes.

'So what's different about me then?'

'You seem more confident.'

'More confident? Thanks,' I said, taking it as a compliment, but the look on his face made me wonder if that's how he meant it. 'So, what did you think of everyone?'

'They seemed nice.'

'They are, and so much fun. Soph's just this big ball of energy. And Joel, well, he's Joel.'

'Hmm, he certainly is,' he muttered under his breath.

'What's that supposed to mean? Did you not like him?'

'I think you like him plenty enough for the both of us.'

I didn't understand where the attitude was coming from.

'I know you didn't get much of a chance to get to know them, but maybe we could hang out with them after dinner so you can spend more time with them. They'll probably go to a party on the beach.'

'Can't we hang out just the two of us? It's you I've come to see. Plus there's no point, is there? Next month you'll be starting uni and you'll have a whole new set of friends that I'll have to get to know.'

He took hold of the belt loops of my shorts and bent down and kissed me on the top of my head. My shoulders were so tense that they were almost at my earlobes. I couldn't imagine he was right. I couldn't bear the thought of not being close to Soph or laughing at Douglas's exploits or seeing Joel again.

'Let's spend tonight just the two of us.'

'Just the two of us,' I repeated.

Scott smiled down at me and I looked into his eyes properly for the first time since he'd arrived. They were eyes that I'd looked into thousands of times before, imagining the future we were going to have, the adventures, the houses we'd live in, our wedding, kids. The dreams we'd once had. Only the more I looked into his eyes the more I could see them slipping away. I kissed him, trying to cling onto them, not wanting to admit to myself that I'd changed or that I wanted different things in life, or that the thought of not seeing Joel anymore bothered me more than it should.

Chapter 18

Soph wasn't kidding when she said Hartland's had gone upmarket. I'd never have known it was the same place. From the purpose-built, air-conditioned brick-walled reception block to the fancy wooden lodges that had replaced the white plastic mobile homes, everything had had a makeover. I had been worried that I'd be flooded by memories of my childhood, or of my time working here and my mum dying, but, ironically, I'm getting upset that it's so different and that it's not triggering any memories.

The lodge we're staying in is beautiful. It's got a sliding patio door at the front that lets the light in and a new-looking kitchenette with sleek black appliances and a long table with benches inside, and a comfortable L-shaped sofa in the lounge area. The three bedrooms are split into a double and two twins. I'm the first to arrive and I bag the twin without bunk beds.

'Hello,' calls Joel and I head down to meet him.

'Hey.'

He walks over the threshold, a bag slung over his shoulder.

'Are you and Miles the first ones here? It's too quiet for Soph to be here.'

'I am the first, and it's just me. Miles has got a conference call tonight. He'll be down tomorrow. Where's Verity?'

'She flew to the US this morning. She changed her flight so she could have a few more days with her family before she flies to Florida.'

'Shame she won't be here.'

'She was sorry to miss it.'

We might have cleared the air paddle boarding but we're still trying to find our feet being friends.

'This place is pretty fancy. Do you think that if we were eighteen we would be able to get jobs here now?' Joel asks, slipping his bag off his shoulder.

'No.' I laugh. 'I imagine they probably have higher standards.'

My phone rings from the bedroom but by the time I get it I've missed a call from Soph. I walk back into the living room.

'Voicemail from Soph,' I say, putting it to my ear.

'Hi Edie, Alfie's not right, he's got a really upset belly. It could be teething or something that he's eaten, or the fact that we were off on an awesome weekend and he thought he'd scupper our plans. Who knows? But what I do know is that you won't want us in a paper-thin walled room with a grizzling baby, or for him to pass on any bug to you guys. So we're going to wait and see if he's better tomorrow and come then. I hope you guys have a lovely time tonight.'

I put the phone down and look up at Joel with a sense of dread.

'Everything OK?'

'That was Soph. Her and Brett aren't going to make it until tomorrow as they're worried that Alfie is sick.'

'Oh no, I hope he's OK.'

He walks over and sits on the arm of the sofa. Joel's always been one of those people who seem incapable of sitting properly on furniture. He's always perching on arms or leaning.

178

I think it's because he can't sit still but he always looks so good doing it.

We look around the lodge that seems quite big for the two of us. 'Shall I phone Douglas and see what time he's coming?'

'Yes,' I say with relief.

He picks up his phone and I open up the sliding patio door and go and sit at the large table on the wooden deck. The sound of children laughing and chattering drifts across the air and somewhere in the distance I can hear splashes from the pool. If I close my eyes it almost takes me back seventeen years.

'He's at Waterloo,' says Joel, coming outside to join me. He sits on the table, resting his feet on the bench. 'He's having a beer whilst he waits for his train.'

'Right, so he'll be about, what, three hours?'

'Uh-huh, just in time for dinner.'

My head's starting to feel light and this no longer seems like a good idea. How are Joel and I going to fill three hours alone?

'Do you fancy exploring the campsite to see if we can find anything that's still here from our day?' asks Joel.

'Yes. That sounds like an excellent plan.'

It doesn't take us long to uncover remnants of the holiday park we remembered. The little mini-mart might have been spruced up but the shell of it's still the same. The park where we used to have campfires and late-night parties is still here, even though fancy new coin-fed barbecues encircle it.

I've spotted what I think is the old portacabin where the reception used to be. It makes sense that if they've expanded so much that they've moved the entrance. There are several golf buggies outside and big metal trollies with bags attached that look full of washing, and when I get outside it, I see a sign that says: cleaning and maintenance services.

'Where are you going?' asks Joel. He stays by the foot of the stairs, his hands in his pockets.

'I can't resist having a peep inside.' I need to see where I wrote the emails. I walk up to the creaky veranda of the old hut. The paint is peeling off the wooden staircase, just like it had in the day, and I peer through the window into the building.

'Can I help you?' asks a women walking out of the cabin. 'Did you need more towels or anything?'

'Um, yes, towels,' I say, jumping in shock.

She heads back in and I follow her into the doorway. The big long desk is long gone and the cabin is full of racks of cleaning products and linen, but the way that the stifling heat hits, the heather-patterned wallpaper and the light fittings are exactly the same.

I can't quite believe that I'm standing in the very spot that I sent those emails all those years ago. It feels so bittersweet.

The woman hands me two towels wrapped in thin plastic and I take them with my shaking hands. 'Is that OK?'

'Perfect, thank you.'

I don't move and the woman raises an eyebrow. I take the hint and smile again, having one last look at the room before I go.

I hurry back to Joel, holding up the towels, and he shakes his head.

We head to the pool terrace bar, gravitating to the same table we used to sit at when we did our night security, although the view's now of the indoor pool complex rather than the campsite.

'Too bad they ripped down the old staff accommodation,' says Joel.

'I know, the new stuff looked all snazzy with its key cards.'

'I bet there's no way you could get into the wrong room and pass out naked nowadays.'

My cheeks begin to burn automatically. I spent far too much time that summer replaying the moment that I'd walked in on Joel in my room, thinking of those abs and the flash of his bum that I'd seen.

'Good thing too,' I say, picking up the menu and fanning myself with it. 'Do they come and take orders or do I need to go up?'

'I'll go,' says Joel. 'What do you fancy?'

'Just a beer, thanks.'

There's a queue at the bar and I pull out my phone. There's something about being so close to where the emails came from that makes me want to re-read them and I pull up the latest one that I got earlier in the week.

Dear Future Edie,

I hope you're doing OK! If I thought the start of the school holidays was busy, I was delusional. It seems like everyone's waited for August. There are people EVERYWHERE! Every caravan and tent pitch is full and the noise has increased tenfold. Luckily we're all dab hands at everything now, and it's running like a well-oiled machine - well, most of the time.

Despite things being manic, we're still finding time to go out and party. A couple of nights ago we went and had a big bonfire on the beach and didn't get home until sunrise. I was exhausted, especially as I had a whole daytime shift to get through. The sunrise was worth it though. I've never seen anything like it. I always thought Westerly would have a good sunset, but it gets its name for being West of Bournemouth and Poole (who says that I don't know my local facts) but that means that the beach faces east and the sunrise blew my mind.

But enough about that. The big news with me is that I've broken up with Scott – I'm guessing that was less of a surprise to you than it was to me. He'd been weird since he came down to visit, and eventually he told me that he'd kissed Annie Barton. I hung up on him and he texted me telling me that he thought that it's best that we call it quits – he broke up with me via A TEXT MESSAGE??!!! To be honest, I'd been cross as he'd been really distant when he came to visit. He'd probably been cheating on me all round Europe. Good riddance, right?

Everyone here has been so great trying to perk me up. Especially Joel, he's been my rock. He always made me laugh before, but now it's like he's trying super hard to make sure I'm not sad. I have laughed more this summer than I ever knew possible and most of the time that's been when I've really

let my hair down and let loose. I'm not
talking about going out and getting really
drunk - I've learnt the hard way that killer
hangovers are no one's friend when you're
emptying campsite bins. I'm talking about
just enjoying yourself, not taking yourself
too seriously and laughing until it hurts.
Give it a go!
    Much Love
    Edie chops x x

I'm guessing that the latest challenge from my eighteen-year-old
self won't be too difficult when I'm spending the weekend with
the old gang.

Joel hands me a beer and sits back down at the table.

'Hey, random question but do you ever still watch the sunrises
down here, like the ones we used to see down at the beach?'

'I haven't done that since I moved back here. This probably
makes me sound so old, but I value sleep far too much. It was
a lot easier to catch them when we were on our way back
from a party or finishing off a night shift. I think my days of
all-nighters are long gone.'

'I can't remember the last time I stayed up later than midnight,' I say, knowing even that's a push.

'Don't tell me you're suggesting we do that tonight? That's
the kind of crazy thing Douglas would suggest.'

'God, no.' I think of the times I'd ended up on the beaches
after all-nighters with Joel and I push the thoughts out of my
mind before they linger. 'Speaking of Douglas, I hope he gets
here soon. I'm getting hungry.'

Joel picks up his phone and swipes, before putting it to his ear. 'All right? . . . When's your ETA? . . . When? . . . OK, OK.'

He puts the phone down and stares at it in confusion.

'Everything OK?'

'He said he wouldn't be long, but it sounded very loud for a train.'

'Maybe he was in the buffet car. Do they still have buffet cars?'

'Not on the train he should be on. He told me he'd ring when he got to Bournemouth. Maybe I'm wrong but I have this feeling that he was in a pub.'

'Really?'

'Yeah and he was slurring.'

'If he's had a few drinks . . .'

'The problem is he's always had a few drinks,' says Joel.

I think of how he seems to age every time I see him. I don't want to connect the dots, but I can't help it.

'Has he stayed a big drinker over the years?'

Joel rubs at the back of his neck.

'It's difficult for me to tell really because whenever we meet up he uses it as an excuse for a big night out. I'm not sure what he's like every day. You'd think with Suz and Isla he'd have reined it in a bit.'

I can see that Joel's worried about him and at some point over the weekend I'm going to make sure that I talk to Douglas properly. This time I won't let him brush me off so easily.

'Has he talked to you much about Suz or Isla?' he asks, taking a sip from his beer bottle.

'No, not really. Only to offer excuses as to why they're not coming somewhere. Why?'

He shrugs. 'I haven't seen her for ages and he's stopped mentioning her to me.'

'Have you spoken to him about it?'

'I've tried, but you know what Douglas is like; he makes a joke out of everything.'

That's exactly what he did to me when I tried to talk to him.

'Perhaps we should go easy on the booze this weekend,' I say.

'Definitely, I think my liver had enough of a pounding the other night.'

'Mine too.'

He holds his beer bottle, tilting towards me. 'To one of not many.'

I clink the bottle back as we toast, and I can't help hoping that we're worrying about nothing.

There's still no sign of Douglas by the time that nightfall takes a grip of the campsite. Joel and I crack and have a takeaway pizza, which we eat back at the lodge with a cup of tea. We're both doing our best not to outwardly worry about what his no-show means for him, and how it's left us here just the two of us. When Joel starts to pace the lodge I suggest we head out to the entertainment centre.

Joel tries Douglas one last time before we go in, worried that he won't hear his phone over the music of 'Daz's Disco', but it goes straight to voicemail again. At first when he got his voicemail we'd thought it was a good sign, assuming it was because he had a dodgy signal on the train, but it's been like that for over an hour.

'Do you think I should phone Suz and see if she knows what's going on?' asks Joel.

'Wouldn't that only worry her? He's not *that* late. He could have got stuck for a while at Bournemouth trying to change trains or it might have broken down.'

'You're right.' He sighs deeply. 'Bloody hell, do you think this is what it's like to be a parent?'

'I imagine it's worse. We just have to remember that Douglas is a grown man. He's probably just run out of battery.'

He nods and we head inside. Daz's Disco is everything that you would expect from a holiday park. Disco lights pulsing, overly cheesy music. Vanilla Ice is pumping out of the speakers and a staff member behind the entrance desk checks our neon-pink wristband as we walk in.

'It's request hour,' she says, with far more cheer than I ever had working here. 'Fill out a form, and you're pretty much guaranteed to have it played.'

She hands us a blank slip of paper and a pen each.

'My mind's gone blank,' says Joel, turning to look at me.

'What about a song that reminds you of this place?' I say, with a shrug. I jot down 'Mr Brightside' by the Killers and I go to look at Joel's sheet, eager to know what song he put down, but he's already handed it to the cheery woman.

'What did you pick?' I ask.

We're right by a speaker and the music's loud. Joel shakes his head to indicate that he couldn't hear. I lean in closer and ask again.

'You'll know when it comes on,' he says, leaning back into me. He puts his hand on my waist and it sends shivers down my spine. 'Let's go and get a drink.'

Once we've got drinks, we settle at a table on the edge of the dance floor and we're instantly mesmerised by the scene in front of us. It's already busy with kids flossing and dabbing and doing whatever other dance moves that I am not cool enough to know. Then there are groups of parents that clearly came in for the happy hour cocktails and are still happy all these hours later.

'You know, this place looks pretty much the same, with the lights down low.'

'I know. That would have been us once upon a time strutting our stuff,' I say, gripped by a sudden wave of nostalgia.

'Oh, your and Soph's choreography, how could I forget?'

'What? At least we had moves, unlike you.'

He laughs and memories of his awful dancing give me an idea. I look over at the dance floor and back at Joel.

'Oh no. You've got that look in your eye that Soph always gets, and I don't like where it's going.'

'I'll tell you exactly where it's going.' I rise to my feet.

'No, no, I am not going on the dance floor.'

'Come on, Joel, don't take yourself too seriously,' I say, proud of myself as I quote my note-to-self email.

He holds my gaze for a second and then he laughs and takes a swig of his beer and gestures for me to go first.

I walk over, trying to find a spot in the middle.

'Let me take you back to a man called Joel, who liked a cardboard box,' I shout.

I start throwing shapes like I'm at a nineties rave.

'You know, I used to do those moves ironically.' His hands are on his hips and he's not joining in.

'Shutting the car door,' I yell, jutting my hips out. 'Basting the turkey.'

He laughs at me, before he finally starts to move.

'You're missing out the best ones. Doing the mowing.'

He pulls an imaginary lawnmower cord before placing his

hands on the imaginary handlebars and strutting around me in a circle and I begin to laugh.

'Changing a lightbulb,' I call out and Joel gives me a thumbs up. It's a little scary how naturally they're all coming back to me.

'Watering the garden,' he shouts, shaking his wrist across his body.

I burst out laughing, watching him in horror, and in between breaths I spurt out, 'Stop! That just looks so wrong.'

He stops immediately and I notice he looks a little embarrassed.

No one else on the dance floor is batting an eyelid as we have a dance-off with silly moves, and we dance until the point where we can't dance any more. We go over to a table in the corner and take a seat. This time when we sit down, we unconsciously sit just that little bit closer.

'You know, I'm going to regret those moves tomorrow. I bet I pulled a muscle,' says Joel. 'With those shapes, I'm not surprised I didn't have much luck with the ladies on the dance floor.'

'Well, whizzing about with that mower, you would have mowed them right down.'

'That's true; when that mower gets started, you better watch out,' he says, laughing. 'I can't believe we used to dance like that.'

'I can't believe we stopped dancing like that. Look how much fun that was.'

My cheeks are aching from laughing, my heart is beating and my muscles like Joel's are sore, but I can't remember when I had so much fun.

'I'm going to do this more often.'

'What dodgy dance moves at discos?'

'No, let myself go.'

'Not take yourself too seriously?'

I look at him for a moment wondering where he got that from before I realise I said it to him to get him on the dance floor.

'Exactly. That's how you live your life, isn't it? You live in the moment and you do what you want to do?'

He shrugs. 'I try to, but it's not a shit or bust scenario. You don't have to be jetting off, living the high life. You can live in the moment wherever you are and whatever you're doing.'

Joel's looking at me and the laughter seems to have been forgotten and it's been replaced by some kind of seriousness.

'It must be nice living a life where you don't have regrets.'

'Everyone has regrets, Edie, especially me,' he says, leaning in closer. I can feel his breath on my neck causing me to shiver.

We sit for a while in silence, watching the people on the dance floor, but I'm busy wondering what regrets Joel has.

The guitar riff of the next song puts a smile on my face.

'This is what you requested, isn't it?' says Joel as 'Mr Brightside' starts to play.

'It was this or the "Cha-Cha Slide".'

'I'm eternally grateful you didn't pick that.'

Joel stands up and holds his hand out to me.

'For a person who didn't want to dance at all,' I say, taking hold of his hand.

He shrugs. 'Seems like it would be rude not to.' He leads me to a space on the dance floor.

We sing and do our best to dance to the song, but it's not the same without the others. We'd always fling our sweaty arms around each other and jump up and down, all the while trying to make sure too many people didn't step on our toes.

By the end of the song and our last final bit of air guitar, I'm ready to sit down, wishing that Soph and Douglas were here to dance with us, when a new song comes on. In an instant the whole mood on the dance floor changes. The subtle beat of the slow song kicks in and couples drift together.

Joel doesn't have to tell me that this was his choice.

'"Lady in Red"?' I haven't heard this in forever.

He takes a step closer towards me and puts one hand on my waist and grabs hold of my hand with his other. I rest my other hand on his shoulder. We start to move to the slow beat; it's awkward at first but we soon relax into it.

'I can't believe you picked this.'

'I panicked, it's the only song that I could always remember the ents team always played.'

When we worked at Hartland's we all wore our red logo-emblazoned polo shirts and at least once a night the entertainment team would play 'Lady in Red' and dedicate it to the female members of staff. Most of the time if I was with Soph, she'd slip her arm around my shoulder and we'd sway to it, but sometimes Douglas or Joel would pull me onto the dance floor. I secretly always wished it was Joel.

If I close my eyes it all comes flooding back to me. How his touch would send shivers down my spine and make my stomach flutter with butterflies. My whole body aching for him.

The two of us are drifting closer and his hand closes around mine a little bit tighter and it's like he remembers it too. Our bodies are almost pressed together and I'm sure he'll be able to feel how rapidly my heart is beating.

'Was this song always this slow?' he asks, practically whispering it in my ear.

'Always,' I reply.

Our cheeks are touching, just like the song sings about, and neither of us moves away. I've never felt a pull to anyone like I have with Joel. I thought over the years that I'd imagined it, but I can still feel it. He adjusts his hand on my back and it drops a little lower and the whole of my body shudders with anticipation.

The song stops as abruptly as it started and 'I Gotta Feeling' by the Black Eyed Peas starts to play. We peel apart and I feel a little bit sheepish that I got caught up in the moment. Joel smiles at me and he starts to do what can only be described as awful dad dancing. Something's shifted. It no longer feels weird that it's just me and him here alone. In fact, I'm almost glad that it is just the two of us. It feels like we've put whatever happened between us in the past and we can be more like the friends that we used to be.

It makes me think that Joel's right. I don't have to always live in the moment, but every so often I need to remember to get lost in it. Like this one where I'm dancing like I did seventeen years ago and loving every single second. It's like the years in between have fallen away and I'm that woman that I was then, the one I should have been. Turns out she hadn't gone away; she was here all along. I just needed to let her out.

Chapter 19

I wasn't sure at what point I fell in love with Joel during that summer. Whether it'd happened over time as we'd got to know each other and our friendship deepened, or if there'd been a catalyst. But all I knew was that one moment he was my friend and the next he was everything.

After I broke up with Scott, I would walk around the holiday park hoping to see him at every turn. I would count down the minutes of my shifts hoping I'd find him after. While heading to the beach, I'd walk that little bit slower to the group so we could trail behind the others and talk. I often found myself trying to sit next to him when watching a DVD together.

It didn't feel one-sided, though, because he seemed to reciprocate the behaviour. During my shifts, he'd show up in reception without any reason. He'd watch an inordinate number of romantic comedies, even though he thought they were a waste of time, and on days when I was tired and grumpy, he'd just happen to pass the bakery and get my favourite ring donuts.

My only other proper experience of falling for someone was

with Scott, and that had taken me by surprise. He was new to our school, so I'd noticed him, but I wasn't one of the girls who had trailed around after him. A few weeks into the first term, he'd walked across the sixth form common room and asked me out. Embarrassed from knowing that everyone in the room was watching, and not wanting to cause a scene, I'd said yes. We'd gone on a date, and then another, and then I'd realised after a while that somewhere along the line we were a couple and I was besotted.

It was a very different experience to the crush I had on Joel and it had left me totally unprepared for how to handle those feelings. I fell for him more every time we talked. Every little touch – the accidental brushes of arms when we walked, the slightly lingering hugs when we said goodnight – drove me crazy. I had no idea how I was going to make a move, until one night when the opportunity presented itself.

There was a clearing right on the edge of the campsite, just beyond the staff quarters, which none of the guests ever used. The staff claimed it as their own, playing frisbee and football in their free time, and, in the evenings, we sat around the campfire and hung out. I loved it there. The grassland was flanked on one side by water and the other by big sturdy trees, making it seem even more sheltered and secret.

There was originally supposed to be a big party, only it got cancelled when Lionel banned us from having a campfire. He'd been worried about the grass being too dry and a wildfire starting. He'd said there were to be no fires until a dedicated firepit could be built. The rest of the staff abandoned the party and headed into town instead, leaving just a few of us in the field.

'Do you think we should have gone to the pub?' asked Joel.

He flicked the CD to the next track.

'What and miss this excellent entertainment?'

I gestured with my hand at the one side of the field where Douglas was practically dry humping Molly from the entertainment staff, and to the other where Soph was sat on the lap of the guitarist known as Green Eyes despite his eyes being brown.

'At least it'll be dark soon, we won't have to watch.'

My phone started to ring and I pulled it out.

'It's my mum,' I said, with an apologetic shrug.

'Get it. I don't mind.'

'Hi, Mum.' I stood up to answer it and hovered nearby.

'Hello, love. Is now a good time? Only I bumped into Denise and she said you'd broken up with Scott. Are you OK?'

Part of me was relieved that she'd finally found out from someone else; I wasn't sure how to bring it up with her.

'I'm fine. I think it's for the best.'

'You do?'

'Uh-huh.' I tucked a loose bit of hair behind my ear. 'Listen, Mum, I'm just with a friend. Shall I call you about it tomorrow?'

'A friend?' she said, her tone changing to one of slight amusement. 'I'm glad that you're OK, sweetie. You know you can always call us. We'll always be here for you, no matter what.'

'I know, Mum. I'll call you tomorrow. Love you.'

'Love you.'

We said our goodbyes and I hung up, slipping my phone in my back pocket.

'Wow. Must be nice having your parents check up on you like that.'

'She bumped into Scott's mum today. I hadn't told her that I'd broken up with him.'

'Why not?'

I shrugged and took a seat next to him.

'I don't know . . . because I'd been so adamant in the past that Scott was the man I was going to marry. I guess I felt a bit foolish that they were right about things.'

Joel reached into the cooler and offered me a bottle of beer. I held up the Bacardi Breezer that I was only halfway through. It was warm and sickly but I hadn't really felt like drinking.

'It sounds like they just wanted to make sure you were OK.'

'I know. I think that makes it worse though. You know, more than them crowing *I told you* so like I thought they would.'

Joel laughed.

'What about your parents?' I said, wanting to change the subject. 'What are they like?'

Joel didn't often talk about them. I knew they were divorced, and Joel had mentioned one time that his dad lived abroad and he'd see him during the school holidays, but he never gave too much away.

'They're not like that. We're not massively close. My mum always seemed to be spinning so many plates when I was growing up, with her work and looking after me on her own, I guess I got in the habit of not wanting to burden her with any of my problems.'

'And your dad?'

He flicked the top off a new bottle of beer with a bottle opener.

'I rarely see him. He doesn't come back to the UK very often, too cold and too rainy for him. He's all right when we do meet, but it's very much out of sight, out of mind with him.'

'He's a captain, right?'

He swigged at his beer.

'Yeah, on a yacht.'

'Is he the one that taught you to sail?'

'No.' He laughed almost bitterly. 'I never visited him for long enough. But I'm sure he'll be good to his word about getting me a job in Barbados with him after my course.'

My heart sunk at his words. I knew that he was going to do a maritime engineering course and that he wanted to travel but it hadn't hit me until then that he'd be going so far away.

'Would you go?'

'Maybe,' he said with a shrug. 'I guess it depends what happens.'

My heart started to beat a little faster, all the while he didn't stop looking at me.

Soph giggled loudly and broke the spell that the two of us were under. I turned and watched as she got to her feet and led the guitarist away, back towards the accommodation.

'And then there were four,' I said, shaking my head.

'I'm not sure I really want to be left with them.'

Joel wrinkled his nose as we risked a glance at Douglas and Molly and wished we hadn't.

'We should have gone to the pub with everyone else,' I said, finishing my bottle. I peered into the cooler box, which was now empty. 'Shall we call it a night?'

'I guess an early night wouldn't hurt.'

We stood up from the logs and started to walk away. I was taking a shortcut across the grass when Joel grabbed hold of my shoulder.

'Careful, that'll still be wet.'

I looked down where I was about to step. It was the concrete foundation for the new firepit.

'Thanks, I should really look where I'm going. Though, could you imagine if I'd had stepped in it and left a footprint? Lionel would have been furious.' I stepped back, making sure that I was far away so no more accidents could happen.

'It would have been kind of funny, though,' said Joel, beginning to laugh. 'No one would have known who was behind it; well, apart from us two.'

'It would become this cool mystery about who the footprint belonged to.'

'I bet Elizabeth would start some kind of manhunt to find out. She'd have us all putting our feet in it one by one.'

'And then she'd get to me.'

'And everyone around would be shouting, "It fits, it fits".'

'Pretty sure you're just quoting *Cinderella* now,' I said, pretending to roll my eyes at Joel's smirk. 'But if the footprint led me to my prince . . .'

Joel held my gaze and I wondered if I was giving away with my eyes that I thought I might have already found him.

'You know, maybe we should do it. It could be fun,' he said, looking down at the concrete.

Joel bent down and flexed his fingers.

'I'm not sure,' I said, staying put. 'We could get into trouble.'

'Come on, Edie! Wouldn't it be nice to do something that was just our little secret? Something that would immortalise us and this summer forever.'

I rolled my eyes at him again at first, but there was something in the way that he was talking that got me.

'OK, but you can't do a handprint; it's not the Hollywood Walk of Fame, you know. Plus, it's way too obvious. Let's do something subtle.' I bent down next to him and I placed my thumb in the edge of the cement.

'Oh, sneaky, OK,' he said, and he overlapped my imprint with his.

I turned my head to the side to look at what we'd done. It looked like a heart, but I was too embarrassed to say; I didn't want him to think that I was reading too much into it.

We got back on our feet and we walked to our accommodation block.

'So, goodnight,' said Joel, leaning over and giving me a long hug goodbye. I wanted to kiss him, or to at least grab his arm to stop him from walking away, but I didn't. I watched him go up to his floor and then I went into my flat, cursing myself.

I could hear Soph giggling from her room and I hurried into mine after a quick brush of my teeth and I slipped into my pyjamas. I got into bed just as the giggling morphed into moaning. I pulled the pillow over my head, but it did nothing to drown out the sound.

I thought of Joel in the bed upstairs and I picked up my phone and texted him.

Me:
Things are pretty noisy down here with Soph and Green Eyes. I don't suppose I could sleep on your floor?

Joel:
Yes. Come on up.

I slipped a cardigan round me and took my pillow before I crept up the stairs; I didn't want anyone to know what I was doing. Joel held the door open for me when I arrived and I hurried into his room. I was embarrassed seeing him in his tight boxers, despite the fact that I'd spent most of the summer seeing him in swimming trunks. I should have been used to seeing his torso, but in that moment it felt different.

'I'll just sleep on the floor,' I said.

'Don't be silly, you can sleep in the bed. There's plenty of room for the both of us.'

'Are you sure? I wouldn't want to impose.'

'You wouldn't be.'

I knew he was probably just being a gentleman, but I was hoping it was a sign he felt the same way.

We climbed into bed and he pushed the cover towards me making sure that it was covering us equally.

'Quieter?'

'Much,' I said.

I lay on my back, my hands on top of the duvet, rigid in fear, wondering what on earth had possessed me to do this. I was now only a few centimetres away from him and he was half-naked, and my pyjama shorts and top were not exactly the Victorian passion killers he'd seen me in before. I was convinced that he'd be able to feel how rapidly my heart was beating.

'Edie,' he whispered.

'Yes?' I just about managed to reply.

'Are you tired?'

'Not really,' I said honestly.

He rolled over slowly to face me and propped his head up with his hand.

'Do you think dreams are windows into souls?' He sighed, cringing. 'That sounded way less cheesy in my head.'

I could hear the embarrassment in his voice and I wanted to

reach out and touch him, and to stroke his face to reassure him that he had no need to be.

'It was deep, I kind of liked it,' I said, inching a little closer to him.

We talked in hushed whispers nose to nose for what could have been hours or just minutes. Time seemed to both race by and stand still all at once. A storm had started to rage outside and the rain was hammering on the tin roof.

'You know, when I was teasing you a few weeks ago about being in love with someone, you never did answer. So, are you?' I asked eventually. It was the one question above all others that I wanted to know the answer to.

The room lit up with lightning and I could see the way that he was looking at me intently, and in that moment I wanted him more than I ever thought possible. He leant towards me and our mouths were so close. I could feel his breath on my lips. We were going to kiss.

But before our lips could touch we heard a scream and leapt apart.

'I think it's Soph,' said Joel. 'It came from downstairs.'

He scrambled out of bed, and I was right behind him. We ran down the metal staircase only to find Soph kicking out Green Eyes. He was only in his boxers and Soph was throwing the rest of his clothes over the balcony. It was pouring with rain and he was soaking already. Thunder clapped overhead and we moved away from the railing.

'He called me Stacey when we were doing it. Can you fucking believe it? He's got a girlfriend.'

'Oh, Soph,' I said, pulling her into a hug.

She sobbed on my shoulder, not questioning why I came from upstairs, or why Joel was with me.

'Edie, can I sleep in your bed tonight? I don't want to be alone.'

'Of course,' I said. I mouthed a sorry to Joel over her shoulder and he shrugged a small smile back.

I couldn't help but wonder what would have happened between us if Soph hadn't interrupted us.

'There's Elizabeth coming back,' he said, peering over the balcony. 'You better get Soph inside.'

He ushered us in to our flat and shut the door behind us. I barely had time to whisper a goodbye. Soph headed straight for my bed and after stealing the pillows off hers I climbed in beside her. I could hear the sounds of Elizabeth's laughter through the cardboard-thin walls. I knew that she was talking to Joel and I felt the jealousy rise up inside me. I remembered Douglas teasing Joel about her fancying him. I tried to cling onto the moment we'd just had in his bed, but lying in mine, wide awake, I couldn't help but feel so vulnerable. It was like he held my heart in his hands and had the power to cause it more happiness than I could ever imagine or to shatter it into a million tiny pieces.

Chapter 20

A faint knocking sound wakes me from my sleep. The bed feels unfamiliar and the room even more so and in my groggy state my brain's slow to realise that I'm at the lodge at Hartland's.

'Joel?' I rub my eyes, wondering what's going on.

'Hey, you're awake,' he calls through the door.

'Are you OK? Did you want to come in?' I pull the sheets close around me.

'Are you decent?'

'Always.'

The door opens and he pokes his head round the side and I blush when I see him. Nothing happened between us last night. After our dancing at the disco, we'd come home, and gone almost straight to our respective bedrooms, but as I lay in bed, I couldn't help but think of that summer. I kept replaying over and over all the memories I have of me and Joel. Last night, our slow dance reminded me of the connection we once had, and since then I've been struggling against its pull.

'What time is it?' I ask.

'Quarter to five.'

'In the morning? What's wrong? Is Douglas OK?'

His hair is sticking up in different directions and he tries to flatten it down.

'No messages and it's still going straight to answer phone. I'm thinking he got drunk at the station in London and went home.'

'Sounds likely.'

'Yeah, I'll try him later on.'

'So if it's not Douglas, why the need to wake me up so early?'

'I thought we'd go and see the sunrise.'

'As nice as that sounds, I'm pretty comfortable here. Besides, you've seen one sunrise, you've practically seen them all.'

I slam my head back down on the pillow. I'd been worried about Douglas but now that I don't need to get up, I'm more than happy to roll back over.

'Edie, come on. Remember last night's living in the moment?'

'That was night-time Edie, she's more adventurous.'

'Come on, if we borrow a couple of those free bikes we can make it to Kestrel beach on time.'

'But that seems so far away when it's so nice and warm under the duvet.'

'It'll be there when you get back. Come on, we've got to get up and moving or else we're going to miss it.'

Ten minutes later I'm standing with freshly brushed teeth, dressed in a pair of jeans and a fleece.

There's a definite chill to the air and I'm glad of the fleece as we walk to the bank of bikes. I pull it firmly over my arms whilst Joel follows the instructions on the computer screen to scan a couple of bikes out. He hands me one and I reluctantly take hold of the handlebars.

'You know, I'm not sure if I can remember how to ride a bike.'

'You never forget how to ride a bike. That's the saying.'

'What if I'm the exception to the rule?'

'Live in the moment,' coughs Joel under his breath.

'You know, you can't just say that to me to make me do everything.'

'Seems to be working.'

Up until now, I thought I'd romanticised in my head how easy it was to be around Joel, but now all the frostiness has slipped away, it's exactly how I remember.

I swing my leg over the bike and as much as I hate to admit it, he's right; after a couple of pedal rotations, and a few wobbles, it does eventually come back to me. We're soon riding the route that we must have done countless times over that summer. Down the main road, up to the nature reserve, down the track, over the wooden bridge to the beach.

When we arrive at the treeline of the beach, Joel points to a small line of colour on the horizon. 'Looks like we're on time.'

He slips his backpack off and pulls out a blanket that he lays on the sand.

'What else have you got in there?'

He crouches down onto the blanket and peers into his bag.

'First-aid kit. Bottle opener. Energy gels.'

'You have it all packed just in case you get whisked off on an emergency adventure. Who are you, Bear Grylls?' I sit down on the blanket, hugging my knees to my chest.

He laughs. 'You just never know. But living down here, it all comes in handy. I'm sure I used to carry a rucksack like this when I knew you.'

'But back then it was full of beers rather than a blanket, *Grandad*.'

'Hey! I can always put it back in the bag.' He stands up and takes hold of it from the edge.

'No,' I say, pressing my hands down on it to stop him.

'Oh, so you can dish it out, but when it comes down to it, you're secretly pleased I brought it.' He sits back down and gives me a shove with his elbow. I can't help but laugh. I hate to admit it, but he's right. It's much nicer than sitting directly on sand.

The sky's becoming lighter but the sun's showing no sign of rising.

'Will Verity have made it home by now?'

'Yeah, I had a text to say she'd landed when I woke up this morning.'

'How long's she gone for?' I ask, hugging my knees tighter.

'About two weeks.'

'I'm sure you'll miss her.'

'We're used to being apart. In our line of work separation is just part of the job.'

'And you think you'll be able to do that forever?' It comes out harsher than I wanted it to.

'You sound like my mum and Soph.'

'Sorry, I didn't mean to. I guess it's hard for me to understand your lifestyle. Doesn't it ever get lonely? I know that my life is too predictable, but I couldn't imagine living from one place to another, not setting down roots.'

'Is that how you see it?'

'Isn't that how it is?'

He shakes his head.

'I'd settle if I had something worth settling for.'

'Looks like you may have already found it, if you're thinking of moving with Verity to the US and setting up home together.'

The sun starts to appear on the horizon and I fix my eyes on it.

'Back in the day, no one would have batted an eyelid if I'd have said yes to living abroad with Verity; people would have assumed I was living the life with no strings attached. But when you get older it's funny how everyone reads so much more into things and takes a different view on your decisions.'

'I get it. It's like we reach a certain age and everyone expects us to go down a certain path.'

'Exactly. I feel like I'm at the crossroads and I've got to pick which way I'm going to go.'

'At least you're a man. You don't have a ticking biological clock or all the societal pressures that women do.'

'Don't I? You were the one that just questioned my life choices. You'd be surprised how much pressure there is. Even from our yachting circles. Most of the stews and the deckhands are ten years younger than me. They pass through for a few years before settling down somewhere and getting a job on land, and starting a family. All my friends the same age are married and have kids and it feels I should be using this temporary break to work out what I want and where I want to be long term.

'Before I broke my ankle, I went to stay with my dad. He's living in Dubai at the moment. He's got this great apartment on the waterfront and it's filled with all the latest tech and he took me out to all these great restaurants. But it hit me that that's all he had. He had so much, but at the same time it felt like he didn't have anything. He's never really had a proper long-term relationship. He doesn't really know me. And he's happy with that, he loves his job and he'd never want it any other way. But all I could think of for the whole trip was that if I wasn't careful, that would be me in twenty years and I don't think I want it to be.'

He rests his head in his hands, almost massaging the back of his scalp.

'I'm sorry, Edie, I have no idea why I'm telling you of all people any of this stuff.'

He looks up and smiles with embarrassment.

'It's fine, really.'

'It's like all my life my mum and my aunt, probably even Soph, have told me that I'm just like my dad and I always took it as a compliment. Thinking it was great that I had his spirit of adventure and I'd inherited his sea legs. But seeing him it hit me what they were really saying.'

I think back to the first time that I met him, when Soph warned me he was just like his dad. I hadn't realised how wrong it was of her to write him off like that at eighteen.

'I don't want to be like him. My mum said to me recently that often the person you're meant to be with is right under your nose; you're just too scared to let your heart admit it.'

I swallow hard. I'm wondering if the phrase stings because I know that his mum is trying to nudge him and Verity closer together, or whether it's because it makes me realise that my heart is too scared to admit Miles isn't the man I'm supposed to be with.

'You know, I probably could have gone back and done the summer season this year. My ankle would have been OK, but I saw a yacht advertised in the boatyard and I just had this urge to buy it, and somehow ended up with that and a job.'

'You bought a yacht?' I'm wondering if I misheard.

'Not the kind of yacht you're thinking of, with that look on your face. A yacht can mean a lot of things in the sailing world. It's not a superyacht with a Jacuzzi or anything. It's just a small

1970s cruiser with a tiny galley and bedroom. It's a total wreck that needed to be completely stripped back and I haven't got the engine running yet.'

'Still, at least you'll have a cool line to impress the ladies with when you ask them if they want to come aboard your yacht,' I say and he laughs, looking embarrassed. 'Well, sounds like you've got yourself a long-term project on your hands.'

'Yeah, it was a stupid thing to buy when I'll be leaving. But I bought it on impulse, and I've been trying to fix *Hetty* as much as I can on the weekends.'

'You named her *Hetty*? After your grandmother?'

'You remember her?'

My cheeks flush. It's become increasingly apparent that I don't need the emails to remember everything about him.

'You know, she died last year.'

'Oh, Joel, I'm sorry. They don't make them like her anymore.'

'They certainly don't.'

He's lost for a moment and he looks out towards the water.

'It's been nice having a project of my own to work on for a change.'

'I'm sure you could buy another one in Florida.'

'Maybe.' He lets out a big breath. 'I'd forgotten how easy you are to talk to. Thank you, I needed that.'

I reach out and rub his arm.

'You'll make the right decision; you'll know it in your gut. You've just got to work out what it is you want.'

He places his hand on mine, gently pinning it to his arm, and I feel a warmth ripple through my body.

'Thanks, Edie.'

'Anytime.'

We sit, our hands touching in silence for a couple of minutes, watching the sun rise through the sky.

'It's even more beautiful than I remember.'

'I know.'

I turn towards him but he's looking at me rather than the view. He quickly removes his hand and faces the sky again, nodding in agreement.

'What about you?' he says, turning the tables on me. 'I can't be the only one baring my soul out here. Are you happy doing what you're doing?'

I let out a deep breath.

'It's fine, I love the people and couldn't imagine working anywhere else.'

'But are you happy?' he asks. He peers at me and his eyes search mine and it makes me feel I can't hide the truth from him. 'When we were eighteen you couldn't think of anything worse than working there.'

'How many people get to do what they wanted to do when they were eighteen?'

He coughs and raises his eyebrows.

'Except you.'

'Soph went into PR, I'm guessing Brett wanted to always play the guitar.'

He's making it sound so easy.

'It just wasn't an option for me. When Mum died, everything changed. It was such a shock and it hit everyone, not just me. My dad was a complete mess, he . . .' I'd usually tiptoe around his drinking but I can't keep doing that any more. 'He started to drink too much. It got to the stage where I didn't know which days were worse, the ones where he showed up to the office still drunk or the ones when he didn't show up at all because he couldn't get out of bed.'

'I'm sorry. I had no idea.'

I know he's looking at me but I keep staring out onto the horizon because if my eyes meet his I'll start to cry.

'I didn't tell anyone. I couldn't tell the people at work and all my friends had left for university. Soph did try and reach out a few times, but I fobbed her off with work.

'Those first years trying to get over Mum's death, helping to keep the company afloat and trying to care for Dad, they were the worst of my life.

'I know he's been sober now for almost fourteen years, but I'm always worried that something might tip him over the edge and he'll reach for the bottle once again. I feel like if I'm working with him and seeing him every day that I'm keeping an eye on him. That this time I'd know when something was really wrong and it'll make up for me not acting sooner the last time.'

I rake the sand with my fingers.

'You can't blame yourself for what your dad did. You were so young and your mum had just died.'

'I know, but I still do.'

'I'm sorry. I shouldn't have pushed. What you've been through, it's no wonder you're still there.'

I swallow and wipe my glistening eyes with the sleeve of my fleece.

'But you're right. I'm not happy. Our company recently won a big tender, but I couldn't even get excited about it. I felt like a fraud because I didn't really want to be there. Every time it looks like the company is going to fail and it might be better to close it, something happens to bring us back from the brink and we keep going. But instead of being relieved I get disappointed as, if it failed then, I'd finally be free.

'How awful is that? I almost want it to fail and all my co-workers to lose their jobs just so that I'll be able to get out and do something different with my life. It's so selfish.'

'Don't be so hard on yourself. You're not wishing for your work colleagues to end up on the street; you're just looking for an easy way out and see it as your only choice. A chance to leave without any guilt. But you do have a choice, you can walk away. You said it yourself that your dad's been sober for years now.'

'I can't.' I sigh. 'I have to be there for him.'

'But maybe you've already done that. You stepped in when things were out of control and it sounds like you've helped make the company into something that's now stable. Maybe that's good enough.'

'It's not just Dad. I'd have to start from scratch with a whole new career. Plus, I'd be leaving my work colleagues behind and they've become like family to me.'

I think of all the extra hours I've done lately with the improv and how much closer it's brought us.

'Well, I'll tell you that the one thing I've learnt from working abroad is that if they're your family, they'll want to see you truly happy, and they'll always be there for you, wherever you are.'

'You make it sound so simple.'

'That's because it can be.'

A boat meanders along the estuary out towards the open sea. I envy it being able to drift away.

'And what about Miles?' he asks, breaking the silence. 'You two have been dating for a while. Do you think you will go the distance?'

There's such gravity to the question, the conversation I had with Miles in the pub at the forefront of my mind.

'I'm not sure,' I say with honesty. 'I think I don't know him as well as I should do. I don't know enough about what he wants and he doesn't know enough about me and my past.'

'Your past is always more a part of you than you realise.'

'Oh, I realise.'

'I didn't mean it like that . . .' he says. 'I didn't mean all the stuff with your parents.'

'It's OK.' I go to ask him what he did mean by it, but he gets in first.

'Does it still hurt, with your mum? I mean, I know that it must do. What I'm trying, and failing, to say is does it get easier?'

'I didn't think it would but over time it does. That doesn't mean I don't miss her any less. I'm just learning to live with the grief and with the knowledge that it comes and goes at various points in my life.

'But it's been hard lately because my dad's got this new . . .' I struggle to get the word out '. . . girlfriend. Julie. She's lovely and I've wanted him to find someone he really likes for so long, but now that he has I'm finding it difficult. It's like watching how he was with Mum, but it's someone else. I sound ridiculous.'

Joel reaches over and wipes away a tear from my cheek that I didn't know had fallen.

'It doesn't sound ridiculous at all. From the sounds of it, you and your dad have been through a lot over the years; it's bound to be hard letting someone else into that relationship.'

I nod and close my eyes. I'm relieved to hear that what I am feeling is natural.

'Is this the stuff that you don't talk about with Miles? Because you should. You shouldn't be bottling all this up.'

'In all honesty, I don't know why I keep things from him. He doesn't even know the details around how Mum died and he only recently found out about Dad being an alcoholic, and not because I told him.' I try and blink away the rest of the tears before they can fall. 'Didn't things used to be so much simpler when we were younger?'

'I don't know, did they? I don't remember it being that easy then either.'

I want to ask him what happened between us at Hartland's, why things suddenly changed between us, but I still can't do it.

The sun is almost up now and it's already starting to get warmer.

'This is better than I remember it being,' I say instead, as the sky explodes into colour.

'Worth getting up at stupid o'clock for?'

'I guess so.'

We sit in silence for a minute or so taking in the scene in front of us. I need to take the time to appreciate things like this more.

'I used to think thirty-five was the age when you become a proper grown-up,' I say, raking my hands in the sand again. 'Where you have everything sorted and you are exactly where you are supposed to be in life.'

Joel whistles through his teeth. 'If there's one thing I've learnt it's that life never goes as planned, and I think that's almost the point. Making it up as you go along, it's part of the adventure.'

'When did you get so philosophical, Joel? All those years looking out onto the sea. You sound very wise.'

He shrugs. 'I don't feel it. Besides I'd choose happiness over wisdom, any day. And I wish you were happy, Edie. If anyone deserves to be happy, it's you.'

Our eyes meet and in that split-second it feels like he can see into my soul. We start to drift a little closer and I can't resist the urge to kiss him any longer and I'm certain that he wants it too.

His phone rings and we freeze. I close my eyes, breaking the hypnotic pull.

'Do you need to get that? It could be Douglas.'

Me mentioning Douglas's name snaps Joel back into action. He fumbles for his rucksack and pulls out his mobile.

'Unknown number,' he says, before he answers. 'Hello?'

His jaw drops and I know instantly that something is wrong.

Chapter 21

Joel looks as white as a sheet and he's blinking rapidly.

'Um, yes, this is he. Can I ask what it's in regards to . . .?'

He stands up, his free hand shaking. A shiver runs down my spine.

'Yes, yes, I'm in Westerly but I'd need to get my car . . . In an hour. Sure, I'll be there. Thank you very much for calling, officer.'

Oh, blimey.

Joel hangs up his phone and stares at it before sighing.

'Douglas?'

He puts his phone back in his rucksack and starts to zip it up.

'He was arrested last night in Westerly for ABH.'

'ABH?' I say, not knowing my police acronyms.

'Aggravated bodily harm.'

'How could that happen?'

'The police didn't say only that. Luckily, it sounds like they're not going to charge him, but Douglas is in a bit of a state. He's hungover and they're concerned about sending him out alone. I'm going to go and meet him at the police station. I'll have to cycle back and get my car.' He slips his backpack on.

'I'll come too. How long will it take?'

'I don't know. Driving from the campsite, maybe forty minutes? It's still early on a Saturday so maybe the traffic isn't too bad.' He shakes his head. 'I can't believe he made it to Westerly after all.'

'Briefly, from the sounds of it.'

'Bloody Douglas. I knew something wasn't right, I should have tried harder to get to the bottom of it.'

'This isn't your fault. Come on, Douglas needs us.'

My legs are stiff when I climb out of the car at Bournemouth. We pedalled back at such a furious pace that my legs were burning by the end of it and being cooped up in a car where I couldn't stretch hasn't helped.

'You OK?' asks Joel.

'Old bones.'

He smiles, the first one since he got the phone call. He spent most of the journey nervously tapping his fingers against the steering wheel. I've always thought of him as being laid-back but now he's anything but.

From the outside, the police station looks more like a media outlet, all modern and light.

Joel pauses and he turns to me.

'I guess we just go in?' he says, and I nod back with reassurance, even though I'm a bit scared. I feel like we're on the way to the headmaster's office about to be told off.

When we get inside it looks exactly like it does on every TV drama. Joel approaches the desk clerk to tell him why we're here, and he points to a waiting area. We go over and sit on the uncomfortable plastic blue chairs and wait.

After about ten minutes, Douglas is led out. He looks even

more dishevelled than usual. He's still wearing his work suit but his tie has gone and his shirt is untucked.

The officer who's accompanying him takes him to the desk, where he's handed a clear bag with his wallet, phone and shoe-laces. He thanks the officer and they shake hands, before he sits down next to Joel and starts to lace up his shoes.

'Wanna talk about it?' asks Joel.

'Not here,' he says, letting out a deep breath.

He makes a right meal out of rethreading and lacing his shoes. His hands are shaking and he keeps having to put his head upright, and I wonder if it's too much for him being bent over with his hangover.

'Here,' says Joel, sliding off his seat and batting his hands away. 'Just try not to be sick on me whilst I do it.'

I lean over and give Douglas's hand a squeeze whilst Joel laces up his shoes. He shuts his eyes tightly and I can tell he's trying not to cry.

Laces tied in double knots, we nod a little goodbye at the desk clerk and shuffle out. Douglas winces at the bright sun that's now risen high in the sky.

'When was the last time you ate?' asks Joel.

'I don't know, yesterday lunchtime?'

Joel tuts and he walks across the road. I've never seen him this angry before, and I put my arm through Douglas's and we follow Joel into the café opposite. It's the kind of café that serves big fried breakfasts and I can imagine it does a roaring trade being so close to the police station.

We find a table in the corner and order full breakfasts and much needed coffee. 'That food will be the make or break of this hangover,' says Douglas.

'I'm sure it will do you good,' I say and Joel shoots me a look but I can't help pitying Douglas because he looks truly awful. It's almost like we're assuming good cop, bad cop roles.

I'm waiting for Douglas to explain what happened but he sits there in silence, his head hanging in his hands.

'So, what happened?' I ask.

He pushes his hands over the back of his head and sits up straight.

'Just a misunderstanding.'

I'm waiting for him to elaborate, but he carries on sitting there like we haven't spent the last hour going out of our minds with worry.

'Mate,' says Joel, leaning forward, 'I got a phone call from a police officer this morning to come and get you from the station after you committed possible ABH and all you're going to say is that it was a misunderstanding?'

Douglas sighs heavily like it's a big inconvenience and the waitress brings over our coffees.

'Thank you,' I say, sliding the black coffee in front of Douglas, followed by the sugar bowl.

'Douglas.' Joel's starting to lose it.

'Fine,' says Douglas with a tut. 'I was on my way to meet you guys and the train was delayed at Waterloo. So I stopped in for a couple of drinks and I missed the train I was supposed to get. Then I eventually got a train and took a bottle of wine along with me for the journey. By the time I made it to Westerly, there weren't any taxis so I thought I'd pop into the pub next door whilst I waited for one and I had a couple of drinks there. I went out for a smoke in the garden and I guess I fell asleep. And the next thing I knew some guy was inches from my face so I punched him.'

I gasp, never pegging him as the violent type.

'I obviously wouldn't have punched him ordinarily, but he was in my face and I was asleep and very drunk.'

'He was probably just trying to make sure you were still alive,' says Joel, shaking his head.

'So he said. But at the time I didn't know what he was doing. I thought he was trying to steal my wallet or take advantage of me. I was just defending myself.'

'Did you hurt him?' I ask.

'They thought at the time I might have broken his nose.' He at least has the humility to hang his head in shame at this point.

'And did you?'

'They don't think so. The landlord called the paramedics after he phoned the police and they told him to have an X-ray just to make sure, but they didn't think it was broken.'

'That's lucky,' says Joel. 'So, they took you back to the police station to interview you?'

Douglas shifts in his seat, looking sheepish. 'Well, when the police started talking to me I wasn't too happy. You know when you're at the stage of drinking when you just want to pass out and be left alone. There might have been quite a lot of swearing on my part and I might have resisted their help. So they took me back to the cells.

'This morning they told me that the guy I punched said it was more of an accident than an aggravated incident and so they didn't charge me. No big deal.'

He shrugs it away and starts to stir two sugar lumps into his coffee.

'Oh, right, no big deal, did you hear that, Edie?' says Joel, his tone so unlike anything I've heard from him before that

I'm expecting steam to come out of his ears any minute. 'You realise that if you had got charged you'd have a criminal record. Do you know how much of an impact that would have on the rest of your life?'

'Look, Joel, I've got a pretty raging headache, and I got zero sleep on that bloody slab that they pass off as a bed. I could do without this right now.'

'You could do without it? Oh, I'm terribly sorry, we'll talk later about how you are taking a pretty privileged life and flushing it down the fucking toilet.'

People in the café are starting to look at us and I can't blame them.

'Tell me what you really think, why don't you? I just had the shittiest night of my life and I could really do with eating some food and getting some sleep. If I needed a lecture I would have got the police to phone my mum.'

Joel looks daggers at him but he bites his tongue. Douglas stirs his coffee with such force that it spills over the edges.

'Have you spoken to Suz this morning?' I ask in a gentler tone. 'Does she know what's happened?'

He continues to stir his coffee.

'You've got to tell her, she's your wife,' says Joel, exasperated. 'You are still married to her, aren't you?'

Douglas stops stirring, but he doesn't look up or say anything and it slowly all fits into place. Why he hasn't called her . . . Why Suz and Isla are always too busy to come down with him . . .

'When?' says Joel, his anger visibly ebbing away.

'About four months ago.'

'Four months?' says Joel.

I put my hand on Douglas's back and rub it.

'Things haven't been good for a while, probably the last couple of years? We kept having the same old arguments. Suz was always on at me for staying out late after work and drinking too much when we were out. It got to the stage where I didn't really want to be around her because she was just nagging. Then one day she told me she wanted me to leave. She got an estate agent round, put the house on the market and that was that.'

'Where are you living?' I ask.

'In a flatshare,' he says with a hollow laugh. 'I share with two other guys from my office, in a flat in Wapping.'

'Why didn't you tell us?' asks Joel. 'We would have understood.'

Douglas pushes the hair out of his face in an attempt to tame it.

'It's embarrassing, having your wife leave you. Having to tell everyone that it's all your fault.'

'People break up all the time,' I say. 'Nearly half of all marriages end in divorce.'

'But I love Suz, I really do. I just didn't realise until she made me leave.'

'And there's no hope that you can work things out? Have you told her how you feel?'

'So many times, but she says it's too little, too late.'

I rub at his arm, wishing it would somehow take away his pain.

'How's Isla taking it all?'

'Oh,' says Douglas, taking a sip of his drink, 'here's the real kicker: I'm not allowed to see her. Suz says she can't trust me with my drinking.'

Joel looks up in surprise.

'Surely she can't stop you seeing her, you're her dad.'

'Yes, she can. It's with the courts now and according to my solicitor the next time I see Isla it'll probably be under supervised conditions.'

I shake my head. What a mess.

'So, you see, Joel, when you're there shouting at me about how I almost flushed my life down the toilet you really had no idea, because all I could think about this morning sat in that tiny cell was how if I got charged I might not be able to see Isla again. It would have been exactly what Suz needed for the court documents for her to get sole custody.'

Joel's jaw hardens and I'm wondering if another lecture's brewing.

'So, what are you going to do about it?' he says instead in a calm voice.

'What do you mean, what am I going to do about it? I'm going to forget it ever happened.'

'You've just had a monumental wake-up call. Suz left you because your drinking was out of control and last night you got arrested for assault because you were blind drunk. If you don't stop now, something much worse is going to happen. You said yourself that it could have implications on you seeing Isla.'

'I'll stop.' It comes out pathetic and not at all convincing.

'I don't think that's enough,' I say.

'Me neither,' says Joel. 'You don't seem to know when to.'

'Come on, guys, you've seen me on big nights out, that's all.'

'You always have one too many. When was the last time you had a night off drinking?' Joel's glaring at him again, the anger returning.

'You're sounding just like Suz. I'm not an alcoholic, if that's what you're getting at. I wouldn't be able to hold down a job, which I go to every day, may I add.'

'I do think you're an alcoholic; I think you're a functioning one,' I say, cross at myself that I didn't try harder to speak to him properly the night we played pub golf. 'That's what they call people who can manage their everyday life but are still dependent on drink. They hide it really well. Look at you, Douglas, your hands are shaking and you're twitchy.'

'Because I'm hungover.'

'Come on.' Now it's my turn to be bad cop.

'OK, so maybe I've been on a few more benders than usual, but that doesn't mean to say I've got a problem. I'll not drink this week, how does that sound?'

'I think it's gone beyond that. I think you need to consider rehab.'

I let too much go with my dad before I got him help and I won't make the same mistake twice.

Douglas laughs. 'I'm not some kind of celebrity.'

He stops when he realises I'm not joking.

'I've seen this before with my dad. He started drinking too much after Mum died. It started small, a couple of glasses of wine, then it became a couple of bottles a day, but by the end of it he had a whisky bottle in his filing cabinet at work and he was drinking after breakfast.'

'What did he do?'

'He got help.'

'Does he still drink?'

'He's been sober for almost fourteen years.'

Douglas is quiet for a moment and then he turns and looks at me and I can see how frightened he is.

'You've got to stop. You need help.'

'No, I can't, I can't do rehab. There's my work for starters.' His joking has given way to a serious tone. 'And also Suz would find out and she'd tell the judge and it would throw more oil on the fire.'

'Or maybe it would prove that you're serious about changing. It might make her trust you more with Isla.'

He puts his head in his hands and Joel gives me a hang-in-there look.

'You need to do something,' he says. 'Come and stay with me.'

Douglas lowers his hands.

'I couldn't. There isn't room and, as much as I love crashing on the couch, it's too far to commute to work.'

'Can't you work remotely?' asks Joel.

'For a bit, maybe, but still, I couldn't stay with you. It would be too much.'

'Is there anyone else you could ask?' I chip in. 'Detoxing isn't going to be pleasant.'

He's silent for a minute. 'My brother, maybe.' He shrugs. 'He lives with his wife in St Albans. They've got a spare room, at least.'

'There you go.'

'But I don't understand how being there will be any different. I'm sure if I was going to get help I could stay where I am.'

'Do your flatmates drink socially in the flat? Do you go for after-work drinks with them?' I ask.

He nods.

'See, that's how being at Jake's will be different,' says Joel. 'He'll be there for you. He looked out for you on the stag do when you—'

'I don't think Edie needs to hear that story.'

I raise an eyebrow.

'I don't think anyone needs to hear that story so early in the morning,' says Joel, laughing. 'Right, so here's what you're going to do. You're going to call Jake and see if you can stay, and then we're going to find you a counsellor in the local area and an AA meeting, and we're going to look up how you safely detox.'

'Yes, that's really important. I remember from Dad that the advice was not to just stop and go cold turkey as it's too dangerous.'

'You're also not going to forget that night in the cell,' says Joel. 'You're going to remember how close you were from royally fucking things up any time that you crave a drink.'

Douglas rubs at his eyes.

'You can do this. I know you can.' My heart breaks to see him in this much pain. 'Life can be really, really shitty and throw some awful things at you, but the one thing I've learnt is that you really are stronger than you think. Even though things seem impossible and insurmountable. You will get over them.'

'And we'll be here to help. I am always on the other end of the phone.' Joel reaches out and puts his hand on top of Douglas's.

'Thank you,' he says, with a nod, and Joel nods back.

The waitress comes over and puts huge plates of food down in front of us. I try and push away the uneasy feeling of how fragile Douglas is and the fear that my dad could go back to this at any moment.

Chapter 22

Douglas has showered and shaved and he's in fresh clothing, but he still looks absolutely shocking. When we arrived back at the lodge, he was able to speak to his brother and they made plans for him to stay at Jake's place for a few weeks at least. He managed to sort out his work situation as well as find a local rehab centre in London that does outpatient detoxes for mild cases, which, luckily, they think Douglas is. He's going for a consultation on Monday morning. Hopefully between his brother and the rehab centre they'll be able to give him the support he needs to take the first steps to quit, and to detox safely. They've already started him with a plan to taper off his drinking.

I now watch him nodding on the phone to my dad before he thanks him and holds the phone out towards me. 'He wants to talk to you.'

I give him a sympathetic smile as I take my phone back. I put Douglas in touch with Dad as I felt like he needed to speak to someone who'd been through it to know that he could do the same.

'Hiya, thanks for that.'

'Anytime. He sounds like he's got his head screwed on right,

I think he'll be fine. You did good, you and your friend, getting him to realise that he needed help.'

There's a wrench in his voice. It's been such an emotional day and I scrunch my eyes shut, willing myself not to break down. I'm sniffing away tears, thinking that I'm doing a good job of being discreet but I'm probably not.

'It's just been a little overwhelming.'

'I can imagine. I'm sure it's bringing back old emotions.'

'We don't have to talk about that.'

'We do sometimes.'

I wipe away my tears; now really isn't the right time.

'I'm going to go, I think we're going to sort out a late lunch,' I lie, but I need to get off the phone.

'OK, I'll speak to you soon. Call me, any time.'

I walk back into the lounge and Joel and Douglas are sat on the sofa with their legs resting on the coffee table.

I'm about to collapse in the middle when the patio door screeches open. Soph bursts through carrying Alfie on her hip.

'Surprise, we made it!' She breezes in and plonks her baby bag on the table. Brett follows behind, weighed down by bags.

'Hey, how are you guys?' I walk over and give them a hug. I'd almost forgotten they were coming. Them and Miles. Shit. Miles, I must give him a ring and see where he is. With everything going on I hadn't given him a second thought.

'How's Alfie? Is he feeling any better?'

'Yes, so much better. It turns out when Brett had been making the purées he'd made a spinach, pear and sprout one, which is what caused the toxic bum situation.'

'That's good news,' I say, grabbing on to his little hand and saying hello.

Brett pulls a face. 'Not for his nappy it wasn't.'

Soph hands him to me and I balance him on my hip as best I can. She makes it look so effortless, but it takes a few shunts to get him on the right bit of my hip bone. 'Hey, little man, glad to hear you're feeling better.' I walk my fingers up his chest and then tickle him under his neck to make him laugh.

'I'll go and get the other bits from the car,' says Brett.

'There's more?' Joel gets up and stares at the pile of kit. 'Do you need a hand?'

'Actually, yes, thanks.'

Joel walks past Alfie and gives his hair a little rustle. I can smell his aftershave and it takes me right back to this morning on the beach watching the sunrise.

'So, what have I missed? Did you check out the entire campsite? Is it all this swanky? What mischief did you get up to last night?'

I turn to Douglas, who puts his head back on the couch.

'What happened? Why do you look so awful?'

She glances between us and her smile begins to fade at the expressions on our faces and I fill her in quickly on what happened to Douglas. She immediately goes and sits next to him and wraps her arms around him.

The patio door screeches again and Joel and Brett are back with more stuff.

'Look who we ran into.' Brett gestures with his head because his hands are full.

'Hello,' Miles says, hovering in the doorway looking around the lodge. 'This is quaint, isn't it?'

'You should have seen the old caravans,' says Joel.

'Right.'

I walk over to him and he gives me a quick kiss all the while eyeing Alfie suspiciously.

'This is Soph's baby.'

'OK.' He backs away slowly and heads over to greet everyone else, pulling a bottle of whisky out of his overnight bag. 'Just a little something to get the party started. Macallan, twelve year, double cask, just like we were talking about the other night. I know it's a little early, but it's five p.m. somewhere, am I right?'

Brett nods appreciatively, but he reads the room quicker than Miles who's slipping the bottle out of its case.

'Um, actually, we're not going to drink tonight,' I say.

Miles laughs. 'Very funny, you had me going there for a second.'

'No, I mean it. Things have changed,' I say, looking at Douglas.

'It's OK, Edie. I've got to get used to telling everyone. In brief, I got arrested, pretty sure I'm bordering on being an alcoholic and my wife left me and she won't let me see my daughter.'

'What?' screams Soph.

I wrinkle my face up. 'Oh, we forgot to mention that part.'

She turns to him, her eyes wide and mouth open.

'How could you forget that?'

She wraps him up in another hug, squeezing him tight.

Miles gently puts the bottle back in his bag and I feel bad that's now happened twice. I'm worried how he's going to react but he seems to take it all in his stride and pulls out a plate wrapped in silver foil. 'How about a cheese platter instead?'

Everyone stares for a moment as he unveils the platter full of different varieties of cheese with crackers and grapes around the outside.

'I thought most people like cheese.' He turns to me and looks worried. 'Or don't tell me, someone's lactose intolerant?'

'A cheese platter is perfect.' I walk over and rub his shoulder and he relaxes.

'I could go for some of that,' says Brett.

Miles cheers up. 'Hang on, I've got some chutney.'

'What else have you got in the bag, Mary Poppins?' Soph laughs as she swoops in for some crackers. Even Alfie is trying to wriggle out of my arms to get in on the action.

Who knew all we needed to cut the tension of a potentially awkward afternoon was a cheese knife?

We'd originally planned to go for dinner at the fancy campsite restaurant and end the night at the campsite disco, but with us all steering clear of alcohol we had a change of plan.

The clearing might look neat around the edges, but it was still the same campfire area we knew and loved.

Soph comes and sits down beside me on the blanket. We're sat just next to the designated campfire area, despite the fact that it's too warm and too bright still in the evening to light it.

'Oh, this is just like old times. Well, I mean some things have changed, obviously,' she says, rocking Alfie in his pram with her foot, 'but it's nice to be back here, isn't it?'

'Yeah, it really is. We used to hang out on this field a lot,' I say for Miles's benefit. I'm doing as much as I can not to make him feel left out. 'We'd host parties down here and even play a game of midnight frisbee or two.'

'Midnight frisbee?'

'Gosh, I haven't thought about that in years,' says Douglas. 'We used to have this frisbee that glowed in the dark, and we'd wait until nightfall and play it out here. It had the same rules as Ultimate.' Miles still looks blank. 'Kind of like five-a-side football but with a frisbee.'

'Remember those glow stick necklaces we used to put on?' Soph leans over and picks at the last of the dessert.

Douglas nods. 'Yes, that's right. It was the only way to avoid bumping into everyone.'

'Not that it worked; we always still ended up on the ground.'

'Sounds like fun, shame we don't have a frisbee tonight,' says Brett.

Douglas shoots Miles a look. 'You don't have one of those lurking in your bag, do you?'

'Sadly not.'

'Perhaps we should organise another meet-up and play together,' says Soph, still managing to scrape chocolate mousse out of the bowl that must be empty by now.

'I'd love that,' I say. 'In fact, I've been thinking of inviting you guys up to mine for a visit, and there's a park we could play in behind my block of flats. I'm sure I could rope in some other friends to fill up the teams.'

'That would be amazing,' says Soph. 'I'm in. It'll be nice to come up and see you.'

Everyone nods and a warm, fuzzy feeling passes over me.

There's a wail from Alfie and Soph groans. She's leant against Brett and the two of them look so comfortable. He goes to move just as she does.

'Let me.'

I stand up and start rocking the pram back and forth on the spot. It doesn't take long before Soph gives me the thumbs up.

'I think he's gone back to sleep.'

'I'll stay here for a bit, just in case.'

'You look like such a natural. Don't you think, Miles?' Soph raises her eyebrows not very subtly.

'Mmm-hmm,' he says. Ever since that night in the pub, there's been this elephant in the room we can't seem to shake.

'Hey, anyone up for playing a game?' says Joel.

'Yes,' I say a little too quickly. I'm relieved of the change of subject.

'I've got the perfect one,' says Soph.

I point at her. 'Do not say truth or dare.'

'You still know me so well.'

'How about charades?' says Brett. 'Could be fun.'

We all nod and agree and he sets about organising the game.

I don't know how it happened but I end up on the same team as Miles and Joel. I'm sandwiched between the two of them and I just feel awkward . . . as to why, I'm not entirely sure. Ever since our conversation this morning, and now with Joel so close by, I feel very self-conscious of my relationship with Miles.

'Edie, your turn.' Soph hands me the baseball cap with balled-up suggestions.

I get up and pick a piece of paper. I groan when I see it. Of all the movies to pick. Brett shouts, 'Go' as he starts the timer on his phone.

I start to mime a video camera.

'Movie,' yells Miles enthusiastically. 'Four words . . . comedy.'

I wish I was as energetic as him. I start to act it out, pulling at my hair, and Miles is desperate to guess.

'*Hairspray . . . Rapunzel . . . Tangled . . .*'

I rub my hands then pretend again to make a quiff in my hair. Miles looks blankly and I do it again.

'*Ace Ventura Pet Detective*? I don't know what this hairstyle is. What movies was Elvis in?'

Joel is trying not to laugh and I point an accusatory finger at him.

'If you know, then share it with us, please.' I'm clueless as to why Joel is being this difficult.

'You're not allowed to speak.' He folds his arms and I take another deep breath. The other team are one point ahead; we need to get this.

I hold up four fingers and then wiggle my ear.

'Fourth word,' shouts Miles. 'Sounds like . . .'

I point at his arms, wanting him to guess 'hairy' and Joel laughs again. I throw him a death stare. I'm convinced he knows the answer.

'Arms . . . Biceps... Muscles?' I point at the hair on Miles's legs before I tug on one of the hairs in frustration. 'Ow . . . Leg hair . . . Hair?'

I point and then move my hands further away from each other.

'Hairy?'

I tap my nose and nod.

'What rhymes with hairy? Scary . . . fairy . . . lairy . . . dairy.'

'Ten seconds, guys.'

I do the quiff once more because I'm out of options.

'*There's Something about Mary*,' says Joel, cool as a cucumber.

'Finally.' I sit down and give him a nudge. 'Did you forget you were on our team?'

'Nope, just didn't want to miss out on you potentially trying to mime what she got in her hair.' At his smirk, I roll my eyes.

Miles leans across to me. 'Well done, Joel. Although it might have been easier, Edie, if you'd just mimed a halo and put your hands together in a prayer position for Mary.'

'I'll remember that for next time.' I grit my teeth.

'I thought you did a great job,' says Soph. 'Now, by my estimations I make that a tie. What shall we do? Sudden death? Someone's name gets picked out of the hat and both teams guess.'

'Sounds good,' says Brett.

'Does anyone mind if I quickly run to the shop before it closes to pick up some more of that fancy artisan lemonade?' asks Douglas. 'Something I never thought I'd hear myself saying on a Saturday night. Anyone else want anything?'

We all shake our heads and he runs off.

'I'm getting a little chilly; I might head back and get a sweatshirt from the lodge,' says Miles. 'Do you want me to grab you one, Edie?'

'Oh, yes please.'

'I might come with you.' Brett stands up. 'I'll grab a blanket for Alfie.'

'And I need a wee,' says Soph. 'Can I leave Alfie in the pram with you guys?'

'Of course,' I say, watching them all head off before I turn back to Joel. 'I still can't forgive you for leaving me hanging on that charade, by the way.'

'Sorry, I just couldn't resist. I forgot how competitive you get. Poor Miles, he really did try as well.'

'I suppose, although sometimes I wish Miles and I were

more on the same wavelength. Seeing Brett and Soph together, especially in that last game, it makes me realise how out of sync we can be at times.'

'These things take time. Brett and Soph have had seven years to figure things out.'

I stretch my arms out behind me and my fingertips graze the concrete of the firepit behind me. I turn and look at it.

'Do you think this is actually the same firepit that they built when we were here?' I run my fingers along the edge, wondering.

'Surely they would have upgraded it over the years.'

'There's only one way to find out.' It's getting a little darker now, but it's still light enough to see and I start to walk around the edge.

'You don't really think it would still be here, do you?' he says.

I stop and bend down when I find what I'm looking for.

'See! Here it is.'

Whilst I can't really make out the lines of the thumbprint like I once could, I can still see the outline of a little heart shape.

'I can't believe it. It's crazy how people walk past this all the time, and yet only we know that this exists,' he says, as he walks over. He bends down next to me and we put our thumbs in it at the same time. They brush against each other and it's like my whole body has come alive. 'Still here after all this time.'

I know he's talking about the thumbprints but a part of me wonders if he's talking about our chemistry too.

'Why are you two on the floor? Has something happened? Where has everyone gone?' Douglas is balancing glass bottles of lemonade in his arms and Joel stands up to help him.

'Nothing to worry about, I just tripped, and Joel was helping me up. The others nipped back to the lodge; they'll be back any second.'

Joel nods. 'Typical Edie, still clumsy.'

I'm not sure either of us needed to lie about what we were doing, but it feels like it should just be our little secret, just like it always was.

While Joel starts chatting to Douglas, I go over and check on Alfie, giving them a bit of space.

'Right, we're back. Let's win this thing,' Soph calls.

'Shhh, you'll wake Alfie,' Brett says, slipping his arm around her.

'Sorry, was he OK?' She leans over his pram where he's still fast asleep.

'Didn't make a peep.'

'Let's get this game going then.'

We all put our names into the hat to see who's performing the sudden death charade, and Joel's name gets picked.

We shuffle a little closer on our seats to get a better view.

'Movie,' shouts Soph as Joel starts.

'Two words,' says Miles.

'Musical.' Brett claps his hands together.

'That's not the mime for musical,' tuts Soph.

'It's horror. Horror movie,' Douglas yells.

It was hectic enough playing in teams but now that there's five people shouting out answers at the same time, Joel looks flustered trying to keep up, but he perseveres.

'Whole concept,' shouts Miles.

Joel starts to turn his head.

'*The Exorcist*,' I shout and Joel jumps up and points at me.

'Got it in one.'

'How did you get that so quickly?' asks Soph.

Miles leans over and kisses my head. 'Who cares how. We won!'

Only I care. For the same reason I felt uneasy that Miles and I weren't in sync with our guesses, I feel uneasy that Joel and I are with ours.

Chapter 23

Big Little Readers night has soon become one of my favourite parts of my week. I left work a little earlier than usual to come tonight, as I wanted to check with Adrian about some specific books I was hoping to bring along with me to Lola's house. We are making progress with her, but she still won't talk in the sessions and I think that Arnold may be right, that talking about my own experience with loss could help.

'I was wondering if you had any books on grief? I have an idea I want to try to get Lola to open up to us.'

'Oh, yes, I think there are some.' He goes to the other end of the children's section and runs his fingers along the spines on the bookcase until he finds what he's looking for. 'Here we go.'

He pulls out a couple of books, checks the back and then puts them into our box ready to take.

'Thank you.'

'You're welcome. I hope the reading goes well.'

Arnold and I pull up outside Lola's house and he turns to me. 'You all right, love?'

'Yes, I'm OK.' I nod back. This has become our little ritual. He gauges my emotional temperature. In some ways the sessions get easier and in others they get harder. I'm more prepared than I was the first day of the initial shock, but it still breaks my heart to think of everything Lola's going through at such a young age.

Kate answers the door with a warm greeting and Lola is sat on the sofa in her usual spot. We pull out our stools and sit down opposite her.

'Hi, Lola, what have you been up to this week?' Every week I ask, and every week I hope she answers.

When she doesn't Arnold fills the silence.

'We've brought a good selection of books today. Would you like to pick one or shall we choose something for you?'

I root around the box of books and pull out one of the ones I've included.

'OK,' I say, holding the book to show her the title, *Rusty and the Memory Jar.* I open the first page and begin to read the story of a young squirrel whose grandfather has just died. I start to get nervous that maybe it's a terrible idea, but Arnold nods in encouragement. *'Rusty was worried, Rusty was scared. What if he forgot Grandpa and all the memories they'd shared?'*

I glance at Lola whose eyes are open wide and I turn the page.

'His mum gave him a jam jar and told him to go fishing, but when he was there he thought of his grandad and all he was missing.

'He sat on a rock and looked out on to the stream. Remembering when he caught a fish and his grandpa's smile would beam.'

A couple of times words get stuck in my throat as I turn the pages and we learn how Rusty went to all the parts of the forest with his jar and, on remembering memories of his grandpa, he wrote each one down and placed it in his jar, which he hung on a branch on his room so that he knew he'd never forget.

When I stop reading I chance a look at Lola but she remains as quiet as ever.

'That was a beautiful story,' says Arnold, and I notice that he's a little choked up.

'It really was.' I didn't expect it to move me in the way it did. 'What a lovely thing to do. I wish that I'd done that when my mum died.'

I wasn't thinking of Lola when I said it. Every year I have to work harder to hold on to memories.

'Your mum died?' Her voice is high and pitchy, and I'm so startled she's spoken that I stutter a reply.

'Yes, quite a long time ago now. I miss her very much.'

She reaches out and takes the book from my hands and curls her fingers around it.

'I miss my mum too.'

My heart starts to crack and I bite down hard on my lip to try and stop myself from crying.

'I'm sure you do.'

'Do you still remember her?' she says, in her little voice.

I nod slowly. 'I do but it was a long time ago now and I wish I'd made a memory jar like Rusty as I'm sure that I've forgotten a lot.'

Lola traces her finger over the jar embossed on the front. I wait for her to say more but she opens the book and turns each page following Rusty's journey again on her own.

I look over at Arnold, not knowing if I should offer to read it again or to read something else, and he does a little movement with his hand to say just let her be. She looks at the pictures again and again and we wait for her to say something, but she doesn't.

When it gets to the end of the session and Lola has read the book twice to herself, Arnold starts to pack the other books away.

'It's time for us to go now. But we'll be back next week. Would you like to keep any books until then? We've got a good one about a fairy who gets stuck in a tree, or one about a talking pencil case?'

'This one,' says Lola. She clutches the book to her chest. 'I want to keep this one.'

'It's a good choice. Rusty is a very wise squirrel,' I say.

We get up out of our stools and say goodbye to Lola before heading out into the hallway where Kate is waiting for us.

'She spoke to you,' she says, trying to keep her excitement at bay. 'Does that mean it's working?'

'It means it's early days.' Arnold pats her on the arm. 'But it's a good sign. Hang in there.'

I do a double thumbs up with my hands and Kate grins. I can't stop thinking about it all the way back to the library.

Claudia's there talking to Adrian when we make it back.

'How did it go tonight?' she asks, whilst she helps us unload the books back into the storage cupboard. Lola's a pupil at Claudia's school and whilst she hasn't taught her, she knows what happened to her mum.

'Yes, it went well,' says Arnold, with a pause. 'Lola spoke to us.'

'She did?' Claudia stops what she's doing and looks up and we explain what happened. 'Small steps, but such an encouraging start. Which book was it?'

'One about a squirrel and a memory jar,' I say.

'Had us both going. I even shed a tear.' Arnold raises an eyebrow and heads off to go and talk to Adrian.

'I think it really struck a chord; she's kept it for the week too.'

'That's brilliant. I'm so glad that you're getting on so well. I thought you would. You were so brilliant that day in class, and Arnold's been singing your praises.'

'He's been a really good mentor.'

'Yeah, but there are some things that you can't teach and building a quick rapport with kids isn't easy, and whilst everyone can read to the kids not everyone can get them to connect to what they're reading. Arnold said that you manage to get through to Lola despite her resisting the sessions.'

'I'm not really too sure what to say to that.'

'You say thank you, as it's a compliment, and then you feel good about what you're doing.' Claudia raises her eyebrows, waiting for me to give it a go.

'Thank you,' I say with a little reluctance. It doesn't come very naturally to me.

'Look at you smiling. Do I take it to mean you've got that warm, fuzzy feeling inside?'

'Yeah, I have. Is that what it's like being a teacher?'

Claudia laughs. 'I wish. Although we do get it sometimes, in amongst all the report writing and the other things we're supposed to do. But yes, every so often you feel like you're making a difference, and those are the moments that in the dark days when you're surrounded by a classroom of kids who aren't listening to a word you say, that's what you have to think about. Those children who will remember your name for the rest of their lives for being the one that helped them or listened to them or made them feel seen for the first time. Those are the moments that you cling to.'

'I'd love to make a difference in my job.'

'I'm sure you do.'

'In the world of office supplies, I make a difference by ensuring data hasn't being stolen when the files are securely shredded.'

'You are too harsh on yourself. I have no doubt you make a difference in other ways. Take your employees, for example. Didn't you say before that it's been a difficult market for you over the last few years? I'm pretty sure that your staff would argue that you've been making a difference by keeping them in a job and their mortgage paid.'

'I've never thought of it like that. And there was me going to ask you about teaching and whether it was too late for me to retrain.'

'Oh, Edie.' Her whole face lights up. 'I think you'd make a wonderful teacher.'

'But what about all the bad bits you were talking about?'

'They don't outweigh the good bits, unless we're having an inspection and then I'd definitely urge you to have any career other than teaching.'

I laugh.

'Listen, there are so many routes into teaching and you volunteering would even count towards work experience for your application too.'

'I'm just not sure if I could handle going back to university, not at my age.'

'You can do what I did and work as an unqualified teacher in a school while training part-time on a course. You learn just as much on the job as you do from the lectures and assignments. It's a great combination. Have a look into it, and any help you need with applications, I'm your girl.'

'I think I'd be a while away from that stage, but I might think about it.'

'Do, Edie, because we all know how short life is. Do you know that Lola's mum was only thirty-three?'

'Wow, so young,' I say, and it hits me that she was two years younger than me. My mum was only forty-two and it's been starting to weigh on my mind that it's not going to be long until I reach that age.

'So young, but a wake-up call for the rest of us.' Claudia locks the store cupboard and I slip on my cardigan, ready to head home. 'Listen, if you wanted to chat more about the teaching stuff, I'm always around to meet for coffee. My boyfriend and I only moved here at Christmas and the summer can be so long when he's at work all day. Perhaps if you were free one day for lunch or for coffee or—'

'I'd love to meet for coffee or lunch. My office manager is always telling me that I need to get away from my desk more.'

'Great, well, you've got my number. Send me a text.'

'OK, I will do.' I'm about to say my goodbyes and head out the door when I stop and turn back to her. 'How do you feel about frisbee?'

'Frisbee?' Her forehead wrinkles.

'Uh-huh. I'm getting some friends together to play a five-a-side game. Some of my work colleagues and friends are coming . . . It might be a good way for you to meet some people in the area.'

I go on to explain about our midnight frisbee plans and she starts to smile more and more. I can't help but smile too because of the journey the past emails are taking me on and the friends that I'm making on the way.

★

Dear Future Edie,

I hope you're having a sizzling summer, and generally feeling like a Jazzy Jeff and Fresh Prince 'Summertime' vibe: cocktails, barbecues and plenty of sunshine. All the things that the holidaymakers are having here when we're sweating our bits off working hard.

I've been having a great time with the guys as per, but I have a secret. I'm actually a little relieved to have someone to tell as I can't tell anyone here, but I've started to fancy Joel. Like really properly fancy him. Like I want to spend as much time as possible with him and I can't concentrate on anything else when he's around type fancying. I'm going out of my mind.

We spend so much time together and we have such a laugh, but I don't know if he only sees me as a friend or as something more. I really want to find out but I'm scared that I'll ruin our friendship.

I feel so much more for him than I ever did for Scott. We have this connection that's really hard to explain. But if he doesn't feel the same I don't want to risk losing him from my life.

I know that it's probably worth the risk and

I know that I'm going to have to get brave,
even though I'm terrified. Which leads me onto
your note to self, which is to be you, just
braver. Sometimes you've got to be brave and
get something out in the open.

Much love,

Edie xx

Chapter 24

I've started to cling to the note-to-self lines like a talisman, chanting them over and over in my head when I need to hear them. Like now, as I will myself to be me only a little bit braver.

'Hang on,' I say, turning to the left. 'You have to get this, it's my best side.'

'It's your only side. That racoon took off the other side of your face,' says Aaron, pretending to recoil in horror.

'OK, OK,' I say, trying to keep calm and remember the rules of improv. Agree with him and add something. 'Unfortunately we couldn't all die when we'd been made up on a movie set, like you.'

He runs a hand over his cheek.

'You had to mention the movie, didn't you?' says Yas, shaking her head. 'Here we go again with that damn story.'

'It was a cold night, and I was getting ready for my big scene. My hair was coiffed to perfection. My make-up flawless, and then, and then . . .'

'And then the rain fell and you tripped over the light and you got electrocuted, we've heard it plenty of times before,' says Dave, pushing Aaron out the way. 'Say cheese.'

He makes a flashing noise and we all pose for our imaginary photo booth picture.

Aaron pretends to be sad, reacting to what Dave has said.

'Don't be too hard on him, guys,' I say, my voice much less shaky than the last time I was on stage. 'It's hard when no one can see us but we can see each other.'

'Dumb living people,' adds Yas. 'They can't see us no matter how hard we try.'

It's my third time competing with the improv team after Hayley had to bow out, because even though her leg wasn't broken her ankle was badly sprained and she needs to be careful whilst it heals. I wouldn't say I've started to relax or that it was becoming natural to me, but I am starting to feel a little more comfortable and I'm contributing more. I'd always assumed it'd be hard without a script but in some ways it's easier as none of us know what's coming next. You can't really get it wrong and there's always someone there with another line straight after to hide it if a line doesn't quite land.

I'm amazed after the judges award us the win. Not that the rest of the group weren't brilliant, but just because it's the furthest that the team have progressed before in the competition. I hear Layla's unmistakeable wolf whistle and I try and spot her in the crowd, and when I do, I also catch sight of the fluorescent yellow tie of the man next to her. It's Dad. He's clapping loudly and he leans towards Julie who's next to him.

After celebrating on stage, I head into the backstage area with the rest of the gang.

'Edie, are you OK?' asks Aaron, tugging at my sleeve. 'Stunned we won?'

'A little, but I was just surprised to see Dad in the audience.'

248

'Oh, yeah, I bumped into him on the way out of work and he was so excited to come along. Hope that's OK?'

'Of course,' I say, wondering what I'm going to say to them after. Dad had made me promise I'd tell him when the next one was and I'd forgotten to.

I can't think when I last popped round to Dad's. I used to visit at least once a week and we'd have dinner together. If I'm honest, it was my way of making sure he was OK; I'd run through my mental checklist, peering into his fridge to see if he was eating healthily and checking for signs he'd been drinking again. I've not been round as much because Julie always seems to be there. I can't help worrying that she doesn't know what warning signs to look out for like I would.

I think of Joel and our conversation down at the beach before we found out Douglas got arrested and how he'd reassured me what I felt was normal, but it doesn't make me feel any less guilty about it.

When we leave the backstage area, Layla makes a beeline for me.

'Congratulations, I thought you were all brilliant, but you were especially,' she whispers, giving me a squeeze.

'I think you're biased but thank you.'

'Right, first round's on me, I'm so proud to know you all.' She leads the way to the bar and I'm about to join them when Dad and Julie come over.

'You were sensational,' says Dad. 'I couldn't believe that was you on the stage.'

'It was a team thing but thank you.'

'He was so proud of you all the way through,' says Julie, 'and he had every reason to be. Well done.'

'Thanks, Julie. It's nice to see you again.'

'You too.'

'Are you staying for a drink?' I ask.

'Only if we're not imposing?' She looks at Dad nervously.

'Of course not,' I say.

'I'm going to nip to the ladies then, I'll meet you in the bar.' Dad touches her back as she goes.

'I'm sorry I didn't tell you that I was doing this tonight,' I say after she's left.

'I guessed you were too nervous to have me watching. That's why I didn't text you beforehand to let you know we were in the audience.'

It was the perfect opportunity to correct him and tell him the truth but instead I nod along, pretending that was the case.

'I'm glad you brought Julie along to keep you company. Seems like she's been doing that a lot lately.'

There's an edge to my voice that I don't want to be there.

'Yeah, she has. Speaking of Julie, I thought I might pin you down for that shopping date you said you'd go on. Are you free this weekend?'

'Actually I'm not.'

'You know, if you're trying to get out of it, or you don't want to go, it would be easier if you just said—'

'No, I do want to go,' I say, lying; the look of hurt on his face is too much. 'It's just that I've sort of organised a summer party, or more like a gathering. We're going to play some frisbee and I was going to cook pasta for everyone. I invited Soph and the gang up for the afternoon, plus Layla and Tim, and Claudia from the Big Little Readers, and Aaron and his boyfriend said they'd stop by.'

He looks relieved that I wasn't fobbing him off.

'That'll be nice. I'm glad you're seeing more of your friends.'

'Yeah, but I promise that I'll get a date in the diary with Julie too.'

Dad puts his hands in his pockets.

'Thanks, I know she'd like that. She really does want to get to know you and it would mean a lot to me. You both mean so much to me.'

I'm starting to feel a little sick, like the adrenaline that was keeping me going on stage is starting to ebb away. Julie walks back up to us and I force myself to smile.

'I was just asking Edie about your shopping trip, but she's busy this weekend; she's throwing a party.'

'Not a party per se, just some friends coming over. My flat's too small for a proper party.'

'Do you want me to make you some cupcakes for it?'

'Julie's an excellent baker,' says Dad.

I think of her banoffee pie.

'Um, I wouldn't want you to go to any trouble.'

'It'd be no trouble.'

She's looking hopefully at me and I feel like the best thing to do is let her.

'Thank you, that's really kind.'

She's beaming and so is Dad. I can see how much me letting her in, even if it is a little bit, means to him.

'Shall we go and get a drink?' I say.

The rest of the gang are delighted to see that my dad came to watch them and everyone makes a fuss meeting Julie. They spend a few minutes chatting and they've already made more of an effort to get to know her than I have. I must try harder.

'No Miles tonight?' asks Layla, coming to stand next to me.

'No, he's got a lot of work on this week.'

My dad's not the only person that I'm avoiding at the moment. It might be true that Miles is working a lot of extra hours, but I didn't even ask him to come tonight. Spending so much time with Joel has only highlighted the issues Miles and I have with communication. I know I have to talk to him but I'm worried what it's going to mean for us when I do.

'That's a shame. He'll be at the frisbee. Won't he?'

'He sure will.'

They'll be no hiding from him then. Or Joel who'll be there too. Joel whom, ever since that morning watching the sunrise on the beach, I haven't been able to stop thinking about.

Chapter 25

THEN

After our near kiss, it was days before Joel and I found ourselves alone. I'd naively assumed that I'd speak to him the next day, but there was always someone around and it wasn't like it was the kind of thing that I could bring up in front of Soph or Douglas or any of the other staff.

Finally, one morning while I was manning reception, he came to see me, and I thought it was our chance. But before I could even bring up what happened, a departing guest wanted me to go and check their caravan against the inventory so that they could receive their deposit back. We had to put our conversation temporarily on pause whilst I headed off with the guest. I thought Joel would have waited for me, but by the time I came back, he'd left.

Usually on check-out days the shifts passed in a bit of a blur, but that shift dragged. By the time I walked back to the accommodation later that afternoon my back ached and my feet were killing me.

'What is with you?' Soph nudged at my elbow.

'Nothing, why?' I rubbed at the base of my spine, trying to massage away the tension.

'It's just you keep looking round; it's starting to freak me out. Did you sleep with a guest or something?'

'No,' I said, 'my name's not Douglas.'

She laughed and then started talking about the party we were heading to later that night; I was relieved of the subject change. If Joel hadn't been her cousin, I would have leapt at the chance of picking her brain. I was desperate to know whether she thought Joel liked me. But then I thought of the first warning she gave me about Joel, that he's the love-and-leave-them type, and it burned in my chest.

Joel was leaning over the balcony of the staff quarters when we got back to our flat.

'Hey,' said Soph. 'Waiting for me?'

'For Edie, actually.'

'I'm hurt you don't want to see your favourite cousin,' she said. 'I'm going to hit the shower. We'll leave about eight? You coming?'

Joel shook his head.

'I'm on night security.'

Soph headed inside our flat and I leant against the railing next to him, until we were side by side.

'Who are you on night security with?'

'Elizabeth.'

I pulled a face. My flatmate hadn't become any more friendly than the day I first met her.

'Fun.'

'Yeah, I'm really looking forward to it.'

'Sorry, have you been waiting long? We stayed a bit at reception after our shift ended. Soph wanted to send an email to that guitar player from the band that she met last week. You know that one that she thought looked like Jon Bon Jovi.'

'Soph thinks any man with a guitar looks like him.'

His hands seemed to be shaking a little. He shoved them in his pockets when he caught me looking at them and he turned to rest his back against the railing so he was facing me.

'It's a shame you can't come tonight.'

'Is it?' he asked.

'Yeah, I mean it's not the same without you; the gang's not complete.'

'Right, yeah, *the gang.*' He sounded deflated and I cursed myself. I wanted to tell him that I'd be disappointed as I missed him all the time when he wasn't there. That I thought about him all the time. That I was falling head over heels for him. But my mouth had gone dry and all of the words that were so desperate to spill out were stuck.

'When Soph was sending her email, did you check yours?' he asked.

'Yeah, although mine wasn't as exciting,' I said with a shrug.

He stared straight at me, his eyes narrowing before he broke away and turned to leave.

'I better get ready for my shift.'

He started to walk away and I was left stunned. What just happened?

'But it doesn't start for half an hour,' I called but he either didn't hear me or chose not to.

I heard him walking up the metal stairs. I nearly went after him, but I didn't know what I'd say. I wondered why Joel was acting this way and where the man that I'd fallen for had suddenly gone.

Chapter 26

I've never had a party at my flat before and I'd always assumed it was too small to hold enough people, but looking around at everyone chatting, there seems to be plenty of nooks and crannies for people to stand, sit and perch. The doors to the balcony are wide open providing a much-needed breeze, and Miles is standing outside on it, chatting to Brett.

'These cakes are amazing. Did you make them yourself?' asks Soph, peeling off the paper case.

'I'd love to say yes, but my dad's friend Julie made them. They're amazing, aren't they?'

Dad brought them into work yesterday and I can't help but feel guilty that when I texted her to say thank you that I deliberately didn't mention the shopping trip. I know I've got to stop putting it off. It just seems like a very mum-and-daughter thing to do. She's slipped so seamlessly into Dad's life but I can't help feeling disloyal to Mum that she might do the same into mine.

Soph takes a large bite and she groans and pulls a face.

'These *are* amazing.'

'Don't you be eating any of those cakes.' Douglas walks up to her with a pointed finger. 'Not until after we've played; you're on my team.'

'Typical Douglas. Always competitive,' I say, smiling up at him. He looks a hell of a lot better than he did two weeks ago. He's still got big black bags under his eyes, but at least he's got a healthier glow.

His brother is watching him like a hawk wherever he goes, but I'm glad that he's got someone to look out for him.

'I just like to win, doesn't everyone?'

'A man after my own heart,' says Aaron, walking over to the conversation. 'I mean, it might be a child's game, but I still play to win.'

'Woah there.' Douglas's hand flies up like some nineties 'talk to the hand' gesture. 'Ultimate frisbee is not a child's game. It's a hardcore sport.'

'Made all the more hardcore as we're playing it in the dark,' I chip in.

Soph groans, staring at her half-eaten cupcake. 'Douglas, you can't expect me to not eat dessert until after we've played?'

'You just had a big bowl of pasta; surely you can't be hungry?'

'I'm still feeding Alfie, I'm always hungry. Besides, everyone knows that cakes go into the dessert stomach, that's separate.'

'I'm with Soph,' says Verity, striding over. She looks as perfect as ever, despite her bemoaning her jetlag having arrived back from the US yesterday. 'One cupcake is not going to hurt.'

'Well, if we lose and it's either of your faults, I'm going to blame the cupcakes.' He puts his hands on his hips and glares at them.

Soph gives him a wink as she devours the rest of hers and picks up another before walking away. Verity picks one up from the stack.

'Oh wow. These are too good. They're easily as good as

anything you get back home.' She's practically drooling as she eats. Douglas walks off towards the boys on the balcony, pretending to be in a huff.

'Julie, the woman who made them, would be happy to hear that.' I rearrange the cupcakes on the plate to fill in the empty gaps.

'I'm so sorry, Edie,' says Soph, interrupting, 'but Alfie's knocked half of my cupcake on the floor. He went to take a massive bite out of it and I wasn't prepared for it.'

'Can't say I blame him,' says Verity. She puts her hands out. 'Give me the little dude. I've finished mine.'

She carries him over to the other side of the room and Joel walks inside to meet them. Alfie giggles as Joel keeps tickling him. It's almost infectious and I find myself smiling at the sight. I sense I'm being watched and I turn to see Miles looking at me.

I hold up the plate of cupcakes, gesturing to see if he wants one, but he shakes his head and goes back to listening to what Brett is talking about.

'Have you got a dustpan and brush and I can get this cleared up?' asks Soph.

'Yes, of course,' I say, going under my sink and pulling it out. I hand it to her and I'm just trying to shove the clutter back in and make sure that none of it spills out when I turn around and see Joel.

'You OK down there?' He holds out his hand and pulls me up.

'Now you know that I'm secretly a messy person.'

'I think your room at Hartland's told me that.'

Joel helps himself to a cupcake.

'Verity told me I had to get one of these.' He bites into it. 'And they are every bit as good as she said.'

'I can't take the credit,' I say, tempted to eat another, but I did test a couple before everyone arrived. 'Douglas is looking well.'

'Yeah, he's doing really well apparently. Jake says that he's been hell to live with because of his mood swings. Grumpy one minute and pacing like a caged tiger the next. But the centre's managing his detox safely and he's been sober properly for over a week now.'

'That's such great news,' I say.

'I think that they were both really pleased that you'd organised this. I think it's nice for them to get out and not have to worry about there being alcohol. You don't realise how many social events revolve around it until you have to cut it out.'

'That's what my dad said when he got sober.'

We both turn and look over at Douglas. He's deep in conversation with Miles and Brett, talking animatedly with his hands about something.

The intercom beeps and I excuse myself from Joel and head towards it. It's Claudia with her boyfriend and I buzz them in and wait for them on the landing. The noise is quite loud coming out of my flat and I figure that we should get going soon before we annoy too many of the neighbours.

'Hello,' I say, opening the door.

Claudia beams at me as she air kisses me on the cheek.

'I'm so glad you're dressed like that too. It felt quite unnatural putting these bad boys on for a Saturday night out.'

She pulls self-consciously at her tight leggings.

'Don't worry, we're all dressed like it. Hello, I'm Edie.' I put my hand out for her boyfriend Robin.

'Nice to meet you, Edie.' He shakes my hand. 'Thanks for inviting us, this sounds fun.'

'I'm hoping it'll be as fun as we remember it being. Come in and meet everyone.'

I take them round the room, introducing them.

'And last, but not least, this is Miles.' I hold my hands out to present him.

'It's so nice to finally meet you,' says Claudia, greeting him.

'You too. Edie has nothing but good things to say about the charity.'

'Well, we have nothing but good things to say about her too. She's such a natural. I was telling Robin on the way over that she's going to make a really good teacher if I can get her to fill out the application form.'

I try and laugh along, but out of the corner of my eye I see that Miles is smiling like he's in on the joke despite the fact it's the first he's heard of it. I've been looking for the right moment to bring it up with him.

'Sorry to interrupt, again,' says Soph, wincing. 'I just wondered what time we're leaving? Alfie's getting a bit grizzly so I thought I'd start walking him in the pram.'

'We can leave anytime now, as we're all here.'

'Great, I'll pop Alfie in the pram outside and then I'll look forward to my power laps around the park whilst you all play.'

'You know that we're going to be taking it in turns to push that pram, don't you?'

'Ha, ha, no,' she says. 'You'll have to prise my hands off it. I'm happy watching you all. You heard what Douglas was like before; I don't want to be on anyone's team.'

I'm about to go round and tell everyone individually that we're leaving when I catch myself thinking how long that will take. I clap my hands to get everyone's attention.

'Right, we're ready to get going. We're playing in a park, and we don't want to leave big piles of shiny goodies for someone to take. So Soph's said she's happy to store any valuables like car keys and phones in the bottom of the pram. So once you've given them to her all you need to bring are your water bottles and yourselves. Let's go.'

There's a few excited cheers and everyone does what I say. When everyone gets ready it hits me what I've just done. It might not be the biggest crowd, but my heart's still beating rapidly. Speaking in front of crowds might not come naturally to me, but it's slowly getting easier.

It's a relief that twilight frisbee has gone down so well. It doesn't have quite the dramatic effect it has when it's pitch black, but there's still a fun to it in the fading light with the frisbee shining bright. There's only a couple of points in it and the game is almost finished.

Aaron's got the frisbee and I see an opening near the goal and I make a break for it, only Joel, who's done such an excellent job of marking me, spots me and runs and blocks me.

'You know, if I didn't know any better I'd have thought that you played netball at school.' I try and keep light on my toes, dodging left and right.

'If only I hadn't gone to an all-boys school and they'd played it.' He stretches his arms out and shuffles sideways, blocking my attempts to escape. 'I learnt my excellent defence moves one summer when there was a superyacht that had a basketball court moored nearby the one I was working on.'

'It did not.' I put my hands on my hips, not knowing if he was trying to distract me.

'It did too.'

Miles is blocked into a corner and he throws the frisbee to Layla.

Joel takes his eyes off me for a second and I double back and run into a space. 'Over here.'

I'm waving my arms and shouting, but Verity's got other ideas.

'Oh no you don't,' she cries.

I jump to catch the frisbee, my fingers making contact, but she does some kind of Michael Flatley leap and slams straight into me and we crash to the ground. Neither of us can stop ourselves, and I tumble over backwards with her almost on top of me.

'Shit, I'm so sorry. Are you OK? Have I hurt you? Did you hit your head?' she asks, scrambling off me. 'I think you broke my fall.'

My body is aching everywhere. The ground's rock solid thanks to a summer of little rain.

'Edie, Edie?' Her voice is sounding more frantic.

'I'm OK,' I say, wincing in pain. 'I didn't hit my head.'

'I'm so sorry, I don't know what I was thinking.'

'I thought Douglas was the competitive one on your team.'

'You guys OK?' asks Joel, squatting down next to us. Verity and I attempt to get up. I sit up and bend my knees towards my chest, and I wrap my arms round them. Everything aches.

'I got a bit overenthusiastic with my jump; it was like I was doing some Hail Mary. I smashed straight into Edie, poor thing.'

'I'll live, but I might need to sit out for a bit.'

Douglas is over and the rest of the players crowd around whilst he squats next to Joel.

'How many fingers am I holding up?'

'It's so bloody dark I can't see . . . I'm kidding, two fingers. I didn't hit my head and I've got no double vision.'

'OK, well, perhaps we should call it a night anyway,' says Joel, and Verity reaches out and takes his hand. 'To be on the safe side.'

'But it's tied at ten all,' says Douglas. Jake gives him a nudge. 'But your health is obviously more important.'

'Why don't Verity and Edie just sit this one out?' says Aaron. 'Seems a shame to get so close.'

'That's a good idea.' I wrap my arms tighter round my legs. I think I've had enough.

'I can sit it out too.' Soph scans the park, looking for Brett whose turn it is to walk the pram around.

'Oh no you don't.' Douglas frowns. 'We're going to be a player down. We'll need you more than ever. This is going to be tough, but it's winnable.'

'Bloody Brett, where is he? I'm sure it's my turn to look after Alfie.' She walks back with the others muttering under her breath.

The rest of the group give me little arm pats and smiles before they head off to their positions. Miles hovers in front of me. I try and blow a bit of hair that's stuck in front of my face and Miles reaches his hand out like he's going to brush it away but he stops short and stands back up.

'You're OK then?'

'Just a little sore.'

He nods and doesn't offer his hand to pull me up before he walks off.

Verity holds her hand out and pulls me up and we walk to a bench that's far enough away not to get hit by a passing frisbee.

'Is Miles OK? He seemed a little cold with you just then.'

I watch him running on the pitch, getting frustrated that he can't get clear of Layla marking him.

'Yeah, things with us haven't been great lately.'

Miles and I haven't really recovered from that night in the pub and neither of us wants to admit it. He's stopped staying over and I've barely seen him in the last two weeks.

'Oh, I'm sorry to hear that.'

'These things happen.' I shrug. I don't feel I know Verity well enough to go into details so I change the subject. 'How was your trip to the US?'

'It was *so* good.' She emphasises the 'so' in a way that Alexis from *Schitt's Creek* would be proud of. 'I didn't realise quite how much I missed the place until I went back. Have you ever had that?'

I thought of how it felt when I first went back to Westerly and I nod.

'It's like you get there and you go, oh, I'm home. Everything's familiar and easy and you understand all the subtext of what everyone's saying.' She stares across the pitch and I follow her eyeline to Joel. 'I can't wait to go back and start the job.'

'So you got it?'

She raises her eyebrows. 'The interview was only ever a formality.'

My hands tighten around the bench. I want to ask her if Joel's going too but my throat is growing tight and I can't get out the words.

The thought of him leaving my life when he's only just come back into it is too much.

Verity points down the field. 'Ooh, it looks like it's getting rough out there. Douglas seems to be taking this game very seriously. Glad we could sit this out.'

'Yeah, me too, although my bones might argue we left it a tiny bit late.'

She winces. 'Sorry, again.'

'It's fine, really.'

There's a loud cheer at the other end of the field; someone must have scored.

Douglas and Joel have lifted Claudia in the air and Verity does a little fist pump in the air in solidarity with her team.

She runs over and joins the celebration and I head towards Miles, who's bent double at the waist and panting. 'It was a tight game.' I rub his back and he brings himself up to standing and doesn't say anything.

'That was so much fun,' says Layla. 'We'll have to do it again.'

'Absolutely,' says Douglas, clearly buzzing. He puts Claudia down and hugs the rest of his team. 'Who knew you don't need alcohol to have fun.'

After the game we drift over to the car park. Joel climbs in the passenger seat of Brett's car, whilst Soph and Verity squeeze into the backseat next to Alfie's ginormous car seat. They're heading straight back as Alfie's fast asleep and they want to get him home. Jake and Douglas also head out and we wave them off.

'Does anyone fancy going out and grabbing a drink?' asks Layla, turning to the rest of us who don't need to drive home. 'We've still got a babysitter for another hour or two.'

'I'd be up for that.' Claudia turns to Robin and he nods in agreement.

'Us too,' says Aaron.

I turn to Miles.

'Do you fancy going?'

'Actually, I think I'm going to give it a miss.'

At his response, I know deep down we can't carry on like this.

'Thanks, Layla, but I think I'll head back with Miles. Do you want to come back to my flat?'

He nods. No one says anything, but I can sense that we all know what's coming.

Layla wraps me up in a hug, squeezing me a little bit too hard, and it makes my muscles hurt even more. 'We'll just be in the pub, if you change your mind.'

'Thanks guys. See you all soon.'

I watch them walk off, wishing I was going with them, but instead I head into the flat, dreading what's to come.

Chapter 27

It's a warm evening and we arrive back at my flat. I pull out a bottle of rosé from the fridge, removing the cockerel corkscrew before Miles sees. I don't want to offend him that the Tiffany one he bought me is still in its original packaging. I grab two glasses and we head onto my balcony.

I sit down at the bistro table that just about fits in the small space, and Miles leans with his back against the railings, cradling the glass in his hands.

'So things aren't great, are they?' I say.

He takes a sip of his drink and then pulls a face.

'No, they're really not.'

I nod, glad that we're on the same page for this at least.

'Something's changed.'

'You've changed,' he says softly. It's not an accusation, merely a statement. I let it sink in. He's right; I have.

'I know.'

'I don't know who you are anymore.'

He sits down on the chair next to me and puts his drink on the table.

'I think the problem was that I didn't know who I was. That's what I've been trying to figure out over the last few months.

I've been trying to remember who I wanted to be in the past and who I want to be now.'

'You mean the teaching? That was a shock. You've never even told me that you don't like your job. I mean, you're a company director, why would you give all that up?'

'I know it probably doesn't make any sense to you.' I take a deep breath because none of this is Miles's fault; it's mine for not being open with him in the first place. 'Do you know that it's what I wanted to do before my mum died? I had a place at the University of Leicester to read English and I was thinking of becoming a teacher. I had it all planned, I got the grades, I was off . . . and then they were in the accident.'

'I didn't know.' He shakes his head and leans over, taking my hand.

'That's because I never told you. Don't you think that's weird that we've been together seven months and we've never really spoken about my mum or about her death or how it completely changed the course of my life? Not to mention I've never mentioned the accident. Or that losing her made me scared to have my own children, even though the older I get, the more I'm starting to want them?'

Miles looks at me with the kind of pity I always try and avoid.

'I just thought you were a private person. I actually found it quite refreshing.'

'Refreshing?' I say, confused.

'Yeah, my ex was a big oversharer; constantly telling me and worrying about every little detail of her life and asking me what I was thinking. I didn't mind it at first, but it was exhausting by the end. I felt like I was more her therapist than her boyfriend.

So, it was a bit of a relief to be honest when I met you and you never wanted to talk about things.'

He picks up his drink and takes a large sip.

'I get that. We've got the same problem of our past experiences tending to . . .'

'Fuck us up?' he says.

'I was looking for a slightly more eloquent way to put it, but that's it, isn't it?'

'I guess so,' he says, before he shakes his head and sighs. 'We were happy though, weren't we?'

I nod, feeling the tears starting to form in my eyes. Whilst I've known this was coming it still hasn't prepared me for it to happen.

'We were.'

'But that wasn't enough for you?'

The question stuns me for a second. I have, on the face of it, a perfect-looking life, good job, nice flat, and a caring boyfriend, but it doesn't feel right.

'I guess, I've felt for a long time that something's been missing. I've often thought that it's my mum. I thought I'd always feel incomplete without her. And I think to some extent that's true – I'll always have bits of me missing and the space in my heart that she should still be filling – but I've come to realise that that's not all of it. There's something missing because I'm not living the life I truly want.'

'So, it's not just about the whole baby thing?'

I purse my lips together; there's so much that we haven't talked about.

'No, it's definitely more than that, but that's a big thing in itself. I still don't know if I will have kids but I know that I can't rule it out entirely.'

'You know, we should have maybe had this conversation when we met. It would have saved us a lot of heartache.'

'Perhaps that's just something we've learnt that'll teach us for the next time. Maybe you'll be the one in your next relationship that'll be making them feel like they've had a therapy session.'

Miles cracks a smile.

'It's so weird that you're talking about my next relationship. We're really doing this whole break-up thing?'

He turns to me and I remember all the good times we've had, all the memories that would make a best-bits compilation if we were on a reality TV show. It makes me wonder if I'm losing the plot, but then I think about why I'm doing this and the life I want to lead and what I want from the future. The future that Miles isn't going to be able to give me.

'I think we're really doing this,' I say, echoing his words and letting out a deep breath, trying to hold my tears at bay. I wrap my hands around my wine glass to ground me.

'It's just so weirdly amicable; I've never had a break-up like this.'

'I know, it's a head-fuck, isn't it? It makes you wonder if you're doing the right thing,' I say.

'Are we?' He looks into my eyes and it only confirms in my gut what I know already: we're not meant to be.

'I think we both know we are.'

A cool breeze whips through the balcony and it makes me shiver.

'Can we stay in touch at least?'

A tear rolls down my cheek and I wipe it away with my fingers.

'I'd like that.'

'Good.'

We sit in silence for a few minutes, trying to digest what's happened. I look out over the houses in the town that are lit up in the distance; it looks like strands of fairy lights across the hill. In any other moment this could be so romantic.

'Now that I guess we're technically broken up, I'm just going to come right out and ask: did something happen between you and Joel when you were at the holiday park?'

My body goes rigid even though nothing happened.

'No,' I say, but it sounds unconvincing and even I wouldn't believe me. 'Honestly. There's never been anything between Joel and me; we've only ever been friends.'

It's the painful truth that I wish wasn't true, but it is.

'You just seemed so . . . cosy.'

'We've always been like that.'

'Did you want there to be anything else?' He looks me straight in the eye and I can't hide it. This time I can tell he can see it in my eyes.

I slowly nod.

'And now?'

'And now, what?' I gulp down a large sip of my rosé.

'Do you want something to happen?'

'He's with Verity.'

Miles shrugs. 'That's not really an answer.'

I think about the conversations with Joel and how he's being so wishy-washy about going to the US with Verity. Even if Joel did like me and he wasn't with Verity, he's never going to commit or settle down. It's best I let any thought of us two together go.

'No, I don't want anything to happen.'

I know that no matter what connection we have, he's not the man I'd need him to be.

Miles finishes his drink and puts his glass on the table. 'You know, it might have made it a little easier if something did happen a couple of weeks ago.'

'Really?'

'Yep, because then I could have made you out to be some kind of monster and sometimes it's easier to get over someone if you don't like them.'

Now it's my turn to lean over and take his hand.

'Sorry I didn't cheat on you,' I say as sincerely as I can.

'That's OK.'

He squeezes my hand before he takes his back.

'OK, I think it was time that I got going,' he says, standing up.

'OK.' I get to my feet and we stand there for a second, not really knowing what to do, before he turns and walks back into my flat.

'What about your stuff? Did you want to take it now or . . .?'

'I can get it later; there's nothing here that I need urgently.'

'OK,' I say, a lump in my throat.

'Did you want me to walk you to the pub to meet the others? It's on my way home.'

'Oh, I'm not going to go now.'

'Come on, what else are you going to do? Sit around and mope? Layla would want to be there for you. Plus Claudia seems great.'

'She is.'

'Go on, get your bag and I'll walk you there.'

I rub at my face, which I'm sure is puffy and red from the tears. But sod it, I've just broken up with my boyfriend; I should be around my friends.

We walk mostly in silence to the pub and when we get there, Miles bends down and gives me a kiss on the cheek and we have the longest hug.

'Goodnight, Edie.'

'Goodnight, Miles.'

He walks off down the road and I start to head over to the pub entrance. I spot Claudia in the window laughing with Aaron.

As I push open the door, Tim spots me first.

'Hey, Edie.'

The others look round and they turn and wave.

Layla gets up and pulls me towards her and Claudia reaches out and pats my arm.

'No Miles?'

'No Miles,' I say, shaking my head.

Layla keeps one arm around me and squeezes my shoulder.

'It's OK, it was a good thing, I think. I don't really want to talk about it now.' My bottom lip starts to tremble. 'But he thought that I shouldn't be alone tonight so I thought I'd come.'

'Absolutely,' says Claudia.

'Let me get you a drink.' Tim stands up and puts his chair underneath me. 'It's my round.'

'Quick, watch the moths fly away,' says Layla, guiding me into Tim's vacated chair.

Tim shoots her a look and then heads off to the bar with our order.

Layla starts to tell a story about when the two of them were first dating and Tim kept forgetting his wallet. Miles had been right, being with other people is exactly what I needed; perhaps he knew me better than I thought he did. It might have been the most amicable break-up in history, but it doesn't mean it doesn't sting.

Chapter 28

I never expected to feel such relief after breaking up with Miles; it's as though a massive weight has been lifted off my shoulders. The best part is that we've managed to keep things amicable between us. Over the last couple of weeks, we've kept in contact, usually messaging to check in on each other, and we met up in person to exchange items left at each other's flats. Yet, despite the lack of tension and drama, I still feel emotionally wrung out. I've had time to really process what happened but I'm still no further ahead with working out what it is exactly that I want from life.

I'm staring at the figures of last month's profit and loss that Nina in accounts has sent over and it's the first time that we're seeing an uptick in profits from the council tender we won at the start of the summer. Orders have started to come in from the different council-run establishments, and whilst many of them have only been small, collectively they've made a huge difference.

At the start of the summer, before receiving the note-to-self emails, I might have felt disappointed that the company was doing well, but now I can't help but feel a little proud. It may not have been my first choice to work at Porter's but I've worked just as hard, if not harder, than I would have done in any other job and I've helped to keep it afloat over the years.

'Morning, Edie, you OK?' asks Dave, walking past my desk.

He's got his tie underneath his neatly pressed jumper with his brown overcoat on top, ready for his work in the warehouse.

'Yes, I'm OK.'

'You look tired.'

'It's Monday morning, don't most people?' I rub at my eyes.

He's got the same look on his face that my dad's had on his face since I broke up with Miles: one of concern and pity.

'You could do with a holiday,' he says, pointing a finger in my direction. 'That's your problem, you're always at work or if you're not you're thinking about it. You need to learn to take a break.'

'Um, says the man who hasn't put in for any leave over the summer.'

'Can't stand the heat. I think we'll head away in October.'

'Back to Spain?'

'Oh, yes. We're creatures of habit. You know, Mary wants us to buy a little place there when we retire. Sell the house and move there.'

'That would be exciting.'

'It would, but I keep telling her, I've got a way to go before retirement. Don't worry, I won't be leaving you in the lurch any time soon.'

An unexpected rush of sadness comes over me. I've known Dave for as long as I can remember; he started work almost on day one with Mum and Dad and I can't imagine him one day not being here.

'Right, better get on. We've got a big delivery going out today.'

He gives me a pat on the shoulder as he walks away and

before I can dwell on Dave retiring I hear the ping of an email notification. My heart skips a beat as it's a note-to-future-self one. I've been missing my little updates and challenges.

Dear Edie,

I hope you're good! You would not believe what happened last night - except that you would of course because you already know. I almost kissed Joel!!!! I ended up in his bed after Soph and Green Eyes the guitarist were way too loud, and I think we would have kissed properly if Soph hadn't screamed. What happens next, Edie? I wish you could tell me as you know the next part of the story. Do we eventually kiss? Is it as phenomenal as I think it's going to be?

I have no idea how he feels about me or whether I'm brave enough to do anything about it. We've only got another few weeks left here and then we're going to be heading off in different directions, and I know we'd be naive to try long distance.

I just wish we had extra time to see what was really there, you know proper time, without work. I've never pulled a sicky before, but I'd be tempted to if I got to spend the day with him. And knowing you, if you're still like me, you won't have ever pulled one either. Edie, always playing by the rules. Never got a detention from school. Always presses the

```
pedestrian button at the traffic lights to
cross. Which brings me to this email's note
to self: bend or break the rules! Go on, be
a rebel - just not too much of a rebel, I'm
obviously not advocating breaking the law.
   Love you oodles, Edie xx
```

My heart almost breaks when I read it. I remember how I felt in
that moment, so full of lust and excitement that something might
happen between me and Joel. Unfortunately I lived through it,
I know what happened. I know that not long after, my world
shattered when my mum died.

I can't help but think of the anniversary of Mum's death,
which is looming large. It's never not painful and I never feel any
less guilty. But this year it'll be especially hard as I know from
that moment on I won't get any more emails from my past self.
After everything spiralled out of control and things got so bleak
I wondered if I'd even make it to the age where I'd receive all
those emails I'd sent myself, let alone writing any more.

I try not to think about that and instead I read today's email
again. My younger self predicted correctly that I've never taken
a sick day. It's never even crossed my mind to do it.

My eyes flick over to the profit and loss sheet; it's not like
the company's doing badly at the moment. I pull up the internal
calendar and my personal one to double-check today's meetings
and if anyone would miss me.

I look over the top of my computer screen at Claire, who's
busy processing a big pile of invoices.

'Claire, do you think you could manage without me today?'
She leans round the side of her computer.

'Yes, of course, everything OK?' She stares hard at me over the rims of her glasses.

'Yeah, there's just something I need to do. I'll have my phone with me if you need me.'

I glance over at Dad's desk, which is empty. I hesitate, feeling a little guilty about what I'm about to do, then I remember that he is often late. He's probably lost track of time with Julie this morning. I'm sure he'll be in soon and that'll ease my guilt.

By the time I arrive in Westerly I've experienced a plethora of emotions about skipping out on work: guilt, excitement, paranoia, happiness, nervousness. On the roundabout at the motorway junction, I nearly turned back to the office, but somehow I made it, and I'm glad I did. Spending the morning with Soph and Alfie was just what the doctor ordered.

'I'm going to really miss these lazy summer days,' says Soph, leaning over on the rug to stop Alfie scuttling off the end. He's almost got the hang of crawling. He shuffles mostly on his tummy, but every so often he pushes himself up and almost manages to go. 'It's going to be a right shock to the system when I return to work.'

'You've got a while left though, haven't you?'

Despite my reservations, skiving off work seems to be agreeing with me and I'm already feeling more relaxed. I can't remember the last time I lay on my tummy on a picnic rug, propping myself up with my elbows.

'Another four months, but I'm two-thirds of the way through my maternity leave and it's flown by. I might have felt like I've lived every single second of them with Alfie not sleeping, but, still, the closer work gets, the faster it seems to go.' She sighs deeply. 'Don't mind me, I always get a bit melancholy at the end of the summer. It's a weird feeling, isn't it? You look forward to summer from January onwards, all the outdoor events and the fun they bring, and then poof, it's over before you know it. Then it gets colder and darker.'

'But then there's Christmas.'

'I know, but for me I always love the summer. You know our time at Hartland's will always be one of my favourites.'

'Mine too. I mean it was my best and my worst summer.'

'Oh Edie, I'm so sorry. I didn't think. It must be soon, right?'

She leans over and puts her arm around my shoulders and gives me a hug.

'Yeah, a week on Wednesday.'

I'm dreading this anniversary because, thanks to the emails, it's made me remember that time in more vivid detail.

'Next Wednesday? That's so soon. Are you doing anything? You're welcome to come and stay with us if you like. We're free most of that week. We've got Joel and Verity's wedding on the Friday morning, but other than that we're free.'

I'm about to interrupt to tell her that Dad and I always spend the day together when I register what she's said. I'm leaning on my elbows and I slowly push myself up to sitting, worried that my arms aren't going to support me any longer.

'Joel's getting married?'

Soph's distracted by Alfie launching himself at the grass with his newfound freedom, trying to curl his mouth around the tips. She doesn't notice that I'm almost shaking.

'Yeah, but don't be offended that you're not invited,' she says, wrestling Alfie off the grass just as his mouth makes contact. 'Brett and I are only going as we're witnesses. It's going to be a small ceremony at the registry office, nothing fancy or anything.'

The world is starting to spin and my chest is burning.

'He's getting married.' I try and come to terms with it.

'I know. It's almost unbelievable that Joel is finally putting a ring on it. They've said that they're only doing it because it makes it easier for him to get a work visa, but of course the hopeless romantic in me thinks that he's telling himself that so he doesn't get scared.

'You know, Verity finally told me the reason that Joel is the way he is. I thought he was just like his dad, but apparently some girl shattered his heart to smithereens when he was younger. She wasn't exactly sure when it happened, but apparently he told a girl that he was in love with her and she completely ignored it. Ghosted him apparently.'

'Poor Joel,' I say, my heart breaking for him.

'I know, awful. It's made me see him in a whole new light. It's why I'm rooting for him and Verity. I feel like he deserves to be happy. Of course I wish he could have found happiness here, and not with someone that's taking him across the other side of the Atlantic, but I guess that's typical Joel, isn't it? Just when we all get used to having him around, he ups and leaves. This one is especially going to miss his uncle, aren't you?'

She picks up Alfie, who has already made it back to the grass. She pulls out the blades of grass hanging out of his mouth, much to his disappointment.

'Do you fancy taking a stroll back to mine? Alfie's going to need a nap soon and I don't want to miss the nap window.'

'Actually, can I meet you there later on? There's somewhere I need to go first.'

She looks at me for a second, before nodding. I wonder if she's guessed where I'm headed.

It doesn't take me long to walk from the main town to the boatyard where Joel works. I'm debating whether to ring him first or just turn up, worried that it's lunchtime and he might not be here at all, when he walks out of a hanger and spots me. He's wearing long shorts and a polo shirt, and his hair is sticking up in multiple directions behind his sunglasses, which are pushed up on his head. My stomach flips at the sight of him.

'Edie?'

'Sorry to just turn up when you're working.'

'I was actually on my way to grab lunch. Have you eaten?'

'I just had a picnic with Soph.'

'Ah, you were eating on Alfie time.' He smiles and my stomach flips again.

'Yeah, I'll probably be starving hours before dinner.'

'That's the risk but always a bit of a treat eating at eleven. I'm going to grab some food at a van further down if you want to walk with me? I mean, I'm being presumptuous that you came to see me.' He turns and gestures to the boats behind him. 'You're not here to buy a fixer-upper?'

'No, no. I came to see you.'

He puts his hands in his pockets and we start to walk back the way I came.

'Busy morning?' I ask.

'Kind of, we had to winch a sixty-foot yacht into a dry dock. They ran it aground and knocked a big hole in it.'

I nod along like it makes perfect sense to me, but I'm too jittery to pay close attention to what he's saying.

'What are you doing down here anyway? Day off?' he asks.

'I skived off work.'

'Aren't you the boss? Can't you do that whenever you want?'

'Technically I could, but I don't. First time ever.'

'Look at you living dangerously.'

'I know. I'm not sure what's next.'

'It's a slippery slope. Let's think, maybe it leads to doing drugs or joyriding.'

'Not sure on the drugs front, but we could steal a boat? If only your boat worked, we could have taken her for a spin.'

'I think much like you skiving off work when you're the boss, taking your mate's boat out for a sail, especially when you're going to make them sail it, wouldn't technically be stealing a boat.'

I laugh and my heart aches. It's moments like this when I'm reminded of the Joel I once knew and loved, and it makes me start to fall for him all over again, and I don't want him to leave now. Since my conversation with Miles, it's made me realise that I'm not entirely sure if all of those feelings ever really went away.

'So, um, did Soph tell you about next week?' He slips his sunglasses down over his eyes.

'About you getting married?'

He takes a deep breath and nods. He puts his hands in his pockets only to take them straight back out again.

'That's quite the commitment,' I say.

'It's not how it looks. It's just so I can work out there. The company that Verity works for seem great and they're interested in my CV but they can't sponsor me for a visa.'

It slowly sinks in.

'So you're marrying her to get one?'

'We looked into the different options a while ago before . . . the summer. It seemed like the simplest way and now Verity's got her job and she wants me to work towards getting mine there . . .'

I try and nod along like it makes sense but it doesn't and I can't stop the pain in my chest. It doesn't matter whether he is marrying her for convenience, or if it's more than that as Soph suggests, the end product is still the same – he's still leaving.

'And you want to go?'

'It's a good opportunity.' He shrugs. 'A new start.'

'Right, there's a lot of that going around at the moment. I've also come to a decision as well, about my job, that is. I'm going to talk to my dad about leaving the company, as I think I want to give teaching a go.'

Joel's the first person I've told and it feels strange hearing it out loud. I brace myself for his reaction.

'Really? That's so brave, but I think you'll be brilliant.'

'Thank you,' I say, breathing out a huge sigh of relief. 'I've wanted to leave for a while, but I've never seriously considered doing anything about it. You know, I haven't been able to shake that conversation we had on the beach about what I want from life, and I guess it made me realise there was nothing stopping me from going after my dreams. I'm just plucking up the courage to tell Dad.'

I wrinkle my nose up. I'm not looking forward to that one little bit.

'That's great. What does Miles think of it all?'

'Er, actually, we broke up.'

'Oh, I didn't know. Are you OK?'

'Yeah, it was the right thing to do. I've been doing a lot of thinking about what I want and I don't think that Miles is the right person to give it to me.'

He bites his lip and we walk along for a little while in silence. I don't know what I expected him to say. He didn't want me all those years ago, he doesn't want me now. I've got to stop imagining that what I feel for him is reciprocated.

'Look at us, adulting, choosing paths,' he says, making reference to the chat we had on the beach while watching the sunrise and us being at the crossroads in our lives.

He turns to me and I'm glad we've got sunglasses on because I don't want to look into his eyes, and I don't want him seeing how sad I am about his life choices.

'I know.'

'So when do you go?'

'Not right away. Verity's heading off next month, and then I'd have to apply for a visa to go, so it'll take a while.' He nudges my elbow with his. 'Why, are you going to miss me?'

'Maybe,' I say, trying to hide in my voice how much. 'Although, I'm more pissed off that I'm not going to have a seafaring adventure on *Hetty* now you're buggering off.'

'Glad you're going to miss me for me, and not my boat.'

'Your yacht, remember; sounds way more impressive.'

'Well, *Hetty* is almost seaworthy, so I might be able to take you out before I go.'

'That's a relief then.'

We reach a food truck on the edge of the marina and while Joel orders his lunch I go over and sit on a bench, looking out along the river. It's so peaceful here, far away from the normal tourists that flock down for the holidays.

Joel takes a seat next to me and he starts to eat.

'What are you going to do with *Hetty* when you go? Will you sell her?'

'I haven't really got that far yet. It seems a bit of a waste to keep her when I might not be back for a few years, but at the same time I'm going to have a hard time letting her go.'

'You seem so settled here.' It tumbles out before I can stop myself. 'I know it's none of my business.'

'No, it's fine,' he says, putting his wrap down on his lap. 'I do feel settled here, first time in a long time, but Key West is a great opportunity for me, and there's pretty much no other way I'd get there otherwise.'

I don't know a lot about the US, but I know that Key West is all palm trees and colourful wooden houses and if I was offered the opportunity to live there I'd probably jump at the chance. 'I've heard it's really miserable there. Bit drab and dull.'

'Are you getting confused with the UK?'

'Probably.' I do a kind of pathetic laugh, one tinged with sadness because how could we compete with Key West.

'I will miss you though, it's been nice becoming friends again.'

He nods. 'Yeah, it has. But I've heard that these days it's easy for friends to keep in touch with each other. Facebook and things.'

'I'm not big on social media but I could email.'

'I never had a lot of luck with you replying to those before.' He laughs an almost bitter laugh.

'What do you mean—' My phone starts to ring and I don't get to finish my sentence. I was going to mute it but then I see it's Claire. 'Sorry, I've got to take this.

'Hi Claire, everything OK?'

285

'Edie, thank god you picked up. Where are you? Are you at home?' She sounds panicked and she's speaking so quickly.

'I'm in Westerly, what's wrong?'

'There's no easy way to say this but Julie just phoned.' Her voice is pitching all over the place and I start to recognise the tone in her voice; I've only ever heard it once before. I feel sick and I'm having to grip my phone so hard because my hands are quaking. 'She said your dad wasn't feeling well this morning and he started to clutch his chest in pain and he was really red so she called the paramedics.'

My heart is pounding so loudly that I can hear the blood pulsing in my ears.

'Is he . . .' The words catch in my throat, I can't say them out loud. I can't lose my dad. I'm not sure at what point the tears start to roll down my face but my cheeks feel wet. Joel puts his hand on my arm, but I can barely acknowledge it.

'He's in the hospital, they think it's a heart attack. Julie's there on her own and she's scared because she doesn't know what is going on as you're his next of kin.'

I swallow hard.

'He's going to be OK though, isn't he?' My voice trails off.

'I hope so,' she says but she doesn't sound reassuring.

'It'll take me at least an hour from here and I need to get my car; it's in town.' I can't think straight.

'I'll look after Julie until you get there and if there's any update I'll phone you.'

I hang up the phone and it tumbles out of my hands. Joel catches it before it falls to the floor. My hands have started to shake and my legs feel weak and any second now I'm going to be sick.

'Dad's had a heart attack,' I say but it doesn't sound real. 'I've got to go and get my car, and I've got to drive to the hospital. I should never have taken the day off, I should never have—'

'I'll take you. My car's at the boatyard, it'll be quicker. Plus, you can't drive in this state.'

'You've got work and—'

'I wasn't there for you before when you needed me; I'm not making that mistake a second time.'

He stands up and pulls me up from under my elbow, forcing me to my feet and he holds me all the way to the car. It's a good job too because I don't think I would have made it unaided. I can't stop thinking the worst.

Joel helps me into the car and then runs round to the driver's side.

'I can't lose him, Joel. I can't.' I push my sunglasses up on top of my head as my tears overcome me.

He takes my hand and squeezes it tight whilst he starts the car.

'It's going to be OK, I'm here, OK, I'm here.'

I hope he's right, because I don't think I'm strong enough to go through it again.

Chapter 29

THEN

The countdown to the end of the season at Hartland's had well and truly begun. The children were back to school and the campsite had grown quieter. We had less than a week until it closed for the season.

I'd spent so much of the summer dreading the moment I'd have to leave, but suddenly it couldn't come quickly enough. It was as if things had switched; one minute Joel and I were spending every waking minute together, and then the next, he was going out of his way to avoid me.

At first I thought I was imagining it, that with fewer staff we were all a little busier and that he didn't have time to see me. But soon I realised he was deliberately leaving the room almost as soon as I entered it.

If Soph and Douglas noticed, they didn't say anything, although I wasn't exactly going to bring it up with them either, as I'd never confessed my feelings for Joel before and it would be pointless to do so when I knew he didn't feel the same.

After a week of Joel's weird behaviour, I'd had enough and decided I needed to break free of the misery and do something to help forget my troubles; I roped Soph into the mission, a night out just the two of us, and I wasn't holding back on the pre-drinks.

Elizabeth was out, thankfully, so Soph had the music cranked up in her room and it filled the flat. She walked into my room with yet another drink whilst I was crouched on the floor applying my eye make-up. I stood up to take it from her and my head spun, and I staggered into the wall.

'You're such a lightweight,' she said and we laughed like it was the funniest thing we'd ever heard. 'We better get dressed or else we're never going to make the pub.'

'You're right.' I took the drink and placed it on the dresser before I flicked through the clothes in my wardrobe. I pulled out various tops and skirts and settled on a dress that left little to the imagination.

There was a pause between songs on the CD and I heard a creaking sound coming from the room above. I glared at the ceiling; Joel and his squeaky ab cradle. I'd just about managed to get him out of my mind as well. 'Hollaback Girl' came on and drowned it out.

'Wow, that dress is hot,' said Soph, dancing her way into my room. 'Where have you been keeping that all summer?'

She looked down at her jeans and her halterneck top and shook her head. 'I'm going to go change.'

She came back a few minutes later with another drink, dressed in the shortest skirt that I'd ever seen. It was almost as small as the wide belts that she wore.

'A toast to us looking fabulous and hot. Tonight we're going to be beating off men with sticks, looking like this. Who needs fucking Brian and Scott?'

I didn't want to correct her that my foul mood had nothing to do with my ex, so I toasted to it and downed my drink.

She stood next to me and admired our reflection in the mirror.

'If we don't pull tonight, there's something seriously wrong with the men in this town. Let's go.'

I slipped my feet into my heels and we picked up our small bags that just about fit our ID, bank card, phone and a lipstick and we headed out the door.

'Do you think we should see if Douglas and Joel want to come?' she asked, slamming the door behind us. Anger rippled over me at the mention of Joel. I'd been heartbroken about how he'd been treating me, but the alcohol had turned it into rage.

I was about to tell her where to go with that suggestion, but now, with my abundance of Dutch courage, I wanted to tell him exactly how mad I was at him.

'OK. You go and knock on Douglas's door and I'll find Joel,' I said, almost hissing his name.

'Excellent, I'll meet you at the end of the block in a few minutes.'

She headed downstairs and I headed up. I should have known how drunk I was when I kept ricocheting like a pinball off the banisters, but I made it to the front door of Joel's flat. I tried the door and, finding it open, I went inside without knocking. I did the same to his room, expecting to find him mid-workout, but I froze in horror when instead I saw Elizabeth lying in his bed.

At first I thought I'd made a mistake, that I'd got the wrong room, but then I noticed Joel's *Sin City* poster on the wall, followed by his overly large tub of protein powder on his dresser and finally my eyes fell on the ab cradle in the centre of the floor.

Elizabeth didn't say a word. She pulled the sheets over her naked shoulders and a small smile spread over her lips.

I stumbled backwards, my head spinning and this time not because of the alcohol. The toilet flushed in the bathroom and I knew Joel would be out any second. I slipped off my heels, picked them up and I hurried out of the flat. I ran down the metal stairs, the lattice imprinting in my feet but I barely registered the pain. I kept running when I reached the ground floor, out of the staff quarters, over the grass where we played midnight frisbee and down the path to the beach. I didn't stop until I was ankle deep in the cold water.

I panted for breath, feeling desperately sick, the image of Elizabeth and her small smile indelible in my mind.

My phone rang and I hurried to answer it, thinking it would be Soph wondering where I'd got to.

'Hello,' I answered.

'Edie? Are you OK?'

'Mum?' I almost dropped the phone in surprise. I couldn't speak to her when I was this drunk.

'Did the caller ID not give that away?'

'I didn't look, I was, I was . . .'

I thought of Elizabeth and rage bubbled up inside me. Why her and not me? I didn't want to worry Mum, so I tried to cover the microphone as I started to sob.

'Edie, what's wrong? What's happened?' Her voice was becoming more panicked and it just made me cry harder because all I wanted was for her to wrap me up in her arms and stroke my hair, telling me it was going to all be all right.

'It's nothing,' I said, stepping out of the water. I sank down onto the sand.

'Doesn't sound like it. Are you drunk? Where are you?'

'I've only had a few.' I could hear the words coming out slurred. 'Don't worry about me, I'm being silly and getting sad over nothing. I'll call you tomorrow.'

'Edie.'

'Mum, I'm fine.'

There was a sharp intake of breath on the other end of the line. 'You'll call me back later if you need me? Your dad and I are always here, *always*. We're only an hour up the road if you need us. Do you want us to come down? We're not doing anything tonight.'

I nodded, relief flooded over me before I stopped myself. This summer was supposed to be me taking my first steps into my adult life. I was going to have to learn to deal with things without running to them. I'd be at university soon and they wouldn't be there to hold my hand each time.

'No, I'm fine. Really. I'll speak to you tomorrow.'

'I'm worried about you. Call me before that if you need me.'

'I will.'

'I love you.'

'I love you too,' I said, hanging up the phone, my heart aching for how much I needed her.

My phone rang almost instantly again and this time it was Soph. I wiped the tears away and told her I'd meet her at the end of the road, I didn't want to go back to the campsite. I couldn't face running into Joel, or seeing Elizabeth with that smug look on her face. I wanted to go into town and I wanted to get so drunk that I didn't remember it at all.

★

I woke up the next morning to Soph banging on my door. I pulled a pillow over my head and writhed in pain whilst she came in and sat on my bed.

'Edie,' she said softly, 'Lionel's here. He needs you to get dressed and go with him.'

'Fuck, what did I do last night? Did I do something really awful? I can't remember anything after us getting to the pub.'

I panicked, thinking that I'd gone and smashed up the place enraged about Joel and Elizabeth, but Soph shook her head. It was then that I noticed that she was shaking and I sat up.

'What is it? What's happened?'

'I don't know exactly, but Lionel said it's serious and there's someone here to see you.'

I slid out of bed, my head pounding at every little movement. I shoved a fleece over my pyjamas and slipped on a pair of flip-flops.

Lionel was standing outside on the walkway and he tilted his head when he saw me. I noticed he wouldn't meet my eyes.

'What's wrong? What's happened?'

'Edie, someone's here to see you. One of your parents' friends.'

My stomach lurched. It could only be bad news.

Lionel led me to the staffroom and when I walked in and I saw Claire, her face confirmed it. It was red and puffy and she looked like she'd been crying.

'Edie,' her voice quaked. She reached over and took both of my hands in hers and squeezed them tight. 'It's your mum and dad. They were in a car accident. Your dad's all right, just a bit battered and bruised, but your mum . . .' Her lip started to tremble and she was fighting hard to blink back the tears. 'Your mum . . .'

She didn't need to finish the sentence.

My legs fell away from me and Claire did her best to hold me up.

'I think I'm going to be sick.'

I turned round and vomited on the floor, I couldn't help it.

'I'm so sorry, Edie.'

'How?' I whispered and she told me but I don't think I really heard. I later found out they'd been on the motorway driving towards Westerly when they'd been caught in a heavy downpour. The rain had caused flash flooding and they'd aquaplaned, losing control.

My fists formed into balls and my lips started to shake. I knew my life wasn't going to be the same. All I wanted to do was be with my dad.

What happened next was a bit of a blur. Soph was there at different points. Lionel cleaned up the floor, which if it was at any other time I'd have marvelled at because I'd never seen him get his hands dirty. Douglas held me whilst Soph packed my things, but Joel was nowhere to be seen. Not that I wanted to see him. If I hadn't gone to his room or got that drunk, then Claire wouldn't be here telling me about my parents' accident. I knew I couldn't entirely blame him, that the fault lay with me for drinking too much and spiralling out of control.

I was bustled into a car and my hastily packed kit put in the boot. I leant my head against the window and cradled the bucket that Lionel had given me, my hangover raging, but that wasn't the worst of my pain.

My mum was gone. All I could think of as grief tightened its grip on my heart was that I was never going to see her again and it was all my fault.

Chapter 30

The car journey to the hospital is the longest I've ever taken in my life. It's only usually an hour to Basingstoke from Westerly but it seems to have taken ten times longer today. Joel screeches to a halt at the drop-off bay.

'Thank you, for bringing me.' I gather up my bag and release my seat belt. I look out at the vastness of the hospital; the sounds of sirens in the background are making it feel all too real.

'Of course. Let me park up and I can come in and wait with you.'

'I couldn't ask you to do that.'

'You didn't, I offered.'

I lean over and I give him a hug.

'No need, I'll be fine. Thank you anyway.'

I get out of the car and hurry to the reception. After enquiring about Dad's ward, I navigate the rabbit warren of corridors to the family room where Julie and Claire are waiting inside.

Julie bursts into tears when she sees me and I do exactly the same. It's written all over her face how worried she is about Dad. I walk over and hug her and it makes her cry even more.

'He's going to be OK,' I tell her. 'I take it there's no more news?'

I pull away and look over at Claire who shakes her head. She hands us both a tissue then gives me a hug.

'I'm sure I sound like a broken record, but no news is good news,' she says. 'Listen, now that Edie's here, do you two want to be alone?'

Both Julie and I reach our hands out and take hers.

'No, stay, please,' I say, my voice shaky.

The door to the family room opens and a young male doctor walks in and I squeeze Claire's hand tighter.

'Is he OK?' I ask. My heart feels like it's in my mouth. I finally understand what that expression means. 'Was it a heart attack?'

'It wasn't a heart attack,' he says. Julie yelps with relief and I stand there motionless, almost unable to believe it. 'But it is unstable angina, which could lead to a heart attack if we don't act. His arteries are blocked and we're going to need to put a stent in; do you know what that is?'

I shake my head, I don't have a clue. The doctor explains that it's a surgical procedure to insert a little balloon-like contraption that inflates to open his arteries.

'We're going to do it at some point today or tomorrow. I'm not sure yet on schedules, but we'll keep you posted. I should explain that there are some risks, as there are with most procedures, but you still need to be aware of them. When we know more about when the surgery will be, we'll talk you and Mr Porter through this all, but I just wanted to keep you in the loop.'

'Can we see him?' I ask.

'Yes, he's having some tests done at the moment, but I'll get a nurse to come and fetch you when they're finished.'

'Thank you,' says Julie. When he's left, she turns to me, wiping under her eyes. 'That's good news, isn't it?'

'I think so.' I nod slowly, trying to process it all. 'It sounds like they caught it in time at least.'

'Yeah, that's what I thought.'

I sit down on one of the plastic chairs and hang my head in my hands.

Claire rubs my back. 'I'll go get us some coffees, OK?'

She heads out and I let out a deep breath. Julie walks over and sits next to me.

'I'm glad you're here,' I say, biting my lip. I feel a little guilty that I haven't taken up Dad's offers to get to know her sooner.

'You are?'

'Yes, it's nice to know that I'm not alone. We can support each other.'

I notice Julie's hands trembling in her lap.

'Dad will pull through, he always does. And we're going to get through this, OK?'

She nods.

'I know it hasn't been an easy time for you, with me dating your dad, but I really do care for him. It might have only been a few months, but he makes me so happy and it just feels right.'

Dad's a lucky man to have a woman like Julie in his life. I can't help but think of Joel. He's the only person who has made me feel truly connected with someone.

'We haven't had much time to get to know each other properly, and that's my fault.' I think of the emails and how they've made me that much braver and how they've been pushing me to be more open. 'Seeing you with Dad is harder than I expected it would be. I didn't realise how him meeting someone that he really cared about would affect me and it left me feeling unsure how I would fit into his new life. I'm sorry; it sounds so pathetic, especially when I've wanted him to meet someone and to finally move on for so long. It's just hard.'

Julie smiles with compassion.

'I know how much you mean to your dad. He talks about you all the time and he is so proud of you. But I understand that it must be hard, especially as your mum sounded like such a wonderful woman and I don't want to get in the way of her memory. I know he still loves her and he always will, and that's OK. He's got a big heart. He's allowed to love her and me, and you. There's room for all of us in his life.'

I don't know how I'm holding it together. She really is the nicest woman he could have picked.

The nurse comes in and tells us that we can go in one at a time.

'Thank you, I needed to hear that.' I smile at her to show that there's no bad blood between us. 'Do you mind if I go first? I promise I'll be quick.'

'Of course, I wouldn't expect it any other way.'

I squeeze her hand and the nurse leads me onto the ward, and behind the curtain to where my dad is.

He looks terrible. He's so pale and he looks so much older than he did when I last saw him at work on Friday. He's hooked up to machines that are whirring away and he just seems so vulnerable.

I sit down, taking his hand in mine.

'Sorry for giving everyone such a fright,' he says, like every word is an effort.

'When you're better I'll give you a proper telling off. I don't know about you, but I almost had a heart attack when I heard the news.'

He tries to smile, but winces in pain as he does so.

'I thought I was going to lose you.' A tear rolls down my cheek and I try and hold it together. 'I thought . . .'

'Edie, I'm not going anywhere, not yet anyway.'

He squeezes my hand back. There's so much I need to say to him but he looks so tired. Now's not the time.

'Julie's here, I'll go so that she can come in. But I want you to know that I love you, and I'll be in the waiting room, OK?'

'I love you too, sweetheart. One thing this experience has taught me is that life's too short. So I know things aren't great between you and Miles but you should call him,' he says in staggered breaths.

At his words, my heart aches at just how little time we've spent together lately. I haven't had a chance to tell him yet the reason for our break-up. I didn't realise he assumed we'd just had some sort of lovers' tiff and that we're going to get back together.

'I'll get Julie,' I say. I promise myself I'll tell Dad everything as soon as he's better.

I let go of his hand, even though it pains me to do so, and I search out Julie, who's grateful for her turn.

I update Claire and talking it through makes everything that's happened start to sink in.

'I think I might go and get a breath of fresh air; this has all been . . .' I can't finish my sentence, I'm too overcome with emotion.

'Of course, you go,' she says.

'I won't be long.'

'Take all the time you need, love. We'll call if anything changes.'

I weave my way back through the corridors until finally I find myself out at the main entrance again. I'm almost surprised that it's warm outside when the doors open and the brightness of the sunlight dazzles my eyes. The air is humid and thundery and it's not quite the fresh air I'd envisaged.

I head away from the main entrance to get some space and I see Joel sitting on a wall, looking at his phone.

'Hey, you're still here.' I walk over and put my hands on my hips like I'm pretending I'm cross but in reality I'm anything but. He stands up and he hugs me tight and I want to stay in his arms forever.

'How is he?'

I pull away.

'He's going to be OK.' My head's feeling light and I perch on the wall to support myself. 'It wasn't a full-blown heart attack, but he's got to have an operation, with a stent or something put in. But they think he'll make a full recovery.'

'Oh, Edie.'

I nod. 'Please don't say anything more. I've stopped crying for the moment and I don't want to start again.'

'But sometimes it helps to let everything out.'

He leads me along the pavement and we walk to a quieter end of the hospital grounds where there's a bench and we sit down.

'When I got that phone call, all I could think was that I was going to lose him like I lost Mum, that history was repeating itself. I felt so selfish thinking that just when I started to dream again it would all be taken away from me once more – that my notes to self would have been for nothing.'

It comes tumbling out like a stream of consciousness and I don't realise what I've said until I spot the confusion on Joel's face.

'What notes to self?'

I take a deep breath. It's not like I've got anything to lose by telling Joel about the emails. He's never been one to judge and has always put me at such ease that I feel like I could share almost anything with him.

'When we were at Hartland's all those years ago, I started writing emails to myself.'

'Right. Like some sort of diary?'

'Sort of, but they were emails to the future.' It sounds so far-fetched. 'I used this site called Note to Future Self that stores your emails and then sends you them at the date that you've set. Sort of like a time capsule. So, I'd decided to write to my thirty-five-year-old self. They were mainly little insights into my eighteen-year-old mind, but the emails would end with these little challenges, which were cheesy and cringey, but somehow, I've found myself doing them.'

'Like some sort of bucket list?'

'Along those lines but more like try something new, do something that makes you laugh, step out of your comfort zone, et cetera.'

'Skive off work?' He raises an eyebrow.

'Something like that, yeah.' I rub at my tear-stained face. 'The emails reminded me of that summer and that's why I looked up Soph.'

'Now it all makes sense.' He runs his hand through his hair. 'This all sounds a bit sci-fi to me.'

'I know. I can't believe it actually worked, to be honest. Usually I'd be sat at reception during a quiet shift and play around with words and notes, never thinking anything would ever come from it. It was just a bit of fun.'

'You wrote them when you were on reception?' he says, sitting up a little straighter.

'Yeah, if no one was about.'

'And you didn't ever receive a copy of these emails when you sent them?'

'No, you'd write your messages on the website, click send and that's the last you'd see of them until they're delivered on the pre-arranged date. To be honest, I'd completely forgotten that I'd even written them until I received the first one on my birthday.'

'And you've been getting them regularly?'

'Yeah, but it'll stop after next Wednesday, as I never wrote any more emails after my mum died.'

'Next week?' His voice has gone up an octave.

'Uh-huh. I'm actually going to miss them. I keep checking my phone, wondering when I'm going to get the last one, if I haven't already.'

I turn my phone over in my hands hoping that I'll get one more before next week and I see that it's not on.

'Shit, I switched my phone off when I went to see Dad in case it interfered with the machines. What if they were trying to contact me?'

I fumble trying to turn it on.

'You haven't been out for long, I'm sure everything's fine.'

I turn and look at the hospital in a panic. What if Claire was looking for me? The sheer number of windows show the scale of how many rooms and corridors there are, and there's such a hive of activity by the main entrance with people coming and going; she'd never have found me.

'I think I need to go back in to check everything's OK.' I stare at my screen coming back to life; it's not beeping with any messages but it doesn't mean to say they haven't tried to contact me. 'Do you want to come up?'

'Actually . . . I should probably head off.'

'Oh, right. Yes, of course.' I try and hide the disappointment in my voice that he's leaving. 'Thank you for everything, I honestly don't know what I would have done without you today.'

I lean over to give him a hug but he's all rigid and tense.

'I hope everything goes well with your dad's surgery.'

'Thanks,' I say, standing up.

We say our goodbyes and I head off back to the labyrinth of corridors, anxious to see Dad. When I get to the main entrance I turn back, hoping for one last look at Joel and I see him still sitting on the bench with his head hanging in his hands. I'm torn between wanting to check he's OK and to see Dad.

My phone beeps and I see it's a text from Claire.

Doctor's on his way to talk to your dad about surgery.
Scheduled for this afternoon. X

I type back that I'm on my way and I hurry through the automatic doors. It's probably just been a long day for Joel. I'll send him a message later, letting him know how grateful I am again for all he's done today, but right now I've got to focus on my dad.

Chapter 31

The days after Dad's heart surgery pass in a blur. The operation was a success and he was back home the following day. It felt so sudden that one minute I was fearing the worst and the next he's at home in his PJs watching daytime TV. I offered to stay whilst he recuperated, but Julie beat me to it and surprisingly it didn't bother me one bit. Since our chat at the hospital, I feel as though we've had a breakthrough with how I've felt; it's honestly a relief and comfort to know she's there to look after him all the time. I've got to make the time to get to know her properly; I owe it to Dad and to her. And now, instead of dreading it, I'm starting to look forward to it.

With Dad resting at home, work has been hectic. Whilst we often joke that he doesn't do any actual work, this week has proved otherwise. Everyone's missing him and we know the sombre mood won't lift until he's sat back at his desk. But the doctor advised against it at least until a few weeks' time, given the severity of his surgery.

I'm not sure when he'll be back but with everything that's happened, I can't leave the company now. Not when they need me. Maybe it's a sign that becoming a teacher wasn't meant to be. Typical, just as I plucked up the courage to tell Dad, this happens.

But just because I accept that my plans have had to change, doesn't mean to say that I don't feel absolutely gutted.

I've been trying my best to pretend that everything's OK, but I'm failing miserably. I've been in a terrible mood and found myself snapping at the staff about the silliest of things, something I've very rarely done before, and it's not fair to take out my frustration on those around me. So, I've thrown myself into an unhealthy amount of work.

'Are you getting any sleep?' Layla deposits a cup of coffee on my desk along with a sandwich. She and Claire seem to have taken it in turns to make sure that I'm eating. 'You look exhausted.'

'I'm OK, it's just lots of things need to get done. A ship misses its captain.'

Claire comes over and sits on the edge of my desk.

'We know these next few weeks are going to be difficult for you,' she says, 'and we're all prepared to do more. Aaron and I have worked here for so long, we practically know the company inside out and can cover for you and your dad.'

'And I can put in extra hours,' chips in Layla. 'Believe me, it's less work being here than it is at home.'

'I'm fine, really there's no need.' I take a large sip of coffee and it makes me realise how dry my mouth is; I can't remember when I last had a drink.

'Edie, you don't need to do this alone. You've said it on numerous occasions yourself, this place is a family. You don't have to be a martyr.'

Claire's never one to mince her words but she's never spoken to me like that before.

'But I can't afford to take my eye off the ball. The last time I did that, Dad ended up in hospital from all the stress.'

'Or maybe it's because he doesn't actually do the exercise he should do, and that he sneaks off to the greasy spoon on King Street and has a bacon butty or a full English most mornings. Whatever you think you did or didn't do, it's not your fault,' Claire tells me.

'Look, we're just trying to say' – Layla looks at Claire like they're drifting off topic – 'that we are here for you and can help.'

My head's starting to throb and I rub my temples. Deep down, the logical part of my brain knows they're right. I appreciate what they're doing for me but I need my work to distract me more than ever, to take my mind off everything, especially the upcoming anniversary of Mum's death.

'I'll let you know. Thanks for the sandwich and the drink, Layla.'

My stomach sinks watching the two of them head back to their desks, and I don't miss the concerned look they throw each other. They were only trying to help and I pushed them away. It's easier this way. My priorities are work and Dad, and I can't allow any more distractions into my life. Not Layla and Claire. Not Joel. It's like I'm constantly acting like a dam to my emotions and I'm worried if I let anyone breach the walls that they'll get swept away in the torrent that comes out.

When I eventually leave the office I head straight over to Dad's.

'You must be starving,' says Julie, opening the door to me. 'You haven't just left work have you?'

'There's a lot to do.'

She frowns and ushers me in. 'I cooked a moussaka, let me heat some up.'

'That'll be great. It smells amazing.' I follow her into the kitchen and see it sitting on the side.

'Did you even eat lunch?'

'I did.'

Julie raises a questioning eyebrow.

'Layla put it on my desk.'

'Good. I'm glad.'

She scoops a big chunk of moussaka out of the dish and places it on a plate.

'How's the patient doing?'

'Better. He's starting to get his sense of humour back, which is the last thing we need.' She rolls her eyes and laughs. 'He's awake if you want to pop your head round and say hello?'

I head on up, lightly knocking at the bedroom door in case he's drifted off to sleep.

'Come in,' he calls.

I find him propped up in bed, the television going, and he puts it on mute as I walk in and sit on the edge of the bed. There might be more colour in his cheeks but he still looks gaunt.

'I was hoping that you were coming to bring me some of whatever smells so good from the kitchen. Julie's stress cooking and she's feeding me none of it.'

'Surely she's giving you food?'

'Oh, she is all right, but it's all meals from the nutritional sheets the hospital gave me. You know, lentils and broccoli and steamed fish. Anything without a hint of taste basically.'

'And without a hint of grease that got you in this state in the first place,' I scold.

He laughs then stops before he hurts himself even more.

'How's the office?'

'Still there.'

He looks blankly at me, waiting for me to elaborate.

'That's all you're going to give me?'

'Yes, you're signed off from work for a reason.'

'I know, but I want to make sure you're all coping.'

'Of course we are. Everyone's pitching in.' Or at least they would if I let them.

'That's what I like to hear.'

I haven't spoken to Dad one on one much since the surgery as he's been quite out of it on painkillers. But now he seems very much lucid.

'I'm sorry, by the way,' I say, concentrating on his grey bed-spread.

'For not smuggling up the food from the kitchen?'

'No,' I say, laughing. Julie was right, he was beginning to get his cheekiness back. 'For leaving you to deal with the company alone while I've been distracted this summer.'

'Edie, you're not to apologise. If anything, I'm grateful for the summer because for once, you've been putting yourself first. No one is at fault except for me and my lifestyle. As much as I hate the new diet, I'm going to stick to it, because this was the wake-up call I needed.'

He takes a deep breath and I'm worried that I shouldn't have said anything when he's supposed to be resting.

'You know, one day you're going to have to realise that life isn't about living with regret, constantly blaming yourself and feeling guilty for everything that goes wrong. You didn't cause my angina any more than you did your mum's accident.'

My stomach drops. How can he not think the accident was my fault?

'But it'd never have happened if I hadn't been stupid and drunk in the first place; I wouldn't have worried her and she wouldn't have needed to see me.'

'And if I hadn't have had a couple of beers, I would have been the one driving. Or if we'd left ten minutes earlier or were driving on a different part of the road, then we might not have aquaplaned. Believe me, Edie, I did exactly the same blame game for years, always thinking "what if", wishing it had been me in the driver's seat rather than Jan. But if there's one thing I learnt while getting sober it's that as much as you want to, you can't change the past, and you instead need to move on with your life.'

Julie calls up the stairs that my dinner's ready.

'I don't want you to blame yourself for what's happened – this is all me and me alone.'

I nod, trying to take it all in. I give him a big hug before walking out.

'And don't forget if there's any spare food going you don't want . . .'

I turn back, leaning on the doorway.

'I'm sure Julie's got some more lentils you could have.'

He gives me a hard stare and unmutes his telly and I head downstairs.

I know he's right, that I can't change the past and I know it's time to accept that and move on, but I can't help thinking that's easier said than done.

Chapter 32

When Thursday rolls around, I'm completely exhausted and all I want to do is go home, have a long hot soak in the bath and go to bed, but I can't because it's Big Little Readers and I wouldn't want to let anyone at the charity down, especially Lola.

Claudia is taking Arnold's place today as he's staying down in Cornwall with his daughter.

'How's the new term going?' I ask, climbing into the passenger seat of her car.

'Hectic, but glad to be back. I know I won't be saying that by half term, but there's always something special about that new-term feeling you get. Everything feels fresh and exciting, and anything seems possible.'

'Sounds amazing.'

I don't mean to sound quite so wistful, but I can't help but feel a little jealous.

'Speaking of new starts. I was going to email this over but I thought it easier to say in person.' She pulls a piece of paper out of her bag. 'A friend of mine is speaking at an event for aspiring teachers looking for a career change. The speakers are all ex-professionals, like solicitors, accountants, IT workers, who have retrained. They're offering advice and tips about the challenges of switching to teaching, as well as giving practical insight into the different training routes and the options available. I thought it might appeal to you.' She hands me the paper with a hopeful smile on her face.

'Oh, um, thanks.' I take it from her, but I feel a rush of sadness at how only last week I would have jumped at this opportunity, but so much has changed since then. 'I'll take a look.'

She places her bag on the back seat and is about to pull away from the curb when she stops and turns back to me.

'I thought you would have been more excited about it. Is everything OK?'

I try and put a brave smile on my face.

'My dad almost had a heart attack recently and needed an emergency operation. He's on the mend now; it just means he's going to have to take it easy for a while and now's not a good time to leave the company.'

'Oh, your poor dad. I'm glad he's OK though.' She opens her mouth as if she's going to say something else but closes it again.

'What? You can say it, whatever it is.' I turn to look at her and she smiles, softly.

'I was going to say that there's always going to be a reason not to do something. It's never going to be a good time to retrain and start your life again. I know it's not like you have to do it. You've got a lovely flat and it sounds like you've got a good job, so in some ways you'd probably be crazy to change.' She pauses and I know there's more.

'But . . .'

'But,' she says, turning to look at me, 'you've got to ask yourself, if you reached your dad's age, would you be happy with the life you've led?'

The question throws me because I know the answer almost immediately. I don't even have to reply, I'm sure she can see it written on my face. She smiles at me with compassion before she slips the car in gear and pulls away.

Her words remind me of my notes to self. When past me asked if I was happy I knew instinctively I wasn't. If I don't do anything to change my life then I can't imagine future me would be any happier.

I read through the printout on the drive and the day sounds perfect, exactly what I'd be interested in.

'I spoke to Lola's new teacher over lunch to see how she's getting on,' Claudia says, interrupting my thoughts, and I fold up the piece of paper and place it on top of my bag in the footwell. 'She said that she's really quiet but that she's participating a little bit. Apparently, she comes alive when they do story time at the end of the day, and today she even put her hand up to ask a question.'

'That's great. Do you think these sessions have made a difference?'

'I honestly do. I wouldn't think that it's a coincidence that she feels most comfortable in school when books are involved.'

I think of Lola and the sadness in her eyes, and the thought that we could be making a tiny bit of a difference pulls at my heart strings.

We soon settle into Lola's living room and she shyly says hello to Claudia.

I pick up a book about witches and start to read, and Claudia follows up with a story about an enchanted dinosaur. We try to engage Lola in some way, both of us asking questions about the stories as we go along, and it is an encouraging sign when

Lola answers every now and again, but there isn't that magical transformation that I was really rooting for. I guess part of me wants Claudia to be dazzled by how much progress she's made, and whilst Lola's made huge leaps from our first visit, Arnold and I still haven't succeeded in bringing her completely out of her shell.

When we've finished reading for the day, Kate pops her head round the door whilst we're packing away the books.

'Lola, did you want to go upstairs and get you-know-what to show Edie before she leaves?'

Lola gives me a look like she's contemplating it, whatever it is, before she slides off the sofa and hurries up the stairs.

'How's it all going, Kate?' asks Claudia, standing up from her stool.

'We have some good and some bad days. We're having slightly less bad days than before so I'm taking that as a small victory. I think it's helped that she's back at school and around friends. Occasionally I get glimpses of the niece that I knew before and it makes me happy.'

'Well, you know that if there's anything more that the school could do to help.'

'Thank you, you've already done so much. And these visits, I know it might not seem like a lot each week, but she'll have a little smile on her face for the rest of the evening, and for those few hours she doesn't seem as sad.'

She goes quiet as the footsteps become louder again on the stairs.

Lola comes back into the room and she's holding a painted jam jar. The glass is painted with rainbow colours and there's a string handle tied around the top. I recognise it immediately.

'Oh, Lola, is that a memory jar? Did you make one like in the book?'

She nods.

'But that isn't your jar, is it?' says Kate.

'Mine's over there.' She points to the bookshelf where there are two jars painted in bright colours and through the paint I can see little pieces of paper folded up inside.

'We had so many memories, we had to make two jars, didn't we, Lola?' Kate gives her an encouraging smile and she nods back. 'We try to talk about Ruth, Lola's mum, every day, don't we? And when we talk of a different memory, we make sure that we add it to the jar.'

I blink back a tear.

'That's so lovely.' I just about manage to keep my voice from breaking.

'So what's the third jar for? Is that for more memories?' asks Claudia, pointing at the jar.

'It's for Edie.' She doesn't look at me as she holds it out. I take it gently and she instantly goes and hides behind Kate's legs.

'For me?' I'm lost for words.

She nods, not quite meeting my eyes.

'Lola told me about your mum, Edie, and she said that you don't have a memory jar and, well, we thought that you might want one of your own.'

Claudia whimpers and I don't dare look at her as I'm trying hard not to cry. My heart feels fit to explode.

I bend down so that I'm on the same level as Lola, holding up the jar and examining it from different angles.

'This is so beautiful. Did you paint it yourself?'

She nods and looks pleased.

'How did you know my mum loved rainbows? It's so amazing. I can't thank you enough. I'm going to go home and fill it up straight away.'

'Don't forget to ask other people for their memories too,' she says, 'like Rusty.'

I'm so taken aback by the full sentence she's just said that I can't answer her immediately. I let it sink in and I smile.

'That's a fantastic idea. I can ask my dad and perhaps some of her friends. Thank you, I think this is the best present I've ever received.' I stand back up and Kate pats me on the arm, my eyes glossy with tears.

'I hope it's as useful for you as it has been to us.'

I nod and Claudia steps in and takes over discussing next week because I'm totally choked up with emotion.

I get into the car and I sit there in a stunned silence, staring at the jar.

'Oh Edie,' says Claudia, climbing into the driver's seat. 'Are you OK? Do you need a hug?'

'I think if you gave me one it might open the floodgates of tears. I honestly meant it, it's the best present I've ever received.'

'I know. I get some nice presents at the end of term, but that . . . What a sweetie.'

Claudia squeezes my arm and then starts the engine and pulls away.

We drive back to the library in silence. My mind is racing with all the memories I have of my mum from my childhood. When we pull up at the library car park we unload the boxes of books back inside and then I head back to Claudia's car to collect the jar.

'Don't forget this.' She reaches over to the printout about the career day.

'Thank you.' I take it and slip it into my handbag. It must have fallen onto the floor as I grabbed my bag from the car.

'Edie, I'm sorry for being so pushy. Robin's always telling me that I get too invested in other people's lives, which is a nice way of him saying that I meddle too much.'

'You don't at all. I will look into it.'

'I hope you do. I mean, watching you today and seeing what an impression you've made on Lola, it only confirmed what I know. That you'd make a brilliant teacher. She's one girl you've been able to help but imagine if you had a class of thirty-five every year.'

'I could make a difference.' My voice is small as the magnitude of possibility sinks in.

'You certainly could. But even if you decide to stay where you are, I hope that you keep volunteering with us, because you're really good at it.'

'Oh, I will.' I slip my bag over my shoulder. 'Right, I'm going to go before I start to cry and I've done far too much of that lately.'

'OK. Hopefully I'll see you again soon. Maybe we could meet for coffee one weekend.'

'Yes, definitely. Or perhaps you can come along with Layla to see the improv competition I've been roped into taking part in?'

'I'd love to. Aaron mentioned it at your gathering. Did you make the final?'

'We did, no thanks to me. But Layla and I will be going for a drink before the show, so you're welcome to join us and we can head over together.'

Claudia's smile is wide and she's nodding along.

'Text me the details, I'm there.'

She leans over and gives me a hug goodbye and I feel like we've really started to form a friendship.

I walk back towards my flat, clutching the memory jar to my chest like it's the most precious item in the world. It's amazing to think that something as simple as reading a book has helped someone. And for the first time in a long time, I can't help but feel proud of myself.

Chapter 33

I can't believe it's not even been a week since I got the call about Dad. It seems like a lifetime ago. Between work and checking in on him, I haven't had a chance to pick up my car – the one I abandoned outside Soph's house when Joel drove me to the hospital on Monday.

But this weekend is the first opportunity I've had to collect it. I spend most of the train journey trying to work out a plan to divide Dad's workload. I desperately don't want him to return to a backlog of work, for fear of making his condition worse, but Layla and Claire are right, it shouldn't have to fall on my shoulders alone. Aaron and Claire are more than capable of taking on extra responsibility and if we hire a temp to pick up some of their admin then it might just work. I finish my notes and, even though I haven't told anyone else my plan, my shoulders feel that little bit lighter.

We can't be far away from Westerly so I pack up my papers and I pull out my phone, ready to check the news, when I realise that I haven't checked my personal emails yet, not since yesterday afternoon. I get that little tingly feeling of anticipation, wondering if I'm going to find one last email before they all stop. I open my inbox and scan through marketing emails, and my stomach does a flip as I see the familiar little words, note to future self: hey!!!!

I'm about to click on it when I spot another one below it, only it's not from me.

I open it up, confused and wondering what the hell's going on.

```
hi edie, surprise! it's me joel. i know what
you're thinking, why am i sending you an
email, especially as i'm sat in reception
whilst you've gone off to check a caravan
inventory and i know you're going to be back
any minute. bollocks if you're reading this
and i'm still in the room - do not read any
further. please!

    if however you're reading this and i have
gone, then that's OK. i've actually been want-
ing to talk to you for some time, but i have
bottled it up so much that i thought if
i wrote it to you it might be easier. i tried
to write you a letter, but i didn't think
you'd be able to read the scrawl and also
i worried douglas or soph would get hold of
it and they'd rip the piss out of me forever
more. then when we were chatting here on
reception and you got called away i saw you'd
left your email open, and your email address
was there, i thought it was a sign.

    ok, i should probably tell you what i want
to say now before i lose my courage.

    from almost the first time i met you i've
```

known you were something special. or almost
the first time i met you, when I sobered up
and realised what was going on. i thought at
first it was because you were cool and we got
on so well. obviously you were with scott and
we became such good friends and i thought
that being friends was enough for me. but
every time we're together, i fall for you
a little bit more. i've never found anyone
that gets me or my humour, like when there's
that tumbleweed moment where no one else in
the conversation laughs and then you do your
laugh where you bark like a sea lion - the
one that's all spontaneous, and honestly,
there's no better sound. and then there was
that moment we had in my room, before we were
interrupted by soph, and i really, really
wanted to kiss you. i guess this is a bit of
a rambling mess and i'm not making any sense,
but i'm terrified you're going to come back
and catch me in the act as it were. so, look,
i'm laying all my cards on the table. edie,
i have fallen for you and i wanted to do one
of those grand gestures, the ones they do in
those romantic comedies you love so much,
but honestly i'm already breaking out into
hives as i write this email, so there's no
way i could do anything as big. but just know
that this is that moment, and even though it
doesn't compare to anything like the movies,

to me this is huge. i've never told anyone
that i've fallen in love with them before.
and i've certainly not written a love letter
to anyone.

so that's how i feel, i guess the next
stage is up to you. you can put me out of
my misery and let me know how you feel (either
way).

love

joel

At first, I think he's clearly playing a cruel trick on me, that, after finding out about my notes to self, he's sent me an email pretending it's from the past. But when I scroll up to the details in the header, I realise he sent it seventeen years ago.

My hands start to shake and my heart begins to pound as I try desperately to process it. I'm stunned by the revelation. Joel was in love with *me*.

I remember the other note-to-self email in my inbox and I click on it, hoping it may shed some insight on what I've just read.

Yo, yo, yo my future self!

How's it all going? I hope your summer
didn't feel like it passed in the blink of
an eye like mine has just done. I've only got
a couple of weeks to go now and I wish that
wasn't the case.

I am still swooning over Joel. He came in
to see me in reception earlier and it's been

so quiet here on the desk that I actually thought that this was going to be a good moment to talk about our almost kiss. I've been working myself up to confess how I feel AND just as I'd plucked up the courage as well, a guest chose the perfect time to come into reception and I had to check them out of the caravan. By the time I got back here, Joel had buggered off. Charming, huh?

Anyway, I will talk to him. Which brings me to the note to self for today – stop putting off conversations that you need to have. I know that I do it with everything in life, but don't put it off, do it today.

I'm going to do this one too – really I am – wish me luck and all the bravery in the world.

Edie x x

I close my eyes as all the pieces fall into place. Joel didn't know that he was sending the email to the future.

I can't quite believe it. Joel told me he loved me and I never received the email. He was waiting for me to answer him and I never did. No wonder he was acting weirdly around me. I don't know how I would have reacted if roles were reversed and he was ignoring my declaration of love. I wonder if that was why he slept with Elizabeth, which now makes me feel a bit sorry for her as I think she really liked him.

I instantly feel sick, imagining the possibilities of what might have happened if the email was delivered to me on that day.

Would Joel and I have got together? Would our relationship have lasted? My brain instantly goes back to the very night my world turned upside down, and I think about how so much of that night could have been prevented: the days of feeling hurt from Joel's sudden disappearing act; the excessive drinking to forget my troubles yet still my desperate need to see Joel; finding Elizabeth in his room and having my heart torn in two; worrying Mum enough for her to jump in the car to check up on me.

The train starts to slow and I search the landscape outside, no clue as to where we are.

The man opposite me stands up and slips his jacket on. 'Excuse me, what's the next stop?'

'Westerly.'

I thank him as I hastily shove my phone into my bag and rise to my feet, gripping the tops of the headrests as I walk to the doors. The train comes to a halt and I follow the other passengers, walking on autopilot. All I can think about is Joel and the lines of that email. I'm vaguely aware of someone yelling and it takes a moment to realise it's my name being shouted.

'Edie, Edie,' calls Soph. I wave back but my feet don't want to move.

She walks up and gives me a quick hug.

'You look tired. I bet you've had a long week.'

'You have no idea.'

'Your dad still recovering well?'

'Yes, thank goodness.'

'Good.' She links her arm through mine and steers me towards the car park.

'We'll go back to ours and have a cup of tea and then I'm making pasta for lunch. Alfie will be pleased to see you.'

'A cuddle with him might be just what I need. How's he doing?'

'He's good, thanks. He's really mastered the crawl now, which I was jumping for joy about for all of five minutes until he started crawling everywhere. It's exhausting trying to run after him.'

She carries on rattling off his exploits but I can't concentrate. I feel like I'm going to explode if I don't confide in someone about what I've just learnt. Maybe it would help to speak to Soph about everything that happened back then and how I feel now. Besides, I can't keep it from her any longer.

It doesn't take us long to arrive back at her place and we pull up onto her driveway. But when we walk into the house, the sound of chattering forces me to stop. I turn to Soph and I go rigid in fear.

'Oh.' She looks just as surprised as I do. 'Sounds like we've got company.'

She leads me towards the lounge, where I can hear Verity. I can only assume Joel will be nearby. He's the last person I want to see.

My whole body feels like it's on fire and I've never felt such a strong desire to run away from anywhere before. Soph's practically having to drag me as I'm digging my feet into the ground like a stubborn mule.

I spot the toilet and I excuse myself, bolting the door behind me. I take hold of the porcelain basin and I scrunch my eyes shut. I breathe deeply, trying to come to terms with things, but I don't know where to start. I've been so caught up this summer thinking that Joel never liked me in that way, that there's no chance, even now, he'd feel the same way as I do. Only that email rewrites all our history. The connection I felt then was as strong then as it is now; what if he still feels it too?

I wish I could hide in here forever, but I know I'm only delaying the inevitable.

Soph's standing in the doorway to the lounge and she ushers me in. Everyone greets me and I try not to look at Joel on the sofa. I wave with a shaking hand at Brett sitting on the armchair, and Alfie crawling on the floor. Soph guides me to the end of the sofa next to Verity.

'Well, this is a nice surprise,' I say, trying to even out my voice.

'Joel and I only popped by to borrow a bike but then when we heard you were coming, we thought we'd stay and say hello.' Verity taps my leg and smiles.

'Lovely.' I put my hands on my lap but I can't keep them still so I end up slipping them under my thighs.

'Right, shall I make the drinks?' says Soph. 'Everyone want tea?'

'I'll have some hot tea, please,' says Verity. 'Black, no sugar.'

Joel pulls a face. 'One of these days I'll get you to drink tea the proper way.' She winks then raises an eyebrow in a flirty move that stabs at my heart. Of course he doesn't feel that connection like he did all those years ago. He's happy with Verity. Whatever he said in his email was all in the past.

'How's your dad, Edie?' asks Verity. 'Joel told me what happened. I'm so sorry.'

'Yeah, he gave us all quite a scare, but he's going to be fine, thank you. He's off work for another few weeks, and changing a few of his lifestyle habits, but he's going to make a full recovery.'

'I'm so pleased to hear that.'

There's a pause, like it's my turn to fill the conversation and I panic.

'How are the wedding plans?'

It's the last thing I want to ask but it's all I could think of.

'They're OK; I mean, it's not really a big affair. My mom would kill me if we planned anything big. It's actually quite nice not having to do the whole bachelorette stuff and the bridal shower. But it'll be nice, intimate, won't it, Joel?'

'What?' he asks. He'd been tickling Alfie who's at his feet. He picks him up and turns him round so that he goes crawling back the other way towards his dad.

'I was just saying how intimate our wedding was going to be,' repeats Verity.

Whilst Verity is talking, Soph walks in with a tray of hot drinks and places it on the ledge of the bay window that's just about out of Alfie's reach for now.

'I think that's so lovely,' says Soph. 'If we were ever to get married — which we're not, for the record — then I'd want it to be a small gathering of people. Minimal fuss and feels more personal.' She perches on the armchair next to Brett and he squeezes her hand.

At these words, Verity wraps her hand around Joel's in affection and I feel a stab of pain in my heart. Brett starts reminiscing about the party at my flat, and I try my best to follow the conversation, all the while avoiding looking at the happy couple.

By mid-afternoon I'm itching to leave. Soph cooked us all a big pasta dish for lunch and I've managed to escape the room by helping Brett with the washing-up. I put the last of the plates back in the cupboard.

'Thanks for helping,' says Brett.

'You're welcome.'

I don't tell him that I'm grateful for him letting me hide away in the kitchen. I hand him the wet tea towel and he pops it in the washing machine.

'I just want to say thank you.'

'You already thanked me once.'

'No, sorry, I meant, I wanted to thank you properly, for helping Soph.'

'With what?'

He leans back on the kitchen worktop.

'For being her friend again and for bringing back some of the old Soph. I think becoming a mum hit her harder than she expected it; in fact, it all hit us both harder than we expected. We had no idea how difficult it was going to be. I've had it easier as I've been able to carry on as normal working while she's had to do everything. But over the summer, I've seen glimmers of her as her old self again, and not just as Alfie's mum. She's seemed so much happier, and I can't help but think that it's because of you.'

I'm so touched because, if anything, she's done that for me.

'I'm so glad we got back in touch,' I say.

We're interrupted by Alfie's crying.

'I think he's due a nap, I'll see if I can put him down,' says Brett. He goes to leave and holds the kitchen door open for me.

'Actually, I need to make a quick phone call.'

He goes back out alone and I stand there, taking a moment. I never thought that in trying to reconnect with the old me, I'd also be making an impact on my friend's life too.

The kitchen door creaks and it startles me. Joel walks in and my heart starts to thump in my chest. I've deliberately avoided him today and the last thing I wanted was to find ourselves alone.

'Hey, can't talk now, I'm just about to head home,' I say, walking towards the door, but he gently closes it before I get there.

'You got the email I sent, didn't you?'

I freeze and I meet his eyes for the first time today.

'Did you know it was being sent to the future?'

He splutters a laugh. 'No, I absolutely didn't. But when you were talking at the hospital the other day about the emails you'd been receiving, I started to wonder if that's what happened. And then you confirmed it today; you haven't been able to look at me once.'

I take a step further away from him.

'Joel, I'm so sorry. I would never have ignored an email like that. If I'd got it . . .' I stop myself from saying what I really want to say.

He runs both his hands through his hair and walks into the centre of the kitchen.

'Fuck, Edie. I spent years hating you for breaking my heart and then I find out that you never even got my email.'

'I know. But if it makes you feel any better, I spent years hating you too after I walked in and found Elizabeth in your bed.'

He turns round and stares hard at me.

'You knew about Elizabeth?'

I nod. I can still see her after all these years with that smug smile on her face.

'I wanted to find out why you were ignoring me. You'd been acting weird with me for days, but when I got to your room she was there.'

'I couldn't stand to be around you. I couldn't understand how you couldn't at the very least tell me to my face that you didn't feel the same way.'

'If I'd have got the email of course I would have spoken to you.'

He takes a step closer to me and doesn't stop staring at me. I can hardly breathe.

'And what would you have said?' he says.

I close my eyes; it's too painful to look at him.

I want to tell him that I was in love with him and that seeing him again has slowly made me realise maybe I never stopped.

'It doesn't matter what I would have said.' My voice is quiet and unconvincing.

'Doesn't it?' he asks.

I open my eyes and the look on his face is enough to break my heart. I know that my dad says that you can't change the past and you've got to move on, but what if I don't want to move on? What if—

The door swings open and Soph marches in, Alfie in her arms, followed by Verity.

'Oh, hello, we wondered where you'd got to.' She picks up a sippy cup from the side and hands it to Alfie, who grabs it and starts sucking on it.

'I was just finishing the washing-up. I'm going to have to head off, I'm afraid.' I wipe my sweaty hands on my jeans. 'I said I'd pop in and see Dad this afternoon.'

'Of course, well, it was great to see you.'

'And I think we should get going on that bike ride,' says Verity. She walks over to Joel and slips her arm around his waist.

Soph starts to ask her about it and Joel looks over to me. We lock eyes and all the hurt that I've ever felt over him comes rushing back. It doesn't matter what we felt for each other seventeen years ago or what I think I feel now – he's getting married and moving to America.

I turn away and make my excuses to go, trying my hardest to sound sincere to Verity when I give her my best wishes for the wedding, but I don't look at Joel again. The pain is too raw.

I try and keep it together walking to the car but as soon as I'm away from them I feel my heart break in two.

Chapter 34

Normally I'd throw myself into work, to help distract me from my problems, but I was determined not to this time around. I went through with the plan I came up with on the train and redistributed the workload across the team so less fell on my shoulders. Aaron and Claire were pleased that they were finally getting to help. Ever since Dad went off sick, they've been pushing for me to share the load, and I'm truly grateful for how dedicated and loyal our staff are. I've said sorry to Layla for being so horrible lately and I only felt even more of a worse friend with how well she took the apology, telling me she understood, and how quickly she forgave me.

I'm also trying to face things head on. Tempting though it was to pretend I wasn't aware of Joel's former feelings towards me, and to fight the urge to bury my head in the sand, this time I've realised that in order for me to move on, I have to acknowledge it all. To accept that he's getting married to Verity in three days' time. It's shitty and it's unfair but that's how it is. When I picked my car up on Saturday, I wanted to read so much more into his loaded questions, but if our past is anything to go by, we've learned the hard way that we shouldn't beat around the bush, and it's quite clear he's made his choice: he's marrying Verity.

'I know you're thinking about him,' says Layla.

'I wasn't.' I'm such a bad liar and she knows it.

'I still don't get why you won't find out how he feels about you. Don't you want to know?'

I drove home from Westerly and went straight to her house on Saturday and told her everything that had happened. I spent the evening frustrated, angry and tearful, and she sat there like the good friend she is, listening to me whilst Tim kept us topped up with food and wine.

'I think it's obvious what he feels about us, as otherwise he wouldn't be getting married. There's no use clinging onto the past.'

Layla bites her lip.

'It just seems such a shame. He's said to you that he's only marrying her for the ease of getting a visa, hardly romantic. It doesn't sound like they're madly in love to me.'

'It's not like the same thought hasn't crossed my mind, but I can't help but hear Soph's voice in my head telling me this is Joel's way of settling down. And if there's a chance that he'd be happy with Verity and with their new life in the US then I can't get in the way of that. It's not fair on Joel or Verity.'

'If there's a possibility . . .' begins Layla.

'There isn't. It's just best for all of us if we move on.'

Claudia walks over to our table with drinks and Layla reaches out to help her put them on the table.

'I'm so excited to see you in action,' says Claudia, and I'm relieved to be talking about something else. The two of them have come to watch the improv final and we've got time for a quick drink before it starts. 'I used to love watching *Whose Line Is It Anyway?* when I was a kid.'

'Don't be expecting anything as good as that.'

'Don't listen to her, the last one I saw was brilliant,' says Layla. 'And Edie is great at it. All those years you told me you were scared of public speaking and then you get up on stage and do that, all off the top of your head. It's incredible.'

'You were scared of public speaking?' Claudia wrinkles her face. 'But you were a natural with the kids during your talk at the school.'

'Maybe I seemed that way on the outside but on the inside I was terrified. Perhaps kids are an easier crowd.'

Claudia almost spits out her drink.

'Are you joking? They're one of the toughest crowds going. You don't know when they'll innocently come out with a brutal comment that would make some restaurant critics' toes curl.'

'That isn't what you told me before the talk.'

'Well, I didn't want to scare you. Besides, you took it all in your stride. It's why I think you'll make a great teacher.' She winces. 'Oh, there I go again. I promised Robin that I wouldn't push anymore.'

'You want to be a teacher?' asks Layla.

This summer's been such a whirlwind that aside from Saturday night's crying on her shoulder, Layla and I haven't had much one-on-one time to catch up about anything other than the emails.

'Since I've been volunteering at Big Little Readers, I've been thinking about retraining as a teacher, or at least I was until Dad had his operation.'

'What? And teach kids like my two all day.' She pulls a mock horrified face. 'Not to mention I'd miss you terribly if you left Porter's.'

'Me too, although I wouldn't miss your weird song choices on the office Spotify.'

Layla smiles. 'Joking aside, though, I think it would be great if it's what you want and it'll make you happy.

'Plus, you'd get all those holidays. Imagine what you could do with that time. You could go travelling or you could babysit, or even tutor my two wonderful children.'

'The ones that you were just horrified that I'd have to teach.'

I can't help laughing at her.

'I'm sure they'd behave for you. What did your dad say about it?'

'I hadn't found the right time to tell him.'

Aaron walks up to the table before she can reply.

'Hello, sorry to interrupt,' he says, 'but Edie, I think we're going to get started on the warm-ups.'

He gives an apologetic smile to Claudia and Layla.

'That's fine,' I say. 'Right, ladies, I'll see you after the show.'

'Good luck or break a leg or whatever it is you're supposed to say for improv,' says Claudia.

We take to the stage for our final challenge and we can hear cheers and whistles from the crowd that I know are coming from our friends and family. I was touched to see that a few people from work also came along, including Claire. There's something really comforting in knowing that so many people in the audience are supporting us and willing us to do well.

I smile and take a few deep breaths, my heart beating even faster. Before I started improv, I never realised I'd be capable of getting such a rush from performing on stage. It's as though when I'm in the moment, I forget to worry about what the audience is thinking and instead focus on what's about to come out of my teammates' mouths, even if I'm slightly fearful of the unknown. I try and quell the pre-performance nerves by reminding myself that I'll be soon feeling that adrenaline rush.

We all hold hands on stage, anxious about what scenario we could get.

'OK, you guys, your scenario is . . . a runaway bride. The location is . . . a dinghy, and the key word is . . . regret.'

My mind has gone blank as all I can think of is Joel and Verity's wedding and the word regret. Here was me thinking that tonight might take my mind off it.

The other members of the team start to get themselves psyched up. Yas is shaking her arms. Aaron's rotating his head left and right. Dave is patting down his neat sweater.

The host starts the timer over and the improv starts. I shuffle to the back, letting Aaron and Yas take centre stage. I start taking deep breaths, trying to calm my thoughts, which are swirling round my brain.

'You can't just run out on the wedding now,' says Aaron, standing next to Yas. He's pretending to paddle up to her.

'I can, and I am. Leave me alone. I can't go through with it.'

'Where are you going to paddle to?' says Dave. 'You're on a boating lake.'

'I couldn't see a horse and I needed to make a dramatic exit.'

'I can see Rodney and the rest of the guests at the church,' says Aaron, waving.

'I can't do it, I can't marry him. He snores too loudly.'

'You can get the most wonderful earplugs these days,' says Dave.

'But he leaves the toilet seat up all the time.'

335

'You're never going to find a man then,' says Aaron and the audience laugh.

'How do you know if that person's the one? What if I get married and later regret my choice?' says Yas, her voice sounding so hopeful, and I snap.

'What if you don't?' I blurt out. 'You only regret what you don't do in life. What if you spend the rest of your life wondering what would have happened if you'd given him a chance?'

Yas goes to open her mouth but I'm in full swing now.

'What's the worst that could happen to you? You put yourself out there and he says no? It's not like it'll stop him getting on with his life. He could still marry Verity.'

I'm met with a stunned silence and I realise what I've said and where I am. I start to panic. This is the final and it looks like I've blown our chances by getting lost in my own thoughts.

'Who's Verity?' shouts Yas. 'Don't tell me Rodney's been cheating on me.'

Dave and Aaron mock gasp. My heart races. They're covering up my mistake.

'Oops, I regret saying that out loud,' I say, and the audience titter with laughter and I get a light-headed rush. I try and catch my breath — it's suddenly feeling too real; I'm inwardly praying that everyone assumes it was all an act but it was far from it.

Aaron and Yas take the Verity line and run with it. And they come up with more and more absurd excuses and rebuttals of why Yas should go back to Rodney and the audience keep laughing harder until the host signals that we're onto our last thirty seconds.

'I'm going to do it,' says Yas. 'I'm going to jump and swim to shore. Three, two, one.'

She leaps into the air and pretends to swim.

'You know, she could have just stepped out; this pond is tiny,' I say, demonstrating.

'But she'd have regretted not doing something big to declare her love. Every love story needs a dramatic ending,' says Aaron.

The host signals our time is up and the audience clap but all I can hear is Aaron's words echoing round my mind.

When the clapping finally subsides, the host calls the other team back on stage; it's not going to be long until we find out who's won.

There's a tense wait whilst scores are totted up. Yas is squeezing me so hard that I'm worried she's going to cut off circulation to my arms. I'm keeping my fingers crossed my slip-up of Verity's name in the act didn't cost us the victory.

'And the winner of this year's Improv Battle Extraordinaire is . . .' The audience start to stamp their feet and the noise echoes off the walls, making it sound thunderous. 'Four's a Crowd.'

After the initial disappointment at not hearing our name called, I start to graciously clap and congratulate the worthy winners. Although there's a part of me that's worried we lost because of my mistake.

'There's always next year,' says Aaron, pulling us into a huddle backstage.

'And Hayley will be back by then so I'm sure you'll be glad to be rid of a beginner like me who unexpectedly goes off on tangents like I did tonight.'

'Edie, that's the whole point,' says Yas.

'Hang on a minute.' Dave points his finger playfully at me. 'Don't think you're leaving us now. We can have up to five in the team, you know.'

'Too right,' says Aaron. 'You're not a temporary part of this team, OK? You're stuck with us. Now that's sorted, let's grab a drink and drown our sorrows.'

The bar is packed when we make it out from the backstage, but our work colleagues have secured a table in the corner. Claire gives her commiserations as I walk up.

'You guys were robbed,' she says.

'The other team were really good.'

'Always a shame that you can only ever have one winner. Anyway, well done, Edie. I'm proud of you and the rest of the team.'

She turns to Aaron and drags him into the conversation, and spotting Claudia on her own I excuse myself.

'So, did you enjoy it?'

'So much. I'm in awe of you and the team. I'm definitely coming again. That last one where Yas kept coming up with reasons not to marry Rodney had me in stitches.'

'I know, I couldn't believe the excuses people would come up with to get out of doing something.'

'I would have thought you'd be well practised at it,' says Layla, raising an eyebrow at me as she hands us both a glass of wine.

Claudia laughs and gives me a knowing look.

'It's like I said to Edie last week, there's always going to be a reason or excuse; sometimes you've just got to give it a go.'

The two of them nod at each other and I can't help but think that my ears should have been burning whilst I was backstage.

Claire and Aaron join our conversation and we start to talk about tonight's performance.

'You know,' says Yas, joining us, 'I feel like we need to toast our success. We may not have won but look how far we came. That in itself deserves recognition.'

'Here, here,' says Aaron, nodding.

Ordinarily, I'd keep shtum and hope that someone else would jump in and do it. It's usually my go-to response when I don't want to do something, but as I look around at our corner of the pub, full of friendly faces from work and their partners, I surprise myself by feeling this sudden urge to say something to the people I consider a second family to me.

'That's a great idea,' I say, and I clap my hands together.

Claire slips her glasses off in shock and helps to quieten our group down.

'Thanks,' I say. Now that I've got their attention, I'm not entirely sure what I'm going to do with it. 'Um, I wanted to say a few words just to, um . . .' I start to stutter, unsure how I could be so calm on stage minutes ago and yet so nervous in front of familiar faces. 'I want to say thank you to Aaron, Yas, Dave and Hayley' – I point to her sitting down on a chair – 'for taking me . . . um . . . into the group. I'm sure none of you would be surprised to say that it was something that took me completely out of my comfort zone. Those that work with me will know that speaking publicly is Dad's forte, not mine.

'But I have really enjoyed being part of this wonderful team and I couldn't think of better teachers to have had. So thank you for letting me join, and thank you to all of you who came to support us. I hope you'll join me in raising a glass to the Impensonators.'

We all toast the team. I might need to steady my glass with both hands but I'm proud of myself for giving a speech.

'Where's the Edie Porter I know gone?' says Claire. She smiles at me, a look filled with pride.

'She's still there; she's just found her old confidence,' I say, smiling back.

I am so grateful for the emails because, without them pushing me, I probably would never have found improv or thought I was capable of overcoming my fear of public speaking.

It makes me feel a little sad at the thought I won't be receiving any more challenges. Without them, I wouldn't have become so comfortable in my own skin. And even if it did come with some emotional baggage, I wouldn't change a thing, because I like who I've become. I've finally found that feeling of contentment I've been missing for so long. I just hope I remember going forward that sometimes in life you need a kick up the bum to remind you that you only have one life, so why not live it?

Chapter 35

Ever since I received my first note-to-future-self email, I've been dreading today more than ever. I can't believe seventeen years have passed since my mum's death and that I haven't seen or spoken to her in that long.

It feels harder this year, what with everything that I've gone through with Dad, and Joel, and the fact that the emails have bought that period of my life back in almost vivid technicolour. It's bought a tidal wave of emotions.

I managed somehow to get through the morning at work, but I'm glad to have escaped for the afternoon. I've headed to Dad's to spend the rest of the anniversary with him like I always do. Only this year I've brought the memory jar with me.

Dad's sitting at the kitchen table, examining the jar like it's a priceless work of art.

'What a beautiful idea.'

'It is, isn't it? I've already put a few of my favourite memories in there. Like the one where the crab latched onto her foot when we were at Swanage.'

Dad laughs abruptly. 'Definitely top ten moment right there. And I take it you got the al fresco wee on that nature hike?'

'Of course.'

My poor mum was mortified that she'd snuck off to have what she thought was a secluded toilet break on a hike only for a coachload of tourists to pull up alongside her.

'I'm going to head out to the shops for a few hours,' says Julie, walking in. 'Let you have a little bit of alone time.'

She rests a hand on the back of Dad's shoulders and he puts his hand on top of hers.

'Or you could stay.' I shrug. 'If you wanted to, I mean I don't know if you'd want to hear stories about my mum, but we're going to write some down to put in the jar as a keepsake.'

Julie pauses and I'm hoping I haven't offended her.

'If you wouldn't mind, I'd love to hear them,' she says.

'The more the merrier,' I say with a smile.

She pulls up a chair next to Dad and he gives me a look of thanks.

'So, what have you got so far?'

Julie sits through all the stories we exchange about Mum, asking questions, laughing a little, and it hits me how wrong I've been about this whole situation. She's sitting here listening to memories of a woman whom she'd never met, who she knew would always have our hearts, and it's not fazing her in the slightest. It's made me finally accept that she's not looking to take anyone's place, and that there's enough room for her in our family without her replacing Mum or usurping her memory.

'I've just thought of a memory I want to add,' says Dad, picking up a bit of paper, 'one I don't think you know of actually, Edie. But when you got accepted into university on an English degree, your mum was so proud of you that she told every single one of our clients. She was boasting for days and spent weeks grinning like a Cheshire cat.'

'She did?' Edie couldn't believe what her dad was saying. 'But I thought she was disappointed that I wasn't doing business studies and that I wouldn't be going into the company.'

'I think that she only wanted you to choose that degree because she thought it would give you more options for work later on. Of course she wanted you to work at the company, you know that she had grand notions of it being a big family affair, but that was her dream and she was proud that you were following yours. I don't think she would have ever expected you to actually start working with us.

'Not that I'm not grateful that you did,' he adds hastily. 'It's funny when you look back though; I'd forgotten that Porter's was not really on the cards for you career-wise.'

I know I need to be honest. Of how I've felt over the past seventeen years. It's time to put in action the final note to self that came through at the weekend. The final challenge: stop putting off conversations that you want to have.

'The funny thing is, I've been thinking about that a lot lately. About what I would have done if I hadn't started work at Porter's—' My voice is unsteady but I take a deep breath. If anything this summer has taught me it's that I'm capable of more than I think I am. 'And volunteering with the kids has made me think that maybe it's time for me to try something different. Aaron and Claire have stepped up brilliantly and I know that if we promoted them, and took on the right member of staff to support them, that you wouldn't even miss me.'

I'm hurrying through a stream of consciousness, wishing that I'd planned it all out.

'After the accident, I joined the company because it felt like it was something I had to do. Everyone was in shock and I knew that you needed someone to do Mum's work. I guess I thought I was the best person to fill in, because over the years I'd seen what everyone did and I knew the company. It was almost comforting because I was surrounded by her presence, and I wanted to be around people who knew her. I needed to be there.'

'Oh Edie, I guess I didn't think about what you'd given up. I was supposed to be the adult and yet back then I was a mess. I'm embarrassed by how much I came to rely on you, even though you were still so young. If you hadn't been there when I was drinking . . .'

Julie leans over and takes Dad's hand when she sees it trembling and they exchange a look with each other. Knowing my dad has someone to turn to for comfort warms my heart.

'It was a hard time for us all and looking back I wouldn't have done anything differently. But the job was only meant to be temporary. I hadn't envisaged being there for seventeen years, or that it would become my career. It's almost like I drifted into my life, and although I'm so grateful for the experience – I've been able to work with some wonderful people and to live a comfortable life – I'm just not sure I want to keep doing it forever.'

I finally stop to take a breath and I risk a glance at my dad. I start to panic that I should have waited until he was better to have this conversation. But to my relief he's actually smiling at me.

'You know, I've been bracing myself for this speech for a long time.'

'You have?'

'Uh-huh. There's absolutely no denying that I needed you in

the company when Jan died. But you're right, Aaron and Claire can cope and we can always bring someone in. You know as well as I do that a company has to evolve to stay alive and I guess that's true of people too.'

I choke on a laugh, in shock at his reaction. 'Dad, what has that operation done to you?'

'I guess it was yet another reminder that life's too short, there's no point in spending your time doing something you don't love.'

I'm stunned. I'd always been too afraid to have this conversation with my dad, fearing that I would be unable to resist his pleas to stay, but this . . . this I was not expecting.

'Are you all right? Didn't you want my blessing?' He laughs and takes a sip of water. He winces a little and it reminds me how fragile he still is.

'I did. I just didn't expect . . . I thought you'd try and talk me out of it.'

'All I've ever wanted is for you to be truly happy and I'd hate to think that you're staying at Porter's out of obligation. So, what is it you're wanting to do?'

'I'm, er,' I stutter in shock. 'I'm thinking of training to be a teacher.'

I'm not sure why I wince when I say it but maybe it's because I'd spent the last few weeks reading forums about teaching as a career and it's hit home how tough it could be. There were so many negative comments online about the workload and school inspections, but for every one of those there was one from a teacher who showed such passion for their job, and that made me want to at least try.

'I think you'd make a wonderful teacher,' says Julie.

Dad nods in agreement. 'You really will.'

345

'Well, nothing's set in stone. I mean, I'd have to apply and there's no guarantee I'll get a place. Especially as I want to do an in-school training scheme. But Claudia who's the teacher that helps with Big Little Readers, she said she'd help me with the application.'

'That's kind of her.'

'I know. And it'll take at least a year because the applications are only just open for next September's intake, so it's not like I'd be leaving straight away. I'll have time for a proper handover and to recruit someone. To help with restructuring the company.'

Dad turns his head and looks at Julie.

'Yes, and who knows, maybe it'd be a good time for me to take more of a step back too. Julie and I have been thinking and we might do a little bit of travelling.'

I'd been drinking my water and I almost splutter it across the table.

'What? Am I hearing you right?'

Julie looks as shocked as I do.

'Well, we all know that I wouldn't want to step down completely, I won't be retiring early or anything. But I guess it wouldn't hurt for me to take a few more holidays a year and maybe longer ones.'

'I thought you hated the sound of those?' she says, surprised.

'Well, I've already given up booze, and now I've got to give up cheese and fats and my true food loves, so I've got to have something in life that's a pleasure.'

'Too right,' I say.

We sit there for a moment in silence and I can't believe how free I feel. All these years I was too afraid to say anything.

'So I guess this means now that I've told you that I'm thinking of doing this, I've got go through with it. Let's hope I get accepted.'

'And if you don't then you'll come up with another plan.' Julie shrugs like it's no big deal. 'I feel like this is some sort of occasion we need to celebrate.'

'Oh, great idea. I think there's usually a bottle of sparkling apple juice lurking at the back of a cupboard.'

'And I could go for a bacon sandwich,' says Dad.

'I've got some fake bacon. You'd never know the difference.'

'Believe me, you know,' he says with a groan.

'Well, perhaps we could have a celebratory meal. I've been experimenting with some of the recipes I found on the website to prevent heart disease and I'm sure I could cobble something together.'

'Surely we could make an exception for one meal. A nice juicy steak or—'

'No, one of those recipes will be fine. Is it so wrong that I want to keep you around for another twenty years?' she says.

'Twenty? I'm going for thirty at least.'

'Even better.'

He leans over and kisses her on the head.

Seeing the two of them loved up, it makes me wish for the same, to have someone in my life who cares for me just as much.

Joel pops into my mind but I know it's time to move on. Instead, I focus on being happy for Dad now that he has found it again.

Chapter 36

It's strange coming into work when I've made such a monumental decision about my future in the company. Dad and I decided that we wouldn't tell anyone I was leaving just yet; we thought it best to wait for his return to work so that we could have a concrete plan in place.

I'm the first one in the office this morning. I woke up at stupid o'clock as I didn't get much sleep, distracted by thoughts of Joel and Verity's forthcoming wedding later on today, and I figured that I was better off going to work early to keep my mind occupied. I sit down at my desk and look at the framed photo of my parents and whilst I'm never going to not feel guilty about how Mum died, I'm slowly starting to move on.

'Blimey, you're in early.' Layla walks in, clutching her sandwich box.

I'm desperate to tell her about my decision to leave, but I promised Dad I wouldn't say anything yet, plus I wouldn't want to risk anyone overhearing.

'Coffee?' she asks.

'I've got one, thanks.'

She smiles and heads towards the kitchen.

I turn my attention to my computer, automatically opening

my personal emails out of habit, like I have done so regularly over the last few weeks. But I know there aren't any more surprise emails in store for me.

I'm sad it's all over. I miss hearing from past Edie, and it gives me an idea that maybe I should pay it forward. Write a note-to-self email to future me so that she can remember everything that's transpired over these past few months, to relive it all in the hope that it can help her in some way as it did for me. I bring up the website and it's totally different to the very basic site I used at the reception desk at Hartland's. It's had a flashy makeover over the years but I'm able to quickly find my way around the page. After resetting my log-in I start a fresh email, selecting seventeen years in the future from the drop-down menu. It seems poetic with the symmetry. I wonder what I should write to my fifty-two-year-old self? I've learnt so much from the ones I've got this summer that it feels there's pressure to write something equally inspiring.

```
Dear Future Me,

    You only went and bloody did it, didn't
you? Did what we said you'd never do: grow
up. Don't you remember, we were supposed to
always be young, always know what's in the
charts, always be down with the cool kids?
But let's face it, I've never been down with
the cool kids, so there's really no hope of
that happening. Unless I've seriously under-
estimated myself.

    My mind is boggling at what your life might
be like. Are there flying cars? Do people live
```

on Mars? Did you finally reduce your unread emails to zero? I can't begin to imagine.

So, what do I hope of me in seventeen years' time? Mainly I hope you're happy. And not the kind of on-paper happy that's all about shiny cars and executive flats. I mean proper cheeks-ache-from-too-much-smiling-and-laughing-type happy. I hope your life is busy and full of love and friendship and that you're finally comfortable in your own skin. I hope that you are being true to yourself and that you've become the woman you should have been and the one that you wanted to be.

But most of all I hope that you haven't fucked it up and that you didn't lose him, again.

X x

What the hell am I doing? Emailing the future to tell myself that I hope I didn't make the wrong decision when I'm not even taking my own advice at present. If there's anything that I've learnt through all this, it's that there's no point in feeling afraid to be open about how you feel because if you don't you'll always be living with what-if.

What would have happened if I'd got Joel's email? We'll never know. But I have to stop living my life based on things that happened in the past. Dad's right; I can't change them. I can't think any longer in 'should have, would have, could haves'.

I shouldn't be writing to future me talking about my regrets when it's not too late to change things. I've spent years thinking

I'd imagined the connection between me and Joel, and yet his email confirmed that I wasn't crazy. And we never lost that connection, I'm sure of it. I've been in denial this whole time, but suddenly moments come to mind that give me hope he feels the same way: watching the sunrise; the night out on the campsite; Soph's kitchen.

My stomach starts to churn at the thought of what I'm going to have to do. Am I really going to break up a wedding? Both Verity and Joel are adamant they're only marrying for the visa, but would Joel still be going through with it if he knew how I felt, both back then and right now? And even if I have got it all wrong, then at least I'd have tried and will have my answer.

It's only eight o'clock. Soph mentioned the wedding was happening at eleven. I could still make it. I shut down my computer and I write a quick note and I prop it up against Claire's PC. Skiving twice in two weeks; past Edie would be proud. I just hope that today doesn't turn into such a disaster.

'Woah, where's the fire?' asks Layla, walking out of the kitchen with her coffee.

'I'm leaving. I've got to tell Joel I love him.'

'What?' Layla almost spills her coffee.

'No time to explain but wish me luck!'

'Good luck,' she shouts, and I channel past Edie and her confidence as much as possible.

The traffic is going to be horrendous, so instead of heading to my car I run to the train station.

I arrive breathless, glance up at the screen and realise that I've got eleven minutes until the next train to Bournemouth. I queue for the self-service machine and I can almost feel the adrenaline coursing round my veins. I manage to buy my ticket and make it onto the platform with a few minutes to spare.

I head down the platform well away from anyone and when the train arrives I watch the carriages pass until the last one stops in front of me. Thankfully, it's relatively empty.

It isn't until the train pulls away that the magnitude of what I'm doing starts to hit me. I close my eyes and start taking deep breaths.

'Edie?' says a very distinctive Scottish voice.

My eyes spring open and Douglas is smiling brightly at me. His hair is as neat as he could probably make it and he's freshly shaven.

'I thought it was you. I saw you standing on the platform.'

'Hello, what a surprise.' I stand up and give him a big hug. 'You look so well.'

'Turns out being alcohol-free is a good look on me. Who knew?' He sits down opposite me, resting his arms on the table between us. 'So, what are you doing here?'

'I . . .' I suddenly don't know what to say. It's probably best not to mention that I'm about to tell Joel I love him. 'I'm just taking a long weekend down in Westerly. Can't get enough of the place.'

'Oh,' he says, looking up at the empty luggage rail above our heads. 'Travelling light?'

'Yes, very light. How about you?'

'I got a phone call from Joel last night, asking if I'd be a witness for the wedding. Brett's got a last-minute gig in Cornwall and I said I'd fill in.'

'Oh.' I'm willing my mouth not to give the game away but my bottom lip is starting to wobble. 'I'd forgotten that was today.'

'Yeah, eleven o'clock. We thought it was safer that I took an earlier train down this morning, less temptation, you know, after the last time. Just in case.'

'Ah, yes. I'm not sure the buffet trolley sells booze at this time of the morning.'

'Silver linings.' He shrugs. He starts to tap his fingers on the table. 'I'm actually a little chuffed that he asked me. Not many people know about the wedding, because of the whole visa thing, so I'm honoured that he trusts me,' he says, lowering his voice. 'I know that his mum for instance didn't want to know anything about it.'

'Is that right?'

'Oh, aye.'

'Douglas, you do realise that you just went really Scottish then?'

'Did I? I blame my mother for that. Suz always used to tell me that whenever there was any piece of gossip, I turned into my mother. We'd always joke and say I'd make the worst spy ever, as everyone would know my tell as soon as I started to open my mouth.'

'How is that all going by the way? Did you speak to her?'

He nods slowly.

'I did, I told her the truth in the end and she actually thanked me for being honest. She's pleased that I'm getting help, and whilst it hasn't changed anything right now – I'm still having to go through the courts to see Isla – I feel like at least we're being honest with each other for the first time in a long while.'

'Honesty is always a good thing.'

'Hmm,' he says. He gives me an extra-long hard stare and

I think he knows exactly why I'm on the train. My cheeks start to burn and I can only imagine I've gone bright red.

We talk for some time about my plans to leave the company, about teaching, and about Douglas's brother Jake and what detoxing at his house has been like – anything to really avoid talking about why I'm really here. But there's no getting away from it in my mind. Every time the train pulls into a station, it's one step closer to the wedding and the nerves are starting to grow.

We're about halfway into the journey when the train pulls to a stop. I look out of the window, expecting to see a station, but all I can see are fields. The voice of the train guard crackles out of the speakers.

'Excuse me, ladies and gentlemen, we're stopping here temporarily as there's a train ahead of us at Christchurch station and we're just waiting for it to pull out. We'll hopefully be moving again in a few minutes.'

Douglas looks at his watch.

'I've still got plenty of time.'

'Are you meeting Joel and Verity in Bournemouth?'

'Yes, they've got a room in a hotel to get ready.'

It hadn't really occurred to me that they wouldn't be at the registry office when I arrived, or that Joel might be with Verity already. In fact, I hadn't thought much about the logistics at all.

'Edie, you're looking agitated; are you OK?'

'Uh-huh, just, you know, I don't like it when trains stop. It means it'll be a bit late.'

'Right, for your weekend, down at Westerly.'

'Uh-huh, yep, lots of relaxing to do there and don't want to miss a moment.'

'Right,' he says slowly.

Before Douglas can probe any further I ask him what he's up

to over the weekend, and I listen to him rattling off his plans. I'm trying to pay attention but all I can think of is how I have zero idea what I'm going to do when I get off the train. How the hell am I going to do this? How am I going to get Joel alone to talk to him? I can't rock up to their hotel suite, and, come to think of it, I couldn't be that person who breaks up a wedding when it's in progress either.

'Earth to Edie,' calls Douglas.

I look up.

'Sorry, I was miles away.'

'Already in Westerly?' he asks.

'Something like that.'

'*Good morning, ladies and gentleman, this is your guard speaking again. I apologise that we are now twenty minutes behind schedule. This is due to a train that is stopped in Christchurch station. The train has broken down and will need to be moved before we are able to pull into the station. We've also got two other trains in front of us. I can only apologise for this delay and we are working to get you on your way as quick as we are safely able.*'

Douglas looks down at his watch and pulls out his phone.

'I don't want Joel to think I've gone on an early morning bender now, do I?'

He puts the phone to his ear and I can't react quickly enough, terrified that Douglas is about to tell him that I'm here.

'Hey mate, it's me. I'm on the train, I'm going to be a bit late as there's a broken-down train, but I'm on my way . . . Not sure, we passed Winchester a little while ago and we've been waiting for twenty minutes already . . . Yes, I'm OK. I'm actually—'

I wave my arms frantically at him and I shake my head, pleading with my eyes for him not to reveal I'm with him.

'I'm actually reading a really good book . . . I know, me reading a book,' he chuckles. 'It's getting to a really exciting part though, so I best go, but I'll update you with a better ETA when I know it.'

He hangs up his phone and puts it on the table, face down.

'Right then, are you going to tell me why you're really on this train, or do I have to guess? Because right now my guess is that you've finally realised you're wildly in love with Joel and you're going to go and break up the wedding.' He laughs and picks up his water bottle and starts unscrewing the top. My face falls at his words. Douglas slams the bottle on the table. 'Edie, don't tell me it's true? I was just joking.'

'Shhh.' I look around self-consciously; there aren't that many people in our carriage, but I don't want them to think I'm some wedding wrecker. I let out a deep sigh. 'I just want to speak to Joel before he marries Verity.'

'Because you love him?' he says, softly, with a slight nod of his head.

'Because I love him.' I scrunch my eyes up. It's terrifying to say.

'I was always surprised that you two never did get together back in the day. Joel had the biggest crush on you and I always thought that you liked him too.'

'We did, we had a connection. But it didn't really work out then.'

'And now you're saying that this connection hasn't gone away?'

'I'll admit it was awkward seeing him again at first, I was still angry at him for breaking my heart. But the more time we've spent together recently, the more I've felt that spark growing between us,' I say, thinking about the events over the summer.

'But I kept thinking it was all one-sided, that given how we left things back at Hartland's seventeen years ago, there was no way he liked me then or now. Then I received an email from Joel.' I'm starting to lose Douglas. He's blinking rapidly, trying to keep up. 'It's all a bit of a long story.'

'I'm sorry, ladies and gentlemen, your guard again here. We've just had an update and the good news is that they're going to be able to move the train. The bad news is they need another engine to do it, and we're going to have to wait for it to arrive from Southampton.'

'Looks like we're not going anywhere for a while, so you've got plenty of time to tell me.'

By the time I've finished explaining, Douglas is sitting stock-still, his mouth wide open. The train still hasn't moved and now there's only an hour until the ceremony.

'I can't believe you guys. That was the perfect moment to tell each other how you felt in Soph's kitchen.' Douglas threw his arms up in frustration.

I give him a look to say, *are you serious?*

'I'm telling you,' says Douglas, just a little too loudly for the carriage. 'From what you've said, and knowing Joel, he was willing you to say something. Bloody hell. Why at no point over the last few days did you not think, oh hang on, I think he might still like me?'

'Because he's moving to the other side of the Atlantic with another woman who he's getting married to.'

'So what's changed now?'

'I realised that I'd regret it if I never told him how I felt. I guess I've been too scared to take risks and to let anyone get too close because I didn't want to lose them, but with Dad's recent health scare and how happy he is since being with his girlfriend Julie, it made me think about my own life and how I shouldn't let fear stop me from going for what I want, for who I love. I mean, what's the worst that could happen? He tells me he doesn't feel the same way and he moves to Key West and I never have to see him again.'

'I suppose,' he says. 'So how are you going to do it?'

'I don't know, I hadn't planned any of this. One minute I was in my office and the next thing I'm on the train and then you were here and—'

'OK, well, I want to make this happen more than anyone, so here's how it's going to go down,' he says, resting his hands on the table and linking his fingers like he's a super villain unveiling a plan. 'I'll arrive at the venue and lead Joel away to where you'll be waiting so that you can both chat about things. That way there's no big scene and no one except me and him will know what's happening.'

'Am I being the biggest bitch in the world doing this to him and Verity?'

'If I'm being honest, I've always felt that Verity and Joel were together out of convenience. And there's no denying that you and Joel have always had chemistry. You never know, you could be saving them from future heartbreak if they're getting married for all the wrong reasons. Especially if Joel does have feelings for you. If you don't tell them then potentially you'd be hurting all three of you in the long run.'

My heart is hammering in my chest now and my hands are starting to shake.

'Maybe I've read it all wrong. I haven't missed the touches, shared glances between them or when they take those soppy selfies together.'

Douglas's eyes go wide.

'You know those were for show on social media, right? To back up their visa application,' he says. 'I honestly wouldn't be pushing it if I thought they were really in love. But no matter what happens, I'll be there for you, the way you were there for me when I got arrested.'

He reaches over and takes my hand and gives it a little squeeze. The train lurches into action and he grins at me.

'This is it. Less than one hour to the wedding,' says Douglas. I can only assume I look alarmed as Douglas squeezes my hand again to reassure me. 'We've got plenty of time. Plenty.'

Half an hour later, we've managed to make it to the next station. I'm having trouble sitting still and keeping my panic at bay.

'*Hello, ladies and gentlemen, this is your guard speaking. I'm afraid we're unable to go any further on our journey at this time. There will be rail replacement buses arriving shortly.*'

'What?' I scream. I'd been holding it together quite well until now.

'I don't think we're going to make it in time. You're going to have to phone him,' says Douglas. He looks crestfallen.

'I can't, it's not the kind of thing that you can say over the phone. *Hello, Joel, I know you're getting married in a minute, but surprise, I loved you seventeen years ago and I think I love you now, too.*'

Douglas picks up his phone.

'What are you doing?'

He taps it a few times and then holds it to his ear.

'Hello, can I get a taxi going from Christchurch station to Bournemouth, to collect as soon as possible, please . . .' I sink with relief that he's not phoning Joel.

It's a good job Douglas booked ahead because the few taxis that were waiting by the entrance were pulling away when we made it outside the station. We get in when ours arrives and we have a nail-biting journey that I spend with one eye on the meter and the other on Douglas's watch.

'We've still got time,' he says, and his phone starts to ring. 'Hi, I'm in a taxi, the train stopped, we— I'm just driving into Bournemouth now. I shouldn't be too much longer. Are you still at the hotel . . . OK . . . OK . . . I'll meet you there.'

He hangs up the phone and he looks at me.

'They're heading to the registry office now. The registrar has to interview them before the ceremony.'

'I won't have time to talk to him.'

'You will. We can do this.'

The taxi creeps through traffic and I know that time is running out. Up ahead are temporary traffic lights and the driver pulls up the handbrake as he stops.

'Maybe it's best to just leave it as we're never going to get there on time at this rate.'

'We've come so far, we can't give up now, Edie.' He leans forward to talk to the driver. 'How far away are we?'

'As the crow flies, it's just down that road to the right, but we've got to drive round the diversion.'

'We'll get out here.' Douglas pulls his wallet out and places his card on the card reader before we exit the taxi. He grabs hold of my hand and he pulls me in the direction the driver was pointing.

'Come on, we can make it,' he says, pulling me along. 'There it is.'

He stops and points at the registry office on the other side of the road and we take a moment to catch our breath. I spot

Soph, and I pull Douglas back towards the shadows. She's chatting excitedly with Verity, who's dressed in the most beautiful, understated but elegant knee-length white dress that goes in at the waist with a full 1950s skirt. Joel's walking just behind and as they reach the building, Verity turns back to him and straightens his tie before he puts his hand on her waist and they smile at each other as they go in.

I'd only just got my breath back from our mad dash to the registry office but the sight in front of me takes it away once more.

'I can't do this,' I say, shaking my head.

'Of course you can, they've only just gone in, you're not too late.'

'But I can't do this. What was I thinking? If he had any feelings for me at all he wouldn't be going through with this. He knew I'd received the email and he didn't say or do anything.'

Seeing the affection as they looked at one another really brought it home for me. It might only be for a visa now, but what if they're both two people scared of commitment who need a nudge like this for them to take the next step. Maybe Soph's right, there is something there after all and I've chosen not to see it because of how I feel.

'Edie, you've come all this way.'

'I know, but I got carried away. I can't . . . Please don't tell him I was here. I don't want him to know. Can you just pretend that you didn't see me?'

Douglas looks pained.

'I will if it's what you actually want.'

'It is. Please don't let him know.'

'OK.' He leans over and he pulls me in close to him. 'Are you going to be all right? Will you get the train home?'

I laugh.

'I don't think I can face another train journey. I'll just get a taxi to Westerly, maybe head to the beach, dig my toes in the sand.'

'I could come with you? I'm worried about you being on your own.'

'I'll be fine. Besides, you've got a wedding to witness.'

He pulls me in tight again.

'You promise you won't tell him?' I ask.

'Promise.'

He pulls out of the hug and crosses the road. He glances back at me when he makes it to the other side. I give him a wave and he waves back before he disappears into the building.

I turn on my heel and I'm proud of myself for holding it together and not letting the tears fall. Joel's getting married and I have to move on. It's the right thing to do, even if it does hurt. Although there's one thing I know for sure: in the future, I'm not going to wait until it's too late to tell anyone how I feel.

Chapter 37

My journey to Westerly was quite dull in comparison to the mad sprint to the registry office. Ironic, really, that there were plenty of available taxis around, no traffic diversions nor any red lights slowing me down.

I know deep down it wasn't a wise decision to return here and pick a beach that was so steeped in memories of Joel and me, but there's something poetic about heading to Kestrel beach just when I've made peace with the future Joel and I have. It's my final goodbye to our relationship. The taxi driver drops me at the edge of the nature reserve and I take my time walking through the heather-lined paths and down the wooden bridges until I can hear the waves crashing on the shore.

I'm cursing the fact that I'm not as organised as Joel to have a backpack; in fact, my small work handbag is of hardly any use to me on this impromptu trip. I sit down on a rock on the edge of the beach, slip off my shoes and dig my feet into the sand.

I stay there for a while, watching the waves crash against the shore, trying not to look at my watch or my phone to see what the time is. I know it's long past 11 a.m. and Joel and Verity will be married by now and probably at the wedding lunch they'd arranged for afterwards.

My phone beeps in my bag and I'm tempted to ignore it, but it might be Dad or one of my colleagues, so I fish it out. It's a text from Douglas asking if I'm OK. I send a photo back of my view and tell him that I'm just fine. I try not to dwell on the fact that if he's texting then that must mean the wedding is over. I'm about to return my phone to my bag when I see a notification for an email I never thought I would see again. A Note to Future Self.

My heart beats that little bit faster. I don't remember sending one after my mum died but maybe I had after all, as a way of trying to feel better in my grief-stricken state. But curiosity soon turns to confusion when I click on it and see that it was sent today at 11.03 a.m.

Dear Edie,

I'm writing you this email as we seem absolutely atrocious at actually telling each other how we really feel and I'm hoping that, this way, there's nothing to stop me from telling you what's going on in my head.

I didn't marry Verity. We got to the regis-try office and I realised I couldn't go through with it. It wasn't fair on Verity and it wasn't fair on me either. I can't keep running away anymore.

Which is why I'm sending this to you now as I'm planning to give you the big scary speech (scary for me – I hope not you, fingers crossed) that has been a long time coming. Just be kind to me, this is not natural for

364

me to say these kinds of things out loud.
But we all know what a mess I made of it
the last time I wrote them down. Anyway, I'm
telling you this, because this way I can't
chicken out of it. So Edie, there's something
I want to say. To be continued . . . (in
person if I've got my timings right . . .).
If I haven't, don't go anywhere, I'm on my
way.

I stand up, my legs a little unsteady, and stare down at my phone
again. I'm not sure what I expect to happen, that he'll magically
appear like a genie, but I start scanning the beach around me.
And that's when I see him.

Joel is standing at the end of the pathway, still in his suit
only now his tie is off and his top button is undone, and he's
barefoot with his shoes in his hand. If the email hadn't stolen
my breath, then the sight of him here sure does.

'You received it this time, I hope?' he shouts, starting to
walk forward towards me. 'I didn't want to take any chances
so I thought I'd deliver the important bit in person.'

It's agonising waiting for him to cross the sand to get to me
but my legs feel like they've turned to stone.

'You didn't marry Verity?'

'No, I didn't.'

'And you're not moving to Key West?'

'I have no plans to.' He shakes his head.

'And she's OK with that?'

'She is. She was understanding after I explained to her what
I'm about to tell you. What I couldn't put in that email.'

He finally stops right in front of me and it takes every single bit of resolve not to close the gap between us.

'And what exactly was that?' I ask.

'Shit, I didn't realise I would feel this nervous or expect to feel this kind of pressure. Maybe I should have put everything in the email after all.' Joel laughs and rubs his palms on his trousers.

'I think I've had enough of emails for a while.'

Joel smiles. 'You and me both. But on my way over, I thought it would be so easy for me to get all the way here, only to bottle it again and never tell you how I really feel.'

My cheeks blush, because that's exactly what I did an hour earlier and I'm guessing from him finding me on this beach, then he knows I was there then too. I silently curse and thank Douglas all at once.

I take a step closer and I'm worried he'll hear the thumping of my heart.

'So how do you really feel?'

I want to reach out and touch him to make sure he's real and I'm not just imagining him.

'I spent that summer falling in love with you, Edie, and I tried for years to put you to the back of my mind and move past it all. Only when I saw you in Soph's garden a couple of months ago, all the same feelings came flooding back. It was as if they never left; they'd gone into hibernation, waiting for the moment you walked back into my life to awaken them.'

It sounds so familiar because that's exactly what happened to me.

'But if you felt that way, then why were you getting married?'

'We'd already started to apply for the intention-to-marry visa by the time you turned up at Soph's, and I carried on with it because it was the easy way out. It's what I've done for years, pretty much since I sent you that email all those years ago. I worked out that it hurts a lot less to not put yourself out there than it does to stay in a situation where you risk getting hurt.'

'I've learnt recently that it's usually better to take the risk.'

'Is that why you left the registry office without coming in?' He raises an eyebrow with a smile on his face.

'Bloody Douglas.'

'He didn't tell me until after, I promise. When Verity and I told him that we weren't going through with it, I told him I was going to talk to you and he cracked and told me that I didn't have to go quite as far to find you.'

'But how did you find me?'

'He said you were going to the beach, and I immediately thought of our place and hoped that you'd be here. I'm glad I didn't have to go far as I've waited so long to do this, and I don't think I could wait a single second more.' He leans forward as if to finally kiss me, but I pull back at the last minute.

'Wait,' I say. 'I'm guessing that with you stood here, and the fact you've spoken to Douglas, you know how I feel about you, how I've always felt about you . . . but I don't know if I can do this. You've just got out of a relationship. You almost got married and . . .' The hurt in his eyes is breaking my heart but I can't not say this. 'What I feel for you is like nothing I've felt for anyone else before and the thought that you could leave at any moment to go on your next adventure, I don't think I could bear it. I want someone who can commit to me long term, someone who wants to make a home with me and settle down, and I'm worried you might not want the same.'

A single tear rolls down my cheek and Joel reaches forward and wipes it off and he leaves his hand there, cupping my face.

'Edie,' he says, so softly that that's almost all he has to say, 'I didn't go through with the wedding because when it came down to it, whilst Verity didn't mind that we weren't marrying for love, I did. When I do get married, eventually,' he says with a cough and it makes me laugh, 'I want it to be for the right reasons. Like I couldn't possibly imagine not spending the rest of my life with the person I love. I want to be different to my dad and I want to settle down. I want to share a life with someone and to grow old with them and to have a proper home to do all that. But I don't want that person to be anyone; I want it to be you. I've only ever been in love with one person and it's you.'

I reach my hand up to the one that's still holding my face and lace my fingers over his. It's exactly what I wanted and needed to hear. He leans forward and our heads are touching and we stay there for a second; the enormity of what's happening sinking in. I've wanted to kiss him for far too long and yet now that we're going to do it I'm suddenly scared.

'What if we kiss and it's really bad?' I whisper. 'What happens if after all these years we kiss and it turns out there's zero chemistry between us? Then everything we've been through would have been for—'

He catches me off guard and kisses me anyway. Not the sort of gentle kiss that we were building up to seventeen years ago back in his room at Hartland's, but one full of passion and urgency, with an intensity that causes my whole body to shudder. He must have dropped his shoes because his hands are on my back and my hands are at the nape of his neck, and then he gently pulls away and stands back and looks me in the eyes.

'Does that answer your question about chemistry?'

He's got a smug look on his face.

'Maybe,' I say. 'But I think we should give it another go just to make sure.'

I kiss him back with such force that I almost push him over. Never have I wanted anyone or anything as much as I do now.

I've thought for a long time that if I played it safe and left things as they were, then there was no risk of feeling hurt or pain. But, in trying to protect myself, I'd forgotten how to live, and I'm certainly not going to make that mistake again.

'You know,' says Joel, taking hold of my hands as he pulls away, 'as much as I like the kissing, which I very much do, I happen to have this boat I've been fixing and it's finally ready to go out on the water. So I was wondering if you wanted to come and sail on it with me?'

'You got *Hetty* sailing?'

'I did indeed. So, do you want to come aboard my yacht?'

'I told you that that was a hell of a line. Was it worth fixing it just so that you could say that?'

'Totally,' he says, before he kisses me again and my whole body melts.

I can't help but think of all those years that we wasted, but I stop myself and I try instead to think of all those years we have to come. We might not be able to change the past, but we can change the future. And what a glorious future it looks like it's going to turn out to be.

Dear Future Me!

About last night! I know that what happened will be etched on your memory forever as I don't know how you'd ever forget it, but sometimes those memories fade over time. So I'm writing this to you as I never want you to forget a single minute of what happened.

As you'll remember, it was our second anniversary, and the week after I started my new job and Joel took me out on *Hetty*. By the way, does the novelty of me actually living in Westerly ever wear off, or the fact that my new school is only a fifteen-minute drive away so that Joel and I actually get to spend every evening together? I know, it's sickening, and Soph is doing her best to make sure it's not every evening, as she tries to drag me out on nights when Brett's feeling brave enough to look after Alfie and baby Poppy.

I'm getting distracted . . . so the boat! Joel took me on it after work, and he'd made a picnic, but not just a few sandwiches and a couple of tins of beer. A proper one – cured meats and fancy salads and champagne – and he went and anchored *Hetty* not far from our beach, you know the one, and then at sunset he proposed. We're getting married! Which I'm guessing you know as I imagine that you're celebrating a big anniversary sometime soon!!

Anyway, I must run – so much to organise!

Douglas is heading down for the weekend to spend it with us, and we're going to have a very fun, and very sober, night out with him and his new girlfriend, the very lovely Lucy, along with Brett and Soph. Then Dad and Julie are coming down on Sunday for a celebratory roast. Let's hope that mine and Joel's wedding is every bit as fun and romantic as theirs was last year.

Oh, I almost forgot – for your note to self – drink in your life more and live every minute.

Love, Me x x x

★

Dear Florence,

I already know you're going to read this and roll your eyes at it, thinking I'm an embarrassing mother to send you such a soppy email. And I know it's definitely not going to be the birthday present you were expecting this year (I can't believe you'll be eighteen and all grown up when you read this). But, hey, as I look down at you right now, asleep in my arms, where you've effectively pinned me down for the last two hours may I add, I realised that the best present I could ever give you is this – to let you know how dearly and unconditionally loved you are.

You have made me and your dad the happiest people on the planet. We cannot wait to watch you grow up into the fine young lady that we know you will become. There are so many firsts to look forward to – your first step, your first word, your first swim in the sea – and whatever you achieve in life, we will forever be proud of you.

There was a time before you were born when I was scared that, if something ever did happen to me, the memories you have of me would fade. It's a feeling I've known too well. But a very wise girl once gave me a special glass jar, one now filled with memories of your grandmother; I'm sure you know the one. And then once upon a time, I used to write emails to myself. Although, I'm sure I'll have told you about that by now too. It's your dad's favourite story, and don't tell him I said this but mine too, about how these emails unintentionally drove us apart but ultimately bought us back together. In many ways I'm grateful to the emails, not only because they led me to your father, but because they led me to you too.

So, you might be thinking, why have I brought all this up? Well, this gave me a brilliant idea for the perfect birthday present. I thought I'd make you your very own virtual memory jar, in the form of birthday emails. Every year, I'm going to send you an email (to this address) with some soppy words and stories to share with you. So suck it up, because I promise one day you'll look back and thank me.

So, Florence, the question is, where do I begin?...

Acknowledgements

Writing any book is such a huge undertaking and involves lots of people who deserve huge amounts of thanks. To my agent Hannah Ferguson for telling me to keep going every time I emailed saying that I wanted to stop when things got tough. And to the rest of the team at Hardman Swainson for all you do.

To Emily Kitchin and Melanie Hayes at HQ, thank you so much for shaping this book into something readable. Edie and Joel's story is all the better for your suggestions and comments! Thank you to Donna Hillyer for the copy-editing – and the much needed timeline. Thank you to the rest of the HQ team – in particular: Tom Wright, Kate Oakley, Katrina Smedley, Becca Joyce, Sarah Lundy, Sara Eusebi and Angie Dobbs.

I really couldn't have written this book without thinking about my own experiences leaving home at eighteen. I read far too many of my old emails from both then and the mid-noughties to get the tone right. I haven't laughed that hard in a long time. I'm so pleased that I am still in touch with so many of the same friends – so thank you Laura, Hannah, Kaf, Jo, Sam, Sarah, Sonia, Christie, Ali and Ross for both the fun and cringey times back then and also now.

I really struggled to write during the pandemic, so I wanted to say a big thank you to the lovely writers that have kept me writing over the last couple of years with both support and much needed word races. Thank you to Victoria Walters, Isabelle Broom, Lucy Vine, Cathy Bramley, Cressida Mclaughlin, Katie Marsh, Rachael Lucas, Liz Fenwick, Katy Collins, Pernille Hughes, Alex Brown, Jo Quinn and all those in the Mirepoix Women's Writers' Group.

Thanks also to my friends and family who have supported me writing and been such enthusiastic cheerleaders when needed. Mum, John, Heather, Harold, Katie, Rich, Debs, Lynne, Janine and Ken – thank you for everything!

The biggest thanks, as always, is to Steve for spinning the rest of the plates when I'm writing, and to Evan and Jessica for putting up with me when I'm 'always thinking about my book'. I couldn't write without having you guys being my number one supporters – thank you, I love you all so much.

Lastly, thank you so much, lovely reader, for reading *Note to Self* – I really hope you enjoyed it! You can keep in touch via my newsletter or follow me on Twitter (@annabell_writes) and Instagram (@anna_bell_writes).

**Turn the page for an exclusive extract
from the hilarious and heart–warming
romantic comedy from Anna Bell**

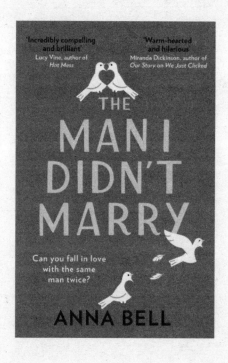

Prologue

When deciding to go to Comic Con this year dressed as Wonder Woman, with a very short skirt and tiny corseted top, I had not factored in the possibility that we would end up in a meat market of a club afterwards. I tug down at my skirt, which seems to have become even shorter in the few minutes since I last pulled it down, before I squeeze through the dance floor, fending off bum pinches and guys trying to grind in my direction. Ugh. To think I've been wearing this outfit all day and I didn't have one unwelcome advance. And yet, I've been in this club less than an hour and I've been slapping hands away left, right and centre.

I didn't really want to come, but my friends dragged me here and I've only gone and lost them. Neither of them are answering their phones, so I've spent the last twenty minutes searching the different floors, which are so dark and full of sweaty bodies, trying to find them. You'd think that dressed as the Incredible Hulk and HawkGirl they'd be easy to spot. It's late and it's been a long day, and if I can't see them on my final scan of the upstairs dance floor, I'm going to call it a night.

I look over at the people standing around the tables at the edge of the dance floor and my heart almost stops. Standing at one of those tables is Max Voss – my best friend Rachel's brother, aka my teenage crush. I haven't seen him in years, but he is every bit as gorgeous as he was when we were younger, perhaps even more so. I can't stop staring. I feel like I'm 15 again, trapped in his power.

It's one thing to be a gormless 15-year-old with an embarrassing crush; it's quite another to be behaving the same way at the ripe old age of 28. Yet, I can't help it. This is exactly why I don't meet up with Rach at her parents' house if I know he's going to be there.

He must sense me staring at him as he looks up and our eyes meet. I expect him to quickly turn away – I doubt he'd recognise me with my hair this long and without the trademark thick glasses that I wore until I was in my early twenties – but to my utter surprise he starts furiously waving at me. I look behind, expecting to see some leggy blonde, but no one behind me is paying him any attention. He points at me again and, thanks to the rum and Cokes I've been drinking, I've got the confidence to go over.

'Hey,' he says, beckoning me closer and shouting in my ear. 'You're here.'

He's so close that I can feel his breath on my cheek when he talks. It's the closest I've ever been to him; he's certainly never been this friendly with me before.

He puts his hand on the small of my back, causing me to melt at his touch. I reach out to hold onto the table beside me to stop my legs from buckling. I hate that my teenage crush still has such a hold on me.

'I thought you weren't coming,' he says.

'I'm sorry?' I say.

'Come and meet Dodge,' he says, ignoring my confusion.

He takes me by the hand, leading me to his group of friends, and places me in front of one who is dressed in a lime-green Borat mankini. Out of all the costumes that I've seen today, this is by the far the worst assault on my eyes. I try to ignore the hair and bits of flesh popping out from where they're not supposed to.

Max whispers something into his friend's ear and his friend looks me up and down; a huge grin appears on his face.

He comes towards me, holding out his hand, and I don't know what to do other than to shake it.

The rest of Max's friends seem to have taken great interest in what's going on and they've formed a circle around me. A couple of them start to shout and sing the *Wonder Woman* theme tune; they're smiling and clapping and, because it seems like a good idea after my rum and Cokes, I start to join in with them, putting my hands above my head and moving my hips to the music.

The chanting starts to change and it's hard to make out what they are saying at first, but then I hear the word 'kit' and then 'tits'. Why would they want me to strip? Unless? I suddenly stop, looking down at my outfit and thinking of Max's reference to him thinking I wasn't coming. The fact that they're all men in their group. The fact that he didn't make any reference to my name or knowing who I was. Oh God. I think he thinks I'm a stripper.

The man in the Borat mankini is nodding encouragingly at me, presumably waiting for the show to start, and I look over at Max in horror.

I watch his facial expression change from one of amusement to one of confusion.

'Wait, I know you,' he says, taking a step forward, his eyebrows furrowed. 'Oh my God!' he shouts. 'Spider, it's you!'

I cringe at the use of the nickname he used to call me. I haven't heard it in years. When I was younger my glasses were really thick and, if you looked through the side of them, it often looked like I had multiple eyes. Add to that my tall, gangly limbs and my flat chest, and Max had once said that I looked like a spider, and the name stuck. Heartache and pain coming flooding back, of having the kind of teenage crush that consumed every fibre of my being, only for the object of my affection to see me as a spider.

Tears start to form as the memories come in thick and fast, Max's friends all still calling for me to strip. It's too much. I turn and push my way through the crowds on the dance floor and down the stairs towards the exit.

'Spider, wait!' I hear as Max thunders down the stairs after me.

I ignore him and find myself out on the pavement, wrapping my cape around me to counter the chill in the air.

'Spider, please. I'm sorry,' he says, turning me round gently from my elbow.

'You thought I was a stripper?' I say, putting my hands on my hips. My cape billows out behind me in the wind.

'I'm sorry,' he says again, taking me by the hand and walking me away from the bouncers who are trying not to laugh at us. 'It was the outfit. My mate Jez said he'd booked one and then you were standing right in front of us and you were looking over and I just thought… Shit, I'm so sorry. But look at you, Spider, all grown up.'

I'm aware that he's looking at my boobs, which are squeezing

4

over the top of my corset, and my cape is no help; no matter how many times I try and wrap myself in it, it keeps flying back in the wind.

'Um, Max,' I say, waving and pointing at my face. His eyes flick up.

'Oh yeah, sorry, it's just. That outfit. Do you always dress...'

'I went to Comic Con today.'

'Comic what?'

'Never mind.'

'Are you here with friends?'

'I was, but I lost them. I was looking for them when I bumped into you. But I think I'm just going to go home,' I say, scanning the street for a cab.

Two bouncers struggle out of the club; they're manhandling Max's friend in the Borat mankini. They practically throw him into the arms of his waiting friends, who have scrambled out after him.

'What the hell happened?' asks Max.

'Rodge's just been sick on the dance floor.'

Max winces.

'We're going to take him home,' says his friend.

'I'll help.'

'Nah, mate, we've got him,' the friend says, tapping Max's chest. 'You stay here.'

He gives me a big grin and then he helps prop Rodge up and they lead him down the street. It's then that I see Rodge's bare bottom.

'Oh, that costume,' I say, wishing I could unsee it. 'Is it his birthday or something?'

'His stag do.'

5

'He came here on his stag do?' I say, raising an eyebrow at the exterior of the cheesy club.

'If you knew Dodge, you'd know it was pretty fitting. So, Spider—'

'The name's Ellie.'

He screws up his face. 'Of course, Ellie. Shit, I'm supposed to be apologising and I'm digging myself a deeper hole. Look, I can't remember the last time I ate, can I make it up to you by buying you some food?'

Max Voss has just asked me if he can buy me food? Didn't I always fantasise about this moment? Play it cool, Ellie. 'Why not,' I say with a simple shrug.

'Great,' he says, turning and walking into the fried chicken shop next door. Not quite what I had in mind.

We order some chicken and chips and when it arrives Max carries the tray over to the red plastic chairs by the window. My skirt is so short that I'm concerned that my skin's going to get so stuck to the plastic that it'll peel off when I stand up.

'Of all the people to bump into here, I never expected to see you in a club. Didn't think it would be your kind of thing,' he says, taking the cardboard boxes off the tray and handing one across to me.

'Oh yeah, and what did you think would be my kind of thing?'

'Oh, I don't know, sci-fi conventions. You always were a geek,' he says with a cheeky grin. I throw a chip at him and he laughs. 'Ow, bloody hell, they're hot.'

'I know, I just burnt my fingers,' I say, laughing.

'I didn't mean to offend you. I just meant that, you and Rach, well, you weren't exactly known for going out. The

6

only time I can remember is when I had to escort you both into a party because you were too scared to get out of the car.'

'Well, I've got slightly more confident in the last twelve years,' I say, cringing at the thought. Him walking us into the party wasn't the embarrassing part…

He gestures briefly at my chest. 'And I see you have no need for tissue paper any more.'

That was the embarrassing part.

I close my eyes and I'm instantly transported back there. Max had driven us to the cricket club and – when Rach and I had been too nervous to walk past a group of cool boys hanging around outside – Max had walked us over. Rach and I were just saying goodbye to Max when he pulled at what he thought was a rogue bit of tissue stuck to my top, only to pull out a long strip of toilet roll that had been stuffed inside my bra.

'I never did thank you for that night, for not laughing at me.'

When Max had pulled the first bit of loo roll from my top, it had torn and left a part of it hanging out. Instead of laughing at me, like most teenage boys would do, he'd stepped forward and hugged me to discreetly pull the rest of it out. I might have been left with wonky boobs, but at least the whole school didn't find out I'd stuffed my bra in the first place.

'I did what anyone would have done.'

'No, you didn't. It was really kind.'

'Well, you were always at our house and you became like a sister to me.'

'Huh, and do you still see me as that now?'

His eyes keep flitting between my outfit and my face and I can see he's still quite drunk by the way he's swaying.

'That outfit's playing tricks with my mind and I don't know what I'm thinking any more.'

My cheeks go red. Is he flirting with me?

'I don't think your girlfriend would like you saying things like that to me.'

'Girlfriend?'

'Sorry, I thought Rach said a few months ago that you were seeing someone and I just assumed.'

'Oh yeah, didn't work out. She moved abroad,' he says, shrugging his shoulders. 'We weren't serious or anything.'

'Oh right,' I say, feeling a little awkward bringing it up. 'So, what did you do for the stag do?'

'Now, I can't tell you that, but it's been a long day, that's for sure. We started drinking at eight in the morning.'

'Bloody hell, how are you still going?'

'Tactical nap at… an undisclosed location that had some comfy chairs. Plus, I switched to vodka Redbulls, so I might not sleep until next Tuesday, but I outlasted Dodgy Rodge, which is sort of an unwritten rule of a stag do.'

'What are the other unwritten rules?'

'I don't think I can tell you them either.'

'Right, I like the fact you're creating an air of mystery for something that, to be honest, is pretty much about you guys getting as wasted as possible and going to strip clubs.'

Max laughs.

'Were you always this funny, Spid— Ellie?' he says quickly as I go to scowl.

'Yeah, you were just too cool to talk to me.' I pick up a chicken wing, planning to eat a small delicate bite, but I've well and truly got the booze munchies and I ravage it like a caveman.

'That's not true,' he says, but we both know it is. Max was one of those kids at school – the ones that everyone worshipped, whereas Rach, his sister, and I... well, we'd struggle to find anyone that knew our names.

'So, aren't you like some kind of rocket scientist?' he asks.

'A data analyst, so not quite.'

'Still impressive,' he says with a head bob. He eats a chicken wing quicker than I did. 'And do you live around here? I know Rach comes up to stay with you, but I thought you lived in Ealing or somewhere out that way.'

I'm slightly flattered that he knows where I used to live.

'Yeah, I used to, but I got a new job and was finding the commute too long. I live in Clapham North now.'

'Oh, not far from me. I'm in Brixton.'

Of course I know this fact.

'Cool,' I say.

We both look down at our food that we've decimated.

'I guess we were hungry,' I say.

'Yeah. I needed that. So, um, did you want me to make sure you get home safely?'

'Sure,' I say, and as we leave to find a taxi I try and stop myself from having a mild panic attack. He's just being polite and he'll drop me off on his way past in a cab.

It turns out that Max wasn't just being polite because he is now standing in my living room drinking a quick nightcap of limoncello, which was the only spirit I had in.

'You know, it's a really long way back to Brixton,' says Max, stretching out his arms and faking a yawn.

'Yeah,' I say, agreeing, even though I know it's a very short bus ride away. 'You know, you can always stay here.'

'Thanks, that would be great. Of course, I'll sleep on the sofa.'

'How perfectly gentlemanly of you,' I say.

'Naturally,' he says, and he takes a step closer to me. My heart is pounding. He's looking at me in the same way he was looking at his chicken before he devoured it.

'But, you know, I think I'm going to have a little trouble getting this costume off.'

'I could help you out of it.'

'Well, that would be the gentlemanly thing to do.'

He nods.

'It might be easier to do it in my bedroom.'

'Of course,' he says, holding his arm out as if to say lead the way. He follows me into my room and, as soon as the door slams shut, he launches himself at me, kissing me furiously.

We fall on to the bed and there are drunken hands everywhere running all over each other's body. It's not the most co-ordinated of efforts but there's a kind of hot and heavy panting that comes from a lot of lust.

'The costume,' I pant.

'Gotcha,' says Max and he starts to wrestle the top, but it won't budge. We sit upright and he gives the zip at the back another tug, but it's stuck.

'Hang on, let me have a go,' I say and I put my arms round at the back, just as Max bends down to have a better look, and I whack him in the face with my elbow.

'Ow, fuck,' he says, cradling his eye.

'Shit. Let me see, hold still,' I say, leaping up.

He's clutching at his face so tightly that I have to prise his fingers away to make sure there's no blood spurting out of anywhere.

'It doesn't look like it's bleeding,' I say.

'It fucking hurts, though.'

'And your eye's still there; that's a good sign, right?'

I curse my Wonder Woman costume. I have dreamt about this moment for years and years and the one time I get Max in my bedroom I accidentally assault him.

'I'll go and get you some peas, OK? Stop the swelling.'

I hurry into the kitchen, find half a bag of peas and wrap them in a tea towel.

I make it back into my bedroom in record time but Max is passed out on the bed. Oh shit. I can feel my heart racing in a completely different way; now it's in a sheer terror – what if he's got a concussion?

I bend over to him to check his breathing and he's lightly snoring. Do people snore if they've got a concussion? The clock on my desk reads 3.32 a.m.; it's the kind of ridiculous situation where I'd usually phone Rach for advice, but I don't think it's quite the time to broach the subject of what I was doing in bed with her brother.

In a panic I go back into the kitchen and fill up a glass of water and I rush back to Max. I check his vital signs once more before I tip the water over his head, wincing as I do it.

'What the...' he shouts, sitting bolt upright and shaking the water off his face and out of his hair.

'Oh, thank goodness,' I say. 'I thought you had concussion.'

'No, I'm just drunk,' he says, and he reaches out his hands and pulls me in, wrapping his soggy arms around me. He nuzzles into the back of my neck and goes back to sleep.

And I just lie there, in my Wonder Woman costume, trying to ignore the worry of the inevitable awkward morning after the night before, because I've got Max Voss in my bed and, even if it's just for this moment, I feel like all my wildest dreams have come true.

**Can't get enough of Anna Bell's books?
Then make sure you don't miss the hilarious and
feel-good romantic comedy from Anna Bell**

Izzy Brown dreams of becoming a big-time influencer and knows she needs help. That's where her colleague and fellow influencer, Luke, comes in – they'll pose as boyfriend and girlfriend to boost their profiles. But Izzy quickly realises this fake-dating business is not all it's cracked up to be.

Then Izzy runs into Aidan, the mysterious stranger who saved her the day her world fell apart two years ago, and major sparks start to fly. Izzy's sure she can have the online success she's always dreamed of, whilst falling in love in real life. After all, Aidan doesn't use social media… what could possibly go wrong?